I0612731

WILLOW GRACE

CREONEX

BOOK ONE OF THE VINDICTA SERIES

ENDERA
PUBLISHING

Editing by Rich Dalglish
Cover designed by Karisa DeLay
Formatting and interior art by Aubrey Joy Rosales (Jai Design)
ISBN: 978-1-936307-55-5
Published by Vendera Publishing

Dedication

To the mother who inspired me, Anndrea, and to the mother who took me in

when I had no one else, Jennifer.

PRONUNCIATION GUIDE

This guide is here for any who wish to use it! This novel is fantastical science fiction, so *of course* you can't pronounce the names. Each word in each category is listed alphabetically. There's both a phonetic spelling of the word and a much easier, simple pronunciation next to it for those who haven't learned the phonetic alphabet (and probably never will).

A note before you begin: An apostrophe in the Delfungaye language denotes a tiny pause when pronouncing a word: a staccato.

Characters

- [ ] **Avenlae** -/'ɔvɛnl,e/ (AH-vehn-lay)
- [ ] **Darinrain** - /d'ɔrɪnren/ (DAH-rin-rain)
- [ ] **Havyeque** - /hɑv,aɪ'ik/ (hahv-EYE-YEEK)
- [ ] **Kaigar** - /k'aɪgɑr/ (k-EYE-gahr)
- [ ] **Klaecyia** - /kles'aɪjə/ (klay-SIGH-yah)
- [ ] **Lieneata** -/l,aɪ'ɛnitə/ (lie-eh-NEE-tah)
- [ ] **Matri Me'leiv** - /m,ɑtr'i mɛl,ɛi'v/ (MAH-tree meh'-leh-EEV)
- [ ] **Notien** - /n'oʊʃən/ (NO-shun)
- [ ] **Novissime** - /nɑv'is,ime/ (nah-VEE-SEE-may)
- [ ] **Saetyl** - /s'etɪl/ (SAY-till)
- [ ] **Sinivir** - /s,ɪnɪv'ir/ (SIN-ih-VEER)
- [ ] **Vindincta** - /v,ind'iktə/ (veen-DEEK-ta)
- [ ] **Xiaye** - /z'aɪj,e/ (z-EYE-yay)

Cultural Names/Labels:

- [ ] **Audritya** - /'aʊdritjə/ (OW-dree-tyah) - Name of the largest river of the Silvacastra forest
- [ ] **Fae'oteek** - /fe,oʊt'ik/ (faye'-OH- TEEK) - Silvacastra's largest

mountain range, divides the plains and Laizuteek forest from the Icelands

- [ ] **Fae'yeerium** - /fej'iriəm/ (faye'-YEE-ree-uhm) - Mother Death
- [ ] **Glae'atii** - /gle'ɑt,i/ (glay'-AH-TEE) - sacred nest of the armorers
- [ ] **Hi'pret** - /h'iprɛt/ (HEE'-pret) - sheet woven from the fireproof core of the deepest jungle trees
- [ ] **Je'quiet** - /ʒɛk'wiɛ/ (JE'-KWEE-eh) - Delfungaye historians. The honor of becoming a Je'quiet is passed down through direct bloodlines
- [ ] **Le'eseia** - /lɛ'isi,ə/ (leh'-EE-see-AH)
- [ ] **Lyceliah** - /l,aɪs'iliə/ (lie-SEE-lee-ah)
- [ ] **Silvacastra** - /s'ilvəkæstr,ə/ (SEEL-vuh-CAS-trah)
- [ ] **Visiocustos** - /v'isiouk,ustous/ (VEE-see-oh-KOO-stohs) - Sloviyankae historians
- [ ] **Wiegt'ri** - /w'igtr,i/ (WEEgt'-ree) - Delfungaye Celebration of the change of Seasons

Food:

- [ ] **A'ta'ya** - /'ɑtɑj,ɑ/ (AH'-tah'-YAH) - Delfungaye wine
- [ ] **Anteel** - /'ɑntil/ (AHN-teel) - Laizuteek tea
- [ ] **Bauete** - /bɔte/ (baw-tay) - fruit from the Laizuteek forest
- [ ] **Graetae** - /grete/ (gray-tay) - Fyr'aeset pastry
- [ ] **J'guaya** - /ʒg'ɔɪjə/ (j'-GOY-yuh) - seed of the cave trees

Creatures

- [ ] **Gueirag** - /g,ɔɪ'iræg/ (goy-EE-rag)
- [ ] **Kreeleur** - /kr'il,ur/ (KREE-LOO-er)
- [ ] **Voxmor** - /v'ɑksmɔr/ (VAHX-more)

Power

- [ ] **Creonex** - /kr'iounɛks/ (KREE-oh-nex)

- **Creovis** - /kr,ioʊv'is/ (KREE-oh-VEES)
- **Genepotentia** - /ʒ'ɛnɛpoʊt,ɛnʃiə/ (GEN-uh-poh-TEN-shee-uh)
- **Excitialium** - /ɛks,iti'ɑliəm/ (ex-SEE-tee-AHL-lee-uhm) - metal mined from the Fae'oteek mountain range

Tribes

- **Delfungaye** - /d,ɛfluŋg'e/ (DEL-foo-ing-gay) - Name for the winged humanoid species of Silvacastra.
- **Fyr'aeset** - /f'irɛs,ɛt/ (FEAR'-eh-SET) - Known for their golden skin, sleek black wings, navy eyes and platinum blonde hair, these people are the Gliders of Silvacatra's plains.
- **Hopyroque** - /h,ɑpir'oʊk/ (hah-pee-ROWK) - Inhabitants of the Fae'oteek mountain range, these people are known for their vivid copper skin, forest-green hair, and small tusks (instead of the elongated canines found in the majority of the Delfungaye species)
- **Laizuteek** - /l'aɪz,utik/ (LIE-ZOO-teek) - The Silver People of the Forest: this tribe is the most abundant after the initial slaughter of the Delfungaye. Their skin is snow white, and they have silver feathered wings that brighten their silver eyes. Their canines are the largest in the species, and are flashed as a sign of dominance or aggression.
- **Sloviyankae** - /slɔv,aɪj'ɔŋke/ (slav-EYE-YONK-aye) - Distant cousin of the Delfungaye species.
- **Y'araye** - /j'ɔr,e/ (y'-AHR-aye) - Known as the deadliest mercenaries and warriors in all of creation, the Y'araye once ruled the deepest jungles of Silvacastra before the Voxmor invaded. They're incredibly similar to the Laizuteek, except for their more muscular build, prismatic eyes, and stronger instincts.

PROLOGUE

Humanity was the last of Creation's civilizations to fall. Not because of their vaunted technology, clever ingenuity, or advanced weaponry. No, the humans survived the interuniversal war for so long because they were simply ignorant of it. It was sheer luck that the Voxmor had left the humans alone for the first decade-and-a-half of the war and the humans had yet to crack the code to interuniversal travel. But the Voxmor were hunters, and all of Creation was full of intelligent, yet helpless, prey.

Queen Novissime had long since stopped feeling anticipation when a scout returned from Earth. The former Queen, Lieneata, had hidden her child amongst the humans so thoroughly that her people were still searching ten years after her death. Although Novissime knew the chances of a child surviving the Voxmor's hunt for a decade were negligible, she couldn't let go of that hope. There was, after all, one last place left to be searched…

Novissime waited on the balcony of her nest, breathing deeply. Her eyes, the color of chrome, followed the path of a Laizuteek scout as he glided toward her, his wings sparkling silver. Smokey scents of Earth filled her nostrils as the scout landed before her, bowing low. Her lip curled—she hated how the stench of the other planet lingered on her scouts, its grime, destruction, and pollution left over from the reign of humans.

"Queen Novissime, we have found her," the scout said, his silver eyes averted.

Novissime stared at her scout in stunned silence. She watched how the light from the two midday suns made strands of the man's braided onyx hair turn a deep garnet. "Get Avenlae."

Novissime stood tall and composed as Avenlae approached her, catching a whiff of rich leather and open skies, the scent of a bloodline she had been trained to fear before the attacks of the Voxmor: the bloodline of a Mercenary. He ducked his head as low as respect dictated and no more. Every aspect of him set the Queen's nerves on edge, but his moonlight eyes - she had known them before he became deadly. Avenlae kept them averted, as the Queen's rank required, but only for as long as necessary.

"It is time," Novissime told him. "I am sending you to Earth."

"There is nothing we can do for the humans," Avenlae responded. "The Voxmor have decimated that planet."

Novissime didn't miss the note of controlled animosity in Avenlae's voice as he spoke the name of their adversaries. "It is not the humans you need to worry about. We found Xiaye."

A muscle near Avenlae's temple twitched. "Am I to bring her back?"

"Alive and unharmed. Lieneata told me her child has the final Creonex. We must get it before the Voxmor do." Before He does. Little white lies—that was how Lieneata had ruled. That was how Novissime learned to take control.

"I am no one's keeper. Send one of your guards. It will be good practice for them."

"You know I trust you more than them. And I know you will complete the mission for the right price." Novissime narrowed her eyes as Avenlae's ears pressed tightly against his temples, daring him to lift his gaze to hers. "I am giving you sanction to use whatever means necessary to bring Xiaye back to the tribe. Kill who or whatever you have to. I do not think we will have another opportunity."

"How will I know who she is?"

"You will smell Lieneata's bloodline."

"And the pay?"

"Name it."

"A bit desperate, are you not?"

Novissime tightened her jaw. *"All of Creation is at war. Everyone is 'a bit' desperate."*

Avenlae's silver wings rustled as he rolled his shoulders. *"Should I leave immediately?"*

"Yes. Kaigar has two void spheres, one calibrated to take you to Xiaye's rough location and one to bring you back here to Silvacastra."

"Rough location?"

"Did you not just state you are not anyone's keeper? I thought you would enjoy the challenge." The Queen fought to suppress a satisfied smile at Avenlae's hardening stare. *"Lower your gaze and get out of my sight. Do not return unless the girl is with you."*

A low hiss emanated from Avenlae's throat as he turned away from Novissime, the breeze from his wings sending her deep black hair fluttering.

The Queen closed her eyes and thought. Little lies, placed here and there, enough that not even Novissime knew the whole story. But she knew her final orders from Lieneata - protect the child, protect the Creonex.

And Novissime, the Final Queen of the Delfungaye, had put the last of her confidence into what few lines she knew of the Prophecy of the Daughter of War: *"The final Queen shall have an heir, not by blood, but by name and sacrifice. That Heir shall either be the salvation or destruction of Creation."*

CHAPTER 1

TWO WEEKS LATER, EARTH

The distant percussion of rain coaxed me to consciousness. I inhaled the wet, earthy scent of the downpour as it seeped through the cracks in my bunker's concrete walls and ceiling. Rain had become one of the few things on Earth that could bring me a sense of calm. Perhaps it was the familiar tap-tap of each drop on the metal hatch, like a friendly whisper in the dark.

Though awake, I didn't open my swollen, burning eyes. Vivid nightmares had again plagued me. My mother's sacrifice of ten years ago had kept me alive, but I couldn't escape MY demons. I couldn't escape the memory of her death.

The cot's rusted springs screamed in protest as I pushed back my threadbare blanket and stood up. Four strides took me across my father's small concrete bunker, unchanged in thirty years save for the moss that sprouted from cracks where the ground outside the walls and ceiling had shifted. I dipped cupped hands into a water barrel in the corner and splashed frigid water onto my face and through my long, dark hair, shivering against the cold.

Staring into the barrel, I studied my gaunt face reflected in the rippling surface of the liquid. My heterochromatic eyes stared back—the left one silver as the stars, the right one blue as the summer sky. My fair skin looked as gray as the macabre stone surrounding me. I could've passed as decently pretty if I hadn't been starving. Granted, my twenty-three years had done nothing to bathe my cheeks in the glow of youth. Trauma had turned the glint in my eyes to sadness and built muscles out of necessity, not health.

I gathered my unwashed hair into a bun, my pointed ears flinching. It was a hunting day—I'd be removing a collection of sticks, leaves, and mud that evening. Why bother with a half-broken brush anyway?

I fell back onto the screeching cot, my nose stinging with the scent of rust, and pulled on a pair of sun-bleached boots. They were tight—their previous owner was smaller than me—but better than the tattered sneakers I'd disposed of. Supplies of any kind were challenging to trade within the Precinct, so stealing the boots no longer felt morally wrong. It was simply survival.

Having strapped a leather pouch to my waist, I reached down to pick up a faded book from where it rested next to the cot. It warmed at my touch, eerie whispers darting around the bunker. This was how the book greeted me every morning before I slid it into its sleeve at my hip. Its pages of scribbled notes held all the knowledge I needed to survive—identification of poisons, medicinal herbs, food, diagrams of weapons, and traps that could be built from sticks and mud. The cover had faded to beige, and divots were left where my fingers held it. But the pages had never curled at the corners, never stained, never torn.

As for the whispers… I had no friends, no one to call me crazy. But I did have a book whose pages had kept me alive. For as long as it proved useful, I didn't question its voice.

I climbed the ladder to the hatch and pressed my ear against a crack between the concrete wall and the corner of the metal, listening for any sound behind the patter of the rain. Hearing only raindrops, I pushed against the hatch, the groaning hinges reminding me that I needed to repair them. There was a chill in the air, the first temperature drop of autumn. I welcomed the cool touch of rain. It would keep me alert as I moved through the trees.

My hand brushed the thin leather pouch as I walked through the forest, my boots squelching in the muddy trail. As the forest lightened from dark and dreary to simply dreary, I approached my garden on the edge of a tiny clearing. There wasn't much growing so close to the end of the season, and I had returned to check the traps I'd set. As the days grew shorter and the air cooler, the rustling of drying leaves foretold the arrival of winter. Fortune favored me—I had trapped several rabbits.

Two hours later, two of the rabbits were wrapped and stored in an ice box, and the other was in my stomach. It had been a while since I'd eaten a decent meal, as my hunting skills were barely adequate. I could trap well enough by following the book's instructions, but the only other weapons I could find and use were knives.

My knives hung in a place of honor on the wall above the cot, but two empty spaces between the weapons set my nerves on edge. The memory of the stag whose meaty flank had stolen those knives swam into my mind's eye. I never did find the damn thing. He had likely become the meal of a Voxmor, the one creature in those woods who needed it least. The pale-scaled aliens were the perfect apex predator, larger than the rusted cars that littered the cracked roadways. Serrated tails could whip over a Voxmor's head to skewer prey before it could react. Voxmor screams could make your ears bleed, pinning you where you fell before it caught you in its tentacled front limbs. I shuddered. The echoes of those shrieks from within the Precinct, the last human market, kept me underground more often than not. Little exposure to sunlight and little food had made me twitchy, irritable, and irrational.

Maybe that's why my routine changed that day.

I headed to the Precinct that afternoon, backpack stuffed with knives, food, and tradeable items. Fortunately, I had extra pelts that would cover the cost of new knives. The rain had stopped, but clouds still sulked dark and low in the sky. A flicker of anxiety arose as it always did when I left the relative safety of the trees. The world was a desolate, sullen place outside of my woods. I passed ramshackle shelters whose muddied inhabitants stared at me with dull, morose eyes in sunken sockets. That's what survival looked like for most humans. Hardly enough food, skin turned to leather from the sun, bodies that'd aged rapidly from constant fear. Compared to them, I should've been counting my blessings, all two of them. Perhaps three, if I included the icebox.

I kept an ear out for the Voxmor's clicks, the sound of their hisses, and the direction of their screams as I entered the Precinct. Small families that had grown into clusters of allied groups peeked out from the windows of the few intact brick or concrete buildings. Survivors slinked out of their shelters and followed the beaten trek to the market. By the time I reached the central hub, I had been slowed by the crowd closing in around me. I watched them from the outer margins of the market, wondering if they knew what easy targets they were for the early-rising Voxmor. A whole buffet, a herd to be scattered to weed out the weak.

I had developed regular stops, merchants who didn't ask about my eyes or stare at the points of my ears. They knew what I came for, and I knew the price of each item I wanted. It was a straightforward transaction that took only moments as long as I stayed clear of the dirty bodies occupying every corner of the central hub.

The sky had begun to blacken by the time I left the pulsing human mass, the smell of sweaty skin lingering in my nose. As I moved through the outskirts of the collapsing city, my eyesight faded into a greyscale. It became more difficult at night to pick out objects, but my ability to spot and track movement was enhanced. My ears twitched as dust swirled in the evening breeze. Earth had become as still as a graveyard, and I listened for the first scream that would herald the rise of the Voxmor.

Something scraped against the concrete behind me. I whirled around and dropped into a crouch, a knife clutched in my palm. My muscles tensed, my heart raced as I searched the shadows. But there were no tentacles wrapped around the corners of the walls, no hiss of a predator spotting its next meal, no glint of moonlight off pale scales or the long spines that extended down a Voxmor's back. I released a breath and turned back toward my forest. Must have just been some scruffy little animal.

What I faced instead was a forked tongue that flicked out to taste my fear and six obsidian eyes that homed in on me as a Voxmor loosened its curled tentacles, saliva oozing from its curved fangs.

CHAPTER 2

I locked eyes with the Voxmor for a mere second and then bolted. But for piles of rubble and pieces of crumbled buildings, there was minimal cover on the outskirts of the Precinct. I dove behind a concrete wall, slamming into rough stone as the Voxmor shrieked behind me. The creature was a scout, a younger member of a Voxmor hive dispatched to search for prey. Panting, I peeked around the edge of the wall, twisted scaffolding camouflaging my movements. Safety in the trees was close, but the Voxmor was directly in the way.

Sweat coated my skin as I leaned against the wall, knowing I would have to face the Voxmor. My heart beat violently—no one survived that fight. But there was no safety in the Precinct, in alleyways the Voxmor had already made its home. I had to fight it. I *had* to survive.

I peered out and checked the position of the Voxmor. The scout flicked its tongue as it stalked the wall, keeping its tentacles curled close to its chest and crouching low on its hind legs. Its serrated tail made no noise as it whipped back and forth through the air. It could slice right through me if given the chance. I would have a quick death, at least.

I took two deep breaths, pulled another knife out of my belt, said a prayer to a God I didn't know, and kicked off the wall in a burst of speed, adrenaline tunneling my vision.

The second my foot appeared out from behind the wall, the Voxmor shrieked and leaped forward, all six tentacles extended. I twisted as I ran by, launching a knife blindly at the scout. Thick mucus pooled down the Voxmor's snout as my blade sunk hilt-deep into one of its eyes. It shrieked as it writhed, wrapping a tentacle around the knife and ripping it out of its eye. My temples throbbed, and I shook my head, my vision pulsing. Crumbling brick walls and twisted metal scaffolding flew past in a blur as I ran. Another scream nearly made me buckle—the Voxmor had begun its pursuit.

A tentacle pummeled my back, sending me skidding across the concrete, peeling the skin from my forearms. I pushed myself unsteadily onto my back as the Voxmor climbed the scaffolding above me. It weaved its head back and forth, vibrating, a scream building in its throat. My feet slipped as I tried to get *off the ground!* The shriek hit me as if the air had turned solid. I gasped for air as the Voxmor lowered itself toward me. Its screech wrapped razor-tipped fingers around my brain, and I held my head as if that could stop my skull from shattering. My own scream joined the Voxmor's. My lungs burned and my nails dug into my skin, drawing blood. My world was unbearable pain.

And then it stopped. I slumped to the side, hardly feeling the chilled ground against my cheek. Something thrummed against my hip, a second heartbeat. *The book?* It burned against my skin through the leather, its whispers morphing into shrieking demands.

Sucking in a breath, I blinked my eyes open. Before me was an abnormally large, hunched-back person in a dark cloak, standing on the Voxmor's head with two swords sunk into its skull. Black blood pooled across the concrete. Wait, swords?

"G-get away," I whispered as my vision darkened again. My head snapped back as I was yanked to my feet, two hands grasping the collar of my jacket. Someone was yelling my name from far away. When my eyes opened, the world spun. "Stop," I murmured, feeling vaguely panicked through the fog in my head.

"What?"

"Don't... g-get away..."

The hands moved to my shoulders and shook me like a ragdoll. "Xiaye, listen! Remember where you are!"

That voice was masculine. I didn't know any men, and I didn't even like any of the men that sulked around the Precinct. A flash of silver from underneath the stranger's hood and a prick of energy from the book at my hip triggered a memory, the memory of two eyes as bright as the stars and a woman's voice, my mother's. *This is all you will need. Everything you need to know is within its pages. You must never let them find you or the Creonex. Guard it with your life, Xiaye. Do you understand?*

"The Creonex?" I heard myself say.

"The what?"

Full awareness returned. My arms stung, my body ached, and blood dripped from my scalp. The hooded person was holding my shoulders, and he towered over me. All I could see were his pure silver eyes—*like mine.*

His pupils were contracted and slit like a cat's. A third eyelid moved over each, from the inner corner to the outer corner of his eyes. Those were *not* human eyes. My hand flew to my belt to find another knife just as another screech sounded from behind the man. Something twitched at the stranger's back under his cloak, and he pushed me behind him.

"Run, Xiaye! Into the forest!"

"How do *you* know—"

He whirled around, his eyes flashing. "If you do not run now, I will *let* them kill you!"

Another screech, closer this time, was all the persuasion I needed. There was no time to dwell on the mystery of the man and how he knew me. I just ran, gasping for air until a sharp pain stabbed my ribs. I collapsed to the ground, retching, my body spent. The rabbit from earlier made another appearance, and I trembled as I wiped my mouth and sat back against a tree trunk. Without realizing it, I ran all the way to my forest. Crickets sang in my ears as if nothing like the Voxmor had ever penetrated the sanctity of the trees, and the book was calm, silent. I squeezed fistfuls of dried leaves, heard them crunch, listened to the burbling of the creek that ran behind my bunker, and let out a sigh. I was home.

My legs shook as I moved towards the creek, lurching from tree to tree. With furrowed brows, I thought about the encounter with the silver-eyed man. He couldn't have been my father—the Hughes I remembered was unremarkably human with his black hair and watery blue eyes. I never saw him after my mother died. After waiting a month for him to find me, I figured he, too, was probably dead. But those silver eyes had been so familiar. My mother had silver eyes and joked that she had given me the third silver eye on the back of her head. But she didn't have pupils like a cat's or third eyelids that blinked vertically. And I had never seen a man in the Precinct who stood that tall.

I waded into the creek and ducked my head under, letting my hair loose from its tied clump and scrubbing dried blood from my scalp. My memory stirred again, another sting of energy from the book, flashes of my mother shoving it into my hands. I touched a damp hand to the leather pouch that hung from my belt. That whisper returned, even more demanding, its language changing. I retrieved the book from its pouch, flinching at the pitch of the voice as I lifted the worn cover to my eyes.

Name me, name me, NAME ME!

Could it be?

11

"Creo," I whispered. A fluorescent blue glow emanated from the book, illuminating the surrounding area. Warmth radiated from the cover, pulsating with energy that vibrated through my body. Startled, I dropped the book, slipping and sliding on the muddy bank of the creek as I tried to escape it.

The book remained suspended inches from the ground, still radiating soft blue light that pulsed with a life of its own.

"That's… not *normal*," I muttered, my mind struggling to comprehend what I was seeing. When the glow didn't fade and the book didn't fall, I scanned the trees and underbrush around me. My ears swiveled back and forth. I heard nothing but the cricket's song, felt only a sleepy breeze. I was alone.

My gaze returned to the book, a whisper still demanding that I name it.

"Creonex." I spoke the word aloud with as much confidence as my weakened body could muster. The glow intensified and enveloped the book until the blue light molded the outline of the cover and pages into one smooth orb. And there it stayed, still floating, but I felt it was observing me. A substance, almost a consciousness, deepened the light of the orb beyond simple colors. All my fear, pain, and questions were forgotten as the light transfixed me.

I reached out and touched the orb with a finger. A shock of electricity, of power, flowed through my arm and into my body, then out into the world around me. Responding to my touch, the orb changed, moving towards my hand as if sucked by the same energy pulsing through me. It weaved around my fingertips, splitting into rays of blue light that twisted over my fingers, palm, and wrist like growing vines. The glow intensified, illuminating the forest, and I felt the power in my muscles, in my bones, in my *being*. With one last flash, the light died.

I smelled the forest, heard the crickets, felt the cool night air. In the moonlight, I turned my hand over, marveling at the blue metal filigree glove covering my fingers, hand, and wrist.

12

As a twist in the metal shone under the light of the moon, a vision flashed before my eyes—*a woman, raven-haired and silver-eyed, run through by the tail of a Voxmor, her blood dribbling down the side of her mouth and out of the gaping hole in her chest. Another flash, and there was a face, eyes as red as human blood set deep into a pale, cracked death mask. A mask with a malicious smile that held yellowed teeth filed into points.*

A shadow shifted in the background. My eyesight refocused, pulling me out of the vision. The silver-eyed man stared at me from across the creek, one of his swords curving across his body as he crept toward me.

CHAPTER 3

I got to my feet, a knife in my hand. My blade was pathetic compared to the practiced way the stranger held and moved his sword. Still, I raised my knife and my left hand to eye level as I stepped backward, preparing to defend myself. A glow illuminated the filigree of the Creonex. I glanced at it, then chose to ignore it.

"Who are you?" I asked the man, apprehension sharpening my voice.

"Why is your hand glowing?" he called back. His voice had the lilt of an accent around its vowels, but not one I could place.

"I don't actually know. But that's not what I asked. Who are—"

"It is no longer safe here, Xiaye." The stranger stepped closer, one of his boots splashing in the creek.

"Don't come any closer! I have a knife."

"I have a sword."

My breath dried my lips as I panted, and I searched the shadows of his cloak to determine how many more weapons he had concealed. Although he must have known I posed little threat to him, he made no move to overpower me.

"Yes, you do." I lowered my knife reluctantly but didn't loosen my grip or relax my stance. "How do you know me?"

"I do not have time to explain. We must leave this place. It is no longer safe."

"It won't get any safer no matter how much you repeat yourself. Save your breath and answer my questions."

"The longer you ask stupid questions, the closer the Voxmor will get."

"I wouldn't have to keep asking if you would answer!" I straightened my spine, confident enough to move half an inch closer to the stranger as I spoke. "I won't follow you anywhere if your intentions aren't made clear."

"Your human side is showing. So simple and arrogant."

"I'm sorry, my 'human side'? Which one is that, right or left?"

"We do not have time for this!" In two strides, he crossed the small creek and was so near me I had caught his scent, rich leather mixed with fresh air. My left hand rose to stop him. In an instant, my whole hand felt warm, as if I'd held it out to a raging fire. Then a warped blue sphere shot out of my palm, close enough to the stranger's head to knock his hood off. The sphere exploded against a tree trunk, leaving a smoldering hole in the bark. Hair black as coal and straight as a blade of grass fell past the man's shoulders as he turned to look. Tips of large, pointed ears sprang up from the hair around his temples, pointing towards the crackling of small fires. His head whipped back around to me, and his opalescent eyes were the brightest orbs I had ever seen in my forest.

The man's face was human in essence but different in detail. Gradually, his slitted pupils dilated until they appeared almost human. Moonlight slid across his high, sharp cheekbones as he tilted his head to the side, a hawk studying a mouse. Claw earrings hung from each ear, and a third black claw was pierced through the septum of his nose. The tips of two long canines

15

pressed gently into the stranger's lower lip as he opened his mouth and cocked his head, ears twitching, much more sensitive than my own. Gold was woven into braids around his hairline, a sharp dichotomy to the brilliance of his skin, as white as the snow that would fall during winter.

"What is that on your hand?" he asked.

"I—what are *you*?" Whatever answer I had died in my throat as his third eyelid passed over his eyes again.

A screech sounded in the distance. "They know you are here. Let's go."

"I don't even know your name—why the hell would I go with you anywhere?" I glanced over my shoulder, watching for the darkness to break along the pale scales of a Voxmor. I had no fear or moment of awe at the power vibrating in the filigree glove around my left hand. At that moment, it was just a weapon, a weapon to protect me from the Voxmor.

The silver-eyed man unhooked a latch at his throat, and his cloak dropped to the forest floor as he glared down at me. "I am Avenlae of the Delfungaye tribe, and I have been sent to retrieve you, Xiaye."

I blinked. "That was quite a proclamation, Avenlae, but it raised more questions than it answered."

"*I* am not the one who is trying to kill you." Avenlae reached over his head and pulled another sword from its scabbard as he walked away from the creek's bank. That's when I saw his wings unfold, feathers as metallic as his eyes, black curved claws on the joints of the wings crossing high over his head. Their feathers dragged behind, dipping into the creek's water and disturbing the underbrush.

"What—?! Those are... *what?*" My shock was cut short by another shriek, this one closer.

"We need to move. The Voxmor are too close. I cannot transport you here."

"Avenlae, I have shelter. In a bunker. I ... uh, *we* could hide there." I still stared wide-eyed at his wings, forgetting my fear.

16

"No, you have led them here. You think that bunker will keep you safe against creatures that live and breathe the underground?" Avenlae's ears were pressed flat against his hair, signaling his growing impatience. His wings twitched as if anxious to take him away from danger.

"I-it's my home." I jogged to catch up to him. I'd never known anything besides that musty bunker. The thought of leaving... *that* fear was strong enough to cut through my shock.

"No longer."

"I can't accept that."

Avenlae halted so abruptly that I almost walked straight into his chest as he whirled around. "Would you rather die?"

Screams shattered the peace of the woods. The Voxmor had finally broken the safety of my forest. I turned, the pain of loss constricting my throat. Voxmor slithered through the trees, obsidian eyes focused only on me, their tails and claws leaving deep cuts in the previously unblemished bark of the towering sentinels. Upon realizing I could never return to my forest, my heart cracked. But I didn't move. I couldn't.

Avenlae shoved me behind him as he spun his swords, angling his wings forward so his claws pointed toward the advancing predators. "Run, you *stupid* human!"

Something flared in my blood. Red-hot *rage* flooded my veins. The Voxmor had ravaged humanity and brought civilization to its knees, but I would not *allow* them to destroy my home without forcing them to face my pain. The burning of the Creonex around my hand was a weapon that craved to be unleashed on the creatures that had taken *everything* from me.

The three Voxmor bared their fangs, their tentacles pulling their bodies toward me. I thrust my left hand out, allowing years of nightmares, anger, trauma, and pain to flood through my veins and into the Creonex, changing the color of the metal from cool blue to fiery red. A magenta beam of raw power exploded from my palm and incinerated the nearest Voxmor. A flicker of fear appeared in the eyes of the other two as they skidded to stop next to the pile of ash that had been their fellow.

I directed my beam of power upon the spined backs of the Voxmor as they turned to flee. I only faltered when tears, cold against my burning skin, slid down my cheeks, a response to a blinding pain that seared my back. My hand fell to my side as if it were weighed down, the fire of the Creonex shrinking to docility. Trees before me were disintegrated, and smoke twirled between me and the Precinct I could now clearly see. Ashes danced in a breeze. A sob wracked my body, and I collapsed to the ground. I felt arms pass gently under my body, brushing carefully against some raw portion of my shoulder blades. My hands shook—my body trembled. I wanted to make Avenlae leave me in the comforting clutches of the leaves, but I had no energy to fight.

"D-don't take me," I whispered between sobs. "This i-is m-my *home*. Don't l-let them d-destroy it!"

Avenlae nodded, ears flat, pupils as thin as a strand of hair, as he carried me somewhere, somewhere far, far beyond my suffering forest.

There was light behind my eyelids. I saw it the way one does when waking at dawn. There was a smell, too, fresh, sweet, and innocent. Something I hadn't smelled before. And there were sounds, a melody of alien birdsong with a harmony of breeze whistling through blades of grass that had long overgrown whatever pasture they claimed.

18

There was peace, a peace I had never felt.

As soon as my eyes adjusted to the light, I took in the deep emerald leaves above me, fanning out wider than any I had seen. They encompassed the world above me, vibrant against the grey-marbled bark of the branch I lay on. Shined surfaces sparkled in the light of two suns that peeked down at me between the shifting of the tree's leaves.

Two suns?

I rose to look out upon a proud, old forest extending up the side of the mountain where I sat and across the rest of the range. These trees stood taller and were vaster than even the crumbling skyscrapers of the Precinct. A river the color of aquamarine carved a broad and deep chasm between the mountains and across the forest. Mellow clouds hung against the sky, and the suns, smaller than the one I knew, shone a soft light on the landscape. Far below me, in the valley, I saw the outline of beings flying, their silver wings twinkling in the sunlight. To the left was a field of gold, tall grasses waving and singing where the wind went to play.

This could not have been Earth. Nothing so beautiful existed there anymore. Calm settled over me despite the pain of my memory returning. I glanced down at my left hand—the blue filigree was still there, swirling around my palm and fingers. It had all been so real. But this, this glove... its warmth was familiar. It was the warmth of the book, my only constant for ten years. The only thing I *didn't* fear.

Leaves rustled above my head. My limbs fumbled about as I pushed myself back against the tree trunk, stopped by something velvety but painful. Panic pumped through my body as I tried to find a better defensive position.

"No, Xiaye, stay down. You will not be used to them yet."

Avenlae descended from the branches, the claw of one wing hooked on the bark of a branch above him. He lowered himself onto the branch I sat on, and I was

19

mesmerized by the jagged lines of the tattoos that swirled down his arms and neck. There was writing in the tattoos, but in a language I didn't recognize. A black vest covered his torso, the material flexible but plated, like armor.

As he settled onto the branch, I noticed his boots allowed his toes to fully extend so he could grip the tree's bark. Avenlae, whatever he was, was adapted to life in the forest. Small sheaths with white-handled knives lined the sides of his thighs, black straps over gray-plated pants. Apart from the sheaths were feathers that folded over themselves from his knees down to just above his ankles. I glanced along his arms, searching for more feathers, wondering if the ones on his legs helped with flight or were some adaptation from a lost ancestor that had yet to be phased out.

"They are traditional, the tattoos. They tell your story and your family's story before you," Avenlae said as he folded his wings and sat with me on the branch.

"You have much to explain, Avenlae," I said.

"I know. It is much safer here. You may ask me questions now."

"I don't need your permission."

"No, because you will ask anyway. You are still too human not to."

I glared at him. My belt was still fastened around my waist, and I felt for a knife, found the last one. My shirt was too soft to be the one I'd been wearing, but at least whoever changed me (I cringed at the thought it was Avenlae) had left my boots, pants, and belt in place.

"Xiaye, I will not hurt you. You see, I have no weapons." He opened his palms and held them in front of me. "But it will not remain daytime forever. If you have questions, ask them now. I need to take you back to the tribe before nightfall."

"Let's start with where we are right now."

"This is my world, Silvacastra. This is the 'Earth' of the universe I live in."

"Universe? This is another universe?"

"Yes, there are four."

"Only four?"

"Should there be more?"

"You're making my head hurt, Avenlae."

"The *Je'quiet* tell it like this. In the beginning, there were Five Brothers. They were the Creators of all things, but they wanted to create one universe full of peace and harmony, where everything was balanced. The Brothers each created a tool with which they could harness their raw power to create their version of utopia. That tool was named the Creonex. They hoped to one day merge all four of their Creations once they had matured and found an element of harmony. But the Fifth Brother created something dark and evil that began seeping into the other Brothers' Creations, causing turmoil. The Four Brothers used their Creonexes to banish him to the dark universe he created. And so there were four universes. However, the Fifth Creator's darkness also gave consciousness to the creatures living within each Creation, so the Four Brothers have allowed us to live."

I couldn't hide my skepticism. "So, this is what your tribe believes?"

"That is the story of the Beginning of Creation. The Brothers then descended to the first intelligent species of each of their universes. They entrusted the leaders with their Creonexes to safeguard, for they feared that if the Fifth Creator found a way to regain power, he might attempt to destroy everything they had created. His own Creonex, the fifth, was lost to time. My people had guarded the third Creonex for generations, until they were murdered by the Voxmor."

Avenlae looked out over the valley, his ears twitching and swiveling. I observed every movement he made, rolling my shoulders against the weight on my back. What he told me felt like a story. Just another tale of creation, something I could deny because it wasn't real.

But he had wings. I could feel them, if I wanted. *He* was real.

"Okay, if I assume that what you're saying is true, does that mean the humans guarded one of the Creonexes as well?"

"Just one family. Your father's family. Only the Creonex's guardian was allowed to know its true nature, as it changed physical forms depending on who it was passed down to."

"So you're saying this," I held up my left hand, "is that fourth Creonex? That's why it appeared as a book to me."

"No. The fourth Creonex was destroyed when your father was killed. The Voxmor have been seeking them out in each universe. If the Creonexes are not in their true form, they are easier to destroy. As far as we knew, the fourth was the last to be found. We believe the one you have is the fifth."

"My mother gave it to me. Did she know what it was?"

"I do not know if the Queen knew what she had. I assume she must have, for that is why she fled to Earth, in the last universe that had yet to be infiltrated."

My brows furrowed. "Did you just—Queen? Why did you call her the Queen?"

"Because that is who she was. Queen Lieneata, first Queen of the united Delfungaye."

For once, I had no response. I had no evidence to prove he was lying, only my own doubts. The new information overwhelmed me. His explanation was an answer, but could I believe it? I rolled my shoulders again and reached a hand back to rub out the tension in my muscles so I could think clearly. I felt something solid, something feathered. Like an extension of my shoulder blade, I could *feel* the touch of my hand, although it did not lay flush against my shoulders.

Avenlae noticed my eyes widening, and he chuckled snidely. "I decided to let you discover them on your own. Would your little mind be able to process it if I told you about your wings?"

I said nothing as I turned to take in the wings, with feathers that fell in a black-to-white gradient and hooked claws crossing high over my head like Avenlae's. Even folded behind me, the bottom of the wings extended a few feet past where my legs dangled from the branch. Their weight was foreign, yet my awareness of them was as natural as my awareness of my own arms.

"They're massive," I whispered. It was the only thing I could think of to say. My mind had become a jumbled mass of frantic thoughts, massive denial, and feeble attempts to process the weight of an entire *world*.

"Your body carries more weight on this world than our bodies. Your wings need more strength to carry you through the air."

"Avenlae, why are they there? Why are they there now? How could they just—just appear?"

"They ripped out of your spine as you killed those Voxmor. You are a hybrid, but your mother had to suppress your nonhuman aspects so she could hide you from the Voxmor."

My vision blurred with tears as my body trembled. I inhaled the clean, fresh air of the forest in shuddering gasps. *This* forest was my mother's home. This was her world, this was where she ruled. These wings, these had been her wings. My hearing, my eyesight, and the grayscale I could see in at night were all because of her. And this power from the Creonex—had she felt it, too? Could she hear its voice?

"Why didn't she tell me?" I choked, not even aware of what I was saying.

"Did I not just explain that the former Queen had to hide you? Telling you this before you could understand the gravity of the interuniversal war would have made her sacrifice in vain. She and the Creonex would have been found."

"What am I supposed to do about this, Avenlae? What if I don't want it? What if I don't want the wings or, or the crown?"

"That is not an option."

"Then make it an option! Take me back. Take me back right now and let me live alone in my bunker. I didn't ask for your protection or help, and I don't want it."

"If you go back, the Voxmor will kill you."

"Let them! If I die, so be it! I don't want the wings, the world, the Creonex, any of it!"

Avenlae stood, towering over me. "Pitiful, selfish human!"

I flinched, expecting a blow, but his eyes cooled, and his wings folded over his back so he appeared less formidable. But his canines still flashed as he spoke, and he curled his hands into fists at his side.

"Do you think *any* of us wanted this war? Do you think your mother did? Because of that Creonex, she never returned to her home! I just spent *weeks* on your filthy planet so I could find you and take you back to the tribe on your mother's final orders. And since you are now attached to that Creonex, you are *never* going back to Earth."

My throat ached as I tried to stem the flow of tears. Part of me knew Avenlae was right despite the venom that laced his tongue. Earth held nothing for me anymore, with my forest gone and my shelter likely overrun by Voxmor. That was too painful to face.

I turned my hand over, the Creonex's filigree glinting in the light of the two suns that hung above me. There, tightened around my skin, was my new reality. Warmth rippled along the swirls and twists of the Creonex. This was *my* weapon. My existence had become even more terrifying and I wanted nothing more than to *run away*, but… could I learn to fight from *his* people? Could I do *more* than just survive?

"If you won't take me back, then take me somewhere safer than here."

"Good," Avenlae growled, facing the lowering suns. "We are losing daylight."

I let him walk down the branch a bit before calling, "Oh, and your favorite insult? It's not accurate, is it? Since I'm apparently not fully human."

Avenlae paused, the muscles in his shoulders rippling as he stiffened. My breath caught as I wondered if I had pushed back too far. He turned so I could only see his profile. "No, you are not. You are Queen of the Delfungaye by blood right, but still human enough for me to smell that you are not one of us."

24

CHAPTER 4

After a few feeble attempts to push myself up the tree trunk, Avenlae walked back to me and held out a hand. I eyed his calloused palm warily.

"If you want to stand on your own, you may try, but it is a long fall from this branch to the ground," he said.

I sighed and grasped his hand. He was right to warn me; I nearly fell back immediately. My wings fluttered as I struggled for balance. As soon as I was stable, Avenlae ripped his helping hand away as if my touch were like fire.

"These will get in the way if I try to climb down," I mentioned under my breath as I acclimated to how my wings folded against my back. They were so alien, yet I could control them without conscious thought. *I don't like them, I don't want them, get them OFF...*

"No, Xiaye, we cannot walk. The distance is too far and too dangerous on foot." Avenlae opened his wings slightly, closing his eyes and letting the breeze run through his feathers.

"You—you want—you *expect* me to fly?"

"Yes."

I shook my head in disbelief. "No. No, I've never—I don't want—*these* aren't even mine—"

"Do you always babble incessantly?" he hissed. "The wings belong to you; they are a part of you. A Delfungaye is strengthened by his wings. He does not refuse to use them out of *fear*—he uses their connection."

"Oh, yes, I feel *so* connected to the wings I discovered *five minutes ago.*" I tried to keep the hysterical notes out of my voice as I threw my hands up. "How dare I not just throw myself off this branch when you ask me to?"

A muscle twitched along his clean-shaven jaw. "Babies are more willing to leap than you are. Flying is an instinct for Delfungaye; we do not need to learn."

"So, this is just what you do, then? Throw children off branches and hope they can fly?"

"Yes."

I blinked at him, open-mouthed.

"They must be allowed to feel the air to awaken their instincts. They only fall a few times. You are more afraid to fall than a child, yes?"

"I'm afraid of *injury.*"

"But the child is not. They learn to avoid it."

Avenlae leaped from the branch, and it swayed under my feet, nearly causing me to loose my footing. He unfolded his wings, catching the wind and soaring in an arc to turn back to the branch he'd leapt from. As his wings extended, so did feathers along the bottom of his legs, like a bird's tail feathers.

I stared at Avenlae. His wings, over twice the length of his body, were magnificent, although I would never dare tell him. He cut through the air with the grace of a sparrow, as if he never did leave the wind. Gusts of air sent my hair flying over my shoulders as Avenlae approached, hovering vertically.

"Why have wings if you refuse to experience flight?" he called.

"I've lived on the ground, and I think I could survive if I stayed that way."

He rolled his eyes. "You cannot do it. You cannot fly."

"I choose not to fly."

"You choose not to fly because that is the only choice your fear shows you."

"Are you calling me a coward?"

"Are you proving yourself to be one?"

My chest heaved as I stared at him. I had survived on my own for ten years with Voxmor hunting me, but he thought he could taunt me for not leaping off a branch into a valley?

I gazed at the sloping tree line below the branch I was stuck to. It really was a long way down, and I was feeling particularly mortal at that moment. When I raised my head to look once again at Avenlae, he averted his eyes as if he couldn't stand to look at me. As much as I wanted to rip the wings from my back, I couldn't deny that... I wanted their *freedom* even more. My stubborn streak flared, and I dove off of the branch without another thought.

The wind rushed up around me, racing across my skin and rushing in my ears. Panic surged into my chest and up my throat, colors blurred in the corners of my vision, and my mind blanked. I fell faster than I thought I would, paralyzed by fear.

No! Catch me, stop me! The second the thought entered my mind, the feeling of the wind in my feathers awakened my instincts and sharpened my focus. My wings extended, catching the wind that held me up like thousands of tiny hands. And then I was gliding. My wings held me as steady as a ship on calm waters, and *this* was where I belonged, in the air, close enough to kiss the sky. Along the bottom of my wings were extensions of feathers parallel to my legs.

27

Since I didn't have the feathers that Avenlae had on my calves, these extensions acted as my tail feathers, balancing me as I flew.

Tilting my body up, I beat my wings to ascend closer to the clouds. Having attained a height that would allow me an overview of Silvacastra's landscape, I hovered, feeling my body rise and fall with the flapping of my wings. The emerald trees of Avenlae's forest melted away into those vast fields of gold in a way I could not have appreciated from a lower vantage point. On my other side were the mountains, covered in lush green, that melted into white snow in the distance. It reminded me so painfully of an ancient Earth, but it was just off, like a glitch: it was *too* beautiful.

For the merest second, the first time in my life, I felt a sense of calm: safety. Here, held by wings and the caress of the wind, was *safe*.

Avenlae rose to meet me. "The suns will set soon. I must take you back to the tribe."

"What happens if the suns set?"

"The Voxmor scream."

"Lead on, then."

Moments later, we were gliding back over the tops of the trees toward the river. Avenlae had mentioned the Delfungaye had settled close to the river, and as we approached, it was apparent why. The trees became fuller, their branches longer and more vine-like the nearer we got to the water, so I imagined it offered more protection. I began to see glimpses of silver wings darting through the leaves beneath us, a few times hearing the whoosh of branches parting as some tribespeople emerged to watch us pass.

Avenlae pulled his wings in and dove into the forest through a small break in the canopy. I followed but came out of the dive with much less grace than Avenlae. Heat rushed to my cheeks as I realized we had dove into the middle of the tribe. The Delfungaye kept their eyes on me as we passed, and other tribespeople paused midway through their chores to stare. I noticed that the tribal tattoos on Avenlae's arms, shoulders, and neck were more aggressive than those on the rest of the tribe. Their jewelry was gold and dainty compared to the garish claws hanging from Avenlae's ears and septum. He was different from them, and their avoidance as he passed heightened my anxiety. Who had I followed into this world?

Hand-woven shelters hung from the branches of trees like so many dew drops. The nests were a work of art, their white and grey marbling matching the bark they hung from, giving the impression that they were part of the trees. Children darted around the forest, chasing each other around the branches and through the juniper undergrowth or seeing who could climb the tree trunks faster. They and their parents would use the claws on their wing joints to help them rise through the trees, like a second pair of arms.

Some women sat in the openings to their nests, weaving, preparing food, watching children, some sharpening knives and polishing bows. Everyone was dressed in the light greyscale of the forest around them, their tops made of a lightweight fabric they wrapped around their torsos. These wraps also allowed for pockets in which to stash weapons and kept their limbs unimpeded in case of the sudden need for defense. Some older children had knives tucked into sheaths strapped across their chests. These people had seen war, and their clothing hid them well in the forest. Perhaps the Voxmor attacks had been as brutal here as they'd been back home.

A tree in the middle of the tribe had vines woven together to create a naturally grown castle. I followed Avenlae to the entrance, which sat in the middle of the mass of vines guarded by two male Delfungaye. They let Avenlae and me pass without comment, and we entered a massive structure with branches serving as different floors. Rays of sunlight poked through openings in the woven nest, creating a beautiful interplay of light and shadow, and small bulbs hung down from different points, serving as an alternate light source. The structure's base was busy with Delfungaye dressed in traditional cloth wraps adorned with beadwork. They flew between the branches, performing their daily duties and creating a bustling atmosphere. Vines of emerald foliage draped across branches serving as walkways, and the vaulted "ceiling" was the reinforced and insulated canopy of the tree the nest wrapped around.

Avenlae led me to the top of the nest, flying where we could and climbing the rest of the way, him hissing out his impatience at my slow progress. It took several tries before I figured out how to use my wings to help me climb, and my muscles quickly tired. We came to a walkway that circled the top of the tree and out onto a balcony on the side of the nest that faced the tribe. I followed Avenlae, stepping over the threshold of French doors, first with a rush of anxiety, then with a gasp of awe.

A woman stood at the balcony, her pure silver wings folded against her back and covered in golden beadwork that flowed along the wooden floor behind her. Her silky smooth ebony hair fell far past her waist, braids connecting and twirling as naturally as vines curling around the branches of a tree. She held her shoulders back, her chin up, her back erect, radiating power.

The woman turned toward us at the scrape of my boots against the wood. Her silver eyes, almond-shaped, had faint lines in the corners as if they smiled before she did. Dainty gold chains swirled down her ears, and she smiled as she saw us, her pointed canines in line with the rest of her white teeth. She wore lightweight white robes whose diaphanous top layers swayed in the breeze, creating an angelic aura as the suns shone the last of their light upon her. I felt as if I could find motherly nurturing in her presence, in her beauty, so calming, so strong.

Avenlae turned his head to the side, tilting his chin up to expose his neck as he bowed. "Queen Novissime. Xiaye Vernet, as promised."

30

Queen Novissime turned her intense silver eyes on me. I was unable to move under her gaze, as I had no idea what the social custom was. Should I bow? Show my neck like Avenlae? Smile?

"Don't worry, child. I take no offense to your hesitation." Her voice was low and melodic, her accent curling the edges of her words. She approached, moving as if the breeze carried her. "You are dismissed, Avenlae."

Avenlae drew himself out of his bow, jaw clenched, frowning. He began to speak to her in their native tongue, whose consonants clicked and whistled like birds' calls.

"English, Avenlae. Be mindful of our guest." The queen's voice held a sharper undertone, a hint of impatience.

Avenlae glanced at me and then looked over Novissime's head. "I fulfilled my end of the deal."

"What deal?" I turned my head towards him, feeling the weight of fear in my stomach. Had I been tricked?

Queen Novissime sighed, her smile dropping slightly at the corners. "Yes, and we can discuss payment later."

"Payment?" I glared at Avenlae.

"That was not the agreement." Avenlae looked Novissime in the eye, his canines flashing. "Did you not say I would complete the mission for the right price? Xiaye is here, yet I am still waiting for payment."

The Queen's pupils contracted to slits, and she flattened her ears back, looking just as deadly as she did beautiful. "Do not hold my gaze, Avenlae," she hissed, and her feathers lifted all along her wings.

Avenlae swallowed and lowered his eyes again, exposing his neck.

"Speak with the guard outside the door. He will get your affairs sorted. You are *dismissed*, Avenlae."

He bowed and turned to leave.

"Avenlae!" I called after him, my voice rising. "You bastard, did you bring me here because of some deal? For some damn money?"

"I brought you here alive," he snapped over his shoulder. "You should thank me, impudent human."

I watched him retreat, my chest heaving. Everything Avenlae had told me was thrown into question. A voice in the back of my head berated me for choosing to believe him so readily. *Stupid, naïve girl. Perhaps you deserve to die here, surrounded by aliens. Or predators?*

"Xiaye." The sound of my name brought me out of my panic. The Queen had spoken it softly but with conviction. "I know much has happened to you today. I ask only that you permit me the time to explain as much of it as I can."

"Avenlae already explained your beliefs. I'm not interested—"

"He only told you what I ordered him to. I may be able to provide you with more of the answers you seek, answers Avenlae was not permitted to know."

I held her in my gaze for a few moments, trying to soften my glare. The idea of further understanding *was* enticing. She spoke so calmly, with such confidence; I was more apt to believe *her* than her warrior.

"I understand if you question my integrity, especially after that display with Avenlae. I do regret that, as I had hoped to discuss matters privately with him so that you would not feel unwelcome or unimportant. I assure you, nothing is further from the truth. It is only that in Avenlae's case, desperate and broken men can sometimes become our greatest tools and protectors."

"What do you mean?"

"Come here, child, and let me tell you." She gestured toward the balcony railing next to her. I joined her and got a bird's eye view of Delfungaye life continuing uninterrupted below me. I clasped the railing, hoping to conceal the trembling of my hands. My skin was pinched along the curves of the Creonex's filigree, but I couldn't feel the pain. It was as if I was no longer a part of my body—I was simply observing someone else's conversation.

"I will start with an observation you may have made," Queen Novissime began. "You perhaps noticed Avenlae's tattoos, how they are different from any you may have seen on my people below, and how the claw piercings he wears are not the same as the gold chains and rings the others wear." She spoke to me but watched the tribe as intently as I did, as if she were searching for the man she spoke of within the lively mass of wings, wrapped cloth tunics, and bodices.

"He told me the tattoos told the story of you and your family," I ventured.

"They did in his tribe. You see, the word 'Delfungaye' only refers to a species, a set of people spread out across the vast expanses of our planet. We had the mountain tribes, the *Hopyroque,* who lived on and around the most dangerous cliffs and mountain peaks. There were the plains people, the *Fyr'aeset,* who populated the fields beyond this forest, and my people, the *Laizuteek,* the people of the forest. We were all Delfungaye, but each tribe had a second name. Avenlae is the last of the *Y'araye,* the deepest jungle warrior tribe."

"The last? What happened to the rest of them?"

"The Voxmor came. That is why there are no more Delfungaye in the plains or deep in the jungle. The Voxmor prefer the darkness and solitude of the jungle on this planet." A hint of moisture glinted in Novissime's eyes as she spoke, and a quiver of emotion colored her voice. *How human.* "Avenlae was just a boy. Old enough to wield a sword but just a boy. The Voxmor found his tribe, his people, his family, his mother and father. They were slaughtered as he watched. Torn to shreds, Xiaye. When we found him, he was covered in the blood of his people so thick we thought the Voxmor didn't know he'd survived. He bears the scars of that night, three down his back, deeper than any weapon can make. I am told he still hears the screams at night. Whether they are the screams of his people or of the Voxmor, I do not know. But he is a slave to the memory, to the nightmare of what happened to him.

"Please, do not judge him harshly. I think his heart has turned cold from the pain and loss he has suffered, but I do not think there is true darkness in him."

"How can you be sure?"

"I helped raise him before being appointed Queen." She faced me, a smirk playing around her lips. "Although he will never tell you that little fact."

I studied her face, searching for deception in her eyes. "Why are you telling me this?"

"I am attempting to soften the blow of Avenlae's evident betrayal. I imagine he told you whatever he could to entice you to follow him willingly, as his instructions were to bring you here unharmed."

"So it *is* because of you that I have been taken from my home? Because of you, I can never go back to everything I have ever known." My voice trembled and cracked at the end of my sentence. I blinked rapidly—I could not allow her to see me cry. Of all the emotions battering the inside of my head, my pain was not one I would share.

The Queen's eyes softened. "I know your heart is looking for someone to blame for the pain, and if it must be me, so be it. But understand that I intended to allow you to choose to come here on your own. I had a duty to your mother, for she had made me promise to bring you back to *her* home when you were ready.

"Unfortunately, a few days ago, we received intelligence that the Voxmor had found you and that they knew who and what you are. You didn't see that Voxmor outside the city by chance, Xiaye. It was waiting for you, and you led the rest of them back to the forest where you had stayed hidden for so long. I sent Avenlae to retrieve you so we could keep you safe here."

Anger flared. "Why do you think I can't care for myself?"

"I don't doubt your capabilities. But can you tell me now that you would've survived an attack from all the Voxmor within screeching distance of your bunker?"

I broke eye contact with her and turned to look out over the balcony. Denial was still so strong in my head that I wanted to find any reason to vilify her and Avenlae for bringing me to *their* forest. Avenlae was easy enough to blame, but Queen Novissime had fought back with such calm reason that she had broken through the dark fog that kept me agitated.

"How are you able to communicate with me so well?" I asked, desperate for a distraction, an excuse to not feel.

"The Delfungaye began to learn your language long before your mother left, hoping to one day introduce ourselves to the humans and arm them against the Voxmor. The creatures had become well-versed in universe-hopping, and we knew it was only a matter of time before they found Earth. Humans may not have been the only intelligent species in your universe, but your oxygen-rich planet was the best place for the Voxmor to form a base. The Voxmor found their way to Earth before we could establish a treaty with the humans, and they did not trust us after something so alien brutally attacked them. I made sure the Delfungaye continued to learn and teach English. I wanted your people to be able to communicate with you when you came back."

"They're not *my* people."

"They will be."

"They'll be disappointed, then," I snapped.

"I think that, with time, you will see that your pain is shared here." The Queen gazed down as families of Delfungaye gathered in the fading sunlight, their nests beginning to flicker with firelight. "We have lost so many and fought so hard. The Delfungaye have seen too much blood spill and have felt the searing touch of death. Your story of survival is not unique among them, and I believe that, if you allow yourself, you may find acceptance and understanding here. You may not call them your people now, but they became your people by blood right the day your mother died. You may choose not to lead them, but allow me the opportunity to show you who they are. Let me teach you about the world your mother left behind before you decide."

"Do I have a choice?"

"Xiaye, you always have a choice. I will not keep you here against your will, but I will tell you to contemplate the consequences of each choice. One learns more about their paths by walking them instead of standing still and reading the signs."

I stayed quiet for a while. Indeed, one may learn more about paths by walking them, but there was a reason there were paths less traveled.

"It is getting dark, child. With your permission, the guard outside will take you to where you can stay tonight or for many nights. In the morning, you may meet that guard here, and he will open a portal for you to go back to your bunker if that is what you wish. Or you may meet another guard along the river, where they can lead you to training."

"Training?"

"To stay is to fight." She gestured toward the entrance, and, left with nothing else to say, I turned and walked away.

The guard led me to my own dewdrop nest, hanging high in a tree close to the Queen's Nest. A fire was burning in a stone firepit in the middle of the nest. Near the entrance was a small bed whose frame looked as if it had grown out from the wall. Shelves lined the opposite wall with cookware, cloth, and tools, and leaves covered the floor around the fire pit. On the far wall was a white basin with swirls of steam drifting up from calm water. It was simple, yet more than I had at the bunker.

I spied my tattered backpack and unzipped it, eyeing the knives I'd purchased at the Precinct. Echoes of the shrieks of the Voxmor rang in my ears, mingled with the sound of the red beam exploding from my palm. I shook my head to rid it of such thoughts and tried not to cry—it wasn't safe enough within that alien shelter to cry.

I saw the feathers of wings out of the corner of my eye. Settling myself onto the ground, I ran a hand lightly along the feathers as a wing stretched out in front of me. My fingers trembled as they marked the fade of the feathers from deep coal to pure snow-white. *My feathers?* I pulled at a feather lightly, felt nothing. The trembling in my fingers intensified. I gritted my teeth and yanked. I stifled a cry as a shock of pain rippled down the wing and across my back, red blood staining feather from where I had ripped one out. Fumbling in my bag, I sucked in quick gasps of air, trying to control my panic as I pressed a rag to the wing… to *my* wing.

It didn't take long for the bleeding to stop. It took only seconds longer to accept the wings were mine. They made me feel pain, too.

I moved to the basin, over which was a small shelf with a mottled blue bar of soap and a coral sponge. The basin was a heated bath, something I hadn't had access to for over ten years. I bent my head and sniffed, wondering if Avenlae was right that I smelled "human enough." There it was, the musty scent of cracked concrete, dead leaves, and Earth's night wind.

I didn't bathe that night. I curled into a ball in the small bed and fought the pain of the realization that my rusted cot had never felt as comfortable as those leaves did in that nest on Silvacastra.

CHAPTER 5

I awoke just past dawn of the first sun, inhaling the fresh smell of the forest. Memories of the previous day rushed back, filling me with restlessness despite the quiet of the forest. Truly, I wanted to stay there, to rot in that bed. To wake up on Silvacastra was too overwhelming.

But staying stagnant was how one died. I didn't particularly want to exist, but I didn't want to die, either.

I went to the shelves that held the folded piles of cloth, pushing the ache of homesickness down as deep as I could. Running a finger across the seam of one of the folds, I stared at the outfits sitting on the shelf. One pile contained a pair of ripped, dirty jeans and a stained shirt from Earth, and the other included a plated vest of marbled white and gray similar to what Avenlae had worn. Those two stacks of folded clothes epitomized the choice I had to make. There was no room for my wings in my clothes from home, so they would never fit again.

I put on the vest and gray pants with sheaths along the outer seams and peeked out the entrance of my nest. Serene silence was broken only by the rustle of leaves and gentle swaying of the dewdrop nests. The suns, slim beams of light on the horizon, cast faint light. Spreading my wings, I jumped from my nest, dropping for only a second before my feathers caught the wind and carried me into the canopy. I wanted to hate how naturally I flew. I wanted to hate it as much as I hated how my mother died without telling me of this world made of bejeweled life. But how could I hate what provided me more independence than the past ten years of solitude on Earth?

I broke through the emerald canopy, my mind calm for a moment. There was only the burning sky, the lone branch I settled myself on, and the two Silvacastra suns that warmed my feathers. A breeze tickled my cheeks and arms, and clouds as white as cotton floated across the burning sky.

Tears stung my eyes, and my vision blurred. I heard the breeze whispering through the trees, listened to the river rushing below me and the stirring of awakening forest animals.

"*This*, this was your home," I murmured, speaking as if my mother was standing before me. "Why would you keep this from me?"

A tear slid down my cheek. I brushed it away, felt the touch of metal. I looked at my fingers, at the Creonex. The lattice curling around my skin refuted my denial. And Earth, despite its familiarity, no longer held the solace I craved. Safety, whether I liked it or not, was with my mother's people, and the answers I sought were with her successor.

I was not surprised to see Queen Novissime waiting for me at the riverbank behind her nest half an hour later. She smiled as I landed and approached her. Three Dutch braids ran across her head and down the back of her stone-grey robes.

"Good morning, Xiaye. Are you ready to begin your training?"

"This early?"

"We are still in a war, child. I must ensure you can protect yourself."

"Is there a reason you call me 'child'?"

"Walk with me, and I'll tell you."

Novissime led me along the river, away from the tribe, her robes swaying as she walked. "I forget how little you know about me, Xiaye, as I knew your mother for so long," she began. "I'm much older than I may look to you, and I spent years with her, mostly here and also through correspondence while she hid on Earth."

"How did you know my mother? Are you—?"

"We are not related, no. You are a child of her blood; she made you a child of my spirit. If anything happened to her, I would take over guardianship." Her silver eyes met mine. "Because of that promise, I had to retrieve you from Earth as soon as we found you. I had to send Avenlae, as he is our strongest warrior despite his personality faults." Novissime gave me a knowing smile. "It may be difficult for you to understand it now, but everything I have done has been out of loyalty to your mother to ensure your safety. I hope to communicate that to you during your stay here and teach you about the people your mother ruled over."

"You say that as if you expect me to leave at some point."

Novissime shrugged. "You always have a choice. I do not want you to feel trapped by expectations, so be aware of the open door."

We walked together silently, the Queen watching the river and me contemplating her words. She knew more than she was letting on. As someone with my own secrets, I understood her reticence. But my cynical side questioned her motives.

"You're not telling me everything," I said, fixing her with a hard stare, "You ask me to trust you, yet you keep information from me."

She stopped walking and faced me. "I do so to give you incentive, not to deceive you. The more time you spend here, the more information I will

40

reveal. I will schedule meetings with you periodically, and in between, you can train with the Queen's Guard."

I looked into her eyes, searching for ill intent. Instead, I found a glimmer of my mother peering at me. I still couldn't decide if I should trust her, but I was searching for answers and couldn't deny that the Queen had them. She held all the cards, and she knew it. Was she a master manipulator or a Queen who would do whatever it took to protect her people? To distrust her words and demeanor was easy, but to distrust the gentle shine of her bright eyes or the smile lines along her cheeks, that was something else.

"I suppose I could agree to that," I said, "but if I want to walk away—"

"Then you are free to walk away, no questions asked."

I nodded but a rush of anxiety gripped my heart.

"I have kept you long enough," Novissime said. "The training grounds for the Queen's Guard are just through the trees across the river. Your instructor will meet you there." She turned and headed back towards the Queen's Nest.

"Should I be looking for someone in particular?" I called after her.

"Do not worry; your instructor will find you." Beadwork along her wings clicked as she took off, and I felt a gust from her wing strokes.

Shaking my head, I jumped into the air and beat my wings to climb above the river. I swooped down into the far tree line, hearing the clicks and whistles of the Delfungaye language. Assuming that a gathering of well-armored individuals meant I had found the Queen's Guard, I landed on a lower branch of a tree that stood to their right. Unwilling to draw attention, I settled myself down to observe the dynamic of the gathering.

It was evident that the Queen's Guard was composed of the surviving warriors from each tribe, as it was the most integrated gathering of Delfungaye I had seen. They were all humanoid and had wings, but the details of their appearance differed depending on their tribe. Those from Novissime's tribe, the *Laizuteek*, most resembled humans. Their silver wings, black hair, pointed ears, and silver eyes were the only nonhuman characteristics.

Others were stockier, broad-shouldered men and women who lumbered around with black wings and mops of tightly coiled green hair. Their skin was the color of rust, accentuating the gold of their cat-like eyes. Males had small tusks that protruded over their lips, and their ears and noses were broader than the other Delfungaye. These must have been members of the mountain *Hopyroque* tribe, as their features indicated they were adapted for a colder climate than the forest.

The Delfungaye that stood out the most had gold skin and hair like cornsilk. They had large navy eyes and sleek onyx wings tucked to their backs. Their feathers dragged behind them a little farther than the other tribespeople. Their wings lacked the curved claws of the *Laizuteek* and *Hopyroque* people, suggesting that they were not meant for climbing but perhaps long-distance flight. These golden people must have been what was left of the *Fyr'aeset* tribe of the plains.

The branch I crouched on shuddered. Avenlae had landed beside me, his silver eyes trained on the warriors milling below us. His hair was tied into a ponytail, and he wore a tightly wrapped black cloth around his waist and shoulders. My lip curled. The Creonex warmed around my hand as disgust tensed my muscles.

"Don't you have money to go spend somewhere?" I spat.

"Perhaps, but I make more by being here," he answered.

"Oh, do you?"

"Yes. You are worth a lot."

I tried to appear indifferent. "Am I supposed to be flattered by that?"

"Would you rather be worth nothing? Nobody would be protecting you then."

"I don't need you protecting me."

"You do."

"I do *not*, Avenlae."

"You do, *human*. I could have killed you just now. You let me sneak up too close."

I rolled my eyes. "I don't care how incapable you think I am. Why don't you do something productive and find my instructor for me?"

He stared at me. Or rather, at my feet. Realization dawned.

"*You're* my instructor?"

"Regrettably."

"How much are you getting paid for this?"

"Just enough. I did not ask for the job, but I can do it for the right price."

"You're infuriating."

Avenlae tilted his head to the side. "I am sorry, I do not understand."

I searched his face, attempting to discern if his ignorance was feigned or genuine, but he refused to look at me. I remembered the Queen scolding him for holding her gaze and wondered if it was a sign of dominance to maintain eye contact. In the end, I just huffed and turned away.

"Come," he said, and I felt the branch move as he stood. "I have much to teach you."

I could have turned and left, walked away from it all, but not when Novissime held a wealth of knowledge over my head. I set my jaw and leaped from the branch to follow him. Even through my hatred, I couldn't deny the importance of learning to kill Voxmor the way Avenlae had on Earth. He led me away from where the others were clustered, far above the trees.

"Why aren't we staying with the rest of the students?" I called.

"They are part of the Queen's Guard. You are not ready to be a member of the Guard."

When we came to a small clearing in the trees, Avenlae landed and walked to a corner of the clearing, rolling his shoulders. I landed soon after, stumbling to the side and catching myself on a tree trunk. Avenlae snorted and said something under his breath in a tongue I didn't recognize.

"You are clumsy. How do I train away clumsy?"

"I'm not used to wings," I muttered, embarrassment heating my cheeks.

"*Your* wings. They belong to you, and I have seen you fly. You know they are there. Accept them."

Avenlae picked up two wooden swords and flung one at me. I caught it awkwardly, nearly dropping it.

"Let me see what you know," he called.

"I used knives back home." Anxiety made my skin prickle as I saw how expertly Avenlae held his wooden sword, like an extension of his arm.

"This is a knife with a longer blade. Show me how you would use it." He took a fighting stance, wings angled down, both claws pointed towards me. I tossed the wooden sword between my hands, trying to figure out how to use the weapon. Avenlae side-stepped and began to circle me. I tested a jab at him. He knocked the sword out of my hand and took me to the ground, his sword against my throat. The scent of new leather with a trace of pine filled my nostrils.

"That was too easy." He pushed himself up and walked away, not offering me a hand. I scrambled to my feet, wings twitching. "It amazes me that you survived so long."

"I knew how to run and hide," I responded, dusting nonexistent dirt from my pants to give myself something to focus on other than my humiliation.

"So you were a good coward?"

My eyes widened at him as he turned, retaking a fighting stance. "You know *nothing* of what I've been through."

"Pick up your sword."

I stomped over to where my sword lay in short grass the color of peridot, shaking my head and breathing deeply. The wooden blade trembled in my hand. This time, I circled first, trying to formulate how I might land a hit on his head. Avenlae made the first move, swinging his sword to my left. I stepped back and swung my sword up, a dull crack echoing through the trees as I parried his attack. He swung his wing over his head, smacking the claw into my right shoulder and sending me to the ground again. I hit the dirt hard, the air knocked out of my lungs.

"That wasn't fair. You used your wings," I panted.

Avenlae rested his sword on his shoulder. "You have wings."

"I haven't spent my life learning how to fight with them." I pushed myself into a sitting position, hating how petulant I sounded.

"You have not spent your life learning how to fight with anything."

I smacked my palms against my thighs. "What is your *problem*, Avenlae?"

He raised an eyebrow and looked away from me. I stood up. "Obviously I don't know how to fight with a sword. Shouldn't you instruct me on proper technique, or do you enjoy humiliating me?"

Avenlae moved to attack again. I swung my sword up and blocked him. I spun away from his next attack and swung my sword into his back. *What sweet satisfaction!*

He stumbled forward but whipped around to face me again. Avenlae's eyes flashed, and his pupils dilated as he tilted his head to the side as if re-evaluating me. Sweat formed on my brow. The day had warmed as the suns rose. The tattoos on Avenlae's arms and neck glistened as he stepped closer, angling his wings forward. His third eyelids flicked over his eyes as he raised his sword, his ears flat against his black hair.

When Avenlae darted forward, I was ready. I couldn't attack, and my parries were weak, but I was agile enough to spin and duck away from his sword. Still, I was smacked with the wooden blade and shoved to the ground over and over. My limbs ached, and I wondered how many green and purple bruises would darken my skin.

Tendrils of Avenlae's hair stuck to his sweaty face as we sparred. He called out corrections and I took them begrudgingly, my frustration growing. Finally, after picking myself up for at least the twelfth time, I held a hand up at his order to continue.

"Avenlae, please, I need a moment."

He narrowed his eyes. "The enemy will never let you rest."

"No, but you can."

"You will never learn if you continue to be weak."

"You're supposed to teach me to be better. Is this not a reflection of your instruction so far? You just call out insults as you beat me down."

"You resist my *corrections*. You will not fight me. You run away, like a scared child."

"You handed me a weapon I have never used before, and you expect me to get better every time you push me down?"

"Picking yourself up is only half the battle. You are not pushing yourself."

I shook the sword in his direction. "How am I supposed to push myself when I *still* don't know what I'm doing?"

"*Listen* to what I say. It is *that* easy." His voice was sharp, but he didn't look at me once while we argued.

I had had enough of him, enough of his insults. The Creonex buzzed and warmed around my hand, and I ran towards him, wooden sword raised.

46

Anger guided my blade, and my strikes were stronger than before. I wasn't quick, and Avenlae had no trouble fending me off, but my attack was furious.

The metal Creonex grew hotter against my skin as I swung my sword in wide arcs, intent on causing damage. Finally, with a flick of his wrist, Avenlae sent my sword flying out of my hand. He thrust his sword toward my chest, indicating yet another win. With the feeling of fire in my palm, I swung my left hand up to block his attack. Instead, a pulse of red energy shot out from the metal filigree around my fingers and grazed Avenlae's side, against his ribs. The shot sent him stumbling back, and he dropped his sword as he fell to his knees, clutching his ribs as the cloth wrap unraveled and fell from his shoulders.

I froze, my anger gone, my mind in shock. I took a step toward Avenlae, my ears ringing and my throat tight. Tribal tattoos were exposed on his chest and shoulders, circling across his abdomen. Scars cut jagged paths through the skin over his shoulders and across his upper back. *I am told he still bears the scars of that night.*

"Avenlae, I'm so sorry." I was horrified at what I had done. I had never hurt another person before, not even to defend myself. Blood dribbled out between Avenlae's fingers, red as human blood. There was still some heat in the filigree of the Creonex, and I used it to cut a chunk of fabric away from my bodice. Holding the cloth out to him, I knelt next to Avenlae, who looked confused at the offering.

"Use it to put pressure on the wound," I said. "I-I'm sorry, I don't know what medicinal herbs will help you."

Avenlae's silver eyes met mine, pupils dilating. His ears were pulled forward as if he were listening intently, but he did not speak or take the fabric from my hand. I pressed the cloth against his ribs, glimpsing the ugly cut before covering it. Avenlae gasped, and his wings curled against his back. I raised my head to apologize again for the pain I had caused, but the words died in my throat.

Pupils once again contracted into slits, Avenlae held himself tensely, chest rising and falling with rapid pants, ears flat against his hair as he stared at where I pressed the cloth against his wound. It wasn't pain in his eyes—it was *fear*.

"I just wanted to help," I said. I released the pressure against his ribs and backed away, watching his eyes. Avenlae grasped the blood-soaked fabric, his body relaxing without me so close to him.

"Do you have doctors here?" I asked.

"Healers," he murmured.

"Where are they?"

"I do not need your help. Take a break, but return in thirty minutes."

Avenlae stood, spread his wings, and took off from the clearing, his shining feathers carrying him above the trees before I could respond.

My mind was chaos. I tried to rip the filigree glove from my skin, to no avail. Tears flowed as I held my head in my hands, images of the fear in Avenlae's eyes spinning through my thoughts. My actions had triggered that fear. *I* had caused that pain, that look in his eyes.

What was this thing, this Creonex, doing to me?

CHAPTER 6

I sat on the riverbank in the shade of a tree, stomach twisted with guilt. Fifteen minutes remained before training resumed. I stretched a wing forward and dipped the tip into the river, feeling the water glide lazily over my feathers. Long aquatic grasses rippled under the surface, and small multicolored fish darted through the blades. A part of me wished to dive into the water myself and let it wash away my anxiety.

Robust songs of birds had been replaced by the soft chirps and buzzes of bugs, much louder by the river. It still reminded me of Earth, but the sounds and colors were off, the way things appear through a screen. I ached for home, even though "home" no longer held meaning for me. Earth, as I had known it, stopped existing in my mind when the Voxmor infiltrated my forest. So perhaps the ache was for the memory of home and the longing for somewhere I belonged. Especially now, when I was terrified of the very weapon I had thought would save me from the Voxmor.

I heard grass rustling and looked over my shoulder. A *Fyr'aeset* woman approached, holding folded clothing. Her sleek, ebony wings dragged behind her, and her blonde hair was cut into a severe bob that angled her diamond-shaped face. She gazed at me with deep navy eyes and had the longest eyelashes I'd ever seen. She stopped and sat beside me, relaxing her wings behind her on the grass. The way she held herself reminded me of a porcelain doll, with round, unblinking, shining eyes.

"Hello. Are you Xiaye?" she asked, her accent thick. Her eyes darted from me to the ground as if she couldn't decide whether she was allowed to look at me.

"I am," I answered.

"I thought so." She spoke carefully and enunciated each word as if aware that her English wasn't easy to understand. "Avenlae sent me. You look troubled."

I turned back towards the river. "I'm fine, thank you." If I stayed still long enough, perhaps she'd get the hint and leave me alone.

"This river spans all the way across the forest," the *Fyr'aeset* woman said, gesturing to the water in front of us. "We call her *Audritya*, which translates to 'strong mother' in your language. You see, she was strong enough to make the mountains part before her so she could travel to the sea."

"I'm sorry," I said, shaking my head and facing her again. "Is there a reason you're telling me this? Why did Avenlae send you here?"

She turned away and looked at the water, holding the clothes out to me timidly. "You are a suspicious person, are you not, Xiaye?"

"It wasn't a trusting nature that kept me alive for ten years."

She nodded, her fair hair glistening in a small patch of sunlight that broke through the leaves. "I am delivering a new training uniform to you. And I wanted to tell you that while *Audritya* was strong enough to make the mountains part before her, she needed the moon's light to guide her at night and the wind to carry her current."

She made eye contact for a second, smiled softly, and continued. "You may have spent your life alone, but you are no longer on your own. You do not have to choose to be alone."

A little lonely part of me wanted to believe her. "What is your name?" I asked.

"Notien."

"Well, Notien, thank you for your, uh, kind words." I returned her smile but imagined mine didn't look very genuine.

"Of course. I thought you might find yourself lonely here. Being introduced to this world you have never known must be overwhelming."

"Yes, I suppose so." I tried to appear friendly, but she stared at the ground next to me. That little lonely part of me was beginning to decide loneliness was less painful.

"I would love to show you around our tribe. Then maybe you will not feel as afraid or suspicious."

"I never said I felt afraid."

"But you know nothing of our ways or people. Why would you not feel a bit of fear if you are also so suspicious?"

I raised my eyebrows. "You put it bluntly."

"I do not understand what you mean."

"I meant—never mind. You're right. I have been feeling overwhelmed. But Queen Novissime has promised me information, so ..." I trailed off, wondering if *now* Notien would take the hint.

"Oh, the Queen will teach you the official side of the tribe. If you want to know the Delfungaye people, immerse yourself in our culture." She copied me and dipped the tip of her wing into the river's current. "There is much more to our tribes than the languages and social obligations Queen Novissime will teach you."

I traced a finger over the Creonex wrapped around my hand. Notien seemed friendly, although I wondered why she wouldn't meet my eyes. Was she as suspicious of me as I was of her? Was this offer an attempt to disguise her wish to discover more about me?

I decided to take a chance—whether or not I liked her, chances were she had information I needed. "I suppose you could show me around. But we won't get far if you can't look at me when we speak."

Notien laughed nervously. "It is out of respect that I do not meet your gaze. We do not make extended eye contact with those whose ranks are above our own."

"If I give you permission, would you look at me as if I were equal to you?"

She blinked, surprised. "I, yes, I may hold eye contact with your permission."

"Fine. You have it." I looked at her as she raised her eyes from the ground. "On Earth, it's considered rude to not look at the person you're speaking to."

Notien bowed her head. "Please forgive me. I meant no disrespect."

"I know." I didn't know what Notien expected, and I had already exhausted my scant social skills. Fortunately, Notien stood and said, "We are probably expected back for training." She held out a hand to me.

I hesitated a moment. But she seemed harmless and eager to please, so I grasped her hand and let her pull me up. She was several inches taller than me, but I had noted that the Delfungaye were significantly taller than the humans I had been around.

Notien raised a hand in farewell and jumped into the air, her long wings allowing her to glide much farther than I had been able to.

I took a deep breath and took off toward the clearing. High above the trees, the feeling of air through my feathers grew more refreshing than the feeling of water across my skin. After a few minutes of weaving back and forth, I spotted the clearing where I trained and descended. I stuck my landing firmly and felt disappointed that no one had been around to witness it. After assuring I was alone, I sneaked behind the thickest tree I could find to change out of my ruined grey outfit and into the marbled training uniform. My arms were bare, but the material was more breathable than my grey top.

I crept back from behind the tree to find I was still alone. A pang of guilt twisted my stomach as I wondered if the wound I had inflicted upon Avenlae was more severe than it had appeared. I wasn't entirely upset that it was Avenlae I had injured since he was a complete ass. But I feared the power that burst from me in anger, a fiery energy as explosive as dynamite. To be capable of inflicting such damage so swiftly with no control—did that make me a monster? Something to be as feared as the Voxmor?

Was that why I was on Silvacastra? To become *their* weapon?

A strong gust broke over my head as Avenlae swooped down along the treeline, landing lightly on the grass. He had changed into a black matte armored vest, and his hair was slicked back into a ponytail again. A part of me lamented that it wasn't falling in long, dark waves over his shoulders, and the rest of me felt revolted that I dared imagine such a thing.

Avenlae walked past me, not bothering to acknowledge me, and stooped to pick up the wooden swords leaning against a tree.

"Look, Avenlae, I—"

"I am fine. Prepare yourself to spar." He held a sword out to me, still not meeting my eyes.

I took the sword, intrigued that Avenlae still had enough respect to avert his eyes. I decided I owed him a morsel of respect as well. "I am sorry, though. I really hadn't meant—"

"I am fine," Avenlae repeated, tossing his sword between his hands. "I needed to test your limits. I brought it upon myself."

I furrowed my brow. "You were trying to make me angry? To see what I would do?"

"I was wondering if you would use the Creonex again. I wanted to see what power you were capable of."

"So, you didn't mean any of what you said?"

"Oh, I did. I am usually better at keeping it to myself."

I watched him. The suggestion of a smile played on his lips—had that been his idea of a joke?

Avenlae flashed his silver eyes at me as he relaxed into a fighting stance. "This time, try to use the Creonex as you spar."

I shook my head. "No. Absolutely not."

"It is the most powerful weapon you have. You must learn to use it."

"I don't want to. I'll learn to rely on other weapons."

"What if you are in a situation where the Creonex is all you have?"

"Avenlae, I said no. I have no idea what this power is capable of, and I can't … I don't want to hurt someone again." I held back telling him how badly I wanted to rip the metal glove off my hand. I was a runner, not an aggressor, and had never started or even finished a fight. A whisper of *coward* licked the back of my mind.

For once, Avenlae held my gaze for a moment. I glanced away first. "You cannot allow your fear or pain to hold you back," Avenlae said quietly.

"It's *not* my fear."

"It is *only* your fear that is stopping you. That power is only dangerous if you do not control it."

"And how do you know I can control it? What proof do you have that it won't always be this dangerous?"

"You have had that Creonex your whole life, and the only time it has ever shown any evidence of true power has been when you let your anger take over. Control your anger, and you control the Creonex."

54

I touched my fingers to my thumb and listened to the soft clink of the metal filigree. "I… I could've killed you. That fast. I could kill *anyone* in this forest with a power I don't understand."

"I have survived worse. We are too far away from the tribe for you to harm anything but me and the trees if something goes awry."

A crackle of blue electricity forked across my fingers, buzzing through the twisted metal glove. "If I can't control it—"

"You do not have a choice," Avenlae said, leaning back against the tree trunk. "That is your most powerful weapon and may become your greatest defense."

"*You* don't even know the extent of this power."

"I do not care how many excuses you find to not use the Creonex. I will force you to."

I mulled the idea over in my head. I wanted to tear the Creonex from my skin as badly as I had wanted to rip my wings off my back. But, my wings were freedom—the Creonex, a weapon. And I wasn't nearly good enough at fighting to entertain the idea of opposing Avenlae. "Fine. But I'll only use it as my last option in a fight."

"You understand that the Voxmor are hunting you down to kill you, do you not? You must learn how to kill them."

"Them, yes. But I do not need to kill or harm you." I tried to meet his eyes, but they darted away again. "Yet."

A smirk passed briefly over Avenlae's face before he ordered me into the sparring position. This time, he worked through the different attacks and parries slowly, correcting my form and emphasizing the significance of footwork in combat. He even remarked that my time spent trekking through the forest had given me the endurance required for a real fight. I couldn't figure out if it was a rare compliment or something said in relief that part of his job had become easier. Either way, that side of Avenlae was a teacher who could show me the merit in being a skilled fighter. That part of him could prove survival was more than having good places to hide.

Towards the end of the afternoon, as the suns dipped low enough to lengthen the shadows of the trees around us, we began warily testing the possibility of using the Creonex as a weapon. If I took the time to focus, I could make electricity crackle across the fingers of the metal glove, but that was all I could manifest. It was as if there was a part of me attached to the Creonex that I could feel but not unlock. A part of me I feared; it was the darkness, the trauma. The things I didn't want to know and refused to remember.

About the sixth time I created crackles of energy across my fingers, I began feeling exhaustion from the day's events. It clouded my mind, and the electricity fizzled out from my fingertips. When I opened my eyes, the world was spinning and my vision was quivering. I blinked and stumbled back, energy sapped. Avenlae reached out a hand and caught me before I fell, his calloused palm pressing against my back between my wings.

"What is wrong?" he asked, his brows furrowed.

My vision cleared with the spike of fear that raced down my spine from his touch. I pushed myself away from Avenlae, twisting to face him but staggering off to the side as my balance was thrown off. "I'm fine. Just tired."

Avenlae looked as if he didn't believe me, but he kept his eyes down as I righted myself. "You are unsteady."

"It's just the strain of training." I glanced away from him, looking at the ground to see if it was still swaying. Thankfully, it was staying in one place, but fatigue enveloped me. *Don't let him see, it's weakness.*

"Xiaye, when was the last time you ate?" Avenlae asked.

I tried to think, but my mind refused to cooperate. "I don't remember."

"Can you fly?"

I nodded, even though I was unsure. But I had no intention of letting him carry me.

"Follow me. It will not be far."

Avenlae leaped into the air, one flap of his wings carrying him halfway up the height of the trees. I had to take a few steps with my wings spread before I could leap into the air after him, and those steps spent my last bit of energy. My body shook, and I felt winded after a few minutes.

Off to the right of our clearing, Avenlae descended into the canopy of a tree whose branches hung low from the weight of bunches of the bright-colored fruit. I attempted to land next to him but faltered. Avenlae grabbed my arm before I fell, and I was torn between letting him hold my arm to prevent me from falling or pulling away because I was afraid of him. He grabbed my opposite shoulder and I gasped. "Don't—!"

"I am not hurting you, Xiaye," Avenlae said, keeping his eyes on mine. He held me there for a moment, warmth radiating from his hands as they held my trembling arms. "Whatever you may have been told, I am not here to hurt you." He blinked and lowered his eyes as he released his grip. I let out a woosh of air, felt the ache of my lungs from holding my breath.

Avenlae reached up toward the clumps of fruit that hung above us, grabbing two magenta fruits the size of grapefruits and offered one to me. Golden juice dripped from the end that had been attached to the branch.

"Eat. It will help."

I accepted it and took a bite. The fruit's skin crunched under my teeth and released a gush of juice that dribbled over my fingers. It was cold and sweet, with a slightly tart aftertaste.

Avenlae sat next to me. "It is called *bauete*. It provides a burst of energy. The food here is rich in nutrients, and you must eat often to fuel your wings." He took a bite of his fruit and chewed. He then turned his head towards me, still keeping his eyes on the bark at my feet. "It is easy to forgot how little you know. I am sorry."

The last thing I expected from Avenlae was an apology, and I nearly choked on the *bauete* juice. "Thank you," I said. "Um, can I sit?"

"You do not need my permission. I do not own this branch or this tree."

Smiling slightly, I lowered myself down to sit next to him. The suns furthered their descent, casting a warm glow across the sky. We sat quietly for a while, enjoying the *bauetes* and watching the ever-changing colors of the suns' set. As time passed, I began to feel a touch more at ease with Avenlae. I wasn't entirely sure why—perhaps the offering of restorative fruit suggested there was a softer side to him below the mask of warrior. Maybe eating in front of me suggested that he was just as mortal as I despite being a different species. Maybe… I wasn't alone.

"Avenlae," I began, breaking the silence. "Why did you return after I hurt you?" I paused, for I could feel him tense next to me. "I'm sorry, I, I just—"

"Could not forgive yourself?"

I swallowed. "I… I know how dangerous my anger is. And I don't think anyone could get paid enough to be around that kind of power. To do so must be a choice."

Avenlae gazed at the treetops below us. "Someone must teach you how to control the pain."

"Did you learn to control it?"

"I am not sure I learned to control it as much as I learned to reroute it when needed," Avenlae answered after a pause, his voice soft as the evening breeze.

I was so stunned that he was opening up to me that I couldn't reply.

"You will not stop feeling it, Xiaye. But you will learn not to be afraid of it.

The pain cannot hurt you anymore now than it has in the past."

I watched as the warm light of the suns reflected deep amber in the strands of Avenlae's onyx hair, his ponytail lying across his back between his wings. He gazed at the trees, and his pupils shrank, his silver irises gleaming like diamonds. He turned to me, and I felt as if I were looking at a different person, as if I were catching a glimpse of who Avenlae was behind the facade. Someone was broken behind those silver eyes, pushed down, and locked away to be protected by the fierce warrior.

Just as quickly, Avenlae looked away, and his expression went blank. He clenched his jaw and lowered his head. He must have been scolding himself for allowing me the slightest glimpse past his protection. I realized that while I was still deciding how to feel about the Mercenary, the broken person behind Avenlae's eyes was someone I could, in time, learn to have empathy for, if not fully trust.

That broken person wasn't alone anymore, either.

CHAPTER 7

The Mercenary took me to a nest where several *Fyr'aeset* prepared the food they farmed along with any meat the hunters brought back. He procured a leaf plate of "real food" for me and escorted me to my nest without a word. Then he was gone. The tribespeople steered clear of him, but they stared after him, even though he hadn't spared any of them a glance.

Soon after, Notien arrived on the branch leading to my nest. Despite my giving her permission to maintain eye contact, she still bowed her head slightly before saying, "Please forgive the intrusion, Xiaye. I wondered if you might like some company."

I hesitated, but her smile held so much anticipation that I nodded and said, "My lodging is right in front of us." *You're too nice, Xiaye. That'll get you killed.*

"I had hoped they made a nest for you. I would want time to myself if I were taken to a new tribe."

"You don't say."

"I do not say what?" she asked, turning to me with a quizzical look in her navy eyes.

"No, that was—I didn't mean you shouldn't—it was just an expression."

"Oh. I did not realize how many colloquialisms there are in your language."

"Apparently, I didn't either," I said as we entered my nest.

"Well, that is something you can teach me, then!"

Notien sat in front of the fire pit and pulled a small metal capsule from her belt. She touched it to the wood, igniting a fire. My eyebrows rose. *I need to get one of those.*

I sat on the floor and picked at the food on my leaf plate, trying to remember how to host guests. *Remember? You've never even had any friends.* I had to stuff a bite of food into my mouth to stop myself from answering my own thoughts. I really had been alone for too long.

"I imagine you have many questions," Notien said. "I am here to answer them." She paused, chewing and then swallowing her food. "Like a friend, I think."

I blinked at her. We only knew each other's names, and she wanted to call herself my friend? *I do not have the energy for this,* I thought. On the other hand, though, I had to wonder how naive Notien really was and how to use it to my advantage. There was no better way to test the theory than to ask about the topic I had been mulling over. "Okay, then answer me this. When Avenlae was with me, everyone was looking right at him, staring even. As a warrior, I would've thought his rank would be above other people in the tribe, but he resides outside the central hub. Why is that?"

Notien chewed her next bite of food slowly. Finally, she said, "That is quite the question to start with. You must understand that before the Voxmor came and killed off most of the tribes, the *Y'araye* warriors were feared above all on Silvacastra. They were fierce and merciless killers, and the peace treaty we had with them was uncertain at best. They were often hired as mercenaries for the highest bidder on other planets, other galaxies, and some other universes before the Voxmor war. Avenlae may have come here young, but he carries the scent of the *Y'araye* bloodline."

I thought about sitting in a tree next to that *Y'araye* warrior and holding his gaze. That broken person behind his silver eyes didn't seem like an emotionless killer. "He's not allowed to stay near here for everyone's safety?"

Notien shook her head. "No, he chooses to stay apart from the tribe. He knows he is feared, and I think the solitude gives him peace."

I took another bite of food, a spicy vegetable. I could empathize with wanting to be alone, but didn't the loneliness sometimes make the pain stronger? *Ah,* I winced, *I don't want to go there.*

"So," I began, changing the subject, "the Delfungaye used to be in contact with other worlds? Seems odd that you live in wooden nests and fight with swords. I'd expected your people would have the luxury of advanced technology."

Notien smiled. "We learned early on that the 'luxuries of technology' come at a steep price. Most tribes agreed to use our technology for commerce between worlds, medicine, and defense only if necessary. We live as simple people so we can survive if an enemy takes our technology from us. The humans are nearly extinct, are they not? Their technology did nothing to help them against the Voxmor." Notien finished her food before continuing. "Bullets do not penetrate the hide of the Voxmor, but *exitialium,* metal mined from our *Fae'oteek* mountains, doles out lethal strikes." She stretched her black wings out behind her, resting them against the ground rather than keeping them folded close to her back. Her long lashes nearly obscured her eyes as she watched the fire before her. A cold brush of a twilight breeze slunk in through the entrance to my nest, rustling a few strands of Notien's platinum hair. It was so alien to me—here was someone who *wanted* to speak with me, to answer my questions. And she was... *kind.* But who was she, really?

"Notien, why do you train as a soldier?"

She took a moment before answering. "I do not have a family anymore. They were killed during the third attack of the Voxmor." When she looked at me, her round eyes were hardened. "I am training as a soldier because nothing will stop me from avenging my tribe should I get the opportunity. I will not be caught off-guard again."

There was a difference between her and me. The death of my mother made me run from her killers for ten years, but the death of Notien's entire family prompted her to run toward their killers with a vengeance. How could one have the perspective of such confidence?

A few forks of blue lightning cracked across the fingers of my left hand, and the Creonex glowed faintly. "I hope you get that opportunity."

Notien glanced at my hand and then into my eyes. "I hope *you* do, Xiaye."

I curled my fingers into my palm, watching the firelight dance along the smooth, blue filigree. "We'll see. I'm still trying to comprehend that this planet is *real*."

"Do not worry," Notien said, standing up and holding out her hand. "I will help you."

I stared at her golden palm for a long moment. *You've never had any friends...* Hesitantly, I took her hand, shaking it weakly.

"Oh, no!" Notien said with a laugh. The sound was like birdsong. "We do not shake hands like that." She took my hand and slid our palms against each other, hooking our thumbs together so that, when we grasped hands, we held them vertically, fingers across the back of each other's hand. She released my hand and patted her palm and curled fingers on the middle of her chest. I repeated the gesture.

"In my tribe, that is how we say goodbye for now to our friends." Notien smiled, bowed her head, and left the nest. Cold silence slithered in at her absence. I'm not sure how long I stared at the empty entrance, sorting through my thoughts. Long enough for one of my feet to fall asleep.

After smothering the embers of the fire, I looked at my bed, which seemed more inviting now that I was alone. A slight movement caught my eye, and I looked to the white basin, saw steam drifting to the ceiling. I sniffed at my arm—the smell of Earth was gone, replaced with salty sweat. Sighing, I went to the basin, hugging myself. It was just large enough to fit my entire body in if I curled up. After ensuring that the cloth curtains were fastened tightly over the entrance to my nest, I undressed and lowered myself into the water. Warmth soothed the ache in my muscles.

I cried as my skin soaked up the clean smell of eucalyptus from the bar of soap, and I scrubbed away dirt with the sponge. I cried out of mourning for the last vestiges of Earth that swirled down the basin's drain. Earth was gone, home was gone, I… I was gone, too.

Notien met me right outside my nest the next morning, shoving a fluffy pastry into my hands before I had the chance to speak.

"You must have this!" she said with too much energy for the early hour. "The plant they use to make it blooms for only a short time this season, and it will wake you up more than anything else we have!"

I felt as if a full blast of Notien at suns' rise was enough to wake me up, but I still took the pastry. During the flight to the training fields across the river, Notien chatted away as I finished the treat, which I somehow figured out was called *graetae*. She told me all the things she wanted to show me that evening after training, and I grimaced as I struggled to find a way to tell her I wanted to be alone. Relief came unexpectedly when Avenlae landed nearby, silencing Notien. Tight braids sparkling with gold fell like ropes down his shoulders, a style likely more effective at keeping his hair tied back than the ponytail he had the day before. His black vest was in place, and two swords were crisscrossed over his back.

Notien gasped when he appeared and averted her eyes, her ears flat against her platinum hair. Avenlae ignored her and said to me, "We have got a long day ahead. Let's go."

"And a good morning to you, too," I murmured under my breath as I took off to follow him, the morning air rustling through my feathers. It was refreshing to be away from Notien's chatter, but it was negated by Avenlae's somber attitude. Upon reaching the clearing (in which I landed quite well, whether or not he noticed), Avenlae pulled the swords from their scabbards across his back, holding a hilt out to me.

"I don't think you should trust me with real blades," I said warily.

Avenlae cocked his head to the side, then swung his blade down towards his leg. I gasped, darting forward as if to stop him, but the blade bounced off his thigh. "The blade is fake. Indeed, I would *not* trust you with real *exitialium* swords. Not yet."

Avenlae balanced the blade on a finger, tossed it up, and caught it by the hilt, hissing with displeasure. "Not as good as mine, but they will allow you to learn how they feel."

He called for me to enter the sparring position. I took a breath as he began to circle. *Do better. Show no weakness.*

I refused to be intimidated by Avenlae's skill as we sparred, parrying his attacks even though I knew he was holding back. Maintaining eye contact, I attempted intimidation of my own, knowing he could not look away in combat. Each of his comments from the day before ran through my mind, anger fueling my attacks. *The pain cannot hurt you anymore now than it did before.* Avenlae's gaze on the *bauete* tree flashed in my mind, and I attempted an attack, electricity crackling across my blade. Avenlae used his wings to push himself back, and the gust of wind sent me reeling. He panted and stared at me, searching for something in my eyes. For a split second, the image of a man racing through the alleyways of the Precinct flashed across my mind. I shook my head. Was that another memory?

"Something is different. You are fighting with passion, and you could not use the Creonex without being provoked yesterday," Avenlae said, remembering his place and averting his eyes.

I readjusted my grip on the sword, deciding not to dwell on the image. "I need to prove a point."

"What point?"

"That you're wrong about me." I relaxed back into the sparring position, my wings rustling as they hovered over my head. "I'm *not* a weak human."

"Work harder. I can still smell humanity in the air around you."

I held my tongue. Pride would never allow me to admit to myself or to Avenlae that his words meant anything to me. Concealing the rippling anger his remark sparked, I rolled my shoulders and prepared for the complicated attack pattern Avenlae used next, which I parried clumsily, even by my own standards.

Avenlae next had me move through different attack and parry combinations, using his sword to correct my stance and swings. His pokes evolved into jabs, and I could sense his frustration growing. I gritted my teeth as I went through the motions of a new combination for the sixth time, sweat running down my back. *Be good enough, be* good *enough!* Suddenly, Avenlae jabbed at my leg, and my knee buckled. I used my sword to catch myself, panting.

"Get up! You have not perfected your footwork yet," Avenlae snapped.

I stood, glaring at him. "You need to let me rest for a moment."

"You do not give the orders here."

"Well, you won't get paid well for me collapsing from exhaustion, will you? One night isn't long enough for me to develop the same endurance as you."

Avenlae set his jaw, then muttered something under his breath as he turned and walked away.

"What was that?" I asked.

"Stay here."

I flopped onto the ground, dropping the sword. For as long as he was gone, I was going to stay on the grass, enjoying the feeling of *not moving*. A slight chill was in the air, and it felt the way my forest on Earth felt before autumn settled in. My throat constricted, and tears welled in my eyes. It was odd how grief overwhelmed me at unpredictable times. I had been keeping it bottled up until I could face it alone in my nest. But something as simple as a slight drop in temperature could crack open that bottle and remind me of everything I'd lost. I felt that pain again, that heavy weight in my chest. I needed to control it, to stop it. It wasn't safe out in the open.

The sound of wings alerted me to Avenlae's presence just before he landed in the clearing. I choked down my emotions, put on a neutral expression. I straightened my spine as I stood to face him, and my tears were dry.

Avenlae held out a crystal water bottle. I took it and we drank our fill silently.

"It is difficult to train someone so new to combat."

I raised an eyebrow at him. "I suppose I could accept that apology."

"I did not apologize."

"Not directly, no. But I won't get anything better than that from you."

67

Once again, Avenlae muttered under his breath. His language sounded harsher than the clicks and whistles that danced around the tongue of the other Delfungaye.

"What language is that?" I asked, picking up my sword, expecting him to tell me to be ready to spar again.

He made no reply, unsheathed his sword and tested its balance again, almost as if to give himself something to do.

"I asked you a question," I said.

Avenlae's ears pressed back against his hair. He moved his head to the side so that I could see his profile. "*Y'araye.*"

"Will you teach me?"

Avenlae shook his head. "No."

"Why not?"

"Not in the contract."

I tensed as he circled me, preparing for the fight. I hadn't expected him to teach me more than how to fight and defend myself. But I wanted to pick apart his facade. I was more curious about what lay beneath the Mercenary's mask than I cared to admit, either to Avenlae or myself.

The rest of training went smoother than the day before. In the afternoon, Avenlae's comments lessened in severity, and by the beginning of the suns' set, he had become *almost* instructive. I could move through some of the simpler attack combinations he had taught me with a suggestion of the grace with which Avenlae fought. I congratulated myself, knowing he wouldn't. Avenlae did, however, begin to watch me with something more than indifference as he ran me through one final round of attacks and parries. I suspected that he, too, was becoming more curious about me now that I had proved I was capable of learning the art of Delfungaye combat. Then again, perhaps the look in his silver eyes reflected a desire to profit more from me.

At least he refrained from calling me human in that patronizing tone for the rest of the afternoon.

I grabbed my crystal bottle when Avenlae dismissed me, drinking the last drops of water. I watched him retrieve two silver swords from behind a tree stump and slide them into the scabbards crossed over his back. They must have been his own swords, for their blades appeared sleeker than those we had been sparring with, and he was more comfortable handling them.

"Are you expecting trouble?" I asked as he neared.

"I am on guard duty tonight. There is almost always trouble."

"What are you guarding?"

"The perimeter of the tribe's territory," Avenlae said, tying his long ebony braids back. "There are still Voxmor within the forest, and they cannot be allowed to reach the interior of the tribe."

I nodded, following him to the middle of the clearing. "I guess I'll sleep easier tonight, then." I hadn't really meant to say it out loud, but I knew the statement to be true. Something told me very little on that planet could get past Avenlae.

His footsteps paused beside me. I turned back to him, catching his studying look. It was only a few seconds before he looked down, quietly saying, "You exceeded my expectations today."

I raised my eyebrows. "Uh, thank you."

Avenlae's eyes darted uneasily around the ground as if watching a field mouse skittering through the grass. "You have potential, and you can learn quickly. You just need to allow yourself to."

"What does that mean?"

"You are limiting yourself. I do not know if it is out of fear or defense, but something is preventing you from realizing what you are capable of when you fight."

The question I really wanted to ask was wavering on the tip of my tongue. Avenlae was acting almost kind, and I was afraid I would chase away that person he protected so fiercely. I took a breath, then took a chance. "What was it for you? Defense or fear?"

Slowly, Avenlae lifted his head, his silver eyes meeting my mismatched ones. "Fear," he answered softly, and what I saw in the depths of his eyes told me it was also fear that kept his voice so hushed.

I thought I should say something more, encourage the openness, but the moment ended, and Avenlae leaped into the air. It was strange to witness those glimpses of Avenlae that were separate from the *Y'araye* Mercenary everyone feared. It seemed as if he wanted someone to see the truth, to see beyond the warrior, but he was too afraid of the intimacy to allow it. I couldn't figure out *why* I was so intrigued by him—he wasn't the only one with secrets to keep. I wouldn't tell him mine if he didn't tell me his.

Would I?

Preoccupied with these thoughts, I had to swerve to avoid flying into a male *Hopyroque* guard waiting just outside my nest's entrance once I'd returned.

"Queen Novissime requests your presence," he said.

I sighed. "Can I choose *not* to go?"

That comment was met with stony silence. So, I changed direction and flew to Queen Novissime's chambers, still in my training uniform and filled with resentment that my quiet evening alone was being so unceremoniously taken away from me.

CHAPTER 8

Queen Novissime was sitting on her balcony when I arrived, relaxing in white silk robes, her wings tinkling with the intricate beadwork woven through her feathers. Her hair, dark as night, fell in swaths across her shoulders. Novissime greeted me with a smile and gestured towards a plush chair opposite her.

Still prickling with annoyance, I did not return her smile, but I sank into the chair, trying to hide how comfortable I felt. *Keep your guard up.*

"So," Novissime began, "you have survived your first two days here."

Unsure if she expected an answer, I stayed quiet.

"I may hazard a guess that you enjoyed your time more than expected. I hear you made a friend."

"Notien? I'm not sure I had a choice."

The Queen laughed, a mellow sound that almost made me smile. "Notien is very eager, that I know. I think she finds you as interesting as you find her. But make no mistake, she is fiercer than she looks and is a strong ally to have."

I nodded again, lifting my spine away from the back of the chair. Something was off about her mannerisms: they were *too* superficial.

"And what about your training?" Novissime asked, tilting her head slightly to the side. "Are you finding it satisfactory?"

I narrowed my eyes. "Surely you didn't ask me here just to make small talk, Queen Novissime."

The Queen straightened her head, furrowing her brows. "Straight to the point, I see."

"I think you owe me that much."

She studied me again before continuing. "You are correct. I did begin this conversation with idle pleasantries, but only because I thought it might make you more comfortable. I see my mistake now." With a flourish, she spread her wings to rest them on either side of the chair and crossed her legs, clasping her hands over her knee. "I've heard that you've used the Creonex during your training."

My interest was piqued despite my sour mood. "There have been moments when I've felt a connection to its power."

"Interesting," Novissime said quietly, as if more to herself than to me. "That shouldn't happen."

"I'm sorry, what was that?"

Novissime glanced at the blue filigree around my left hand, then back at me. "From what we know about the Creonex—mind you, that is very little—the only beings that can channel or use energy from the Creonex are the Creators themselves."

"But I'm not—"

"Oh, no, of course not, child. I'm not implying that *you* are a Creator. I'm merely stating that we have never seen the Creonex used before."

"Do you know why I can use it?"

"No, I don't," the Queen said, turning away from me, her eyes unfocused as if lost in thought.

"But you have a working theory, don't you?"

"I have a guess. Nothing more substantial than that."

"What is your guess?" I asked, my impatience coming out in my voice more than I intended.

"I will tell you when I have more evidence." The Queen didn't flinch at the glare I gave her. "I know it's frustrating, but you are still amid an incredible transition into this new world and your new role. I do not need to add to the emotions you have yet to process, especially if I cannot confirm what I may or may not know."

I lowered my eyes, another surge of grief gripping treacherously at my heart. I clenched my jaw with the effort to push it away. *Don't you* dare *cry.*

"It will get easier as time passes," Novissime murmured. "I hope you continue to spend that time here, where you are safe." Although the pressure of her gaze grew, I did not resume eye contact, watching instead as creatures with four wings along their elongated bodies flew across the suns' set, moving through the air the way eels swim through water.

"For now, I will," I said with an edge to my voice. It was still so easy to walk away from that world. But I needed answers—I needed to know *who* I was, what I was meant to do, *why* it felt like I was chosen to use the Creonex's power. Those answers weren't on Earth, and Novissime knew it. She knew she had me trapped.

The Queen dismissed me, and I flew off. The night air in my feathers did nothing to ease the growing pain in my chest. I hated my need to know *why*, and the weakness it created. I hated, too, that the acknowledgement of my pain broke my resolve as easily as if it were glass. I didn't *want* to hurt anymore, I didn't *want* to cry. I didn't want *anyone* on that planet see the worst of me and exploit my vulnerability. *It's not safe, it's not safe...*

By the time I landed and stumbled into my nest, tears were falling. With the entrance to my nest firmly shut, I lost myself in the full intensity of my grief, in the anger, the desperation, the loneliness. I lay curled in my bed as the fire slowly burned out, feeling drained from how desperately I had fought to internalize my emotions. I wanted—no, I *needed* to stop feeling. I stared into the growing darkness with burning eyes. *Move forward,* I scolded myself, *you* have *to keep moving forward. You still have to survive.*

A shriek tore through the silence. I froze, terror shooting like ice through my veins. It was the shriek of a Voxmor. I turned towards the entrance of my nest, not daring to blink. All was quiet, as if the Voxmor's screech had stilled the forest.

Another scream sounded. I jumped, my hands shaking. I made a move towards the entrance, then stopped. Outside was the threat. Ultimately, I did what I always had, stayed in the nest, stayed hidden. More screeches sounded throughout the night, but they were softer, miles off. Still, I didn't sleep much, as fear of seeing those cold black eyes and slimy white tentacles kept me staring at the entrance of my nest every time I heard any sound. As soon as the first rays of suns' light shone through the tiny spaces between the wood of the nest, I was up and flying through the trees towards the river.

My wings carried me with the breeze that followed the river's current, droplets from the rushing water kissing my feathers as I sped past. Aquatic animals followed my progress below me, their two-foot-long tail fins waving in the water. Two leaped from the water, their iridescent scales shimmering in the early morning light. They spread their fins, caught the wind, and glided next to me for a moment before diving back into the water.

I angled myself up towards the canopy of the trees, and burst through, sending up a swirl of green bird-like creatures with butterfly wings. They whistled and clicked as they flocked back down to their nests, the sounds reminiscent of the Delfungaye language. I stayed there for a while, pumping my wings, rising and falling as I soaked up the suns' rays. I hadn't realized how tense I had become over the night until I rolled my shoulders back and tilted my head to each side, feeling a burning ache from the stretch. Yet this was warm, this was freedom. *This* was safe.

"You should not allow me to sneak up so close."

Gasping, my wings lost their rhythm, and I dropped a few feet. Avenlae hovered behind me, a bandage around his bicep. There was a glint of gold at either tip of the small claw pierced through his septum as he tilted his head.

"I'm sorry, I was preoccupied," I said, slowing my breathing.

He looked past me towards the suns. "That is not something you can afford. I could have killed you easily if I had wanted to."

"I suppose I'm lucky you don't have a vendetta against me." I tried to keep the tired frustration out of my voice, but I saw Avenlae's nostrils flare. I took a deep breath, deciding I had no energy for another fight.

"Long night, last night?" I asked instead, nodding towards his arm. He glanced down at the bandage, nodding.

"The Voxmor got closer than I liked."

"Are you okay?"

Avenlae's eye flicked towards me briefly, and there was a slight pause before he answered. "Yes. Flesh wounds heal quickly here."

"What do you mean?"

"Our healers are gifted, and the cut was not deep." He nodded toward the clearing where we had made our own training ground. "We have work to do."

Turning away from the suns, I began to feel a slight strain in my wings from staying in the air so long. With quiet relief, I followed Avenlae over the forest, away from the river. A few minutes later, we landed in our clearing,

Avenlae heading for a tree to our right to switch out his swords. I stretched my wings, let them relax.

"How close were the Voxmor?" I asked, trying to sound curious, not fearful.

Avenlae looked at me as he unsheathed his swords. I averted my eyes, looking at my hands as I massaged my wrists and palms, giving myself a distraction. I felt he could read the fear in my eyes if I looked at him. The sound of Avenlae's swords sliding back into their scabbards and the brush of grass beneath his feet and wings made me tense.

"Not close enough for you to worry," he said.

I nodded, still not looking at him. We were quiet for a second longer. I counted my heartbeats. *One, two, three, four…*

"I would not have let them hurt you," Avenlae said quietly.

I huffed, uncomfortable at how calming the sound of his voice was. "You wouldn't get paid if you let the Voxmor get me, right?" I looked up as he frowned and turned his head away from me, flattening his ears against his braids. I was taken aback, understanding his stance to indicate offense.

"I'm sorry," I said. "That was said in poor taste."

Avenlae turned and moved away from me. I watched him, unsure if I should follow him, let him leave, or say more. I wasn't even sure if I felt guilty for what I said or if I meant it. The conversation dynamic had me flustered and scrambling to find something to do or say to move us past the moment.

"No, but had I allowed the Voxmor close enough that I had to save you, perhaps I would have been offered a little bonus," Avenlae said.

I glared at him, but when he turned his head to the side, the anger left me as quickly as it had bloomed. There was a soft smile, just his lips, a dimple appearing on the part of his profile that I could see.

"As if I'd have needed you," I scoffed, knowing I never would've left my nest, anyway.

Avenlae faced me, one eyebrow raised. "Two days of training, and you deem yourself capable of standing against a Voxmor?"

I raised my chin, trying to appear more confident than I felt, and met his bright silver eyes. They were piercing but no longer intimidating. His smile faded, and he blinked and broke eye contact. *Look longer, let me see you.* I cleared my throat, silencing the whisper in my mind.

Avenlae took a breath and folded his arms over his chest. "If you are that eager, then you need to focus more on learning how to use that Creonex."

I clenched my left hand, hearing the clank of the metal glove.

"That is your most powerful weapon, and you will not have time to decide if you want to use it if you are surrounded."

"I know," I answered. "But it's too dangerous. I still can't control it."

Avenlae handed me a sword. "You will learn to today."

True to his word, we spent that day trying to understand how the power of the Creonex could be intertwined with basic combat tactics. My mind felt as if it had been wrung dry by the time the shadows began to lengthen. I had finally figured out how to tap into the Creonex's power and allow it to flow down the metal blade of my sword in long arcs of blue electricity, but that may have been facilitated by the conductivity of the metal. The rest of the time, the power of the Creonex still felt just out of reach.

Fortunately, electrifying my blade was progress enough for Avenlae, as he didn't act as frustrated as he had with our previous training sessions. I didn't allow him to spar with me when my blade was ignited, however.

"You're already hurt, and I'm not going to make it worse," I told him as he hissed, his canines showing. "This power is still too new."

We ended training with a few rounds of sparring without the Creonex's power, Avenlae attempting to suppress the winces he made when he used his right arm. I knew he was in pain despite his efforts to hide it, so I faked exhaustion and pointed out the lateness of the hour. He offered no resistance.

"Do your Healers have anything for pain?" I asked as he sheathed his swords.

A look of concern flashed over Avenlae's face. "They do. Are you hurt?"

"No, I meant for you."

"Oh." He retracted his shoulders and shook out his wings. "I am fine."

"Ah. Pain is part of the life of a warrior, or something like that, isn't it?" I said, giving him an amused smile.

Avenlae's soft smile reappeared again, even though he kept his eyes averted. I discovered there were *two* dimples, one on either side of his lips. *How out of place for such a severe man.*

"Something like that. How can I learn from a pain I cannot feel?"

The strangest feeling of triumph came over me, strong enough that I had to lower my head to hide my smile. I had made a crack in the Mercenary's mask—I'd seen him smile. I followed him into the air and watched him fly, his feathers sparkling as if they were made of little chrome pieces. I wouldn't admit it to him, but I enjoyed watching him fly before me, leading me back to his home. Instead of descending into the trees that formed the central hub of the tribe, however, Avenlae veered off to the right towards a crop of darker trees.

"Avenlae," I called after him, slowing and hovering over the back of the Queen's Nest, "where are you going?"

He looked from me to the tribe, lights beginning to shine through the leaves as the sky darkened above us. "I cannot reside in the central tribe. But I trust you can find your way back."

"Oh." The darker trees must have been where he had flown off to after leaving me at my nest the second night of my stay in the tribe. I wanted to question him further, but the somber look he gave the tribe warned me against it. Avenlae turned away to return to his nest.

"Avenlae!" I called again, surprised at my own daring.

When the Mercenary paused, he looked disgruntled.

"I just—today was good," I said, though my confidence slunk away.

He raised his eyes to mine, and a slight furrow appeared in his dark brow. Avenlae's gaze was analytical, with his pupils widening and shrinking. The silver of his irises seemed to glow in the falling light. "Today was good," Avenlae agreed, then he flew off, leaving me to wonder, alone above the tribe, what had possessed me to allow him eye contact for that long.

CHAPTER 9

A flash of gold in the corner of my eye stopped my descent into the Delfungaye tribe. Notien soared up to me, her navy blue eyes wide. With a sting of guilt, I remembered her telling me everything she wanted to show me the night before.

"I was looking for you," Notien said as she approached, "and I saw you behind the Queen's Nest with Avenlae. Is he giving you trouble?"

"Oh, no. We just got back from training." I glanced around at the lively tribespeople flying from tree to tree around us. "I guess the rest of the Guard finished earlier."

Notien nodded, then gestured back towards the river. "If you would like to talk somewhere quieter, we could fly just outside the tribe. It is still far enough from our boundaries to be safe."

"All right. I'll follow you," I agreed, knowing I owed it to her, having not spent time with her the previous night. She smiled and flew off, checking to ensure I was following behind. As we neared the river, the landscape faded, the colors blending into a subdued gray, with the suns fully set beyond the canopy of the trees.

I landed on the river's shore, stretching my wings and dragging them behind me. Moments later, Notien landed, keeping her wings folded close to her back.

"Sorry, I've just missed walking," I told her. I could see in the way her eyes darted around the treeline that she wasn't comfortable on the ground. At that moment, though, I didn't want to be part Delfungaye: I wanted to be human and decompress by taking a walk.

Eager to talk, Notien made no complaint. "So, you were with Queen Novissime yesterday?" she asked.

I raised an eyebrow. "Not much gets past you, does it?"

"I like to know *things*. I have been told I meddle too much for my own good."

I chuckled. "Yes, I did visit with the Queen last night."

"You do not sound like you enjoyed it."

I remained silent for a while, listening to the gentle flow of the river beside us, thinking about how to respond. I wasn't confident I could be candid since we were discussing Notien's Queen. And if Notien really did "meddle too much for her own good," I imagined that whatever I said would make its way back to Novissime before I returned to my nest for the night. "I just haven't formed an opinion about the Queen yet," I said, an open enough statement to allow interpretation.

"I can understand what you mean," Notien said. "It took the Delfungaye a long time to accept her."

"What does that mean?"

"She is of the *Laizuteek* tribe, the Silver People of the Forest. They are the last tribe to survive completely from the attacks of the Voxmor. The rest of us are misplaced from other tribes of the *Fyr'aeset*, the *Hopyroque*, and the *Y'araye*."

"Was it difficult to unite the tribes?"

Notien shook her head, blonde hair waving back and forth. "Not so much as it was to unite them under her specifically. Novissime is not of the royal bloodline—she does not smell like a queen to us. She was Queen Lieneata's highest guard before she fled to Earth, and when Queen Lieneata died, she hadn't appointed anyone to take her throne, nor had she mated a male of the tribe. That meant Novissime was next in the line of succession, just when the *Laizuteek* began taking on refugees from what was left of the surrounding tribes. There was a lot of outcry about having a soldier as our queen, but I think when the tribespeople realized how few of us were left, they began to trust her knowledge of defenses. Many who opposed a Guardian Queen now say she is the only reason there are Delfungaye left on Silvacastra at all."

I digested what Notien said. So, Queen Novissime had recently been accepted by her people. Could that mean she was still willing to do anything to keep her throne? Did she see me as a threat?

"I can't figure out what Novissime wants, what her end goal is," I admitted. *Tell me more.*

"She is the queen of a dying people," Notien answered, looking at me with the faintest flash of fear in her eyes. "Her end goal includes anything she can do to keep us alive, no matter the cost."

"Do you think that includes me?"

"I think it revolves around you and the power the Creonex holds."

I looked back at the river, watching the night sky's reflection swirling on the water's surface. "Why gamble on a power nobody understands?"

"Because, Xiaye, that Creonex is our last hope. We may have a fighting chance against the Voxmor if you can wield that power. The people you see in these trees—we are all that is left of the Delfungaye. I think the prospect of your power is enough for our people to believe we have a chance at survival."

"It's not enough for everyone," I said, remembering the stares I received when Avenlae and I arrived at the tribe's central hub.

"Maybe not, but if you are looking to be accepted by every person you meet, you will be searching a long time." Notien relaxed her wings, letting them drag behind her through the leaves, creating a trail. "Even with as much hope as you represent, there will still be some that will believe you will only bring more bloodshed to the tribe."

"They shouldn't make me a symbol." I didn't try to hide the bitterness in my voice. "So far, the safety I've been given is the only thing keeping me here."

"You will see your importance in time," Notien said, sounding like the Queen. "That tribe is yours by blood right. They will become your people when you show them what kind of queen you will be."

"And if I have no interest in taking on the throne?"

"It is too early for you to make a final decision. Let yourself explore this world. You may discover why your mother loved this planet and its people."

I opened my mouth to ask another question, but was silenced by a soft clicking. We stopped in our tracks, my ears twitching, hers swiveling. A hiss swelled from beside us, within the shadows of the trees, sending ice down my spine.

Then Notien's hand was wrapped around my wrist, pulling me up into a tree in front of us, her wings beating. I arced my wings over my head and sank the claws of my wing joints into the bark to pull me from the ground. Within seconds, we were huddled on a branch twenty feet high, watching as a Voxmor, its scales the sickly color of ash, dove out of the treeline to where we had just been standing. The blades of its tail clicked as it arced over its head, and the creature's tongue forked out along the ground before it. A shriek ripped through the forest as another Voxmor crashed through the undergrowth, joining the one we were watching. It hissed as it flicked its tongue along our wings' trail, and membranes slid over each of its six obsidian eyes. Claws on the Voxmors' back feet sank deep into the soft bank of the river, and moonlight glistened along their backs, broken up by the spines that stood erect from their necks to their tails.

"How did they get so close?" Notien whispered, her eyes wide. "I've never seen them within our boundaries. Where is the Night Guard?"

With a hiss, one of the Voxmor flicked its head around, fangs bared. My breath caught in my throat—every exhalation was *too loud*. The Voxmor cocked its head to the side as it slunk towards our tree, keeping its body low, dragging itself forward with its tentacles. I felt Notien shrink back beside me, and a small branch broke, sounding like the crack of a gunshot. The Voxmor froze, twitched its head, and its black eyes met mine. In half a second, it had leaped onto the trunk of the tree, screeching as it slithered towards us.

I felt the warmth of the Creonex on my hand and moved as if instinct had taken over. Diving down, I touched my left hand to the tree trunk, a blue mist flowing from my fingers. It spread across the bark and into the tentacles of the Voxmor just as the creature came close enough for us to smell its putrid breath. It slowed to a halt, tentacles half-wrapped around the trunk, mouth open but no shriek in its throat.

A man with a mop of dark wavy hair had been hunted down by Voxmor, his body ripped to shreds as bloody pages of a book floated back to the concrete. Miles away, a raven-haired woman ran through a forest on Earth, her footsteps crashing over dead leaves, and when she turned, her stark silver eyes filled with terror. In the blink of that woman's eye, I was back in the forest, staring at the Voxmor suspended in time. *Go away,* I thought, *get away from here. Leave us alone.*

Remarkably, the Voxmor *obeyed*. It backed down the tree, closing its mouth and lowering its spines. When it reached the ground, it clicked at the second Voxmor, and they crossed the river as if in a trance, disappearing into the trees opposite us. I straightened, my limbs trembling, and turned to Notien, who crouched behind me. Her eyes, round as dinner plates, met mine.

"What did you do?" she whispered.

"I-I don't know," I stammered. "I just, I just did it. I didn't think; I just acted."

"Did you know?"

"D-did I know?"

"Did you know you could do that?"

"No. I-I've never done something like that before." I glanced back at the disturbed underbrush and claw marks gouged into the riverbank, my mind whirring. "Notien, we have to tell someone, do something. There have to be more Voxmor than just those two."

Notien nodded. "I will alert the Queen. You need to find Avenlae."

"Find—why?"

"He is the best warrior we have. And he will listen to you."

I shook my head as Notien took off, gliding towards the Queen's Nest. I wanted to question Notien's words, to try to understand what would make that Mercenary listen to *me,* but I knew time was of the essence. No one knew how long we had before the Voxmor returned with reinforcements. I clenched my jaw and took off, heading towards the dark crop of trees Avenlae aways flew to after training.

I dove into the canopy, calling out Avenlae's name as soon as I was beneath the leaves. Noticing a flicker of light through the leaves of a tree to my left, I descended and landed on its branches. Using the claws on the joints of my wings, I climbed towards the light, which revealed itself to be a firelight from a dwelling woven into several of the tree branches, its leaves making a roof. Avenlae stepped out as I pulled myself onto the branch connected to his nest's entrance. His chest was bare, and his tattoos seemed to writhe across his skin in the dim light.

"Xiaye, what are you—"

"They're here," I gasped, panting with the exertion it had taken to climb. "The Voxmor."

"What?"

"They're in the boundaries. I saw them just now!"

His ears flattened back. "Where?"

I looked around, realizing I couldn't figure out where I was in relation to where the Voxmor had been. Avenlae walked closer to me, likely assuming my stuttering was due to my fear rather than my disorientation.

"Xiaye, where are the Voxmor?" he asked again, his voice low and laced with venom.

I blinked several times and shook my head as if that would align my mind to the Creonex. *Creonex!* The blue filigree warmed around my fingers again. Acting upon instinct once again, I raised my hand to the side of Avenlae's face, touching my fingers to his temple. He sucked in a breath as his body flinched, but then his eyes unfocused and his pupils dilated. I envisioned the events of the evening, the river, the Voxmor, and the mist flowing from my hand that controlled the Voxmor. A pain throbbed in the back of my head, and I lifted my hand away from Avenlae's face, unable to focus on the images anymore.

Avenlae blinked several times, his pupils contracting and his ears swiveling towards me. He stared at me, chest rising and falling, silence stretching between us.

"How did you—"

"Did you see?" I asked. "Did you see where they were?"

"Yes, but—"

"I don't know what I just did, but you must go. I don't know how many there are. I've never seen just two lone Voxmor on Earth."

86

Avenlae narrowed his eyes, staring at me for a moment longer before returning to his nest. Seconds later, he returned, the straps of his scabbards crossing over the black-plated vest he wore. "You need to tell the Queen what you did," he said, not looking at me as he stretched his wings, preparing for flight.

"Why? Why does she need to know?"

"She is the only one who might have answers about what happened."

And then he was gone, his powerful wings carrying him away. Frustrated by everyone else telling me what to do but unsure what I *should* do, I leaped from the branch and flew above the trees that formed Avenlae's home just in time to see the lights darkening in the tribe ahead of me. *Suppose her nest is safer than my own right now,* I scoffed as I glided around the Queen's Nest.

I landed on Novissime's balcony just as she burst out of the French doors. She held a sword with a twisted golden hilt at her hip and wore a silver breastplate, a vined design woven throughout the metal.

"Are you all right?" she asked in a harsh whisper.

"Yes," I answered, glancing around to ensure no one else was on the balcony.

"We are alone," Novissime said, noticing my unease. "What has happened?"

"I don't know." I ran through the night's events, avoiding mention of the images that had sprung into my mind. Although I searched for an answer to what sort of influence I held over the Voxmor, I didn't trust the Queen enough to hint at what I had seen from the Creonex. The Queen's answers were frustratingly guarded.

"You seem to have unlocked another ability from the Creonex," Novissime said, walking past me towards the balcony's edge. "It would appear your instinct for protection and self-preservation led to this discovery."

"But what did I *do?*" I asked, annoyed by her pointing out the obvious. "How did I do it?"

"Child, that is for you to determine on your own. I am not in your mind. I do not know how you performed that telepathy, shall we call it. But I do think it is a skill you should practice and develop."

Irritation rose in me like a flame on dry grass. "And how am I supposed to determine what I have done? I can't always access this power whenever I want. I still haven't learned how to."

"I think, in time, you will improve." She spoke as if distracted, unwilling to give her full attention to me. "There are instincts and emotions at play here, too, and you must navigate those as well."

I stared at the beads in her wings, wanting *so badly* to rip them off in anger. *You know* nothing, *do you? You're just stringing me along for as long as you can!* I seethed in my mind, but a scream tore through my thoughts before I could act on them. Queen Novissime's ears perked up towards the direction of the sound, and more shrieks from Voxmor echoed in the distance.

"They *are* close," Novissime breathed, her grip tightening on her sword. Her eyes scanned the trees, and I glanced behind us, realizing just how dark the tribe had become after dousing all the lights. At night, the tribe was invisible within the trees.

We heard more screeches, even closer, and a few trees swayed. Then there was silence, so absolute that not even the leaves rustled. Every living thing in the forest had stilled at the sound of the first screech. Novissime and I stared out at the black-and-white trees, so still that I may have been staring at a painting.

Wings sounded above us, and two Voxmor heads crashed down onto the balcony, their tongues flopping out from between their fangs. The soft whisper of the forest's nightlife returned, as if the whole of Silvacastra knew the threat had passed. I stayed back against the balcony railing as Novissime turned and stepped forward, her hand still resting on the hilt of her sword. Avenlae landed, the wood trembling beneath my feet as he straightened and sheathed his swords across his back. Black Voxmor blood was splashed across his face and smeared over his arms and torso. Some blood still dripped from the ends of his braids, and I found myself searching to see if any of it could've been his.

"There were only two," Avenlae said to the Queen, keeping his eyes down. "The Night Guard has been alerted. They are scanning inside the boundaries."

"Good. And how did these two get in?" Novissime looked down at the heads in disgust, her lip curling to expose one elegant canine.

"No idea. There are no more in the area. Scouts, maybe. Their bodies will be burned in the plains."

"You have done well, Avenlae. Ensure Xiaye gets to her nest safely, and you will be dismissed for the night." With that, the Queen strode back into her chambers without glancing at me. I couldn't believe Novissime could dismiss Avenlae so readily with the deadly gleam in his metallic eyes. His muscles pressed against the confines of his vest, and I could no longer follow the lines of his tattoos amidst the blood that soaked his skin. This was the *Y'araye* warrior, the Delfungaye's deadliest mercenary. But when he turned to face me, gesturing in the general direction of my nest, that deadly gleam calmed to a cool silver glow. I followed him from the balcony without comment. I had no interest in disobeying the man who had personally delivered two Voxmor heads.

The fatigue from flying across the tribe that night felt heavy on my wings as we landed next to my nest. I curled them close to my spine, feeling safer with the warmth of my feathers. My mind was racing with questions about the new power I had used and the memories that came with it. For that's what they were, right?

That raven-haired woman was my mother. I had seen her last moments. *I watched you die...*

"Are you all right?"

I turned, startled, and caught Avenlae's eyes before he lowered them.

"I-I think so." I looked at him again, still trying to discern if any of the blood covering him was red instead of black. "Are you?"

"I have no new injuries," he said, looking over his arms. "The Voxmor didn't fight back. They were still in whatever trance you put them in."

I wrapped my arms around myself to calm my nerves, but I didn't respond. Not out loud, at least.

"I think you put the Voxmor into a trance because you were trying to protect Notien," Avenlae said. "When you showed me what happened, it felt like a defensive action."

I frowned. "You felt something, too?"

"I felt flashes of your emotions as images passed through my mind."

"So I was able to transfer memories *and* emotions to you." The back of my head throbbed. I reached a hand back and massaged it. *This is too much, everything is too much.*

"You need rest," Avenlae said.

"I know." My eyes flicked over the black blood drying on his skin. "So do you."

"Sleep is for those with no trauma in their past," he whispered. I had to look away to quell the vivid grief that tightened my chest. *You return to them, too, don't you,* I thought as I secured the entrance to my nest after Avenlae flew off. *Every time you close your eyes. You're not even alone in your nightmares.*

90

CHAPTER 10

"Did you discover what you did last night? I still cannot believe what I saw. Can you? It was incredible how that Voxmor just turned and left like you had told it to."

"What?" I rubbed my eyes as Notien prattled beside me on our way to the training grounds the following day. My mind kept me tossing and turning all night, resulting in brain fog that refused to comprehend everything Notien could say in one breath.

"That mist you made, what was it? Were you communicating with the Voxmor? Did it talk back to you?" She gasped, covering her mouth as her eyes widened. "What did it *sound* like?"

"Notien, please, one thing at a time," I said, squinting my eyes against the bright morning suns.

"I am sorry." She lowered her eyes. "It was so fascinating. I could not stop thinking about it last night, and the more I thought, the more questions I had."

"You and me both," I agreed as we landed in the first training field a few feet off from where the rest of the Guard had gathered. "I still don't fully understand what I did, but I know I was communicating to the Voxmor somehow. And no, it did not say anything back to me. It just obeyed the order I gave."

"What was the order?"

"I just told it to leave and not to hurt us."

Notien was quiet, scowling as she thought. "Was the Voxmor obeying you or the Creonex?"

"What do you mean?"

"The mist came from the Creonex. You used its power to communicate with the Voxmor, but was it obeying *your* order or staying away from the power it sensed in the Creonex?"

"I hadn't thought of that," I said, quickly becoming lost in thought. The last Voxmor I saw on Earth had fled from my power—could that mean the Voxmor here sensed and feared it?

"Notien, why are you talking to that thing?" A deep, raspy female voice rang out behind me. I turned and watched as a *Hopyroque* woman advanced towards me, a deep scowl disfiguring her face. Her dark, forest-green hair hung in ringlets just past her shoulders, and her golden cat eyes bore into mine. She towered over me, the black fur pelt across her shoulders widening her stature. A strong jawline, heavy brows, and long chin made her features masculine, except for full lips twisted into a sneer. Broad, black wings with thick feathers spread on either side of her as she neared, as if to intimidate with her sheer size.

"Saetyl," Notien said as the large woman stopped just in front of me, looking down her hook nose. "Remember who you are talking to. You can smell her bloodline."

"Pah. The bloodline of a traitor," the woman spat.

"The bloodline of a *queen,* isn't it?" I retorted. I didn't actually care much about my social standing, but I did crave an outlet for my anger.

"Your mother left us in a flight of cowardice, and our tribes were slaughtered. She is nothing but a traitor in the eyes of my people."

"And who are they, exactly?" I peered over her shoulder, but the rest of the Guard stood far behind her.

Saetyl narrowed her eyes. "Do you know why the Voxmor were in the boundaries?"

"Because *you* weren't on guard duty last night?"

"They came here because of you, because of your stench. And you could not even kill them!" She spat at my feet. "You will bring nothing but bloodshed here, just like your mother. I, for one, will not allow that to happen."

"But you allowed the Voxmor into the borders of the tribe?"

"Shut up, you insolent—"

"Saetyl," Avenlae growled.

I hadn't noticed his approach but didn't take my eyes off Saetyl. Her large ears swiveled back at the sound of her name, and her eyes slid down to the ground as she tilted her head towards him.

"Saved by the Mercenary," Saetyl hissed. She took a step back and glared at me again. "You are lucky he is here to protect you."

"I find it amusing you think I need him to protect me." I felt energy crackle over the Creonex wrapped around my hand, fed by the anger pounding behind my eyes.

Saetyl bared her teeth like a dog about to attack. "Your mother was too weak to protect us. You will understand why I do not believe *you* will be any different." She turned and lumbered back to where the rest of the Guard stood, watching the exchange with varying reactions of apathy, shock, and nodding heads.

I watched her go, my chest heaving, mind whirring with retorts I should've said. Notien glanced at me, then hurried away, getting into formation with the rest of the soldiers without another word. *Little coward.* I glared at Notien's back. I couldn't tell if I was irritated at the prospect of Notien no longer giving me the information I needed or…or the idea that she never had wanted to become a friend. *You have no friends. You have no trust.*

"Let's go," Avenlae snapped. I gritted my teeth and took off without looking at him. My blood was still boiling when I landed in the clearing, and the Creonex became even hotter against my skin. Saetyl's face, her scowl, and her disrespect flashed across my mind, and with a surge of anger, I yelled and swung my left hand in a wide arc. Four blue blades flew from my palm and sank hilt-deep into the trunks of four trees at the edge of the clearing. Smoke swirled lazily from the hilts of the knives as Avenlae stared at the charred bark.

"That was new," he said.

"I was angry," I muttered, looking at the ground, ready for him to scold me about controlling my anger.

"And we have confirmation that the Creonex is controlled by your emotions."

"Explain what you mean." *Give me an excuse to breathe, to control myself,* I thought wearily.

"Just now, you discovered you could create those knives because you were angry. You created that burst of energy the first time we sparred because I provoked you. Last night, I believe you learned that you can use the Creonex to communicate telepathically because you were afraid and used it as a defensive tactic."

"So I have to get extremely emotional to use the Creonex?" I scoffed. "How cliche."

"I do not think that is necessary, but it helps. You may need to focus on the emotion behind the action to unlock more of the Creonex's power and harness it."

"Focus on what?" He was making my head hurt.

"Imagine you are back in that tree with the Voxmor stalking you. How would you feel?"

"Afraid?"

"Thus, you would act defensively to protect yourself, correct?"

"Well, yes."

"Focus on that emotion now. Pull from that power again."

I sighed and lifted my left hand, trying to put myself back into the mindset of the previous night. It wasn't difficult to remember how to feel afraid, but it was hard to focus on the emotion in the warm, shining suns, with Avenlae staring at the Creonex, waiting for something to happen. An idea, one that nearly repulsed me, popped into my mind. *You're absolutely crazy. Completely sleep-deprived.*

"Avenlae, look at me," I said forcefully. He flattened his ears straight back before lifting his silver eyes. His pupils dilated, and suddenly, it was him in the tree next to me instead of Notien that I envisioned. The Creonex warmed and sent tingles up my arm and into my temples. I glanced down, seeing the blue mist circling my hand. I smiled and looked back at Avenlae, who broke eye contact immediately.

"I did it!" I said.

Avenlae nodded. "You need to focus on the emotion that provokes you take action with the Creonex. That seems to allow you to use its power."

I swallowed. The past several days I'd been fighting to suppress and control my emotions. *You only feel when you're safe,* I thought, studying Avenlae as he reached over his head. *Is he safe?* "You'll have me working with the Creonex more now, won't you?"

Avenlae unsheathed one of his swords and handed it to me. "Yes. Hone your ability to use your weapons simultaneously."

When I took the sword in my right hand, a shock of energy passed across my shoulders, and forks of electricity covered the blade. Avenlae's eyes flashed—this was what he wanted. Was it what *I* wanted? To become *more* dangerous? *To fight is to survive, Xiaye. That's how your world is now, isn't it?* I let out a breath, feeling the buzz of power spread unimpeded through my body.

"I think I'm ready," I said, gripping the hilt of the sword tighter. The Creonex's power felt different, within reach—compliant. I still didn't feel as if there was much strength behind what power I could control, but as Avenlae darted forward to begin our first round of sparring, a challenge shining in his silver eyes, it was good enough.

The next few weeks were filled with discoveries of how I could weaponize the power of the Creonex. Every morning, Avenlae would spar with me and correct my sword technique. Every afternoon, we spent hours practicing with a new power I had learned the day before or experimenting with something I had discovered during sparring. Accessing the power of the Creonex became easier the more I practiced, until I could feel its buzzing energy all the time. It became as familiar to me as the book had been on Earth. As I learned to accept my emotions, they and my power became safer—easier to harness and use. By the end of those weeks, I had mastered throwing knives, created a weak shield, shot bursts of energy, and fashioned a chain of electrical energy that I could use like a whip.

I also garnered a new appreciation for the warrior in Avenlae. He expertly used every weapon I created and taught me to fight with each one. I found myself wondering what it would be like to see *him* fight. Not in the practiced way we sparred, but in something raw and wild.

During one sparring session he actually started to smile, as if he were beginning to enjoy the fight.

"Good," he said. "You need more of a challenge."

"That sounds more like a threat than an invitation," I panted.

"It is always an invitation."

Avenlae pushed me back, and without giving me a chance to react, he attacked again, and it was all I could do to parry him. My parries were quick but weak, and I backed rapidly into the treeline. Feeling cornered, I leaped into the air, beating my wings to take me higher.

But Avenlae was as dangerous in the air as he was on foot. He was quicker than I was, swooping around me to avoid my attacks. Taken off-guard when he came at me from behind, I turned and raised my left hand, and a luminous blue shield expanded from the back of my wrist and encircled my body. Avenlae's sword bounced off the shield and leaped from his hand as he lurched backward. He stabilized himself in the air as I lowered my shield, chest heaving.

"I'm sorry, you overwhelmed me," I said, sweat dripping down my back.

"*That* was cheating," he called, his slight smile in place again.

"No, *that* was beginning to use every weapon in my repertoire," I replied. "Isn't that what you've been trying to teach me?"

Avenlae lowered his eyes and nodded, huffing. *Was that supposed to be a laugh?* He looked up at the suns. "We should return to the tribe—you should eat and rest after everything you have done today."

I followed Avenlae to the ground, retrieving his other sword. There were moments when I felt as if we were forming an acquaintanceship, but every time he lowered his eyes, I thought perhaps I was searching for something that was never there. I was *trying* not to be alone, but he was simply working for money. *There's always Notien, right?* I sighed to myself. She'd stayed by my side despite Saetyl's taunting remarks, and I'd begun to regrow a shaky trust with her. But Avenlae...I couldn't shake the need for his approval, even though I didn't understand the feeling.

"What is troubling you?" Avenlae asked. I realized I had been standing still, holding his sword at my side. I blinked and handed the sword to him.

"Sorry, I was distracted."

"I could tell." He studied my face before I looked up at him, then lowered his eyes, as always, to the ground. "But I can also tell something is bothering you."

"How?"

"I have had to be around you daily for nearly a month. After so long, a person learns things about another."

"'Had to?'" I asked. "You've 'had to' be around me? Is the money no longer good enough?"

Avenlae frowned. "*That* is what bothers you?"

"I—yes. It does." I couldn't look at him as embarrassment colored my cheeks.

Avenlae remained quiet momentarily before saying hesitantly, "This is not a paid venture anymore."

My head whipped around. "Why are you here, then? Haven't I been worth as much money as you could—"

"You are a person, not a mission," Avenlae snapped, but he kept his head low. "I am not as heartless as they say."

I stayed silent as he took off, watching as the shadow of his body was swallowed by the setting suns. *I never did think you were heartless. Not really.* I should've told him. *He would've hated you for it.* Unable to argue with myself, I leaped into the air, heading for my nest where, hopefully, Notien was waiting with something to eat and drink—I needed something to silence my thoughts. Sure enough, she was just outside the entrance to my nest, balancing two leaves of food and crystal bottles of iced Delfungaye tea in her arms. The evening was lovely, the weather tranquil, so we took our meal to a nearby tree.

"Your form is improving," Notien said between mouthfuls. "I watched you spar Avenlae before lunch. You make him break a sweat now."

"Don't flatter me too much," I said as I sipped the tea.

"I would not dare." Notien smiled. "Avenlae meets few people who make him work during sparring. You should be proud of your progress."

"And what about you? Will they assign you to a Night Guard squadron?" I asked, moving the topic of conversation from myself. She had told me the week before that the Night Guard was for elite Delfungaye soldiers, and her training was for a spot in one of the squadrons.

Notien sighed and shook her head. "I will not know until next week. I am nervous that I will have worked hard for nothing."

"Keep your chin up," I said, swallowing the last bite of my dinner. "You've still got time to prove you deserve a spot."

She nodded, taking a long swig from her own crystal bottle. "Have you had any more meetings with the Queen?"

I shook my head. "Doesn't seem like she has time for me."

"Perhaps she is waiting to see how your training progresses. If she wants to instruct you on leading the tribe, she may want to ensure you can protect yourself first."

"Notien, while I appreciate *your* support, there is little else on this planet that will convince me to take the throne."

"I told you before and will tell you again—you will see your potential in time."

"You said that almost a month ago. I still don't see it."

We went back and forth like that several times a week. I had no interest in taking Novissime's rule, but I was keen on harnessing the powers of the Creonex and honing my fighting skills. That was all that kept me on Silvacastra. I endured the glares and scathing whispers of tribespeople Saetyl controlled only because I had no intention of taking my "blood right". Feeling safe and remaining fed was more than my musty bunker on Earth could offer, if it was even still there.

Notien rolled her eyes. "If you say so. Here, let me take your braids out."

For the past several weeks, Notien had been braiding my hair traditionally before training. I made no protest, having only ever piled it on top of my head. The natural dark waves of my hair were accentuated by the texture left from the braids each night, and it had grown long enough to brush my waist. I closed my eyes and relaxed as Notien ran her fingers through my hair and against my scalp. *Little trust, little trust.*

A boot connected with the right side of my face, and I fell, wings flailing as my vision blurred. I smacked into another branch, pain exploding in my ribcage. Gasping for air, I tried to roll onto my left side, the world spinning nauseatingly. The branch shook as a dark figure landed before me.

"Aw, look at this. She cowers before me." Saetyl moved towards me, and I tried to push myself back, still gasping. *Get away, GET AWAY!* My thoughts screamed, but panic kept me silent. My scalp burned as Saetyl wrapped her fingers around my hair, yanking my head back and dragging me forward, cackling as a strangled scream stung my throat.

"I needed to show them how weak you are," Saetyl whispered, grinning. Behind her stood several members of the Guard, not one attempting to help me. My eyes were streaming with the burning of my hair being pulled from my scalp, and I panted through my teeth.

Saetyl turned back to her group. "This is who they want to put on our throne? This is who they want to call our queen? Our *last hope?*"

She threw me down onto the bark of the tree, and my nose hit wood. Blood poured from both nostrils. "She will not even fight back. Pathetic!" Saetyl spat. The warriors in front of me laughed. They *laughed* as I retched, the taste of blood filling my mouth.

"Enough!" Notien cried as she landed on the branch, drawing her sword and advancing on Saetyl as I tried to push myself into a seated position. Saetyl's group stopped laughing and backed away.

"Why do you defend that *thing?*" Saetyl growled.

"Because attacking her when her back is turned has no honor." Notien spun her sword in her left hand. "That is not the way of the Delfungaye warrior."

"You say that like we are one tribe."

"We *are* one tribe! You know there are not enough of us left to have multiple tribes anymore. We are united against a common enemy. *She* is not the fight you want to pick."

Saetyl glared at Notien, her canines bared, and leaped off the branch, the rest of the group following her. I stayed seated, taking shallow, painful breaths, shaking too badly to stop the bleeding from my nose. My face hurt, my ribs hurt, my throat burned. Notien sheathed her sword and knelt down, her navy eyes wide and glistening.

"Oh, Xiaye, I am so sorry," she said. "Saetyl had another *Hopyroque* hold me up there for as long as they could so I could not help you and… she cannot get away with this. I-I will tell someone, I can get Avenlae now and—"

"No," I said sharply, wincing as the movement of my head made my temples throb. "I don't need anyone else knowing." I couldn't deal with the tribe knowing one of their own had beaten me down as if I were a bug under her shoe. *You weak, pathetic human!* Avenlae's roar reverberated between the throbs in my temples. *You didn't fight back. You can't fight back.*

"But, Xiaye, this is unacceptable. She cannot just be allowed—"

"Notien, she *was* just allowed to do that! Did you see who was with her? A

101

good chunk of the Queen's Guard watched and *laughed* at what she did." Hot tears stung the gash on my cheek where Saetyl had kicked me. "And you know what? *That*, that right there, is why *your* tribe will *never* be mine. I am *not* one of *you*."

Tears fell from Notien's eyes as she flattened her ears. She shrank away from me as if my words physically hurt her. "At least let me help you to your nest," she said. "I can get something for the pain from one of my Healer friends. I... I will not tell her who it is for."

A wave of guilt pressed against my heart that *I* had hurt Notien, but she couldn't deny the ugly truth the attack revealed. The Delfungaye didn't accept me, no matter how strong the scent of my bloodline was to them. I didn't *want* their acceptance... did I? *Loneliness is so intensely painful when you're surrounded by people.* So it was. That was what made me fight for Avenlae's acceptance in training, what made me try to learn to trust Notien. No longer the pursuit for information, but for an end to the loneliness.

Notien remained silent and lowered her eyes, her tears glistening as she stopped the flow of blood from my nose and iced my cheek. My guilt over the effect of my words on Notien grew stronger as she ministered to me. Still, I couldn't find the words to tell my only friend that she was becoming one of the most important people in my life.

Back in my nest, I lay awake, vowing that, in time, I wouldn't prove I could be queen, but I would prove I could control Saetyl. There would come a day when *she* would cower at *my* feet.

CHAPTER 11

sickening ache woke me early the morning after the attack. Deep purple bruising spread across my ribcage. Swelling along my cheek made my blue eye puffy and difficult to open, but I didn't look at my reflection in the white basin to see how bad the injury was. I left my hair down to hide my face and changed into my training uniform. My top was tight, and I felt stabs of pain despite medication from a Healer. Shuffling through my nest, I found a light grey tank top that I tucked into the front of my uniform pants so it wouldn't rise when I flew or sparred. It wasn't convenient for vigorous training with Avenlae, but it would be harder to hide my pain if I trained in the heavier uniform.

I didn't wait for Notien. I didn't have the mental energy to talk through Saetyl's attack, which I knew Notien would want to do, and I didn't want to see the hurt look in her eyes again. *You don't even know how to apologize to her.*

I headed straight for the clearing Avenlae and I trained in. Tears stung the corners of my eyes as I walked towards a tree, raising the Creonex, the filigree burning around my hand. *Weak, pathetic little HUMAN!* Early morning suns' light was still warm as I aimed the Creonex. *You couldn't fight back!* The forest's peace mocked my anger, now impossible for me to control. *You'll never FIGHT BACK!* A burst of energy shot from my palm and blasted into the tree, a chunk of wood flying off to the side. I sent another, then another. Tears fell down my cheeks, and my chest tightened as the Creonex's power shredded the wood, sending the tree swaying.

"You are starting early today."

I didn't respond to Avenlae. I flicked my wrist down, and the electrical whip flew out of my hand. Stomping toward the tree, I cracked the whip, envisioning Saetyl's face in the bark. Or was it mine? *FIGHT BACK, COWARD!*

I flicked the whip at the tree, once, twice, three, four, five times, until it fell with a groan, its stump blackened and smoking. Choking back a sob, I raised the whip, ready to strike again, but was stayed by a hand closing around my wrist. Its palm was rough with calluses, but its touch was gentle, too gentle for how much rage had been burning through my body.

I gasped, turning my head slowly to see black tattoos wrapped around the wrist of the hand that held mine. Avenlae applied soft pressure to my wrist, backing me away from the fallen tree, then side-stepping to move in front of me, his silver moonlight eyes narrowed in concern. They widened as he saw the bruising on the right side of my face. I lowered my head to keep him from seeing my tears, wanting to wipe them away but unable to pull my hand from his grasp.

"What happened?" Avenlae asked.

I clenched my jaw, shaking my head as my throat constricted. Avenlae's grip tightened as I attempted to pull my wrist out of his fingers. With his other hand, he forced my chin up, his pupils constricting as he saw the gash and swelling along my cheek. He let go of my hand and chin, his face darkening and his ears lying flat against his temples.

"Who did this?"

"I'm fine," I said, my voice shaky. *Hide from him.*

"Xiaye." Avenlae took a step forward, his canines flashing as he spoke. "If I find out who did this to you—"

"I said I'm fine, Avenlae," I repeated, my voice more assertive. "Besides, it's not your fight."

"Was it Saetyl?"

I kept my mouth shut, staring at the grass. Electricity crackled across my fingers.

"Was it Saetyl?"

I took a shaky breath, raising my head towards the opposite tree line. "She said she had to show the rest of the Guard how weak I am."

Avenlae hissed. I looked at him, feeling renewed enmity. The hatred was so strong, I no longer knew if it was directed at Avenlae, Saetyl, or myself.

"Saetyl attacked while my back was turned and my guard was down. She blames me for the suffering of her people and thinks I should atone for the actions of my mother." I felt a tear slide down my cheek and shook my head. "I hardly even remember what she looked like. I don't even remember what my own mother *looked* like, Avenlae! How can I be associated with a woman I barely knew? How can *any* of you compare me to someone I *can't remember?*"

Avenlae stayed about a foot away from me, his ears flat, his eyes on the ground, his hands balled into fists at his side. My rage exploded because he was just there, just standing there while turmoil ripped through my mind and body. It tumbled from my mouth in chaotic, unfinished thoughts. "And you! You can't even look at me! How am I supposed to know if it's out of respect or hatred? Where I'm from, the reason you don't look at someone is because they're a *freak.* That's probably what I am to you, isn't it? Just some freak human you were paid to retrieve. And now half your people want me to be a queen, and the other half

105

want me gone because of my mother who I *can't* remember! All these expectations, but nobody gives a *damn* about what I want. Nobody cares that I *hate* being here! I can't find a way to trust anyone in this forest because now I know no one besides Notien in your world would *dare* come to my defense. I'm too weak to even fight back—just some puny, *pathetic* human! And you still won't even *look* at me!"

Avenlae's silver eyes flicked up to meet mine, pupils constricted. My next rant died in my throat.

"Is this what you wanted?" he asked quietly.

"Yes," I whispered. "I'm tired of feeling invisible."

He lowered his wings, stretching them behind him, his eyes never straying from mine. "All right. Now, follow me." Avenlae turned and walked away. I blinked, bewildered by the sudden change in subject and dismissal of everything I had just yelled at him.

"Wait! Did you not listen to anything I just said?" I called after him, jogging to catch up.

Avenlae whirled around, glaring down at me, his wings curled high above his head. "It was difficult *not* to hear you shouting at me." His canines flashed as he spoke, and I shrank away. At this, he lowered his gaze, perked his ears up, and stepped back. "You need a break. Follow me."

Avenlae took flight, clearing the tops of the trees in seconds. Afraid to disobey the look in his eyes, I leaped into the air after him. The wind caressing my feathers quickly calmed the monster that had risen in my chest. I breathed the subtle sweetness of sun-warmed leaves as I watched Avenlae's wings carry him along the air currents in front of me. *Be calm; this is safe.* I caught up with him as he reached the river but was perplexed to see him arch his back to tilt his wings away from the tribe, following the river's flow deeper into the forest.

We descended, gliding within the canopy of the trees, their emerald leaves a rustling blur as we passed. River water as clear as glass rippled below us, and aquatic plants dissolved into the color of sapphires, swaying in the current. My hair flew behind me, whipped by the wind. I was buffeted by Avenlae's slipstream a few times, so I rose above him, beating my wings to match his speed. Deeper into the forest, the underbrush near the bank of the river became thicker and wilder. The colors changed from emerald green to a darker jade, and the bark of the trees slowly transitioned to slate gray. Whitecaps appeared in the river as it rushed over rock formations hidden below the surface.

A rushing sound filled my ears as I came level with Avenlae. The whitewater below us forced him upward, close enough to me that I could've touched him. *So close.*

"Are you ready?" he called up to me, his low voice carrying over the sounds of wind and water.

My pulse quickened. "Ready for what?"

He pointed towards a tree bent low over the river, the white water jumping high enough to hit its leaves. "You see that tree coming up? You have to dive there."

"Dive?" I shouted. "Dive into the water? Are you insane?"

"Keep your wings in close and dive straight down."

"Avenlae, there's no way that water is deep enough."

"No time to argue!"

"I never learned how to swim!"

Avenlae twisted and wrapped his arms around me to clasp his hands together just under my shoulder blades, pressing my cheek against his chest as he pulled me down. The world went silent. Water splashed against my face and through my hair, and his pulse kissed my skin for a mere few seconds. *So... close.*

The river dropped into a waterfall whose mist rose in brilliantly shimmering rainbows amidst a vibrant cavern in the middle of the forest. Avenlae released his hold, pushing me away from him as he spun into a dive close enough to the white water that his body appeared to dissolve into the mist that swirled behind his wings. Squinting against the spray of the waterfall, I grinned and followed Avenlae in the dive, tasting the minerals of river water. Exhilaration filled me as we sped up, falling faster and faster, water rushing beneath us. It was a feeling I could never forget—the weightlessness, the rush of the wind, the water against my skin, the wild awe of placing my mortality in the strength of my wings and the current of the air from the fall of the water.

Avenlae pulled out of the dive, spreading his wings and zooming up to glide up the cavern wall, his body so close to the rock that it looked as if he were sliding up the surface. I copied him, gritting my teeth from the force applied to my wings to tilt my entire body straight back up the vertical walls. Near the entrance to the cavern where the waterfall began, I slowed down, held in place by the current of the air being pushed up as the water fell in a torrent to a cave river.

Plants were set into crevices that lined the cavern walls. Trees with aquamarine leaves jutted from the rock, and vines the color of amethyst twirled down the cavern's depths, some brushing against the opal rocks of the riverbank below. Ruby moss softened the stone walls, sparkling with tiny orbs of water droplets. Flowers the color of tourmaline, topaz, and citrine glittered in bunches that fell over the edge of small ledges and in the rough bark of the trees that swayed like willows on the bank of a still pond.

I smiled again as I took in the colors, sounds, and tickle of mist. A soft whoosh of air against my shoulder reminded me that Avenlae hovered beside me. His shirt was soaked, plastered to the uneven surface of his muscles, and the water on his skin made his tattoos more striking. His long hair dripped, lying across his chest in dark ringlets. His silver eyes glowed, and a vague smile brightened his expression.

"Is this better?" Avenlae asked, his voice as calming as the air that held my wings.

I nodded, looking down at the flourishing life below me. Without another word, Avenlae dived again, spreading his wings at the bottom of the waterfall and gliding out of sight along the new river. Curiosity led me down the waterfall as well, but instead of following Avenlae, I landed on the smooth opal rocks of the riverbank, where the waterfall splashed into the current. Before me was a cave with the same plant life as the cavern, but down there, it glowed. My eyes were dazzled by luminescent leaves, flowers, mosses, and trees. Crystals hung from the cave ceiling, splitting the light from the plants across the ground.

I strolled along the river, the sound of the waterfall receding behind me. Closed off from the forest, the only sounds were the flow of the current and the tinkle of water dripping from the crystals on the cave ceiling. Avenlae emerged from behind three trees that grew together, their canopies extending far along the crystals above them, indicating their age.

"Are you hungry?" he asked, holding out a large round object as he walked towards me. It was red, and its surface looked as rough as sandpaper, almost resembling a rock.

"What is that?" I asked, taking it from him. It was heavy as a rock. *If it looks like a rock and feels like a rock, it must be…*

"The seed of the *j'guaya,* the cave trees." Avenlae took a knife out of his belt and stabbed the seed, twisting once. It cracked in half, revealing a moist, black interior. Avenlae reached over and cracked mine open before walking to the bank of the river. I followed, frowning at the *j'guaya* seed. It had no odor, and its blackened pulp had the texture of an orange.

"You may not like how it looks, but it is among the most nutrient-rich food in the forest," Avenlae said before scooping out a bite from the seed. "In my tribe, it was a delicacy."

I pinched a small amount of the pulp from my own seed. Though ugly, it was juicy. I put it in my mouth and was shocked by the splash of flavor, tart as a green apple but with a sweet aftertaste. I happily continued eating in silence and, once finished, felt as satiated as if I had eaten a three-course meal. Avenlae cut up the skin of his seed once he was finished and threw the pieces into the river, watching as bioluminescent fish, looking like so many little stars, darted around the bits of food. I chuckled as I handed him mine.

"This place is like its own little world," I said, watching him.

"Indeed. There are very few caves on the planet, and each is unique to its region." He tossed more pieces of seed skin into the river. "I found this one a few years ago. It is a good place to come to clear your mind."

I nodded, turning back to watch the fish eat. Silence spread between us again. A drop of guilt spread through my thoughts.

"Avenlae," I ventured, looking over at him. "I'm sorry. About earlier." I swallowed, felt my cheeks warm. "I was just so angry and…"

Avenlae slid his knife into his belt and spread his shining wings back against the cool stone ground behind him. "You were not angry; you were hurt. Your anger was secondary to your pain."

My hands lay clasped in my lap as I stayed quiet, unsure how to answer him. It was odd, him telling me how *I* felt, but he wasn't wrong. "It still wasn't your fault," I said.

"Yes, it was. I brought you here."

I glanced up at him. Was that an admission of guilt? Could Avenlae have regretted bringing me to Silvacastra after witnessing what someone in his tribe had done to me? "You were following the Queen's orders. I don't blame you, not really."

"Who do you blame? Yourself or the Queen?"

I frowned. Avenlae turned his silver eyes towards me. "We could sit here for as long as you want to discover who is at fault for the pain you feel, but it will not bring you peace."

Will you tell me? "Are you speaking from experience?"

I held my breath, wondering if I had pushed too far, but I needed to know. A vulnerable part of me craved the reassurance of someone who could empathize with my trauma. *You don't have to be alone.*

He looked across the river, and I saw a muscle in his jaw twitch before he answered. "I know who to blame for the slaughter of my tribe. What brings me peace is knowing that I can do something to avenge them."

"Thank you," I said after a while, "for bringing me to this place."

Avenlae nodded once, tossing a flat stone across the river's surface. "You needed peace."

"I did," I agreed. "It's easier to understand things when I'm calmer."

Avenlae threw another stone, not answering and not meeting my eyes. He had figured out that his abrasive approach did nothing to guide my fractured mind through my trauma and had switched to kindness to persuade me to listen to his teachings. *Kindness...*

"Avenlae, if I give you my permission, will you look at me from now on?"

His ears twitched, and, gradually, he turned his gaze to me. "Yes."

I nodded. "You have my permission."

Avenlae held my gaze a moment longer. There was so much in those moonlight eyes, so much I wanted to know. *You're not alone. He... he's safe.* Avenlae looked at the purple gash across my cheek, and his hand twitched. A gasp of chilled cave air rushed into my lungs, a breath of anticipation.

And then a flash of the raven-haired woman passed before my eyes. The glow of a sapphire necklace at her throat, the tendrils of light leaving her skin, re-

forming into a book's dull cover. Her trembling fingers made the pages shake as she placed them into smaller, younger hands. "Guard it," she whispered desperately, "guard the Creonex with your life, Xiaye."

Avenlae stood, unaware of the vision that had bloomed in my mind. I blinked rapidly to clear my thoughts. I heard the rush of the waterfall behind us, felt my damp shirt prickle my skin. The moment was gone, the memory already fading. I stood to follow Avenlae, rubbing my sweaty palms on the rough material of my uniform pants to lock myself in the present.

As I walked forward, a crackle of energy reached my ears. The Creonex warmed around my hand, and with it came a sudden rush of power that made my breath catch. Raw energy surged through my limbs with each beat of my heart, and the metal filigree glove glowed against my skin. It was as if the Creonex had finally relinquished its hold over its power. The energy was *mine*. Not just something I felt, but instead a part of my very being.

Avenlae turned to me. "Xiaye?"

My eyes roved over the swirls of filigree coating my left hand as I turned it over. A shock of energy shot down my arm, and a blue flame lit upon the tip of my index finger. I extinguished the flame and looked at Avenlae. "Just now, the power of the Creonex shifted. It's mine, now."

"It has always been yours. You just needed to accept it."

As we left the cave, I wondered if, to gain control over the Creonex, it was my acceptance I had needed... or Avenlae's?

CHAPTER 12

In the evening, instead of returning to my nest, I went to the Guard training grounds to find Notien. I needed to apologize to her for the pain my words had caused. I hadn't the strength before, but I knew I owed it to her. *A friend. Keep her.*

Avenlae insisted on accompanying me, his eyes darkening at the prospect of me going by myself anywhere near Saetyl. Although I abhorred bringing him along as if he was my personal guard, I knew there was no convincing him to stay away. I didn't like his sudden protectiveness, but I also didn't have it in me to fight him. *Besides, it is advantageous to have someone as deadly as him in your favor, isn't it?* I shrugged inwardly as we landed on the bank of the river.

The Queen's Guard had just been dismissed, and they were forming their usual cliques. A hush fell as I walked foward, probably owing more to Avenlae's presence than to mine. Several men and women of the Guard stared at him as if to remind him of his "place." I held my head high and ignored their stares, refusing to give them the satisfaction of seeing my fear. Notien approached, averting her eyes from Avenlae behind me.

"We should talk somewhere else," she whispered when she was near. "Saetyl is here, and I do not know if it is safe."

"Did she try to hurt you today?" I asked, feeling the heat of hatred on my skin.

"No, but—"

"Brought a guard with you this time?" Saetyl's raspy voice interrupted our conversation. Notien's ears flattened as she turned to face Saetyl, who pushed her bulk to the front of the group. "Did you not learn your lesson last night, little human? Decided to come here for round two?"

A hiss came from behind me. Avenlae bared his canines at Saetyl, and she stopped short, a crease between her heavy brows. "I have no fight with you, Avenlae."

"Back away," Avenlae growled, his ears flat against his hair and his feathers bristling along his wings.

Saetyl stared, a sneer sliding slowly across her face. "Do not tell me you have gone soft for *her*?"

There was a fluttering of wings, and Queen Novissime landed between us. Her sword was in its sheath at her hip, and she wore a crisp white uniform. A diaphanous cape of iridescent silver flowed off one shoulder, and her dark hair was twisted into an intricately woven bun. Notien crossed her wrists over her chest and knelt when the Queen landed, and I heard a rustle as the rest of the Queen's Guard followed suit. I glanced around, uneasy and still unsure of what *I* was supposed to do in her presence.

"Have I interrupted something?" Novissime asked.

"No, Your Highness," Saetyl answered, keeping her head down. "It is just friendly banter."

"Since when did 'friendly banter' result in bruised ribs, Saetyl?"

"I, I do not understand what you mean," Saetyl replied.

"You know *exactly* what I mean. You were there last night, were you not?"

Saetyl chuckled nervously and glanced at me from the corner of her golden eye. "I am not sure what you have heard, Your Highness."

"I've heard *enough*," Novissime hissed, her wings moving into an arced position with the claws at her wing joints pointed down at Saetyl. "You are removed from the Queen's Guard until further notice."

Saetyl gasped. "But, Your Majesty!"

"*Don't* test my patience. I will summon you when you are to be reinstated. Until then, you train alone." The Queen narrowed her eyes and looked around at the rest of the Guard kneeling before her, as if daring them to protest. "You are all dismissed."

Notien stood, glancing at Novissime before whispering, "Find me in the morning before training." She took off with the rest of the Guard, evidently unwilling to appear even remotely opposed to the Queen. Saetyl glared in my direction before taking a running start to hoist herself into the air and back towards the tribe. *Ha, obey, little puppy.* I tried to hide my smirk.

Novissime turned to face me and raised her eyebrows when she noticed Avenlae behind me.

"Come, child, we have things to discuss," Novissime said, gesturing for me to follow her as she walked towards the river.

"We do?" I asked, my temper flaring at being ordered to obey when she'd ignored me for weeks.

"Indeed. I apologize. I have been busy, otherwise I would've met with you sooner and more frequently. The Voxmor have been getting bolder, and their scouts have been coming closer to our borders." She kept walking, not bothering to check if I was at her heel. I sighed and started after her, hearing the sound of Avenlae's wings dragging across the ground as he followed me.

115

"What is it we need to discuss?"

"Your training." Novissime led me along the bank of the river, angling back towards the tribe. "I hear you have been able to access more of the Creonex's power."

"I have." I glanced back at Avenlae. *What are you telling her?*

"Good. I have told Avenlae to focus your training on harnessing and using that power."

I knew my reasons for harnessing the Creonex's power, but I didn't think they were the same as here. "Why?"

"I believe the time for you to use the Creonex is approaching." The Queen stared at the river that flowed beside us. "It may be our best weapon against the Voxmor."

"You want to use me as a weapon?" My voice rose. "Did it occur to you to ask me first? I thought you brought me here to protect me and teach me to defend myself."

"I have no intention of using you as a weapon."

"You just said—"

"I don't think either of us will have a choice in the end." Novissime turned her gaze on me, her eyes silver as the blade of her sword. "The Voxmor know that your power with the Creonex is growing. They can sense your bond with it. That's why they're trying to cross the borders now when they've been lying low for so long."

"You think they're trying to get to me?"

"I do." Novissime stopped walking as we neared the looming structure of the Queen's Nest. "The rising threat of the Voxmor has forced me to ensure your training is well-guided. The people must know my successor can protect them."

"Your *successor*? Novissime, I told you I didn't want—"

"You may not get a choice in that, either." Her voice became stern. "I will not hesitate to defend my people if those Voxmor enter the tribe. We've managed to keep them at bay for years, but they're becoming more viscous in their attacks. I must know that someone will protect my people if I cannot."

I stared at her, searching for words to express the disbelief cascading across my mind. Growing desperation from the imminent threat to her people had driven Novissime to drastic measures, and I could see the fear behind the warrior's glint in her eyes. *I am not one of you.* "I cannot be their queen," I whispered.

"Then be their defender. Because if something happens to me, this world will have no one to protect it."

I lowered my eyes. Silvacastra was her world—my mother's world— not mine. Novissime didn't seem to appreciate what she was asking of me. As if I could agree to take over leadership of a tribe that didn't accept me.

"You may go now," the Queen said, taking my silence as an answer. "Take Avenlae with you. I'll assign him as your guard to command."

Avenlae said something in his native tongue. I couldn't understand it, but I could tell he was protesting. Her response, in his language, was aggressive. He flattened his ears and shook his head. I didn't wait for her to dismiss me again. I leaped into the air and headed toward my nest, irritation growing. *I almost prefer my sadness to this ceaseless anger,* I thought, clenching my jaw.

Avenlae followed me to my nest in stony silence and stayed on the branch as I walked towards the entrance. "Aren't you leaving?" I asked, not bothering to disguise my aggravated inflection.

"I cannot," he said through gritted teeth. "I am yours to command."

"Is that right? Didn't you tell the Queen you'd rather be out there killing Voxmor than babysitting?"

"As if you need me," Avenlae scoffed. Then, in a quieter tone, as if I wasn't meant to hear, he added, "You do not even want me to protect you."

117

He kept his eyes trained on the movement of tribespeople out in the middle of the tribe, their wings twinkling in the evening light. I could only watch him, running his words through my mind. It was as if he was implying that my acceptance of him was as important as his acceptance of me. When had that happened? As quickly as it burned, my anger died. *Tell him. Tell him he's not alone.*

"If it has to be someone, then it had better be you who has to guard me," I said, calming my tone. "I just think you deserve more than that."

"I do not want to be controlled," Avenlae responded, his head still turned away.

"I don't intend to control you. I'm not interested in forcing you to follow me everywhere on this planet, nor do I want you to. Report whatever you need to Queen Novissime, but as far as I'm concerned, nothing has to change."

Avenlae's eyes slid to mine, the soft glow returning to the silver of his irises. His hair, almost dry, fell over his shoulder as he turned. He dipped his head in a slight bow and said, "In that case, I will bid you good night."

"Don't bow to me."

When Avenlae straightened his spine, a smile softened his face. "Never again."

The next morning, Notien was sitting on the branch just outside my nest. She held two crystal cups full of a steaming green liquid.

"There is a chill in the air this morning with the change of season approaching, so I thought you might enjoy *anteel,* a heated *Hopyroque* tea." She frowned. "I think that is how you would describe it."

I sniffed at the steaming liquid, smelled the aroma of sweet spice. I took a sip and felt warmth spread through my bones. The tea tasted like spiced matcha. I smiled softly. "This may be my new favorite."

"You can finish it while we talk about the last few days," Notien said.

I nodded, watching the green drink swirl. "I meant to tell you I was sorry yesterday. I was too harsh towards you the night Saetyl attacked me."

Notien lowered her cup. "You were in pain. You lashed out. I would not have behaved differently if it were me instead of you."

"Thank you for understanding." I took another sip, eager to move on. "I know you heard something behind the scenes you want to tell me."

"Behind what?"

"Behind the—never mind. You heard something you probably weren't supposed to. That's the only reason you wait for me first thing in the morning. What was it?"

Notien's navy eyes brightened. "You know me too well. The Queen wanted to suspend more than half the Night Guard for allowing Saetyl to attack you, but Kaigar, her general, would not allow her. Said the integrity of our borders was more important, and we needed the full strength of our Night Guard. So she only suspended Saetyl, but I heard she threatened Kaigar that she would make an example out of anyone else who tried to hurt you."

I narrowed my eyes. "Notien, how well do the Delfungaye take care of their weapons?"

Notien blinked. "We survive because of our weapons. *Exitialium* blades never dull."

"I thought so," I said, imagining Novissime's anger stemmed more from her fear that her "greatest weapon" would be compromised than her concern for my well-being. I sighed. "Anything else?"

"Yes. The Night Guard has brought back heads and bodies of Voxmor the past three nights. I have never seen so many."

"Novissime said the Voxmor were getting bolder."

"I think they are getting restless. Those two scouts we saw within the boundaries communicated to the others within the forest." Notien looked out into the tribe ahead of us, watching other tribespeople fly from tree to tree. She pointed. "See there, they are bringing more bodies."

A group of Delfungaye carried the headless bodies of three Voxmor through the middle of the tribe, suspended on ropes. Others were stringing up a metal sheet-like material across several of the largest trees in the tribe below us.

"What are they doing?" I asked.

Notien grinned. "That is a sheet woven with *hi'pret,* the fire-proof core of some of the deepest jungle trees. We burn the Voxmor bodies on it so their scent cannot be tracked. If the warriors bring it here, it means our hunters have made a big kill. It means there will be a feast tonight!"

"I thought the tribe was already well supplied with food."

"We are." Notien shrugged. "But there is an animal, the *zrafejek,* that sometimes wanders close enough for us to hunt. It is the largest animal on this planet, and its meat is a Delfungaye delicacy. It is traditional for the tribe to dine together when it is caught."

"What does it look like?"

Notien laughed. "I am not the best at describing, but I will try. If the *zrafejek* walked up to us right now, you could reach your hand out and pet its thick fur, which is the color of our trees. All down the front of its snout are eyes as white ash, and along the crest of its head are tightly coiled horns—almost like a crown. It moves through the forest on four long, clawed legs and grazes on the very tops of our trees. Ah, I almost forgot: it has a tail twice as long as its body that it can use as a whip for defense." She frowned. "That is really its only defense. The *zrafejek* is so large that the Delfungaye are its only predators on Silvacastra."

120

My interest in the *zrafejek* was short-lived, for at that moment, a guard swooped down from over our tree, the wind from his wings rustling my hair. He dropped three Voxmor heads into the *hi'pret* sheet just after it was fastened to the trees. The guard made a wide arc through the trees to circle back to where Notien and I sat, and I recognized the golden, twisted hilts of the swords crossed over his back.

Avenlae hovered just before us, his wings beating gusts of wind into our faces. His silver eyes shone through the tilted slits in his black helmet. *Exitialium* blades lined the top of his wings, reflecting the suns' light against the leaves above us. He removed his helmet, and his onyx hair, tied back into a long plait, fell down his back. He was covered from head to foot in a tight black material, flexible plating across his chest, torso, and vulnerable parts of his limbs.

"I see I missed all the fun last night," I said, nodding towards the bodies the guards were piling on the *hi'pret* sheet.

"It was not fun," Avenlae said, sounding disgusted. "There was little fight. The kill was too easy."

I raised my eyebrows. "I didn't realize you were a thrill-seeker, Avenlae."

"There is no honor in killing an opponent who cannot put up a fair fight."

"How noble of you."

Avenlae narrowed his eyes at me, and then a soft chuckle escaped his lips. "Training is in ten minutes. I expect you will be a better challenge than those Voxmor."

He left with another vigorous swirl of wind, and I drank the rest of my *anteel* in one long swig. Notien turned to me, her eyes narrowed. "You seem to have become close with him."

"Close? Notien, I have to train with him every day, and all I know is that he is a warrior, and his name is Avenlae. I wouldn't say we were *close*."

121

"You let him look you in the eye."

"You know I can't stand it when people don't, whether or not it's out of respect. I can't get used to it."

"I do not think I have ever seen Avenlae laugh in any form."

"I don't think you've seen much of Avenlae at all. He mostly stays away from the tribe, right?"

Notien kept her eyes on me as if she knew something I didn't. I gave her my empty cup and stood, stretching my wings. Something about the look she gave me made me uncomfortable. "Think what you will, Notien, but you're reading too much into it. I'll see you tonight at the feast. You can tell me who all the people are." I leapt from the branch and flew over the trees towards the river. The chill morning air was refreshing as it filtered through my feathers, rejuvenating me better than any drink or food could. By the time I landed in the clearing, I had already forced myself to forget Notien's knowing look.

Avenlae had already changed into his black training vest and was pacing along the far side of the treeline. His hair hung loose over his shoulders, its waves shining in the daylight. His wings still sparkled silver, but they seemed dull without their blades.

"You told me yesterday you felt in control of the Creonex's power," Avenlae said as I walked towards him. "Do you still feel that way now?"

I closed my eyes and turned my attention inward. The Creonex warmed my hand, and I felt its energy buzzing within my chest, eager to be unleashed. I lifted my head, extending my arm straight out, and energy crackled from my fingertips, taking the form of a brilliant blue sword. "I do."

Avenlae smirked and he drew his swords. "Challenge me, then."

My attacks held new power behind them when I sparred with Avenlae that day. I became faster and more intentional with my movements, and we spent hours locked in combat. My ability to control the Creonex allowed me to embody all that Avenlae had been trying to teach me during our sparring sessions. I wasn't afraid of the weapons I had anymore—just as I had discovered how to wield the Creonex, I had discovered how to *fight*.

Avenlae's hair flew around his head as he spun, ducked, and dove. The black ink of his tattoos glistened with sweat, and his chest heaved as he parried and attacked. I could feel my hair sticking to my forehead as the heat of the day neared, but my muscles didn't fatigue as we danced around the clearing, in the air, and on the ground. Avenlae used his wings as weapons in ways I hadn't figured out yet, but the Creonex blocked his attacks with well-placed shields. I finally got to watch him fight, and the way his muscles contracted with each movement, and his intense silver eyes followed me was beautiful. Avenlae was fluid, the epitome of strength and grace, his mind in tune with his body. That was what got me in the end—watching him. For a split second I was distracted, and then I was on the ground, Avenlae's knee on my left arm and his swords crossed over my neck. We stayed there, each panting, staring at the other, realizing the fight had ended.

"You hesitated," he said. "Why?"

"I don't know," I lied.

Avenlae pushed himself up, placing his swords on his back and extending a hand to me. The blue sword was reabsorbed into the Creonex, and I grasped his hand. He pulled me up with more force than I expected, and suddenly, I was standing with my face inches from his. His pupils dilated as his eyes narrowed, studying my face. My nostrils filled with the scent of him—*how can someone smell like the wind over the trees?*

Avenlae released my hand and stepped back. "You must concentrate. Trust your instincts. This was just practice, but you would have been dead if you had done that in a real fight."

"I know. I won't let it happen again."

"Show me, do not tell me," he said. I stepped back at the sound of his tone. "You have to prove you can survive a Voxmor attack."

"Do you think one is likely?"

"It is becoming more likely, and we are running out of time to prepare you." Avenlae checked the suns' position. "Take a break, rest, and drink. We will start again." He looked me in the eye. "And if you hesitate, you will regret it."

Avenlae ended our training early that evening as we both caught the tantalizing scent of meat over a blazing fire. I didn't let on how grateful I was for the break—he had put me through my paces with the Creonex, and my mind was exhausted. I could feel there was *more* to the power I had unlocked, but for Avenlae's safety, I had been gritting my teeth to keep it under control. *That* was what truly drained my energy.

The forest was bathed in a golden glow from the suns as they sat level with the canopy of the trees. The smell of the roasting meat grew stronger, and my mouth watered as my stomach rumbled. The last fresh kill I had ever eaten was rabbit on Earth, just before my forest had been infiltrated by Voxmor. I swallowed down a bubble of anxiety. *This will be different.*

Avenlae and I passed over the Queen's Nest, and a roaring fire lit up the trees surrounding the *hi'pret* sheet. Several logs rotated over it with giant hunks of meat skewered on them. It was the first time I saw how big the tribe was, as every branch had Delfungaye perched on it, watching the fire. There were *thousands* of tribespeople there, most of them *Laizuteek*, but several *Fyr'aeset* and *Hopyroque* were spread throughout the crowd. Whistles, clicks, and shouts echoed far over the trees as latecomers flew around, trying to find a spot to rest. Unlike the grime of the Precinct, this gathering was colorful, lively, and almost joyful.

"I think you have someone waiting for you," Avenlae said, nodding to where Notien had raised a hand to wave at me from a branch a few yards away.

"Are you staying?" I asked.

He tilted his head to the side. "I must eat, too."

"Yes, well, this doesn't seem to be your kind of thing."

"Food is more important than my personal comfort." At that moment, a man's voice called for Avenlae in the *Laizuteek* tongue. Avenlae's ears swiveled towards the fire before his head did, and he dove down to meet with a man who had seen years of war. One of his wings, silver and mostly intact, was folded against his large, scarred shoulder. His other wing was made of metal with a material I didn't recognize strung across to mimic the shape of his intact wing. When he turned to speak with Avenlae, I saw wires in his skin along his spine and up his neck. Three red scars cut deep lines from the base of his head to his white, damaged right eye and into his long salt-and-pepper hair. There was no eyebrow over the white eye, but a heavy black one over the silver left, and his nose was crooked. He had tattoos, but they were the smooth-flowing kind of the *Laizuteek* and were misshapen from scarring along his arms and shoulders. The man raised his left hand, gesturing as he spoke, and I was shocked to see that his hand, too, was made of metal.

"Notien, who is that?" I asked as I landed next to her, transfixed by the oddity.

"Kaigar, our general." She handed me a crystal glass of iced Delfungaye tea and huffed. "One of the few people Avenlae listens to."

As she said it, Avenlae flashed his canines. Kaigar stood to full height and bared his own gold canines in Avenlae's face. Avenlae kept his eyes down as Kaigar hissed some sharp words to him.

"Listened to," I corrected before sipping my drink. It was hard to imagine there being a single person who could completely control Avenlae. A

125

small part of me wondered what that kind of independence would feel like—to be strong enough to defy all others.

Once their discussion had concluded, Avenlae stepped away from the General, ears still flat against his hair. I caught his eye and tilted my head almost imperceptibly toward an empty branch that arced behind where Notien and I sat. He glanced back at Kaigar to ensure his presence was no longer required, then took off and headed toward us.

Despite my surprise at his acceptance of my invitation, I said nothing to Avenlae as he landed on the branch. The intensity of his eyes warned that he should be left to stew on his own. Notien shifted beside me, but she, too, refrained from acknowledging the Mercenary's presence. A hush fell over the crowd as an elderly *Fyr'aeset* woman with a shock of white hair flew to hover over the fire. Her wise, golden face was heavily lined, and the feathers of each tribe formed a mask around her small navy eyes and over the top of her head. Her body was decorated with extravagant and kaleidoscopic beadwork. Long ribbons the color of the emerald leaves fell below the bottom of her coal-colored wings, fluttering in the wind. She began to speak to the tribe, her voice strong despite the fragility of her body.

"Who is that?" I whispered to Notien, voicing the question of the hour.

"That is the *Matri Me'leiv,* our spiritual leader."

I frowned. "Spiritual? But your tribe knows about the Creators."

"You misunderstand. We know the story of the Five Brothers, and we know they had contact with our ancestors. The *Matri Me'leiv* connects us to the spirit of the forest and the land around us. Right now, she is blessing the food and thanking the forest for providing it."

The *Matri Me'leiv* began to sing. Her voice was mesmerizing, even though I could not understand the words. She sang in a rich alto, her voice rising and falling, flowing like the current of the river, her whistles and clicks reminiscent of birdsong. When she finished, the tribespeople around me called to her, whoops, shouts, whistles, and tribal yells. She bowed to Queen Novissime before swooping down to sit near her, and several male Delfungaye flew to the still-rotating hunks of meat, beginning to hack out portions.

"And now, we wait to be brought our share of the kill," Notien said, her eyes gleaming.

"That's going to take a while," I said, watching the fifteen men at work.

"Usually not. They have a method to feed many hungry mouths."

Sure enough, within minutes of our conversation, I had a warm plate stuffed full of food. As soon as Avenlae had his plate, he began to push himself up on the branch.

"Leaving so soon?" I asked.

"It is as you said. There are too many people."

"But this is supposed to be a chance for you to relax, isn't it?"

"Look around, Xai. They do not want me here—that is not relaxing."

I raised my eyebrows at the shortening of my name, and Notien frowned, her eyes meeting mine. "I—what did you call me?"

Avenlae took a breath, frozen momentarily as if unsure how to proceed. Then his ears pressed flat against his hair and he averted his eyes. "I apologize. I forgot my place."

I blinked a few times. I didn't remember anyone ever calling me something other than "Xiaye". I didn't remember what it was like to be close enough with someone that they could use any other name. *But is that safe? Are we...close?* "I'm not offended. Just surprised." I said softly. Feeling insecure, I glanced around at the Delfungaye shifting away from us. "Sit, Avenlae. You're making everyone else uncomfortable."

He shot me a look, raised one eyebrow, and plopped himself back down on the branch above where Notien and I sat. "As you wish, Your Majesty."

"Don't," I snapped, and he smirked at his plate, taking a bite of food before I could say anything else to him.

Notien's eyes shifted back and forth between him and me, and she took a small bite of her food. "There's no reason to be afraid of him," I told her as I started on my own plate, deciding to simply ignore what had just happened. "He's just as, uh, normal as you are."

This time, they both gave me skeptical looks. I rolled my eyes.

"He could kill me in two seconds if he wanted to," Notien whispered as if this was an excuse for her behavior.

"You would already be dead if I disliked you that much," Avenlae said between mouthfuls, not bothering to look up from his plate.

"See?" I gestured to him with my utensil. "Not that scary."

Notien shook her head slowly as she took several more bites from her plate. The rest of the evening passed pleasantly, with Notien and I locked in active conversation and Avenlae sitting silently behind us, glowering at the crowd among the trees. With Notien's help, I began to understand the role of several groups of Delfungaye around us (hunters, farmers, weavers, healers, etc.) and how the tribes had combined when the Voxmor first attacked the planet. The tattoos of each Delfungaye were not only familial but also noted what job they performed and what status they held. Notien had only a few black and white tattoos around her wrists and ankles, the designs made of complicated but delicate linework.

"Mine are done in the style of the *Fyr'aeset*, but they are only the first tattoos of a warrior. My family died before I could get their familial tattoo, so this is all I have." She rubbed a finger across some of the lines on her wrist.

My own fair skin appeared bare compared to the artwork that adorned the bodies of the Delfungaye. I didn't remember seeing any tattoos on my mother growing up, but I also didn't remember that she had a pair of wings. Then again, Novissime had no noticeable tattoos, so perhaps queens remained bare-skinned. I decided to ask Notien what she knew about it.

"Novissime did have warrior's tattoos before she was Queen," Notien said as she sat back to enjoy what was left of her drink. "As soon as she took the throne, she removed them, for a queen is meant to be pure-skinned since she represents and protects all her people."

"You can remove the tattoos?"

"We can, here. We have a lot of technology that we do not flaunt to remain connected to the soul of our home and ancestors."

I nodded, looking down at the bonfire that had begun to die as twilight fell. The crowd was thinning, and the Queen had retired. A few minutes later, Notien excused herself, and I stood, ready to take off toward my nest. Avenlae stood as well, angled as if to follow me.

"I do think I can make it to my nest from here without assistance," I told him, knowing I had already kept him from his comfortable solitude for too long.

"I would hope so. You could easily climb up there from here."

"You're free to go, then," I said, awkwardly. He nodded, then turned his silver eyes on mine.

"We will train again tomorrow, but not the next day. I'm on the Night Guard again tomorrow night."

"Ah, so I get a long-awaited break?"

"*I* get a break. *You* will join the rest of the Guard in training."

Anxiety bloomed in my chest as I sucked in a breath. "That's—that's a lot of people I don't trust."

"You trust Notien, do you not?"

"I... I do, now."

"Stay near her. And if *anyone* tries to hurt you, they know who they will answer to." Avenlae's eyes darkened as they passed over my bruised cheek.

"You don't need to protect me."

"That is what I was ordered to do yesterday, was it not?"

"Perhaps, but I won't ask that of you."

The silver in Avenlae's eyes seemed to glow with moonlight as night crept into the forest. "You do not need to."

I huffed, breaking eye contact with him as resentment prickled in the back of my mind. "Because the pathetic human isn't strong enough to fight back."

Avenlae's ears twitched back when I used the insult against myself. "Any human who can make me sweat during a fight does not need my help." He paused, lowering his head and appearing almost embarrassed. "But it is offered."

I felt a smile tug at the corners of my mouth. Quietly, I responded, "Thank you, Avenlae."

He nodded once, not raising his eyes to mine, and turned to fly off into the night. A sudden rush of warmth caused me to stop him. "Hey!"

When he faced me, his dark hair flowed as if it had arisen from the shadows. I offered him my smile and said, "Sleep well."

Avenlae's eyes, as bright as the stars above us, widened. Then he smiled. "You too, Xai."

CHAPTER 13

The sky was a deep pink, tinged with purple at the edges, and the night's first stars flickered above Avenlae and me as we finished training the next evening. He led me, unnecessarily, back to my nest, but I allowed it without comment. There was a rising sense of unease in the tribe as members became more aware of the Voxmor testing the strength of the Delfungaye's borders. The feast the night before was a needed reminder of warmth, but fear slunk slyly back through the shadows the very second the bonfire had been extinguished.

"Are you leaving for the Night Guard rotation?" I asked Avenlae, wondering why he didn't veer off towards his nest or some other place he was supposed to meet when we got back to the tribe.

"I will be." Avenlae turned to face me as I landed behind him. "I am supposed to first inform you the Queen wants to meet with you tonight."

I felt my shoulders drop. "I hoped to spend the rest of my night in peace."

"If you were not with the Queen, I am sure you would be with Notien, and I would not describe that as peaceful."

"It would be better than spending my time trying to read Novissime," I muttered, glancing at the Queen's nest.

Avenlae followed my gaze, taking a breath. "You will learn to trust her, Xai."

"Do you?"

He met my eyes. "I trust her enough."

"That's right. Trust no one."

"Almost no one," Avenlae muttered. The branch swayed under my feet as he leaped from it, soaring behind the Queen's Nest. I stood there for a while, trying to understand the meaning behind his words. The look in his eyes... Could Avenlae have been implying that he trusted *me*? Did I even trust *him*, yet? I knew he could protect me in the event of an attack, but I wasn't sure I believed he would *choose* to do so. *You allow him to call you "Xai". And you're not alone when you're with him.* I frowned inwardly at myself. Why was *I* trying to convince *myself* how to feel?

Because you spend too much time in your own thoughts.

It was hard to argue with the logical side of my mind.

Tired of dissecting my feelings, I flew off to meet the Queen and reached her door a few minutes later. It swung open, and Kaigar stood just inches from my face. The top of my head was barely above his chest, forcing me to tilt my head up to look into his good eye. His mouth was misshapen by crackles of scars, giving him a permanent sneer. The top of his left ear was gone, but it hadn't been replaced by metal like his wing and left hand had been. There was a soft whir of machinery as he studied me. His mere presence kept me silent—this wasn't a man I wanted to offend.

"You have another visitor, my Queen," Kaigar said gruffly, not taking his silver eye off me.

"Let her in, Kaigar. Our discussion is finished." Novissime's voice sounded singsong compared to the General's. I stepped back to allow Kaigar to pass, but he watched me until I entered the Queen's chambers.

"Please excuse my general," Novissime said as I entered. "A lifetime of war has imprinted upon him a mistrust I cannot break."

I made no reply, instead taking in the gray room. It was modest compared to what I had expected for the Queen's quarters—two small plush chairs, a bed, and the French doors leading to her balcony. I supposed she didn't spend much time here, since many of her responsibilities probably dictated that she be in other places at all hours. *How odd: it's as simple as my bunker was.*

"Please, sit," Novissime said. Her hair was up, a few small braids falling just over her shoulders and lightly brushing the waist of her white and silver robes. There were faint lines along her forehead and some darkening under her eyes that I hadn't noticed before.

I sat, crossing my legs and keeping my spine straight, not allowing myself to get too comfortable. "Avenlae said you wanted to see me."

"I wanted to explain some things to you," Novissime said, moving into the chair across from me. "I may have come off too strongly towards you during our last meeting."

I raised my eyebrows. "The one where you asked if I would lead your people?"

"Yes. I'm afraid I let my emotions get the better of me. I hope you can forgive the part of me that was protective of you."

I nodded once. "I understand that Delfungaye take good care of their weapons."

"I take good care of my people," she responded, ice in her voice. "I have sat on this throne for ten years, and I have kept this tribe alive, if not entirely safe. My focus has always been to keep the Voxmor at bay and stop the brutal attacks that killed off more than half of the Delfungaye population on Silvacastra. Even saying that, I had begun to wonder if it was too late." She lowered her eyes and looked at her hands. "I wondered if we were just sitting here, waiting to be slaughtered, if the Voxmor presence became strong enough again. We didn't have enough people or power to counterattack, so we remained defensive." She raised her head, facing me once more. "And then we found you. The power you have harnessed from that Creonex is something I have never seen before, and I can't help but feel hope."

I made no reply. Her shoulders gradually lowered, and her eyes held more emotion the longer she spoke. By staying quiet, I hoped I could get her to drop her guard long enough to discover who she was behind her smiles, riddles, and orders. *Show me who you are.*

What I found was that her emotions were as intensely human as mine.

"I'm sorry if I become too protective, too harsh, or too desperate," Novissime continued. "It is only that I am clinging to that bit of hope with everything in me because we are running out of time to strengthen our Guard. The other worlds are running out of options, and more than half have given up the fight because they have died off or been forced into hiding. And here I am, still holding on, because I can't—" Her voice faltered, and she took a shaky breath. "I can't allow Lieneata to have died in vain. Her death has to mean something, and if I cannot protect her people then what was the reason behind her death? Does it become pointless?"

"She died to protect me," I said quietly, lowering my gaze. "Her death will never be pointless."

"No. Because she gave us that hope, did she not?" Novissime's iridescent eyes were pleading with me. "You are the embodiment of everything we have to fight for. I protect you not because you are a weapon, Xiaye, but because you

134

represent a light at the end of the dark and bloody journey my people have been on for too long. I'm left grasping at anything I can to ensure the continued survival of the Delfungaye species." The Queen rolled her shoulders back as she assumed the position of royalty, spine straight and shoulders back, trying to hide the emotion she had expressed so plainly. "All that I ask is that you attempt to understand my impetuosity in light of the horrors the Delfungaye have faced."

I thought of the things I had been driven to do out of insane desperation on Earth when I was learning how to survive alone. I thought of everything I had been told about the Creators, the Creonex, and the universes when no alternative explanation was available to feed my denial. I thought back to the moments of solitude in my nest, ripping out feathers to convince myself that the wings on my back were real. Suddenly, Novissime's call to name me as heir didn't seem so outlandish.

"I am grateful that you can join the Queen's Guard tomorrow," Novissime said. "The recent Voxmor activity has everyone on edge, and they need to see what you're capable of."

"For a morale boost?"

She furrowed her brow, thinking. "I would say more to be someone they can rally behind. They will only follow me so far. You can show them something new, something powerful."

"I'm not sure about that. Saetyl has turned many of them against me."

"Prove her wrong."

The reminder that I would be joining the Guard the next day sickened me, so I searched around for a different subject. "You mentioned the Voxmor's recent activity. I know they're trying to get into the tribe because they sense the Creonex, but what's their end goal? To destroy the last Creonex?"

135

The Queen raised her eyebrow. She answered readily, as if relieved to have moved on in the conversation. "You're asking the right questions now. When the Voxmor first began to attack, we thought destroying the Creonexes was their goal. But I don't think they're intelligent enough to plan something like that."

"They've apparently laid waste to several worlds," I said, questioning how the Voxmor had gained control over entire universes if they could not think for themselves.

"They're capable of carrying out a plan, yes. But they act with a hive mind—something, or someone, is controlling them. While their attacks are strategic, each individual Voxmor's fight is crazed and disordered. They're like cornered animals fighting for their lives. No, I think someone is orchestrating everything behind the scenes, and it is his goal that we need to figure out."

"You said *his*." I narrowed my eyes, the image of bloody eyes set in a white death mask coming to my mind. "What are you not telling me?"

Novissime stared at me for a long while before she spoke. "I have a hunch, we'll call it, about who is really in control, but I have no concrete evidence to support it. In the last communication your mother sent before she died, she told me she knew who was hunting her—not what, but *who*."

"A man with bloody eyes and crimson hair."

Novissime's eyes widened. "How did you know?"

"I—I've seen him. His face. Just a glimpse." I didn't know why it felt safe to divulge the visions I had been seeing to Queen Novissime, but the thoughts whirring around my head did nothing to stop my mouth. "But I don't know who he is."

A look of concern crossed Novissime's face. "I haven't received any intelligence on him, but with how hard the Voxmor are trying to get the Creonex, I'd hazard a guess that—"

136

A shriek sounded from behind the nest. Novissime's ears stood straight up, and her pupils constricted to slits as she turned towards the balcony. I felt a rush of adrenaline, and the tips of my fingers quivered. My heart pounded, my vision pulsed.

Another Voxmor scream sounded. Novissime threw off her robe, revealing a tight white bodysuit, her sword hanging on her hip. I held my breath. *Avenlae is out there.* An image of him drenched in blood flashed into my thoughts. My mind reeled—*hide, fight, hide, fight, hide fight hide fight hidefighthidefighthide FIGHT!*

I leaped forward, crashed through the French doors to the balcony, and jumped into the air. I barely heard Novissime's yell for me to stop. My wings made no noise as they sliced through the wind, and the Creonex crackled in my palm. A third scream split the silence, and I turned sharply, my ears pinpointing the Voxmor's location. I landed in a tree and used my wings to descend from the top branches, trying to find a good vantage point.

I spotted two Voxmor, their pale scales reflecting the scant moonlight seeping through the leaves above them, their fangs dripping saliva as they hissed and clicked, encircling Avenlae. He hovered, both swords up, ears twitching, following each Voxmor's movements. Deep gashes oozing black blood mangled the heads, bodies, and tentacles of the Voxmor. Their tails clicked as they flicked their blades together. *One breath, two.* A Voxmor attacked with a shriek.

Blades flashing, Avenlae dived, twisted, spun, and slashed out with his wings, avoiding the Voxmor claws and tails by inches. He sliced the tentacled arm off a Voxmor as it attacked, and the creature let out a piercing screech. Another darted towards him from overhanging branches, and he sank his swords up through its lower jaw, twisting himself and the blades out as the Voxmor fell. Chest heaving, Avenlae turned to face a third Voxmor, not seeing the fourth creeping up a tree behind him.

Without thought, I dove from my branch and pulled my left hand back. A crackling blue whip shot from my palm. As the fourth Voxmor hissed, I threw my arm forward, wrapping the whip around its neck and pulling myself onto its head. I sank the claws of my wing joints deep into the Voxmor's temples, holding on fiercely as it thrashed, screaming and arching its tail high over its head. One of the blades of its tail sliced into the flesh of my right arm. Gritting my teeth against the pain, I pushed myself off its head, reached up with my left hand, and grabbed its tail. Using my wings, I pulled my body back down against the back of the Voxmor's head, sinking several inches of its own tail into its skull. Its shriek reached a new pitch as its thrashes became convulsions, and thick, black blood sprayed over my face. My own scream of exertion answered its screech and a pulse of energy burst from my chest and through my limbs.

The Voxmor went limp beneath me, and I ripped the claws of my wings out of its head as it dropped to the forest floor, but not before noticing that deep blue flames had erupted over my feathers.

My wings were *on fire*. Yet I could not feel heat or pain.

As my adrenaline calmed and the forest became silent, the flames disappeared. Blue fluorescent smoke flowed into the Creonex in a steady stream. My mind was, for once, shocked into emptiness.

"That was different," Avenlae said, hovering before me. He looked over my wings through the slits in his helmet, but my feathers were back to their black-to-white gradient.

"Did you see what happened?"

"There was a pulse of light from your chest out to your limbs. Then the Voxmor was dead, and your wings were on fire."

We hovered in the darkness for a while, reflecting on what had just occurred, the soft whoosh of our wings the only sound in the still forest.

"You alright?" Avenlae asked, tilting his head towards the gash on my right arm. I glanced at it. The blood had run down to my fingers, but I felt no pain.

"I think so—it doesn't hurt."

"When your adrenaline wears off, you will feel it. Come, we should get you to the Healers."

I followed Avenlae as he rose above the treetops, realizing how blasé his attitude was towards the fight. Of course, Avenlae had probably spent many nights on rotation with the Night Guard, so perhaps combat no longer fazed him. *My* heart still raced, and I was astonished at my own daring. I had flown into the middle of a Voxmor attack without taking a second to plan. Yet I had won. I had killed a Voxmor for the first time in my life. My mind jolted back into a whirling mass. *You killed one, you actually* killed *a Voxmor,* you *really just dove in and—*

"What were you doing out there?" Avenlae looked back at me just as if he were listening to my thoughts.

"I was with the Queen when I heard the screams."

"And you thought you would take a look?"

"I thought you…" My voice died in my throat. Had I really jumped into action because I thought Avenlae had been hurt? It seemed stupid now, knowing what kind of warrior Avenlae was. But his back had been turned on that fourth Voxmor.

"You didn't see that fourth one," I said as we entered the tribe. "Does that mean I just saved your life?"

Avenlae raised an eyebrow. "You and I both know I did not need you there."

I felt my eyes widen as we landed before a large nest built between two trees, its outer walls smoothed and reinforced. Avenlae turned and took his helmet off, his hair falling on either side of his face, and he smirked as he walked backward toward the nest. "You just made my job a bit easier."

I rolled my eyes, sighing at his lack of gratitude. Upon entering the nest, I was struck by white lights bright enough to simulate daylight. I blinked several times, noting the nest's pristine interior. A *Laizuteek* woman appeared, her coal-colored hair braided tightly back and her skin nearly the same white as the walls and floors. She smiled and spoke to me in the Delfungaye universal language. Before I could respond, Avenlae spoke to her, his words accented. He spoke the language with the gruffness of his own *Y'araye* tongue, but the woman next to me seemed to understand him, for she nodded and grabbed the upper part of my left arm, leading me towards a small sectioned-off room. I sat in a chair, and she tapped a side wall.

The wall lit up, revealing that it was a screen. The woman, dressed in a white full-body suit as pristine as the rooms around her, touched more buttons, and a drawer opened near me. Herbs were organized in jars, and gleaming metal tools sat on small pedestals next to them. She walked to the drawer and poked through the jars, placing some on a wheeled metal table.

I turned to Avenlae. "What is she going to do?"

"She is a Healer. She will patch up your arm." He cocked his head to the side. "Are you afraid?"

My eyes flicked back to the Healer as tools clattered onto the table, which she wheeled around to my right side. "I, no, I just—"

The Healer interrupted, pointing towards my arm and asking Avenlae something. He nodded, said something to her, and continued to lean against the wall to my right, his helmet under one blood-splattered arm. The Healer turned back to me, smiled again, and began to clean my right upper arm with a cooling violet paste.

"What's she doing, now?" I asked, trying to keep my voice calm.

"Cleaning," Avenlae answered, watching her progress. I got the impression that he didn't have patience for my questions, so I lowered my eyes and focused on a tiny speck of dirt that one of us had tracked in. I felt the Healer wipe down my arm with something soft and dripping with warm liquid, and then I felt air on my bare skin, raising goosebumps across my upper body. There was silence, then the Healer asked Avenlae something else. I looked up at him as he narrowed his eyes and stepped away from the wall. He responded, and the Healer shook her head, looking down at my arm, gesturing and babbling.

"What is she saying?" I asked.

"She was asking when you received this injury."

I furrowed my brows. "Shouldn't it be obvious? It was bleeding when we walked in."

"It was not, Xiaye. There is no blood trail behind us."

I looked at my arm, seeing for the first time how the corners of the gash were pink, the skin already knitting itself back together, the middle of the gash dark with congealed blood.

Avenlae crossed his arms over his chest, his eyes full of curiosity. "She told me the wound is at least a week old."

CHAPTER 14

"It looks like you had a more interesting night than I did," Notien said the following day, shoving some *graetae* into my hand the second I stepped out of my nest into the light of daybreak. I took a bite, needing whatever energy I could get, for I had lain awake most of the night, trying to figure out how my arm had partially healed. I decided it had to be connected with the power of the Creonex—specifically, the pulse of energy I experienced. I was itching to explore it, knowing how important a skill like that would be on the battlefield, but I wasn't going to be with Avenlae that day. Somehow, I didn't think anyone in the Queen's Guard would be interested in testing the strength and abilities of the Creonex's power. My stomach twisted at the thought, and I no longer had the appetite to finish the *graetae*.

I sighed and relented at Notien's expectant look. "I met with the Queen, and we were discussing the motives behind the recent Voxmor infiltrations."

"Did you hear them last night? I have never heard the Voxmor that close before. I stayed near the entrance to my nest, watching for them, but I did not see any get into the tribe."

"Avenlae and I killed the group before they got to the Queen's Nest," I said.

"*You* killed one?"

I studied her shocked expression. "Yes, I did. Surely *you've* killed many."

"I have, but it is not the act of killing alone that has shocked me." She beamed at me, her navy eyes bright. "Xiaye, that was your first kill as a Delfungaye warrior! You should be celebrated!"

"I think there are more important things going on right now. No need to make it a special occasion."

"No, it is important! It is a rite of passage for a warrior to make their first kill."

"Novissime was too angry with me for rashly acting to care about what number kill it was." I recounted the night's events. By the time I was done, bright morning light was shining through the leaves, and it was time to head to the Guard's meeting place. My mouth had become dry, and I wondered how Notien had the endurance to talk as much and for as long as she did without a constant water source.

"Well, you will have to permit me to take you for a drink after training this evening," Notien said as we leaped from the branch in front of my nest. "You may be happy with no acknowledgment, but I am not! We must commemorate your first Voxmor kill."

"If you insist," I said warily.

"I do. And as for your arm, I have not heard of anything like that. There are no creatures on this planet capable of regeneration that quickly." We crossed the river and neared the Guard milling around the far bank before the tree line.

"I will have to look into that for you and see what I can find," Notien said as we landed before the assorted men and women. Silver, navy, and gold eyes turned towards me when my feet hit the muddy bank. Each looked away as I tried to make eye contact, none as bold as Saetyl to look me in the eye. A

143

rustling shifted through the crowd, and silence fell as Notien and I neared. I kept my head up, knowing I was half the size of most warriors there. I couldn't wield the power of my presence the way Queen Novissime did, but I tried to channel the most queenly power I could from within myself.

"Stay close to me," Notien whispered as we entered the middle of the group, "so they won't attempt anything."

"Are they afraid of you?"

"No, but they know each of our warriors is precious, and we do not have the numbers to lose soldiers over internal disagreements."

I tried to appear indifferent but felt tension rising. The warriors were as unwilling to accept me as I was them, but I blamed myself in part—I never learned how to make myself likeable, and still didn't care to try. With deep breaths and a blank expression, I buried my fear as deep as I could. But the skills I had learned in training with Avenlae suddenly seemed inadequate compared to the venom the Queen's Guard held in their eyes.

A loud cry echoed from the front of the group, and everyone around me snapped to attention, arranging themselves into rows before I could react. I sidestepped behind a man to stand next to Notien, trying to copy her stance, my feet together and my arms across my abdomen, left over right, hands balled into fists. The cry had been a call to order in Delfungaye, for no one moved a muscle once in formation. The whir of machinery rose, and Kaigar appeared in front of the soldier before me. The General's white, damaged eye focused on me.

"Avenlae told me you would be here today." Kaigar's English was excellent, and his voice was gravelly from yelling orders his entire life. I didn't answer—I just kept my eyes on him. "You are in the Queen's Guard now. I expect no mistakes, no matter where you are from."

"I don't think it is *me* you have to worry about," I responded, feeling the other soldiers' eyes on me once more.

"You have some nerve." Kaigar flashed his gold canines.

"So do you." I knew he could smell my bloodline and knew precisely who he held eye contact with. I had hoped that perhaps he, as an older tribe member, would be more apt to adhere to cultural expectations. Kaigar narrowed his eyes at me, then barked out an order in Delfungaye. The warriors around me burst into action. I didn't move until Kaigar turned his back on me, and then I searched frantically for Notien.

"What the hell are we supposed to be doing?" I asked.

"Morning warm-up sparring. Stay here; I will be your partner," she said, grabbing my arms and pushing me back into place in front of her. I winced at her grip on my right arm, then just as quickly tried to hide the pain. *Do not let them see your weakness.*

"Notien!" Kaigar called out, and in a string of words, clicks, and whistles, he changed my partner from Notien to a male *Fyr'aeset* warrior, his skin as golden as Notien's and his wings just as black, but he had no hair. His bald head was covered in jagged, twisted tattoos from forehead to occipital, and his deep navy eyes were set and determined. He was over a foot taller than me and held a staff in his hand, its white wood embellished with the same jagged designs on his scalp. It was then that I noticed all the warriors around me had brought their own weapons, each unique to its soldier. *How fortunate that mine is permanently fused with my skin,* I thought, annoyed as I flicked my left hand, a sapphire sword materializing from the lattice of the Creonex. The *Fyr'aeset* warrior took in the blue blade but did not seem perturbed. Another order left Kaigar's throat, still one I did not recognize, and the *Fyr'aeset* soldier was on me, staff spinning. A moment later, I was looking up at him from the ground, the wind knocked out of me and a dull ache in the back of my head where it had hit the dirt.

I coughed as I got back to my feet, refusing to remain in a vulnerable position long enough for my body to recover. The *Fyr'aeset* warrior sneered as I shook my wings, using the air they pushed forth to help refocus my senses. I glared at him, but before I could prepare myself a second time, he was back, the staff connecting with my left shoulder, right ribs, and sternum before swiping my legs out from under me. I hacked again as I rolled onto my stomach, shock clouding my thoughts and dust irritating my throat. I heard snickers, the other Guard members satisfied that one of their own so easily made an example out of me. The *Fyr'aeset* warrior spoke to them, smirking and waving his staff at my still-prone figure. Although I couldn't understand the tongue he spoke in, I recognized mockery.

My anger flared. *I'm* done *being weak!*

The sword in my hand buzzed and lengthened into a whip, which I cracked as I pushed myself up, the sound like the zap of lightning. The warrior's tattooed head whipped around, his navy eyes holding a flicker of concern at the electricity forking across the whip. He readied his staff and sprang forward, the glow of victory in his eyes. I snapped the whip forward, wrapping it around the top of his staff and pulling it into my hand, a fork of electricity burning a stripe into the back of the warrior's hand. His eyes widened as I threw the staff into the river beside us before my whip reabsorbed into the Creonex.

"Try again," I said, the Creonex glowing with energy.

The *Fyr'aeset* warrior circled me, raising his sleek, black wings into an attacking position even though they had no claws at their joints. I raised my own, although I still had not gotten used to using them as a weapon. After a few moments of circling and sizing each other up, the warrior pulled a knife from his belt. He ran at me, and I used my left hand to block his first attack, knowing that the metal filigree would protect me. Several more times his knife clanged against the Creonex as I twisted just out of reach of his attacks.

I was focused and angry, determined that his blade would not touch my skin. I ducked under a wild swipe and pressed my hands against his chest, a burst of energy pulsing from my palms, sending him flying back. He hit the riverbank and slid on his back through the mud, his wings flailing. He stayed where he was when the slide stopped, chest heaving, eyes popping. I straightened from my crouch and tilted my head, staring down my nose at him.

"You got too cocky," I called out to him as he dragged himself to his feet, his golden skin smeared with mud. The rest of the sparring partners had stopped, watching and waiting to see how their soldier would respond. He walked back to me, shaking his wings to try to dislodge the mud clumping his feathers together. I ignited the Creonex. *Don't touch me.*

"I heard rumors that you held power from that Creonex," he said as he neared, his booming voice as heavily accented as Notien's, "but I did not think they were true."

"What a way to test that theory," I remarked, becoming more apprehensive the closer he got. He opened his hands and showed me his palms.

"Truce? I do not want to feel the fire of that power again so soon."

I looked him up and down, checking for more hidden weapons. Slowly, I nodded. "Truce."

The other soldiers began to spar again, their attention gone now that there was no new fight to watch.

"That knife you had was a sharp blade," I said.

"Indeed."

"Aren't you supposed to use dull blades for training?"

"Yes," he said, raising his head. "But I wanted to see what powers you would use against me."

"You could have asked. If you threaten me, I won't care how badly I hurt you."

"I can see that now." He bowed his head slightly, averting his eyes for the first time. "I am called Darinrain."

I cleared my throat, unsure how to respond. It felt odd to go from fending off his attacks to having him introduce himself as if we were to be on friendly terms. "Well, erm, Darinrain, shall we continue?" I asked, a new staff of wood the color of bluebells materializing from my palm. I wasn't good at making friends, but I had grown a talent and comfort in combat. I tossed the staff to him, then created my blade again from the twists of the filigree of the Creonex. Darinrain tested the staff, spinning it around his body several times.

"You make good weapons," he said, easing into the sparring stance, "but I did like my old staff. I will not make this fight easy because you lost it."

Electricity crackled down my sword. "I didn't think you would."

I sparred with Darinrain the rest of that morning and ran drills with Notien that afternoon. Having been accepted by Darinrain, the rest of the Queen's Guard seemed less wary of me, but they would not speak to me, look at me, or utter a word of English, even though I figured they all knew some. My anxiety dissipated as the day wore on, and I wondered if, by putting me up against Darinrain, Kaigar wanted to force me to show what powers I had from the beginning. If so, it was a good move—the Queen's Guard knew whether or not I could fight back, and it may have diffused any rising tension to do something to the newcomer.

Notien flew with me back into the tribe that evening, telling me her perspective on the sparring match. I found myself smiling, even chuckling a few times at the enthusiastic gestures she made as she spoke. The more time I spent with Notien, the more I began to feel with her. *Almost a friend, I think.*

"Do not forget, I owe you a drink!" Notien said as we neared the market.

"You really don't have to, Notien. I can get myself some water on my own."

"Water? Xiaye, no! Tonight, I will show you *a'ta'ya*!"

"I'm sorry?"

"Alcohol, Xiaye!" She blinked at me. "That is what it is called on Earth, yes?"

"Oh, uh, is it?" A seed of unease sprouted in my mind. As more humans died in increasingly violent ways, alcohol had become a well-sought after delicacy on Earth. "The drink to forget," it had been called. Then, "the drink of death". Too many people tried to make something they didn't understand so they could forget the things they didn't want to see. It became poison.

"You must try *a'ta'ya*. It is not very strong, but it is the perfect way to end a successful day." Notien gave me a bright smile. It couldn't be that bad, right? Notien was becoming safe. So, that meant the things she showed me were safe. *Please, be safe.*

After eating a quick meal, Notien led me to a tree in the middle of the tribe whose branches were well-lit with prismatic bulbs. Delfungaye from each tribe perched all along the tree's height, lounging, laughing, dancing, and, I assumed from their lazy smiles and floppy limbs, drinking. Unlike the humans, though, these tribespeople were *alive*. They appeared *happy*.

The beat of tribal drums echoed down from the upper branches as we landed, and Notien went to one of the small bars along the tree trunk. I was mesmerized by the fluid movement around me and didn't notice Notien holding a crystal cup out to me until a cold drop of condensation fell on my arm.

"This will loosen you up. Try it!" she called over the noise as she sipped from her glass. I sniffed the sweet-smelling violet liquid, tiny bubbles floating up and bursting at the surface. Taking a breath (*please be safe, please be safe*), I touched the glass to my lips, trying to take a minuscule sip, but Notien used a finger to tilt the glass up. The liquid filled my mouth, cool and carbonated, sweet, rich, and with an aftertaste of citrus and strawberries.

149

"Wow," I said as I swallowed, noticing a hint of another taste, something fermented. And, I didn't immediately drop dead.

"Is it not great?" Notien grinned as she took another large swig of her drink. "I am sorry, though. This is not usually how we celebrate a warrior's first kill, but I hope it is good enough."

I smiled back at her, trying another gulp of my *a'ta'ya* and beginning to feel a bit less worried about the world around me. A warm feeling spread through my limbs at Notien's determination to find a way to include me in the traditions of her culture. "This is more than enough."

Notien proved to be an avid drinker of *a'ta'ya*, for as I finished my first glass, she was starting her third. She got me a second, and I got away with taking very small sips as her attention to detail had disappeared along with her second drink. She was quick to giggle at everything that happened around her and told me stories of her childhood in the combined Delfungaye tribe, much to my delight. I tried to follow along with her, but it soon proved difficult as Notien became distracted, and I started to notice that I, too, was struggling to keep track of our conversation. That was when I decided to stop sipping at the drink in front of me and began discreetly pouring small amounts into Notien's cup when she wasn't paying attention. Not that it would've bothered her—I figured she was past the ability to feel discomfort.

Just as I swirled the last few dregs of my drink, wondering how I could convince Notien it was past time to head back to our respective nests, a fist slammed down on the bar next to me. I turned and looked into Saetyl's fiery golden cat eyes. She flashed her canines at me, lowering her head so that her face was inches from mine.

"Enjoying the time you have left?" she rasped.

"I was until *you* arrived," I said, tipping the rest of my drink back into my throat and questioning why my words sounded more slurred than usual.

"You've put a damper on the party."

Saetyl smacked the glass out of my hand, and it shattered at my feet. "Your tongue is going to get you killed."

"Ah, but remember what happened last time," I said. "How much honor is there in being removed from the Queen's Guard?"

Dark patches appeared on her copper cheeks. I was provoking her, but I didn't care. "You think you are untouchable because of the Queen? You think she is always going to come running to protect you?" Saetyl sneered. "That is the way of a coward, hiding behind people stronger than you. You have not changed since they first brought you back, a small, weak, little—"

She didn't finish her sentence before I leaped out of my seat, pinning her left arm with the claw of my wing and pushing her down on the bar, a blue blade from the Creonex against her throat. The claw of my other wing was hooked into the bark of the tree, holding me suspended in the air as I pressed my knee against her chest, suddenly as sober as if alcohol had never touched my lips. "Call me a coward again, and I will show you *exactly* how much power I have gained training here."

"Xiaye," Notien said, a warning. The other Delfungaye had stopped dancing, and their chatter had died. I lifted my knife, then used my knee to push myself back onto the branch, slamming Saetyl back into the bar. She rolled off it, clutching her chest as I turned and flew away, stretching my wings and heading back to my nest, fuming. I didn't even look back to see if Notien had followed me. My boiling anger at being part human didn't give a *damn* about friendships or celebratory drinks. And for Saetyl to use it like an insult, the way Avenlae used to... I gritted my teeth to bite back tears of fury.

Away from the bar, the forest was dark, and the stars were bright in the sky. The stillness of the night seemed to rebuke the echoing chatter and drums of the bar. This, coupled with the furious thoughts swirling around my head, made

151

me lose track of where I was, and I overshot my nest. I hovered in the air above the trees for a moment, looking for the river, the forest around me seeming to sway more than it should have. Instead, I saw the crop of dark trees where Avenlae's nest was, which was enough for me to orient myself.

I had just turned to head back to the tribe, breathing deeply to clear my mind, when a blood-curdling cry drove fear into my heart like a spike.

CHAPTER 15

I stayed frozen in the air, waiting for the sound to come again so I would know if it was real. Every single one of my muscles was tense with fear. But I wasn't afraid of the sound—I feared what *caused* it.

It did come again, this time quieter but no less anguished. It echoed from Avenlae's nest below me. I twisted and dove straight into the trees. *No, no, no, no...*

Leaves smacked my cheeks and scraped my skin. Wind roared in my ears and stung my eyes. I didn't slow my dive until I burst through the canopy. Faint light of a dying fire glowed from the entrance to Avenlae's nest, but no branches were broken, no deep scratches were in the bark of the trees, and not a single panel on the nest was out of place. But Avenlae hadn't come out. Where was he? Why wasn't he waiting for me on the branch, swords crossed over his back? Why wasn't he glaring at me, asking who had made the cries I heard? *Unless...*

A strangled yell burst from his nest, and I bolted to the entrance, a feeling of dread heavy in my stomach. Stepping over the threshold, my eyes widened as I saw Avenlae on the floor, blankets strewn around him. His ribs heaved as he sucked in ragged breaths, and his skin was coated with sweat. Silver feathers shimmered with dim firelight as his wings trembled. His onyx hair was loose from its braids and flopped in front of his face. My own hands shook even more. What the hell could terrify *him?*

I crept into the nest, a voice in the back of my mind telling me I had no right to enter without Avenlae's permission. I knew it, knew he would *hate* me for the intrusion. But I had to see more. I needed to know he was unharmed.

As I neared where he crouched, the trembling in his wings became convulsions throughout his muscles. "Avenlae?" I said into the silence. His muscles tensed, the three scars on his back pulled taut. I stepped in front of him, extending a shaking hand and gently touching his shoulder.

Avenlae sprang up, one hand wrapped around my right wrist. He slammed me against the back wall, his forearm across my neck. I coughed and sputtered, seeing stars, my hands scraping futility across his chest. Avenlae stared at me, his lips curled, canines bared, his pupils tiny slivers. His ears were flat against his temples, and the claws of his wings sank into the wall above me as his nostrils flared.

"Av—Avenlae, you—I can't breathe!" I choked out, trying to claw at his arms, but it was as if he couldn't hear me. I raised my left hand to his face, my fingers pressing against his temple, and then I was in his mind, in his thoughts, in his *nightmare.*

I was watching the slaughter of his family, his people, their blood coating him so thick he could barely breathe. His back, my back, I wasn't sure which, pulsed with a pain so intense that he began to black out. There were so many agonized screams gurgling, filling my ears. There was his mother, her head gone. His father, half his body hanging from the fangs of a Voxmor who bounded past. He should've protected them; Avenlae should've stopped this slaughter. That was what he was trained to do, to kill, to protect, but he couldn't. He hadn't. Grief wrenched through his chest, suffocating, endless pain, despair, and aching loneliness.

154

"Stop!" I shouted. "No more."

The scene froze. Blood stopped flowing, the screams died. There was Avenlae, a boy, his hair touching his shoulder blades just above where his wings sprouted from his back, three long gashes ripping his young body apart, deep enough to see bone. He raised his head, the whites of his eyes so innocent in the blood that soaked his skin. I crouched down so that I was eye-level with where the boy had collapsed.

Tell him, Xiaye. Tell him.

"You... you aren't alone. You don't have to do this alone anymore," I whispered, my throat tight. My fingers pressed to the boy's temple, and I filled my mind with thoughts of the river, the sunsets, the warmth of the fire, and the feeling of a mother's hug. All the comfort I so desperately wanted to give him.

Then I was back in the dim room of Avenlae's nest, an ache in my head and upper back, a tingling in my right hand from where he held it against the wall. Gradually, Avenlae's pupils dilated as the man I had come to know returned. His ears flicked forward as he realized how he was holding me, and the strength in his wings and arms failed. He stepped back, staring at his hands as if they had betrayed him. I sank down the wall, coughing, and tears fell hot against my cheeks. Avenlae stared at me, a look of horror on his face. I covered my mouth, trying to stifle a sob, realizing that this was probably what he relived every night.

"Xai," Avenlae rasped, stepping forward. I tried to push myself up, but fear made my legs weak. He crouched down, a pained look in his silver eyes. "I do not understand."

"I saw it," I gasped, holding out my left hand. As he looked at it, comprehension dawned.

"How much did you see?"

My chest tightened. "Everything." More tears blurred my vision. "I saw *everything.*"

Avenlae's shoulders, wings, and entire being dropped as if he'd been punched in the stomach. This sadness, this awful grief, filled his eyes as he looked at me. "Oh, Xai. No."

That nightmare, that trauma, was something I was never meant to see. I had witnessed him at his most vulnerable, had seen the broken man the Mercenary protected. And it nearly broke *me* to feel his pain, to see how he still trembled now, to watch the torture in his eyes.

"I didn't want you to hurt anymore," I murmured.

Avenlae's throat fluttered as he swallowed. "That is not your responsibility."

"No, but it is my choice."

Avenlae's eyes met mine, that gentle moonlight glow returning to their color. He raised a hand, brushing a tear off my cheek. I didn't realize I had held my breath until his hand dropped.

"You should not have come here. I could have hurt you."

"You didn't."

"I had you pinned against the wall."

"I'm fine. You didn't hurt me, Av," I said, my voice stronger. His head snapped up at the shortening of his name. I pushed myself onto my knees and moved closer. Avenlae looked at me with widening eyes, straightening his spine like a nervous animal.

"I—I'm not alone anymore because… because of you. And you don't have to be alone anymore because of me."

"Who are you to tell me this?" he asked. Even crouched, he was so much taller than I was.

"If I can be brought into another universe and told that I no longer have to try to survive on my own, then you can accept that you… that you have someone to help you now," I replied, somewhat lamely.

156

The faintest smile at my pathetic attempt at support touched his lips, but as I raised my left hand closer to his face, Avenlae flinched away.

"Let me help you," I whispered. Avenlae's terrified silver eyes stayed on mine, his nostrils flaring as he took panting breaths. I'd never offered this kind of intimacy to anyone before, but I *knew* he needed it. I wasn't afraid of him anymore. "Av, you are safe. I would never hurt you."

Something stilled behind his eyes. Then, ever so gently, Avenlae laid his head against my open palm. I focused on the most tranquil memories I had—the smell of autumn on Earth, the scent of fresh rain, the sunny days with no clouds, the sunset, the sunrise, and the sound of my mother singing. At the sound of ocean waves, Avenlae closed his eyes, and his shoulders relaxed, the tremors finally subsiding.

There was a flash of one silver eye and one blue eye reflecting the bioluminescence of the plants in the cave, and I lifted my palm from his temple. I blinked, fleeting confusion at the image making me pause. Avenlae's eyes opened, his pupils returning to normal as he looked down at me.

"I ... I apologize for—"

"Don't," I said as I stood, "You would've come to find me if I were crying out like you were."

He flattened his ears as he stood with me, keeping his eyes on the darkened wood floor.

"Av, we all have demons. Just because yours are worse than mine does not mean I think you're weak. It means I wonder where you found the strength to endure all this time."

It took some coaxing, but Avenlae finally returned my small smile just before I left his nest. But he said nothing to me as I took off, and I said nothing to him. In the comfort of my bed, I replayed the night over and over, reliving the shock of his trauma, wondering why he wasn't angry when he realized how far I had intruded into his mind. And why the simple return of moonlight glow to his eyes made my heart flutter.

Next morning, Novissime summoned me. I resented being called as if I were one of her subjects, yet I never ignored the summons. Was it the thirst for information that kept me returning? I had Notien for much of the information I wanted about the tribe. Perhaps, then, it was curiosity that had me sitting on a plush chair on Novissime's balcony when she brought tea. *No, it's a protective instinct. Find out whatever you can about known enemies and those whose intentions are unclear.*

"*Anteel,* child?" the Queen asked in her calm voice.

I nodded, taking a crystal cup from her. She sat across from me, her lengthy hair not yet braided. Her ivory skin appeared warmed by the drink in her hand, and her almond eyes were bright with the colors of the waking forest as she spoke. "It has come to my attention that Saetyl approached you last night."

"She tried. I put her in her place."

Novissime smirked. "Oh, don't misunderstand, I approve." She sipped at her *anteel.* "I also warned her that she would be removed from the Queen's Guard permanently if she touched you again. I could—"

"No. I can fight my own battles."

"Very good. You *are* becoming your own warrior." She bowed her head to me. "I would also call your training with the Queen's Guard an unqualified success."

"Because I survived or because I sent one of your soldiers through several feet of mud?"

"Both, I think," Novissime said with a grin. Then, all the emotion was gone, replaced with royal power. "You must split your training time between the Guard and private sessions with Avenlae. It is imperative that you enhance your skills with the Creonex with Avenlae in a location secluded from prying eyes. You can demonstrate your weaponry skills publicly to showcase your growing proficiency with Delungaye weapons."

I raised an eyebrow. "You don't want the tribe to know the extent of my power?"

"I want them to wonder about your abilities with the Creonex. The Queen's Guard must regard you as a skilled warrior so they don't fear your power if you're forced to use it."

Not one part of me wanted to continue to train with the Queen's Guard. However, I did understand her intent with that approach—her warriors *only* respected other warriors. If I was to be accepted, I would have to earn it *their* way. *That's how you survive here.* "If I'm to spend time with the Guard, then I think I should be going. They start training early."

"Take the *anteel* with you," Novissime said as she stood with me. I walked to her balcony, pushed the doors open, and took a large gulp of *anteel* before stepping onto her railing and taking off. Novissime really had a way of saying everything and nothing at the same time. My head hurt every time I tried to decipher our conversations, so I pushed my thoughts to the back of my mind as I neared the Guard's training grounds. No need to start my day off at a disadvantage.

Notien trotted over as I landed on the riverbank behind the Queen's Nest. "Were you okay last night? I just wanted to celebrate the occasion, and I had no idea Saetyl would be there. I promise, I didn't mean—"

"Notien, everything is fine. *I* should apologize. I shouldn't have left you there alone."

"Do not worry about me. Saetyl knows I am too fast for her to beat in a fight." Notien tossed her hair.

"Are you still that fast after three or four glasses of *a'ta'ya?*" I asked, smirking.

If she had been capable of blushing, Notien's cheeks would've been red as roses. "No, perhaps not."

"I am sorry, though. I'm not really good at—that is, I'm not used to having, uh, someone else. A friend. I think." *Oh, you awkward little thing,* I cringed inwardly.

"Do not be ridiculous, Xiaye! I know you are the best kind of friend you know how to be, and I will always appreciate you for that."

Kaigar's voice rose above the whistles and clicks of the Queen's Guard to my relief. Notien translated to tell me they were supposed to be warming up with sparring sessions as they had the previous day. Someone cleared their throat behind me, and I turned to see Darinrain, who bowed his tattooed head before saying, "Shall we spar again, Xiaye?"

I glanced at Notien, who gave me a nod I understood to mean he was safe. Then she headed off to find a partner. I stepped back, my sword forming from crackles of blue energy that curled around the Creonex. "I suppose, if you haven't learned your lesson from yesterday."

"Try to keep up," Darinrain grinned, raising his staff, the blue one I had conjured, "I have more to prove than you do."

The beginning of our sparring passed pleasantly, as Darinrain and I were nearly equally matched with our respective weapons. As we continued, it became clear that Darinrain relished the challenge. The thrill of combat was alight in his deep-set navy eyes, and he was engrossed in the moment. Darinrain's energy was contagious, and I almost laughed each time one of us beat the other. Sparring with Darinrain was so different than with Avenlae. With the Mercenary, the

160

fights were intense and he… he was beautiful to watch. With Darinrain, though, combat was *almost* fun. He was a skilled warrior, for sure, but he had none of Avenlae's intensity. It felt much easier to master the use of my weapons when I didn't fear the disappointment of my partner.

Darinrain had just begun to teach me how to wield a staff like he did when a gust of wind blew the hair of my ponytail into my face. Darinrain stepped away from me, his eyes averted, wings pulled close to his back as if to decrease his size. I frowned, wondering what higher-ranking official had landed behind me, and turned to see Avenlae straightening his spine as he folded his silver wings. I smiled, and he nodded as he walked past, face stern. I blinked, dropping my smile and reprimanding myself silently.

"I will take it from here, Darinrain," Avenlae said, pulling one of his swords from its scabbard.

"Of course," Darinrain responded, keeping his eyes down. He moved past Avenlae, ducking his head to say to me, "I look forward to sparring together again."

I watched Darinrain move through the pairs of warriors, patting some on the back and joining in combat with others. When I turned to face Avenlae, he was staring after Darinrain with narrowed eyes and ears tilted back against his long onyx braids.

"Is there something wrong with Darinrain?" I asked, frowning.

"A *Y'araye* warrior does not cut his hair," he said, as if Darinrain's bald head was reason enough to dislike him. I sighed, re-forming my sword and settling into position for sparring.

Our steps were almost synchronized as we twirled, darted, spun, leaped, and danced with our swords locked in combat. Despite the intensity of the fight, I felt a sense of clarity. The weapons I conjured were *mine* to control, and I fought with more ease than I ever had. Still, even with my bolstered confidence, in the end, Avenlae held both his and my swords in his hands, an arrogant smirk twisting his lips.

"You hesitated again."

"I did not," I lied as the image of him fighting rose to my mind, his muscles rippling and tattoos shining in the light of the suns.

Avenlae raised an eyebrow as he tilted his head to the side. The sound of Kaigar's voice made me jump, and the General seemed to materialize out of a tree next to us. Avenlae dropped his gaze as he moved his hands to hold the swords to his sides.

"You dare look her in the eye?" Kaigar hissed. "You know who she is?"

"I have been training her for over two months. I hope I know who she is."

A growl rumbled deep in Kaigar's throat. "You think you can disrespect me, boy?"

Avenlae clenched his jaw but did not answer.

"That is what I thought." Kaigar took a step back from him. "I do not tolerate disrespect from my warriors."

"He has my permission to look me in the eye," I said, and the wires diving through Kaigar's neck whined as he twisted his head towards me. "*You* do not."

Avenlae flicked his eyes up to me, his expression a warning. I couldn't explain the protective anger I suddenly felt, but, at the General's glare, I bristled even more. Slowly, Kaigar turned the rest of his body around. I did not drop my gaze, nor did he, until he was less than a foot away from me.

"You have the nerve of your mother," he growled, finally lowering his eyes. "I hope you do not have her heart as well."

On that puzzling note, he left us, barking orders at the rest of the Queen's Guard.

"That was our cue to leave," Avenlae said, throwing me my sword and sheathing his. I absorbed the sword into the Creonex before turning to follow Avenlae over the trees toward our training grounds.

My thoughts wandered to the night before when I saw the tops of the scars from underneath the neckline of Avenlae's black vest. Would he continue to hide himself from me, now that I had seen the darkest side of him? Or would he become even *more* protective of himself *because* of what I'd seen?

Which do I even prefer?

My rumination was interrupted as we landed in the clearing. Avenlae fixed his silver eyes on me, studying me as if he were wondering if I would mention anything about that night. Were my thoughts so loud that he could hear them?

"Are you okay?" Avenlae asked hesitantly.

"I am. I told you that you didn't hurt me last night." As soon as I spoke, Avenlae lowered his eyes, and some of his braids slipped over his shoulder to brush against his cheek. I dipped my head to catch his gaze. "I also told you that you didn't have to look away anymore."

The corners of Avenlae's mouth twitched. "Force of habit," he said, then raised his head, breathing in the fresh scent of the mid-morning breeze. The day was beautiful, and the blanket of humidity had begun to lift over the past few weeks. The change of season was nearly upon us.

Avenlae moved to the middle of the clearing, stretching his wings so the breeze ruffled his feathers. "Your time with me will become more mentally taxing. Our main focus is strengthening the power of the Creonex. The Guard will take over your weapon training."

"You want me to be able to heal on command like I did after the fight with the Voxmor, don't you?"

"That, and the pulse of energy you released. I think that was a taste of the raw power in the Creonex. You can create weapons, but I think you can do much more."

I turned my hand over, watching the suns' reflection dance along the twists and turns of the metal filigree glove. Energy prickled through my limbs as if itching to be used. I *knew* I could do much more. "Don't make me use it against you," I said quietly.

"I am only here to direct you, not to be a target," Avenlae answered, his voice as soft as the breeze.

I raised my head. "Is that what Novissime told you?"

He scoffed, the warmth in his voice gone. "She still tells me I am your guard."

"Did you tell her I wouldn't give you any orders?"

"I did." The blue energy of the Creonex flickered in the silver of his eyes.

"Are you still obligated to train me, then?"

Avenlae curled his wings closer to his back. I sighed, shifting where I sat to refocus my energy on the power of the Creonex. Avenlae was closing himself off; there was still a line I couldn't cross. I wanted to push it, though. I wanted to see more of the man I found the night before.

"I choose to stay, Xai. I do not trust anyone else to train you."

A smile tugged at the corners of my lips. *Finally.* "I don't trust anyone else to train me, either."

Somehow, the broken Mercenary and I, who had spent so many years fiercely independent, had learned to trust each other.

CHAPTER 16

Notien waited for me at my nest that evening, a plate of food next to her on the branch. I found comfort in seeing her at the end of the day, patiently waiting to speak with me. Our little routine had quickly become my clarity in a sea of wild expectations.

"I did it!" Notien said as I sat. I wracked my brain, trying to figure out what she meant.

"You, uh, did what?"

"I am in the Night Guard." She raised her right arm to show a new tattoo, something like a branding, on the inside of her forearm.

"Oh! That's wonderful, Notien!"

"My first shift will be in a few days," she said, stuffing her mouth with some meat on her plate. "I will tell you what happens. I think there is a lot we will learn from my time in that unit."

"What do you mean?"

"You already have access to the Queen. I will see what is happening on the front line. I think we will uncover secrets about what is really happening."

I gave her a searching look. "You think the Queen hasn't been truthful with me or her people?"

"I do not think she is telling you the *entire* truth. You have been here almost three months, yes? And how much do you know? How many of your questions have been answered?"

Notien made an intriguing point. I had learned there was a reason I could use the Creonex, but I didn't know what it was. I had learned that the bloody-eyed man had hunted my mother, but I didn't know who he was. Novissime had once asked me to take her throne if she were to die, but she had not explained that moment of desperation. "You think she has something to hide?"

Notien nodded. "I do not think she is withholding information with bad intent. The Queen probably believes she is protecting us and you, but from what I do not know."

The Queen says everything and nothing at the same time. The war against the Voxmor was bigger than a promise Novissime made to my mother. There was a *reason* why I was there, and it was more than just protection. The Queen's vulnerable moments of desperation proved that much, at least. And to have Notien *agree* with my suspicions was as validating as it was terrifying.

Notien and I spent a few hours on that branch, contemplating what the Queen might be hiding. Notien wagered that Novissime knew more about the objective of the Voxmor attacks, which was old news to me. I brought up the question of my ability to control the Creonex, and Notien repeated what Avenlae had told me: as an inter-universal hybrid, I had a unique connection to the Creonex's power. Her answer seemed like a practiced one. The true answer, I knew, lay with the Queen. *Guess I'll be a here a while longer, then.*

Just as the first stars began to sparkle in the deepening violet sky, Notien set a hand on my arm. "I should return to my nest—tomorrow will be a long day."

"What do you mean? Extra training?"

"Oh, no! It is the *Wiegt'ri,* the celebration of the change of seasons. Training will end early, but we will celebrate long into the night."

"Is that wise?" I asked, thinking it would be a great opportunity for the Voxmor to penetrate the tribe.

"Our borders will be well fortified," Notien said, correctly translating the worry in my voice.

"And why celebrate the coming autumn? It happens every year, doesn't it?"

"Oh, no. On Silvacastra, the climate cools once every two years. Celebrating the change of the season is traditional for the entire Delfungaye people. It used to be the one time all the tribes came together." Notien lowered her eyes, nostalgia making them glisten in the moonlight. "If we do not continue our traditions to remember where we came from, what is left for us to fight for?"

I set a hand on her shoulder and tried to give her a reassuring smile. "I look forward to you showing me everything there is to this *Wiegt'ri.*"

Notien's face split into a wide grin. "You will love it, I can promise you that!" She sprang from the branch, waving as she left, and I felt that I might find a way to enjoy celebrating with the entire tribe just as much as Notien seemed to.

"It is not as exciting as she makes it sound." Avenlae's voice, deep and soft, rumbled from beside me.

It was the first time I wasn't startled by his presence. "How long have you been there?"

"I just arrived."

"Were you sent here? Does Novissime 'request my presence' again?" I asked mockingly. Avenlae shook his head, then his gaze slid to the firelight of the nests around us. I frowned. "Is there something wrong?" I asked, using the claws of my wings to help lift me from where I was sitting.

Avenlae shook his head again, but he didn't meet my eyes, and I could see the clench of his jaw. "The night... it is too quiet," he muttered, "I cannot..."

"Av," I said quietly, trying to catch his eyes as they darted around. Empathy twirled in my chest—I knew the quiet made the echoes of the past *much* louder. "Will you let me help you?"

Avenlae's chest expanded as he gulped in a lungful of night air. The prospect of my touch to help him seemed almost as terrifying to him as the nightmares he faced each night.

"It's not weakness, Avenlae. I *want* to help you," I whispered.

His pupils dilated as he looked into my eyes, and tension tightened his shoulders. Finally, he allowed his head to rest against my raised left hand, and my fingers sank into the smooth hair that fell over his ear and down his chest. His eyes closed as I transferred memories of the reds, yellows, and oranges of autumn leaves, the rainbow after rain, the warmth of a roaring fire after a cold storm, and the silence of a world blanketed in the first snowfall of winter. The silver of his irises glowed when his eyes opened again, and a thrill of something, some emotion, bloomed in my head. The look of his smile, the flash of silver in his eyes, and the glint of sweat on the black and white of his tattoos darted before my eyes. A soft gasp escaped my lips as I flicked my fingers away from his temple. Avenlae twitched his ears back slightly, the only sign that he may have seen what I had.

"Xai." His voice was low, calm.

"Yes?" My own sounded so unsure, almost afraid.

Avenlae's pupils dilated and contracted, and I was sure his mind was working to understand those images just as much as mine was. After a few seconds, he let out a sigh and said, "I will see you at training tomorrow. We will stay with the Guard since we will not have as much time as usual."

"Oh, okay," I said, feeling disappointed. There was no gratitude, no acknowledgment, not even a question about what he had seen. Avenlae just leaped from the branch, hovered in the air a moment as if contemplating whether he should say more, and left.

I entered my nest, trying to decipher my emotions over the encounter. I hated that he was still so afraid of any form of intimacy, even platonic. Why a part of me wanted to be close to him was still something I didn't understand. What I actually *wanted* from Avenlae was even more of a mystery. Maybe it was empathy. Maybe it was a deeper form of trust—complete transparency.

Maybe… maybe I just wanted *more.*

What an absolutely vile thought.

CHAPTER 17

Kaigar called a halt to training a little over halfway through the next day—he knew his soldiers wouldn't perform optimally with such a big event occurring in a few hours. Avenlae reached back to tie his hair out of his face as I reabsorbed my staff into the Creonex.

"Good work today, Xai," he said, and I felt the urge to smile at the use of my shortened name. I'd finally stopped denying to myself that I liked the sound of it in his deep, rolling voice.

"Thank you," I responded, tossing him his crystal bottle of water. He caught it and took a long drink. The gold at the top of the claw earrings in his ears glinted in the sunlight as a few drops of water swirled around the tattoos racing up his neck.

"Come," he called, jumping into the air as the rest of the Queen's Guard took off around us. "I think Notien is waiting for you somewhere."

I followed him to the edge of the tribe and stopped as he veered off toward his nest.

"Av!" I called, and he whipped around. I hid a smile at his reaction to his own shortened name. "Aren't you going to the *Wiegt'ri*? Notien told me it was a traditional celebration."

"It is, one that is important to our culture. But I am tired of feeling their eyes on me. They do not want me there." His eyes hardened as he looked towards the tribe.

"I do," I blurted. *That is something we* think *but don't say!* I scolded myself as anxiety bloomed in my chest. *What is* wrong *with you?*

Avenlae stared, as shocked by my words as I was.

"I-I want you there." I swallowed, my palms sweaty and an uneasy feeling in my stomach. I should've just stayed quiet. *Just turn away. Just leave, you idiot. Move, do something, ANYTHING but sit here and stare!*

After several long moments, Avenlae found his voice. "I will find you tonight." He bowed his head and flew away. I stayed hovering where I was, watching Avenlae's silver wings disappear behind the trees as he dove toward his nest. Complete mortification colored my cheeks and ran rampant through my thoughts. But there, too, was a drop of something else—was that *excitement?*

Finally, I took several deep breaths and glided behind the Queen's Nest, hoping my thoughts would reform before I found Notien.

I spotted her as she waved from the entrance of a white nest tucked against a tree trunk. Landing on the branch, I fought back and forth with myself about whether or not I should speak with Notien about my interaction with Avenlae. She would be offended if I *didn't* tell her. Ultimately, I held my silence. Oddly, I found I wanted to keep Avenlae and me just that. Just Avenlae and me. *Notien, forgive me.*

Notien beamed as I walked to where she waited on the branch. "I have everything picked out for you! You are smaller than I am, but we have time to make adjustments before the celebration begins."

"You have—w-what am I wearing?" I asked as she ushered me into her nest.

Two elegant garments hung on the opposite wall of the nest as we entered, one white, one black as Notien's wings. I ran my hand along the silk cloth of the white dress, feeling wary. The skirt had high slits on either side of the seams, and the aquamarine beadwork that hung in between the slits would be flush with my thighs. There was a belt of silver where the skirt was attached to the bodice, and the silk extended up from the belt into a plunging neckline, the sleeves long but open. More traditional webs of aquamarine beadwork hung between the gown's neckline, showing a significant amount of skin. Not only would the lack of coverage offer little protection against the elements, but I was not that comfortable in my own skin. *I* couldn't wear something like that, something so… beautiful.

"Notien, this is very revealing."

"It is the traditional tribal dress. It is alright; mine is similar." Notien shrugged as if to say she would be showing skin with me in solidarity. Her dress, indeed, left little to the imagination—however, the red accents of her dress were around the waist and down the back rather than the front like mine. She turned her navy eyes on me with a soft smile. "White is the Queen's color; knowing your bloodline, I thought it was fitting."

I didn't have it in me to fight her on it, not when she was already trying so hard to include me in her culture. So, Notien spent the next several hours braiding my hair, lifting it off my shoulders and back into an intricate updo. She inlaid beadwork on my feathers and told me everything that would happen that night. There would be the blessing by the *Matri Me'leiv,* the feast, music, dancing, and the like. She described the food and drink that would be offered, including items that wouldn't be available until the forest warmed again. She told me of the tribal dances, which I insisted I would take no part in, no matter how much she protested. She was already getting me to wear the dress, and that was about as far out of my comfort zone as I was willing to go.

The light pouring in from the entrance of Notien's nest became warmer as day became evening and the suns sank lower in the sky. The calm breeze that danced into the nest normally calmed me, as it brought with it the promise of seclusion as night neared. Then, however, it just made my limbs tremble as it warned of new experiences.

"It is almost time!" Notien said, taking down the white and aquamarine dress from where it hung. "You can use your wings to shield yourself as you change. I will step outside until you are ready."

I sighed, looking at the dress I held in my hand. Embarrassment rose in my cheeks as I began to undress, removing layer after layer of comfort. I donned the dress, careful with the beadwork, tying the silk cloth down my open back. It fit me well, the material hugging the curves in my waist and the skirt dropping from my hips in elegant swaths. Beads pressed against my thighs, and the dips of my hips were visible from where the cloth hung from the silver belt. The web of beadwork down the plunging neckline laid flush against my breasts, concealed enough by the fabric to protect some of my modesty. I pressed my wings against my back, comforted by their warmth, and turned to call for Notien.

But I caught sight of myself in a mirror. The white of the dress accented the ivory of my skin, and the beadwork complemented the color of my blue eye. My dark hair, lifted off my shoulders, lengthened my neck, which fell into my collarbones, smoothed by the beadwork that rested upon them. There was soft muscular definition down my arms, legs, and sternum that I had not been aware of, having not seen myself in a mirror in years. Was that even *my* reflection? Was that what *I* looked like?

"Beautiful." Novissime's voice floated in from the entrance to the nest. I looked into her silver eyes through the mirror, seeing one small tear trek down her soft cheek. She brushed it away and entered the nest, her own beadwork clicking as she moved. The Queen wore a white and silver gown of many layers, each moving like the waves on the river that flowed behind her nest. A headdress of intertwined beads and feathers covered her hair and fell far below her wings. Her eyes had been lined with kohl, accentuating their shine against the severity of her cheek and brow bones. But still, they smiled before her mouth did.

"I brought something for you," the Queen said, raising her hand to show me a hairpiece. It was made from the same aquamarine beadwork on my dress. I bowed my head, allowing Novissime to place it in my hair, laying two strands of beads across my forehead.

"I used to help your mother get ready for the *Wiegt'ri*. I used to braid her hair like Notien did yours, and we would laugh over the memories of previous *Wiegt'ri* we attended." Novissime swallowed. "It is too cruel that I spent so much time with her and you had so little. It should be her showing you this tribe, these traditions."

"She trusted you to show me."

Novissime's smile was tinged with sadness. She set her finger under my chin, gently tilting my head up. "I only hope you can love this world as fiercely as she did."

With a whirl of silk and beads, Novissime left, possibly to conceal the tears that had threatened to drop while she looked at me. Notien came in, her head turned to stare at Novissime as she flew back to her nest. "What did the Queen—oh, *Xiaye!*"

I tried to smile at Notien as her eyes widened. "Well, it fits." I said, unable to find anything more to say with the questions and anxiety plaguing my thoughts.

"'It fits'?" Notien raised an eyebrow at me and crossed her arms over her chest. "Xiaye, it does more than just *fit*. You look absolutely—"

"I know; I looked in the mirror. Just get changed and I'll meet you outside the nest."

Notien watched me as I brushed past her, but used her stretched wing to stop me from leaving the nest. "You are allowed to know that you can be as beautiful as you are strong and deadly, Xiaye."

I turned my head, acknowledging her but unable to answer.

Notien dressed as I looked out the entrance of her nest, enthralled by the change in the central hub of the tribe. There were so many colors around me; everyone dressed in subdued shades of black, gray, beige, and brown cloth but with brilliant beadwork around their arms, legs, and chests. It appeared traditional that men wore beadwork across their bare chests, and the piercings of the warriors shined gold. The heart of the tribe was alive with a roaring fire, its heat providing warmth and light to the gathering. Every branch was adorned with lamps and multicolored flowers. The smell of food wafted through the air, and my stomach growled. It was a sensory feast that left me spellbound enough to forget that I felt almost naked.

"Do you love it?" Notien asked as she appeared beside me, her dress wrapped tightly around her thin frame.

"Yes. This is amazing."

Notien led me down to where a group of the Queen's Guard had gathered on a net strung between the branches of several trees. The sights of the Delfungaye tribe in celebration were nearly as breathtaking as my first sight of Silvacastra had been. The members of *Laizuteek* had outdone themselves with beadwork and flower decorations draped across the branches of every tree near the bonfire. Within these flowers shone the brightest neon-colored lights, bathing the people in multicolored glory. As we landed next to the throng of the Queen's Guard, Darinrain appeared, holding three drinks.

"I wondered when you would arrive!" he called over the noise, holding out two cups. "Do not worry, it is only *a'ta'ya*," he assured me as I gave the glass a wary look. I accepted a cup and took a gulp. The beauty of the *Wiegt'ri* was not enough to quell the anxiety that rose in my throat from the number of people surrounding me and the amount of my skin that was exposed to the night air. *Make my limbs floppy and my worries disappear,* I thought as I took another drink from my cup.

Darinrain had a similar style and color of beadwork as Notien. A black loincloth held in place by a leather belt hung from his waist, and a large, beaded necklace wrapped in several layers down his neck and over his chest, with four strands extending down his ribs and wrapping around his back. Tattoos in the same tribal style as Notien's wrapped around his chest, indicating that he was a more decorated warrior than Notien was. They were, however, a different style than the jagged ones that ran up his neck and over his bald head.

I searched through the faces of the Guard in front of us but didn't see the moonlight-silver eyes I was looking for. I took yet another sip of the *a'ta'ya*, wondering if it would also chase away the new sting of disappointment.

"He never comes to these things," I heard Darinrain tell me. I looked at him as he drank, the lights above us darkening the tattoos across his head.

"Who?"

"Avenlae." He furrowed his brows. "That was who you were looking for, yes?"

"Oh. Uh, not really. This isn't his kind of thing," I said as raucous laughter burst out from the group. *Real smooth, Xiaye. Good cover.* I had to fight not to roll my eyes at the sarcastic tone of my thoughts.

176

"Drink more," Notien said in my ear as the *Matri Me'leiv* flew to the middle of the tribe to a roar of cheers, whistles, and clicks. "You will feel more comfortable."

I finished my first drink as the *Matri Me'leiv* began her blessing and started on my second as she sang to the crowd. Tribal drums pounded a beat under her voice, and the entire tribe swayed, calling out and whistling. For the last few minutes of her song, the whole forest was swaying along, as if the trees bent to hear her rich voice. As soon as she finished, Novissime flew to hover next to the *Matri Me'leiv*, and silence fell over the massive crowd. She addressed the tribe in her language, and Notien translated for me as Novissime welcomed them to the celebration, thanking the hunters for the meat, the warriors for protection, the mothers for the decoration, and the farmers for the drink and the rest of the food. She opened the feast at the end of her speech, raising her glass and looking directly at me. I tipped my glass towards her, then Notien pushed a plate of food into my hand. Another tribal beat struck up around us, and the tribespeople bobbed as they ate.

I had relaxed my shoulders and was swaying to the music while Notien and Darinrain told me stories of their time in the Queen's Guard. I found myself smiling, even laughing a few times with them. Notien kept handing me things from her plate, telling me I "needed to try this!" and that I "would feel better if you ate this!" *Is this what it feels like to have friends?*

"So, Xiaye, you must tell us about Earth. How often do your seasons change?" Darinrain asked me halfway through his meal.

I blinked. "Um, four times a year."

"That is too much," Notien said, shaking her head. "I could not handle the cold that often."

"It snows in the winter where I'm from," I told her, smiling at the look of shock on her face. "You know, frozen water droplets falling from the sky."

"It must be painful when they are falling," Darinrain said, frowning.

177

"What?"

"The frozen water droplets. That must be painful if they fall on you, a solid object like that."

Notien nodded, her eyes wide. "We are not close enough to this planet's poles to experience snow."

"I have heard it is quite peaceful." A deep voice interrupted our conversation. Darinrain's eyes flicked to the ground, and Notien coughed, choking on her drink.

I turned, looking up into bright silver eyes. All the tension left my shoulders, and suddenly I was smiling easily and *really* feeling the calm of the *a'ta'ya*.

Avenlae tilted his head. His eyes roved over my body, taking in the beadwork against my skin and the silk of the dress that hugged my curves. My palms began to sweat. "I told you I would find you," he said softly.

"Yes, but you're late."

"I told you I would be here, not when or for how long." Avenlae's hair was braided down his back, and his claw septum piercing had been changed to a slim golden hoop. Two black straps crossed over his broad chest, holding the scabbards of his swords, and golden beadwork looped down his arms and across his abs, twisting every time he breathed.

"Hmm," I said as I took another bite of food, my skin suddenly feeling as hot as the fire that blazed before us.

Notien flashed a smile at me.

"Who told you about snow?" she asked Avenlae.

"It is more like a memory I have," he said, looking at me from the corner of his eye. "But it is soft as down and cold as ice."

"That's because it *is* ice," I muttered.

Darinrain shook his head. "I would not be able to tolerate something that cold all around me. It does not get cold enough here in the forest for the river to freeze, so I cannot imagine the whole world becoming cold enough that water freezes in the sky."

"There is very little you can imagine, Darinrain," Avenlae said under his breath, and I stifled a laugh. Even Avenlae's dimples appeared momentarily. Darinrain smiled good-naturedly and finished his plate.

The beat of the drums changed, and the sound of flutes and strings fluttered down from the tops of the trees. A cheer rang from the branches, and some tribespeople took flight, moving their bodies in such a way that I recognized they were *dancing* in mid-air. Notien discarded her plate and waved her arms, stretching her wings and moving to the beat of the music. "Xiaye, you must dance!" she called as she moved closer to the gyrating mass of Guard members.

My eyes widened, and I stepped back, trying to find some excuse to stay far away from the dancing crowd. My heart raced as Notien was sucked into the pulsing bodies, and I felt claustrophobic from watching them. Avenlae's calloused hand brushed against my arm.

"Do you want to go somewhere quieter?" he whispered.

Apprehension about where he meant was nothing compared to the constricting fear of joining the dancing tribe. *Too close, too close.* I nodded. "But what about Notien?"

"She has Darinrain," Avenlae said, then looked at him. "Right? You can keep her busy."

Darinrain raised his eyebrows as Avenlae led me away but did not protest. We flew up to a thick branch a little ways above the celebration, close enough to hear the music but far enough not to be suffocated by the dancing bodies.

"Thank you," I breathed as we landed, sitting to watch the tribe below

179

us. Somehow, being alone with him had become much safer than immersed in the crowd of Delfungaye.

"You see why I do not join in these celebrations," Avenlae said as he watched the members of the Guard laugh and jump to the drums. Something stirred in his eyes as he stared down at the tribe. I sighed, empathy heavy in my chest.

It was yearning that glowed in his gaze.

"I think you want to, in your own way," I said calmly. "You want to be accepted."

He looked over at me. "Do you not?"

I shrugged. "I don't need to be accepted by everyone. I never have been, so I have no longing for what I haven't lost."

Avenlae lowered his eyes again, watching the fire. "I have lived so long on the outskirts of this tribe that I have forgotten what it is like to be a part of them."

"You *want* to be part of that dance?"

"I do not want their stares. Knowing they will never trust me keeps me away."

We stayed quiet, letting the noise of the *Wiegt'ri* float up to us. I felt the cool evening breeze flow over my bare skin and tried to suppress a shiver.

"I trust you," I whispered, feeling as if I were confessing a dark secret. I knew I shouldn't have said it, but I also knew it to be true. And the *a'ta'ya* I drank wasn't doing *anything* to help hold my tongue.

Avenlae lifted his bright eyes to mine, searching my face. "And I, you."

I smiled. The drums ceased, and flutes and strings took the melody. Below us, members of the tribe began to break into pairs. "What is happening now?" I asked Avenlae, trying to ignore every emotion that began to twirl through my mind.

180

"Traditional partner dance," he said, taking a deep breath. "It represents the tribe's will to survive the cooler season."

"You're all very sensitive to temperature changes."

"We live on a planet with high humidity and high temperatures for two years at a time. We do not need to adapt so much to the cold."

Maybe it was the drink talking—actually, it was *definitely* the drink talking—but I stood and held my hand out to him. *So much for ignoring your emotions.* "Shall we?"

Avenlae frowned at my outstretched hand. "Shall we what?"

"You said the partner dance was traditional."

He stood, keeping his silver eyes on me. "Do not tell me you want to dance?"

"Well, no. Not at all." I shrugged. "But I accept you. And this is your tradition."

He stayed there, facing me, and I let his eyes move over my dress again, feeling the rhythm of my heart change. Then Avenlae took my hand in his rough palm, pulling me closer with a soft pressure that spoke of the heightening of his nerves. I was close enough to feel the heat of his skin, and it became difficult for me to suppress the shivers that moved across my muscles. Goosebumps erupted up my arms as Avenlae slid his other hand around my waist, his fingers pressed against my spine at the small of my back. I placed my other hand on his shoulder, feeling the muscle underneath my palm. His skin, his touch, his body—it was all so *warm.* He leaned his head forward, and his lips brushed against my ear as he whispered, "Breathe, Xai. I am not going to hurt you."

I let out a whoosh of air, trying to disguise it with a poorly timed laugh. "I know you won't."

"You always tell me I am safe. Now it is I who has to tell you." He began to sway slowly to the music echoing from below us, and I followed suit, albeit less smoothly.

"I, I'm sorry," I stammered, nerves eliciting another shiver, "It's a lot cooler up here than it is closer to the fire."

"So you say." Avenlae's hand applied gentle pressure to my back, and then my breasts were flush against his bare chest. I searched desperately for something, *anything* to talk about. My heart seemed to thrash against my chest as my mind yelled frantically, *WHAT THE HELL WERE YOU THINKING?*

Fortunately for my flailing brain, Avenlae spoke first. "You look—"

"Different?" I volunteered, eyes tracing over the jagged edge of one of his scars passing over his collarbone.

"That is one way to put it."

"So do you." I focused on breathing, trying to relax my muscles.

"Your hair is falling," Avenlae breathed, letting go of my hand and brushing his fingers over my neck as he moved a curl.

"I hadn't noticed," I said hoarsely, looking up into his moonlight eyes. His hand froze where it was, cupping the nape of my neck, attempts to replace the curl of my hair forgotten. Suddenly, my mind was no longer yelling anything, but my fingers trembled. The silver of Avenlae's eyes intensified as his pupils dilated slowly and darted to my lips. I could almost *see* the pounding of my pulse. His eyes stayed on my mouth, and then I was wondering what *his* lips would feel like, how they would taste. The music faded, replaced by the sound of my breathing. No emotions were whirling around my head, no anger, no pain. There was nothing but Avenlae's silver eyes, his hand on my back, and the feeling of his heart beating against his chest, so close to me, *too close. No, closer.*

For the first time, there was no fear in his eyes.

And then his nose brushed against mine with a quiet grace, his warm breath spread across my face, and my nostrils filled with the smell of him, the scent of leather and the forest. His lips brushed gently against mine, like the touch of a feather, a feather spreading the sensation of tingling warmth across my skin.

A loud *crack* echoed from the fire below us as a log broke, sending sparks swirling up through the crowd of dancers. I gasped and flinched away from Avenlae, the shouts and laughter of the tribe rushing back to my ears. Avenlae had released me, his ears up towards the crowd, ensuring the source of the noise was not a threat. I felt the cold of the night, and my mind whirred back into action.

Did that just happen? Did I just dance with Avenlae and allow myself to be *held* by him? In his arms, in his touch, in his warmth—

"It is late," Avenlae said, not looking at me. "You should rest. No matter how late the Guard celebrates, training will still happen tomorrow."

I blinked, trying to understand the abrupt dismissal of what had just happened. Perhaps he was choosing to ignore it. *Perhaps I should ignore it, forget his hands, his lips...* "Will you be able to sleep?" I asked, pushing down my emotions.

A calm smile spread over his lips. "I will be fine, although I appreciate your concern. Goodnight, Xai."

And just as he always had, Avenlae left in a whoosh of silver feathers, leaving me alone on the branch, wondering what the hell had just happened.

CHAPTER 18

Stretching my wings in the crisp morning air, the suns having just appeared over the tops of the trees, I left my nest to enter into an almost still tribe. Decorations still hung from the branches around my nest, their colors becoming more subdued the higher the suns rose. Other than the streamers of flowers, there was little evidence that the entire tribe had been out that night.

The morning called for hot *anteel*, which I purchased from a small market built into a tree adjacent to my nest. I perched high in a tree that faced the suns' rise. The smell of the forest had changed—no longer was it sweet, but now rich and full. Clouds were darkening on the horizon, slowly, not threatening. I wondered if the rain on Silvacastra felt like the rain on Earth. Would it smell the same, too?

Another soft breeze caressed my cheeks, and I thought about the night before, remembering the tingles of cool air and Avenlae's hands on my bare skin. He felt so strong, so warm, so... *safe.*

But what had that been? Had the alcohol affected our ability to think rationally about our decisions and control our actions? I touched my fingers to my lips, remembering the feeling of his as they brushed against mine. What had that meant? My body didn't hesitate to tell me just how much I wanted to find out. But then Avenlae had left, as if he couldn't handle those moments. Another sip of *anteel,* and I tried to forget the night, told myself it had been nothing more than the alcohol and the setting. It was the music, the shouts and laughter, the food, nothing real. Because I didn't want it to be real.

Did I?

"You look deep in the throes of rumination."

I started, the sound of the morning birds suddenly ringing in my ears, and saw that Novissime had joined me on the branch, her long hair braided. Her silver almond eyes were questioning as she watched me, her spine erect and shoulders back. I nodded and sipped once more from my crystal glass.

"I thought you might like some company this morning." The suns' light glistened on her cheeks and shone down the frame of hair around her face.

"If you insist."

Novissime smiled, and her small laugh sounded as sweet as the tinkle of wind chimes. "I also wanted to apologize for being overcome with emotion yesterday evening. I shudder to imagine what you think of me now."

"I think you're more human for it."

"I have my moments. It's not easy, trying always to appear as if I know what I'm doing."

I frowned and glanced at her, trying to discern sarcasm in her voice. "Don't you?"

"I was put on the throne with no prior training other than with the Queen's Guard. I was young, only a few years older than you are now. I'm always trying to figure out what I'm supposed to do. They call me their Queen, and after so many years, I have gained the trust of the tribe, but I am only their leader."

185

My eyebrows knitted together as I watched the clouds slowly sail closer to the suns. Was she confessing her shortcomings, her own vulnerability? What was her motive?

"I know you remain suspicious of me. I can see it in your eyes every time we are together," the Queen said as she turned again to the suns' rise. "I do not know precisely how this is supposed to go. I don't know what I should and shouldn't tell you, when I should tell you what, or how."

I felt her hand on my shoulder and turned to study her silver eyes.

"I mean to tell you that I am doing the best I can with what I know, and that is very little," she continued. "I know there is no easy way to convince you to trust me, as I'm sure I will misstep and make more mistakes down the line. I cannot conceive and so shall never have a blood heir. Your mother tried to explain to me what it was like to raise a child, and sometimes I wonder if she felt the way I do now, with little idea what I'm doing."

But that's how I've felt, too. The Queen suddenly didn't seem so deceitful. She didn't even seem as powerful or domineering. She was... imperfect. "You're doing well enough," I said, nodding down toward where the tribespeople had begun to exit their nests and travel through the forest. "The tribe is still alive and practicing your traditions. There are children down there who haven't known the fear and pain I have. That's enough."

"I hope it will remain so."

We sat in silence for some time, knowing we could no longer have strict expectations. To move forward, we needed to let go of our biases. I still struggled to find it within myself to trust her completely, but it was easier to trust her intentions, if not her actions or words.

"You should probably be off to the Queen's Guard," Novissime said, breaking the silence. "Kaigar still expects full attendance."

186

"Of course he does," I said, finishing the last drops of my *anteel*. I bade the Queen goodbye and dove towards the river. Most of the Queen's Guard was milling around its banks, but their activity was restrained. The faces of some revealed how long a night they'd had as they winced in the suns' light. Notien stood on the outskirts of the crowd with Darinrain, an unexpected addition to my typical welcome party.

"You sure look bright and energized," I said as I landed, smirking at the dullness in Notien's eyes as she shot me a glare.

Darinarin laughed, the sound booming over the groans of the Delfungaye nearest us. "I had to take the last glass of *a'ta'ya* from her last night. And right before Challenge Day. Notien, you should know better."

She hissed at him, rubbing her temples. "I did not know it was Challenge Day. And neither did you, Darinrain, so for that, I promise I will beat you."

"Challenge Day? What is that?"

"Kaigar told us first thing this morning," Darinrain said, keeping his eyes averted. "It is how he ranks us in the Guard. You fight until you are beaten against partners he chooses."

Notien groaned. "It is how he tests our skills. If you rank low enough, you are dismissed from the Guard."

My stomach twisted. The last thing I needed was for the entire Guard to watch me beaten *again*. "Is Avenlae going to fight?" I asked. *He doesn't need to watch this, either.*

"No," Notien responded, pinching the bridge of her nose before muttering, "I hope this medicine starts working soon."

"Kaigar knows Avenlae can beat all of us with one arm tied behind his back," Darinrain said. "It would not be fair."

It took a moment before I spotted Avenlae where he stood speaking with Kaigar. He was not looking the General in the eye but was scanning the crowd. Was he looking for me, like I was him? *That is an incredibly stupid thing to think,* I scolded myself, but as I did, Avenlae locked eyes with mine, and a twitch of a smile played along his lips.

"No, it's not fair," I said, momentarily holding Avenlae's gaze, unaware of what I was responding to. When I turned back to Notien, one of her slender, perfect eyebrows arched.

"Now that you mention him, where did you go last night?" she asked.

"Somewhere quieter."

Her eyebrows made a bid for the sky. "Is that all?"

"Notien! What are you implying?"

At that moment, Kaigar called the Queen's Guard to attention. Notien flashed a smirk at me before finding her place in the formation. The General then split the Guard into four groups. In the middle of each was a bare circle where members would enter for the Challenge. Kaigar paced back and forth between groups, watching the Challenges, his expression unreadable. All the while, restless energy buzzed in my chest, warming the Creonex around my left hand. Its power fought to be released, fed by my rising anxiety as I watched the Challenges commence.

The Delfungaye warriors were ruthless. They knew when to yield, as they couldn't afford to lose multiple soldiers to injury, but they sometimes skirted the line. My hands began to shake as my chest tightened—I knew I wouldn't see any mercy from my opponents. The warriors were still too curious about my powers and unaccepting of my strength with their weapons. Befriending a few of their own would only get me so far.

Notien was in the group next to me, and she lasted through eight Challenges before she was beaten. She was nimble, and several of her opponents were beaten without having the chance to block or parry. I couldn't see Darinrain enter the Challenges, but I hoped he was doing well.

"Xiaye!" Kaigar's voice snapped after a particularly brutal battle between a *Hopyroque* man and a *Fyr'aeset* woman. I looked at the General. He nodded towards the middle circle.

It was my turn.

"Control, Xiaye." Avenlae's whisper against the back of my neck made my breath catch in my throat. "They do not need to see everything you are capable of."

I nodded once, then entered the circle, the shouts and jeers of the Guard echoing in my ears. The *Hopyroque* warrior stood panting in the circle, two thick swords in his hands. His tusks pressed against his cracked lips, amplifying his sneer. I flicked my left hand as I entered the circle, my blue blade extending from my palm. The mountain warrior spun his swords to tumultuous applause. The crowd quieted when I ignited the electricity that crackled down my blade. *Didn't expect that, did you?* I took a breath, letting the power of the Creonex move through my veins. I didn't really care for caution—I cared about survival.

The warrior charged with spinning swords. Despite his strength, he lacked speed, making it easy to dodge his attacks. The sound of metal against metal cracked across the tightening circle of onlookers as they called and jeered. Had I not been so much smaller than the lumbering *Hopyroque* soldier, the fight may have been more difficult. In the end, a few expertly placed attacks and easy parries won me my first Challenge without the need to tap further into the Creonex's power. The places of impact from the warrior's swords still ached along my back and legs as he left the circle, growling, and I had just seconds to catch my breath before Kaigar called a *Laizuteek* warrior to join me.

He, too, fought with a sword, a long curved blade. Half his head was shaved, the other half left long, and tattoos swirled around his temple. Our swords clashed, the crack of energy forking down my blade. He fought with the intent to test my abilities. *He's looking for a weak spot.* I controlled myself, waiting for a mistake. Darting around the warrior's attacks, I watched the way he used his sword. He flashed his canines—he was becoming frustrated. Finally, he made a wild swing. I ducked and thrust my sword up, the blade splitting into links and wrapping around the soldier's wrist. I yanked the whip down, punching his other shoulder back as he fell on his back. I pinned one hand with my right leg and the other with my left knee, a ball of energy crackling in my right palm pointed toward his head.

"I yield!" he called out.

A half-hearted cheer rang up from the onlookers—not acceptance, but better than the silence that followed my first Challenge. The crackling energy calmed as I stood, and the Creonex reabsorbed the whip into its filigree. I turned to face the other end of the circle, ready to meet my next opponent, when the shadow of wings appeared on the dirt.

Saetyl landed in a cloud of dust, her golden eyes alight with the fire of hatred. "You *dare* fight against our warriors on Challenge Day?" she roared, straightening and pulling her ax from its scabbard.

"Just couldn't wait for the chance to get a piece of the action, could you?" I called back, reigniting the crackles of energy across the filigree glove.

She sneered, beginning to circle me. "I could not wait to be the one to beat you."

"Ah, but you're still not in the Queen's Guard. This fight will mean nothing."

"It will mean *everything* to me. The chance to show everyone who you really are. A weak, pathetic little human!" She charged forward, and I braced myself for impact. A slap of wind tore across my face, and Avenlae had Saetyl pinned to the ground, one of his swords across her throat.

190

"Try and hurt her. *I dare you.*" Avenlae's hiss was laced with venom and his canines were bared. The entire Guard had gone silent.

"Avenlae, stand down!" Kaigar barked, the crowd parting before him as he neared the circle. Avenlae stayed where he was, eyes narrowed as he pressed his blade against the skin of Saetyl's neck, a bead of blood blooming.

"Avenlae," I snapped. His ears flicked towards me. Gradually, with intense control, Avenlae stood, moving away from Saetyl without ever taking his eyes off her. His pupils were constricted, and his knuckles were white around the hilt of his sword.

"Always saved by your little guard," Saetyl spat as she stood, wiping blood from her neck. "How sweet."

My anger flared, burning the metal of the Creonex. "You want a Challenge?" I looked over the faces of the Guard. "You *all* want a damn show? Fine. You'll have it." I jerked my head at Avenlae. "I don't need him."

"Tonight, then. Sunset." Saetyl pointed. "The meadow a mile from here."

"I'll be there."

"I am counting on it."

She shoved her way back through the warriors behind her. There was a ringing silence as members of the Guard exchanged glances.

"You will allow this to happen?" Avenlae growled at Kaigar.

The General narrowed his eyes. "Saetyl made an official Challenge. Xiaye agreed. You know the rules."

"Saetyl is a disgraced member of the Guard!"

"Do not make yourself one as well, boy!" Kaigar flashed his gold canines at Avenlae and turned to me. "It is time you showed us all the secrets that Creonex holds, is it not?"

I glared into the scarred face of the General before turning and pushing my way through the warriors surrounding us, not bothering to answer. Kaigar's attitude proved that within the Guard, the Queen's protection meant nothing. *You survive alone.*

"Xiaye!" I heard Avenlae call out behind me. A hand grasped my arm, and I whirled around, my anger breaking.

"Why did you stop her?" I shouted.

"You may think that Creonex makes you untouchable, but Saetyl is fueled by hatred, and she is a warrior. She will have your *head* if she wants it."

"Let her try! You made me look weak in front of everyone."

"I protected you!"

"I am *not* yours to protect."

Avenlae flinched as if I had struck him. I stood my ground, looking up at him, fury raging through my body.

"I have nothing to lose," I said. "I will not sit back and let her disrespect me anymore. If she wants to prove a point, let her try."

"You are angry, and it is making you irrational."

"What right do you have to say that to me? She has no fight with you, yet you just pinned her to the ground. You would've sliced her throat if I hadn't stopped you."

"She was threatening you."

"Since when have you cared?"

"I have *always cared!*" Avenlae breathed deeply, chest heaving. His ears pressed back against his hair, and he leaned forward, his canines visible. "I am not interested in watching her hurt you."

"Then leave. I'm not asking for your help."

Hurt flickered in the depths of Avenlae's silver eyes. Guilt constricted my throat as soon as I said it, but I spoke no more. With a hiss, he turned and flew away. I didn't know what hurt more: my guilt, or watching his back as he left me to stand alone on the riverbank.

192

CHAPTER 19

I paced anxiously in the clearing that had become my personal training ground. Electricity forked between my fingers as the power of the Creonex fought for release.

"I can't fight you," I said to Notien and Darinrain, who had insisted on joining me to prepare for the Challenge with Saetyl. "I could hurt either one of you with the Creonex."

"That is a risk we are willing to take," Notien said, her thin, curved sword already in her hand.

"Saetyl may seem like she fights only out of anger, but she is a Delfungaye warrior, and she is ruthless," Darinrain said, leaning on his staff. His skin had a gray hue, reflecting what little light was coming through the dark storm clouds that obscured the suns. "You need all the help you can get before she arrives."

"Oh, so you two *and* Avenlae think I can't do this?"

"You are more merciful than Saetyl," Notien said. "You are more willing to fight to yield than she is. I do not think she will hold back on any of her attacks in deference to your health."

I looked up at the clouds, spotting a flash of violet lightning in their depths. "You both realize that I can't always control this power?"

"Then you should practice now. Suns' set is sooner than you think it is," Darinarin said.

"Xiaye, I cannot watch you enter this Challenge knowing I did *nothing* to help you," Notien murmured, just for me to hear. Her navy eyes were wide, but determined.

I took a deep breath, the scent of far-off rain seeping into the air. "Fine. But if I hurt either of you—"

"We will know we asked for it," Notien said, raising her sword and holding the blade horizontally in front of her chest. Sparring with Notien was very different from sparring with Avenlae; her attacks were less powerful, but she was quick. Over and over she tapped her blade to my arm, legs, ribs, and chest, signaling my defeat. I'd never seen anyone move with the grace and agility she had.

"Do not hold back!" she called as she readied for another round. "I have already killed you six times!"

I rolled my shoulders. It was my fear of hurting her that prevented me from using the Creonex to its full extent. If I immersed myself in the fight, would my power burst out unexpectedly like it had in the past? *Don't you dare hurt her.*

Again, Notien dove forward. I dodged her first attack, parried her second, and swung my sword around to her left. She parried, locking our swords together in a cross.

"Fight me, Xiaye! Fight me!" she urged through gritted teeth. I released some of the pent-up energy, and blue electricity cracked down my blade, causing her to throw me back. Threads of blue energy curled up my left arm and traveled across my shoulders to my right hand. Notien darted into another combination of attacks, and I swung my blade up to block, firing a ball of sapphire light from my right palm. She spun out of the way, flinging her sword out as she stopped her momentum with her knees. I leapt, pumping my wings a few times to gain height as her wings swiped under me. Notien was on me as soon as I landed, going for my ribcage, but my movements became faster, stronger. My last parry sent her skidding back, and she sank her sword into the ground to stop her slide. My blade split into the chain links of the whip, which I wrapped around her sword before yanking it out of her hand.

As soon as her sword was in my hand, I felt an impact on my back. I was nearly sent to the ground, stopped by only my right hand and a beat of my wings. Darinrain stood behind me, his staff raised. I gained my footing, the electricity passing from my right hand down the blade of Notien's sword. I dove toward him, my blades catching both sides of his staff as he swung it up. He moved to twist it, muscles bulging. I jumped, spinning with the momentum of his staff and pulling with all my might to the side as I landed, dragging the staff and Darinarin to the ground. Setting one foot on the side of the staff, I pulled Notien's sword free. He swung himself up and kicked the side of my head. I hit the ground hard, and the world spun. Stumbling to my feet, I panted as Darinrain threw Notien's sword back to her.

I shook my head a few times, trying to get the ringing out of my ears. *Better me than them.* Darinrain advanced, staff spinning. I rolled my left wrist, and the sword lengthened into my own glowing blue staff. I parried first to the left, then right, then ducked under the end of his staff and felt it brush the top of my head. I swung at his ankles and sent him to the ground again, but when I stepped forward to signal his defeat, he smashed the blunt end of his staff into my cheek. My head whipped to the side and another surge of power flooded through my limbs. My glowing staff pulsed with the beat of my heart, and every time our weapons connected, a shockwave of blue energy sent Darinrain staggering back. It was all I could do to try and keep the power contained as it thrashed against my skin. For the third and final time, I pinned Darinrain to the ground, chest heaving as my skin *burned*.

"That is the power you need to tap into to beat Saetyl," he panted, keeping a hand between his chest and my staff. I spun the staff up and held out a hand to help him to his feet. Gusts of wind and a light rain turned to steam against my skin. I turned to tell Notien to take a break when someone new landed in the clearing. My pulse beat red in my vision as another surge of power threatened to rip itself from my skin.

Avenlae straightened, an intense glare glowing from his moonlight eyes. He reached back and pulled his swords from their sheaths, the deadly claws of his wings tilted toward me. My staff melted into a sword as I moved away from Darinrain. Avenlae was someone I wanted to fight. *He thinks you're the same pathetic human Saetyl sees you as,* a voice sneered in my head. A few crackles of electricity left my fingers and hit the ground as I bridled with anger. Avenlae started towards me, spinning his swords on either side of him so the blades cut deep rivets into the ground. My power intensified, and energy surged out to crack against the trees on the edge of the clearing.

Avenlae was unforgiving. There was such strength behind each of his attacks that my parries only pushed me further back. In seconds, I had fallen to my knees, ribs heaving, muscles trembling.

"Get up," Avenlae hissed, walking around me, the metal of his blades singing against the grass. I gritted my teeth and pushed myself up, thrusting my sword toward him to attack, only to be thrown back as if my sword were a twig. I spun, jumped, ducked, and parried but was slammed to the ground repeatedly, the air forced out of my lungs. *Nothing* I did slowed the barrage of attacks or calmed the fire in his eyes. The rain really began to fall as I gasped for breath, soaking my hair in seconds.

"Get up!" Avenlae shrieked. "You are not even trying!"

With a cry of rage, I leaped to my feet, my power ricocheting off the tree line from my arms and wings. Rain lashed our bodies as we locked in combat. I met his attacks with crackling parries and streams of electricity from my right palm. Every ounce of anger in my body erupted, but he would not let me rest. He kept fighting, kept spinning his blades around my body, always just close enough to nearly end the fight a third time. The acrid smell of smoke filled the air as the crackles of energy from my wings bored into trees and grass. Then, with a swipe of his wings, Avenlae sent me sliding across the mud. I coughed, choking on the rainwater that dove into my throat the second my head was up to the sky.

"Saetyl is going to *kill* you!" Avenlae roared, his voice louder and deeper than the thunder that rumbled above us. "And you are just going to let her! You cannot even beat me, and you think that is good enough to go against her? You think you are *strong* enough to fight *her?*"

I rolled onto my knees, fire burning in my chest. As Avenlae moved to strike, my control broke. I raised both hands, releasing my fury and letting it stream from my palms in a vivid red pulse of energy. It caught Avenlae in the abdomen and sent him flying backward, wings flailing as they tried to catch him. The ground beneath me trembled with the impact of his body, and immediately, all of my rage evaporated. The energy from the Creonex faded, leaving the clearing smoking despite the rain. I stared at the place where Avenlae's body lay, willing it to move. Hesitantly, I stood, my feet pulling me towards him, my heart thrashing mercilessly against my chest. Finally, when I was a foot from him, Avenlae stirred, coughing and pushing himself off the soaked grass.

"What is *wrong* with you?" I yelled over the sound of the rain and thunder.

"I had to push you!" he shouted back, coughing a few more times before rising to his knees. A drop of blood trickled down his chin, and he winced as he took a deep breath.

"Had to? *Had to?*"

"I had to know you could beat me. Because then I know you can beat her." Avenlae's voice was ragged and strained as he staggered to his feet. His silver eyes pierced mine as he stepped towards me. "Saetyl is not the only one who has something to lose in this fight."

"Xiaye." Notien's voice silenced us. I blinked rainwater out of my eyes and turned to her. "You need to rest. Suns' set is only a few hours away, and you will need all your strength."

"We need to leave before the Guard arrives," Darinrain said. "You know they will want to see this, along with whomever else they decide to bring."

I looked between the three of them, still reeling from the intensity of my power and the fight. Sighing, I acquiesced, allowing them to lead me away from the clearing. Avenlae followed but kept his distance. An hour later found us in the shelter of Notien's nest, a warm cup of *anteel* in my hand. I sat on the floor in front of the entrance, watching the rain cascade through the canopy. Notien came to sit next to me, letting Darinrain carve into his staff in peace and leaving Avenlae to pace in circles around her lit fire pit.

"Why didn't Kaigar stop Saetyl from challenging me?" I asked, finally able to focus on something other than my anger. "He said it was an official Challenge, but I would've thought the threat of the Queen's wrath would make him think twice."

"I think he wants to see this fight as much as the rest of the Guard," Notien said, a hint of harshness in her tone.

"He wants to see her powers," Darinarin said without looking up. "Do not lie, Notien; you know they all do."

"She should not be made to feel like some attraction for them to gawk at."

"Then she probably should not have agreed to the Challenge."

"And *she* is still sitting right here," I grumbled. "I don't understand *why* Saetyl wants to fight me. She's called me a traitor, told me my mother betrayed the tribe, but never told me *how*."

"There are some in the tribe who agree with her because Queen Lieneata left so suddenly," Notien said. "But I think Saetyl is driven by her own pain, not her anger at your mother's abandonment of the tribe."

"You agree with her? You think my mother abandoned these people?"

Notien shook her head slowly. "I do not really know what to think. I only hear the whispers of others, for I was too young to understand and make my own opinion when she left."

"It was very abrupt," Darinrain piped up from his corner. "Few people understood what could be more important than staying to protect your tribe, and even fewer were willing to listen to explanations for their pain and anger."

"What do you know about pain?" Avenlae hissed. Darinrain merely glanced at him, not dignifying his comment with a response.

"I think the Queen may have the answers you are looking for," Notien said. "I know you do not trust her, but she may be able to explain the behavior of our people better than we can."

"Assuming I survive this evening, she'll be the next person I'll talk to," I said, holding the *anteel* closer to feel its warmth. A low growl rumbled deep in Avenlae's throat. The tension radiating from him was palpable. As I finished the last drops of *anteel*, a beam of golden light pierced the canopy, and ice entered my veins.

"It is time," Notien whispered, her navy eyes wide with anticipation. I nodded, a sudden dryness in my mouth. Notien stood, gesturing to Darinrain as she stepped to the edge of the entrance. "We will meet you there," she said, her eyes resting on me for longer than necessary. Then she dove into the humid evening air, Darinrain seconds behind her. I stood and watched them arc around the trees to head back to the clearing, my stomach clenching.

"Is there anything else you'd like to say before I go?" I asked, recognizing Avenlae's scent as he appeared next to me. *Stop me, hold me, anything.* My fingers trembled.

"I told you to control yourself during the Challenges today. This time, *do not* hold back. They should know who they are dealing with. *Dominate*, Xiaye."

I said nothing as I sank back into a feeling of dread. I dove out of the nest, knowing that if I didn't leave then, I wouldn't ever, and I would choose once again to hide. I don't remember the short flight to the clearing—the trees passed in a blur. Upon reaching the clearing, my ears were assaulted by jeers, shouts, whistles, and clicks. The tree line was filled with spectators, most from the Guard, the rest ordinary tribespeople, wanting to see if the newcomer really had any power.

They should ALL know who they're dealing with.

Saetyl waited on one side of the clearing, rolling her shoulders and stretching her wings. She sneered as I landed across from her, and pulled her ax from her back. "I wondered if you would have the confidence to show up, human."

A gust of wind beat down from above us, and Avenlae landed off to my side, stepping back to join Notien and Darinrain. Saetyl tilted her head towards him. "We will see how long you last without your pretty guard in the way."

My ears twitched as I heard Avenlae's hiss. I narrowed my eyes and let the Creonex materialize my blade. "Let's get this over with."

"So be it."

Saetyl began to circle me. She moved in for the attack, and I was quick enough to parry and spin out of the way of her ax. She watched me with her golden cat eyes, sizing me up. Again, Saetyl darted forward; again, I prepared to parry, but I wasn't as quick, and the handle of her ax met my temple. I staggered away from her, fighting the dizziness. Saetyl cackled as she paced around me, the crowd's taunts growing louder in my ears.

"I cannot believe *this* is who the Queen wants to take over the throne! I can already see how easy it will be for me to beat you in this Challenge."

"Then do it! If you're so confident, then just finish it. Quit toying with me!"

Her eyes narrowed as a wide, malevolent grin slid across her face. To my right, hands wrapped tightly around Avenlae's arms, struggling to hold him back. A growl was my only warning before Saetyl rushed towards me, ax raised and muscles taut. I blocked the attack but stumbled from the force. Saetyl hooked a claw under the sleeve of my top and used her wing to fling me across the clearing. Pain seared across my back as I landed, rolling a few times before pushing myself out of the mud. Saetyl's boot struck the back of my head, sending my face back into the ground as the crowd roared. I struck out with my wings, a claw connecting with her jaw and giving me enough time to get to my feet a third time.

Do not hold back.

Power surged into my arms as Saetyl shook her head, ignoring the stream of blood that dripped from a gash along her jaw. I gritted my teeth, trying to push through the darkness that crept into the corners of my vision as my head throbbed.

"What are you waiting for?" I growled. "End it."

Saetyl hissed, darting towards me with her ax raised. I swung my blade up to block her, and the blue energy that crackled down my sword threw her back a step. Taking advantage of the misstep, I darted in for an attack. I swung my left hand around, the whip forming mid-air and wrapping around Saetyl's wrist. Yanking the whip back, I dragged her forward into the ball of crackling electricity in my right palm. She shrieked, covering her face as she stumbled forward, and the whip loosened from around her wrist.

Each link of the whip knitted together, and my blade was once more in my hand. My veins glowed blue and pulsed through my skin. For a second, my eyes locked with Avenlae's, where the crowd barely contained him. His canines were bared, and there was fear in the intense chrome depth of his irises.

Dominate, Xiaye.

I stepped towards Saetyl as she staggered backward, the burn across her face enough to end the fight. *But not enough to end her.* I swung my sword up, holding the hilt with both hands, the energy along the blade glowing brighter. She recovered fast enough to parry my blows, but only just. The crowd had gone silent and began to duck as forks of sapphire electricity shot towards the tree line.

Saetyl dragged herself backward through the mud of the clearing, her pupils so small that I could only see the gold of her irises. I kept bringing my blade down on her ax, determined to keep her down. I needed to show that *I* could do it, that I could fight as well as one of their own, if not better. I needed them to know I did *not* need protection and would continue to be a force to be reckoned with.

I needed *no one.*

With a howl of fury, beams of electricity burst from my body, felling trees on either side of us as I brought my blade sweeping down once more, flinging Saetyl's ax out of her trembling hand. I sank the claws of my wings deep into the softened earth, kneeling on her chest, my blade hovering just over her heart as azure flames from my feathers licked the grass.

"Yield," I demanded, "and I will let you walk away."

"You choose mercy, little human?"

"I *do not* have to."

The onlookers fell silent, holding their breath, waiting for her answer. The fire in Saetyl's golden eyes flickered. "I yield!"

I pushed myself up, resentment still burning as I stared at her. Suddenly, a roar went up from the crowd around me—not of anger but of *acceptance.* The flames sank back into my feathers as Saetyl lurched to her feet.

"Satisfied?" I asked her, my blade shrinking back into my palm.

"Nearly."

"Well, then what was the point of that? If it wasn't enough for you, why did you challenge me?"

"Someone had to see what you were!"

"What—*what* I am? If you wanted to see my powers, there was no need to challenge me. And it doesn't explain your animosity toward me."

"*You* are the reason our Queen abandoned us!" Saetyl's voice rose quickly, but the excited chatter among the crowd prevented anyone but me from hearing her.

"My mother fled to Earth to protect the Creonex. I meant nothing until I was born years later."

Saetyl tilted her head, her signature sneer back on her face. "Ah, is that what you have been told? How does it feel to be lied to, little *heiress?*"

My eyes widened as she sniggered, walking away from me. I couldn't believe what she had said, could not fathom it. To have been lied to, not just when I arrived on Silvacastra but for the entirety of my life—it made no sense. And how did *she* know? *She doesn't know anything. She's just mad. She's lying, trying to get to you...*

Notien had rushed up to me, was speaking to me, but I didn't hear her words as I watched Saetyl's retreating back. What was I supposed to do? How was I supposed to figure out what was true, what was real?

What if Saetyl *wasn't* the one who was lying?

I leaped out of the clearing, felt the air rushing through my wings and my lungs burning as I raced to the Queen's nest. I landed on the Queen's balcony and threw open the French doors, cracking them against the walls of her chambers.

Novissime whirled around, her ears flat, her hand flying to the hilt of her sword. A guard came forward from the corner of the room, gesticulating and speaking to me in the *Laizuteek* dialect, but I threw him against the back wall with a flick of my left hand.

"Why did my mother leave, Novissime?" I snapped.

Apprehension swam in her silver eyes as she stared at me, her jaw clenched. "Leave us," the Queen ordered, and the guard, along with three ladies in waiting, swept from the room.

"I asked you a question. Why did my mother leave?"

"I've already told you it was to protect the Creo—"

"Do not lie to me!" I shrieked, my wings igniting.

"Xiaye, why don't you take a breath, and we can discuss—"

"I just had to *fight* to prove myself to your people over a *lie*! Tell me *why my mother left.*"

The Queen swallowed. "To protect you."

I shook my head. "No, I am half-human. She stayed *away* to protect me. She left because she had the Creonex. I was born on Earth."

"You weren't."

"I was."

"You couldn't have been."

"I am half human!"

"You are not because that human was *not* your father!"

I stared at her, open-mouthed. A deafening silence blanketed us, and the fire of my wings was extinguished. I tried to process how the man I grew up with had not been my father, had not shared my blood. Novissime breathed deeply, her shoulders drooping as if confessing the truth had cost her half her energy.

"All I know is that your mother came to me the night she left, cradling you in her arms. You were so small, so delicate and innocent. She was adamant that she had to protect you, had to leave to protect you—not us—you."

My breathing became uneven. "Th-then who is my father?"

Novissime shook her head, made no reply.

"Novissime, *what* am I?"

She raised her head, her eyes swimming with tears. "I do not know."

CHAPTER 20

I dove down the side of the waterfall, my wings tight against my back. I wanted to feel something, *anything* beyond numb disbelief. The impact on the opal-stone floor of the cave was so hard that I staggered and fell, my hand splashing into the clear water of the river. I couldn't even feel that pain. My eyes caught the rippling reflection of my tear-stained face in the water. Neither of my eyes felt as if they were truly mine. The silver eye of a tribe to which I was supposed to belong and the blue eye of a human I never was. Pain pressed hard against my heart, forcing tears out of my eyes. I let out a cry of frustration, of fear, of grief, of confusion. A burst of energy flew out of my wings, reverberating through the stone. I gritted my teeth, wondering if the pressure would stop the tears. *Hurt me, hurt me enough that I won't feel my heart.*

"Xiaye."

I gasped, raising my head, trying to quiet my ragged breathing. Turning slowly, I saw the silhouette of Avenlae moving away from the waterfall into the colored lights of the cave. There was a crease of concern between his eyebrows, but a flurry of anger writhed in my head.

"Did you know?" I asked, standing. "When Novissime sent you to find me, did she tell you what I was?"

Avenlae shook his head slowly as he stopped, searching my face. I looked away from him, anger morphing into frustration at myself for allowing him to see me in the state I was in.

"She doesn't know what I am. No one does. *I* don't even know." I heard the crack in my voice, and my self-hatred grew. "That's why she had me train with you, away from everyone else, right? Because she didn't know what I could become. She couldn't risk having me so close to the tribe if I became some … some wild *freak*. And you, you're the only one strong enough to kill me out there if I were a threat."

"No." Avenlae's voice was sharp, threatening enough to cut through my pain. "You know I could never do that, even if I needed to."

"And what is that supposed to mean?"

"You do not know?"

"Avenlae, I hardly know anything," I hissed. "But I know you were trained to kill. So don't act like you care too much to kill me if Novissime ordered you to."

His ears flinched back against his hair. "Do not force words into my mouth, Xai."

"Don't call me that! Stop lying to me!"

"I am not—"

"You don't even know what I am, Avenlae! You've only seen half of what I'm capable of. You should still hate me as much as you did when you brought me to this damn planet!"

"Stop, Xiaye!"

"Stop what?" I taunted. "Stop speaking the truth? Stop explaining why you fought so damn hard to get away from the crowd during that fight?

207

Not because of me. No, you've been trained to protect them, right? You had to protect *everyone else* from me!"

"I needed to protect you!" The shout echoed against the walls enough that I thought dust might fall from the trembling crystals. "You are *mine* to protect."

"Because of your orders."

"Because I *chose* you." Avenlae flashed his canines as he moved closer, almost closing the gap between us. A flicker of fear entered his eyes as silence fell. Only one thought rose in my mind: *he... he could choose me?*

"What—what does *that* mean?" I asked, my voice a whisper, my pain forgotten.

At that, Avenlae's confidence seemed to fail him, for he looked around as if an explanation would appear on the walls behind me.

I clenched my jaw. "Of course, you're too afraid to tell me."

"Look, Xai," he said, grabbing my left hand before I could pull away from him.

"Let go, Avenlae."

"No, you *look*, Xiaye!" Avenlae's wings extended forth to encircle me, the soft pressure of his feathers pushing me closer to him. Keeping his nervous silver eyes on mine, he raised my hand to his temple. "Look, because I do not know how to tell you."

Each of my fingertips touched his skin, and images bloomed in my mind. *A girl, intriguing, that he found in the forest on Earth. Her long, wavy hair, dark as the night, and her skin ethereal as the moon. The power that burst from her, a power to revere. Her eyes, mismatched, held so much pain. He was training her, and she was excelling quickly, giving him a challenge that ignited a thrill within him. She had a profound understanding of him he had found in no other, and suddenly, there was comfort in her presence. An unexpected solace that stirred a deep yearning. And she could end his pain, his terror every night, and that only drew him irresistibly closer.*

Then she was there, in front of him, in traditional tribal dress, her alabaster skin reflecting the light of the fire, the shadows dancing along her collarbone, her waist, her breasts, and he was drinking to distract his eyes because it was wrong. Those emotions, that need, it was terrifying. But she was alone with him, and she was warm, her tender skin inviting against him. And her head was resting on his chest—he could've held her for eternity. Then she looked up at him, and from then on if those eyes met his, his heart would beat faster, his lips would part in a smile, muscles he rarely used, and he couldn't think straight. There was just her, her smell, her eyes—one blue, one silver. And he didn't care if it was wrong, spared no thought for conventions or consequences; all that mattered was her—everything she embodied and everything she promised to become.

"You have only ever been Xiaye in my eyes." Avenlae's soft voice brought me out of his thoughts, and he was so close, his skin so warm. "I do not care what you are or what you will be. I chose *you*, Xai."

Tears fell as I stared into his silver, moonlight eyes. He released my hand, and I let my fingers caress his cheek and down his jaw. He didn't flinch at my touch, and I wrapped myself in his acceptance. *He chose me.*

Avenlae's hand slid down my arm, and tenderly, he wrapped his arm around my waist. He brushed the tears from my cheek, and I felt his heartbeat as he pressed my body against his.

"What do you choose?" His voice was deep, and his breath whispered across my cheeks.

"You."

And then Avenlae's lips were on mine, and his hand was on the back of my head and in my hair. My mind went blank, and the world became him: his lips, his hands, his body. His kiss was *not* the tentative brush of before. I slid my other hand over his chest and around his neck, craving the heat of the skin

209

beneath my fingers. With a growl he pressed his hand against my back to bring my hips flush with his. I gasped against him, trying to force my sluggish mind to comprehend the feelings and sensations of his embrace. He moved his lips up my cheek, then bent his head to nuzzle my neck, and my eyes cracked open as my skin burned with the caress of his mouth.

"Avenlae," I breathed, seeing the light of the cave for the first time. The colors were the same but so much brighter, as if each plant were a star plucked from the night sky. Small, golden orbs of light flickered and floated sedately throughout the cave, dancing away from my glowing feathers. Avenlae raised his head, his ears twitching forward as he watched an orb float past him to join the others twinkling throughout the space. Nothing in that cave even came close to the vibrancy of his eyes when he gazed at me again.

Avenlae pulled my hands forward, placing one on each of his shoulders so I had to move with him. His wings stretched over his head, the claws of his wing joints grabbing the ruby moss that clung to the cave ceiling. He bent to nuzzle my neck again, fluttering kisses against my skin, sending tingles down my spine and stomach. I couldn't think about anything past the feel of his lips and tongue across my neck and collarbone. In mere seconds, Avenlae had pulled down enough moss to blanket the cool opal shore next to the river. He lowered himself to the ground, caressing calloused hands down my thighs and brushing the feathers of his wings across mine. A shiver ran across my back and into my core—a shiver of anticipation, of *need*.

He guided me down onto his lap, one of his hands cupping my thigh and the other anchored on my hip. And then Avenlae's mouth was over mine, his kiss desperate enough to blur the entire *world* out of focus. I let my hands slide down his back, tracing the battle scars etched into his skin and feeling the ripple of muscles beneath. His tongue darted out against my lips, and I sucked

210

in a breath. Avenlae angled his mouth so that his tongue pushed past my lips, and the sweet taste of him was intoxicating, enough to make my skin quiver. All I wanted was *more*, more of his heat, more of his body.

He broke away, pulling his vest over his head in one swift movement, his abs rippling. Mesmerized, I traced my fingers along the tattoos that covered his torso, curving around each taught muscle. Avenlae let out a soft groan and set his forehead against mine, fingers tightening on my thighs, every muscle in his body coming alive under my touch. His hand crawled up my thighs, over the curve of my hips and I sighed, a sweet shudder rippling through me. Keeping his eyes on mine, he slid his hands under the tight training top I wore. I didn't resist—I was both thrilled and terrified by his audacity. Gradually, he lifted the top over my head and I hugged myself to cover my breasts, the golden glow of my skin and feathers gone. I had never allowed anyone else to see me so intimately, and my anxiety tightened my chest. Avenlae caressed my arms before wrapping his fingers around my wrists, encouraging me to open up to him.

"Shh, Xai," he whispered, "You are safe. I will not hurt you."

Panting, I allowed him to move my arms away from my body. His eyes roamed over me with a carnal hunger before he claimed my mouth with his own, his hands venturing boldly across every inch of my exposed skin. Curling his tattooed arms around my bare back, Avenlae tugged me down onto him as he reclined onto the soft moss beneath us. My mind circled around the hard pressure pressing insistently between my thighs where I straddled him. *More, MORE.* I pulled away from Avenlae's mouth, seeking the tender spot where his neck met shoulders. A purr of approval met the soft kisses I applied along the length of his neck, but then I bit down, sinking my teeth into the sensitive skin just above his collarbone. A guttural groan echoed from Avenlae's throat as he

211

bucked his hips against mine, craving more friction.

I gasped as his hands wrapped around my waist, moving me to the side of him. Muscles rippling, Avenlae held himself over me, the rest of his and my clothes discarded somewhere in the middle of the sweat, moans, and kisses. His moonlight eyes shone as bright as the Silvacastra suns as they took my naked body in—every last alabaster inch.

"What do you choose?" Avenlae asked me again, his voice a purring growl.

"You, Av."

He laid his body over mine, and I couldn't breathe. Was it pain? Fear? Shock?

"I, I've never—"

"Xai," he groaned my name against the hollow of my neck, his wings sweeping down to cradle me, "I *need* you. Let me feel you."

There it was—need. That was what fought against my anxiety, what kept sweat on my skin, what kept him throbbing between my thighs. I cupped Avenlae's jaw as I pulled his lips against mine, the only permission he needed. With an intense control that made his muscles tremble, Avenlae pressed into me, his warmth, his smell, his taste consuming me. Between ragged breaths, I allowed myself to melt into him as Avenlae began to move, each thrust of his hips against mine intensifying the glow of his eyes. His lips danced across my neck and mouth between his moans and my gasps.

And then we both lay together, skin on skin, heartbeat to heartbeat. For the rest of the night, nothing was between us, just his and my bodies, tangled together in sweat, exploration, and experiences. It was new. I relinquished control to him, and he opened himself entirely to me, and it was beautiful.

A ray of suns' light fell lazily across my eyelids. I cracked my eyes open, seeing the hazy gray ceiling above me. At some point during the night, we'd decided stone wasn't as comfortable as a bed, and had moved to Avenlae's nest.

My gaze rolled down to see a heavily tattooed arm lying across my waist, and the exhales of slow, deep breaths tickled the skin along the back of my neck. I shifted to look at Avenlae. In sleep, he was more peaceful than I had ever seen him, his lips parted slightly as he breathed. His eyebrows were creased as if he were beginning to stir. Obsidian hair fanned out across the pillows behind him, and as I rotated my body, the blanket under his arm moved, revealing more of the tattoos crisscrossing his abs. I propped myself up on one arm and traced a finger over the lines of his tattoos, feeling the uneven surface of his muscle and remembering the night's events. *He chose me.* I sighed. Somehow, his acceptance was enough to quell my self-hatred at never knowing the truth of my lineage.

Avenlae stirred and opened his silver eyes, looking straight into mine. Then he smiled a natural, genuine smile. This look from him felt like a privilege to witness, and I couldn't stop myself from returning the smile.

"Good morning, Xai," Avenlae murmured, his voice rough from disuse.

"Hello, Av," I whispered, still resting my fingers on his abdomen. His hand passed rhythmically up and down my spine, and he tilted his chin up, glancing down at my lips and twitching his ears forward. I leaned down and pressed my lips against his, enjoying the sweet taste of his mouth.

Avenlae rolled himself up onto his knees, holding himself over me, his hands sinking into the pillow on either side of my head. The glow of dawn peaked through the swaths of hair that fell over his shoulders. Avenlae lowered his head and nibbled at the sensitive skin of my neck, and I tried to cling to the vestiges of my self-control, remembering that training with the Queen's Guard waited for no one. *Really, I should fight someone to burn off this energy.*

"Av, we need to go," I said, a treacherous waver in my voice. "You know training will start soon."

"I will tell them you were otherwise occupied." He ducked his head to the divot of my neck and breathed in deeply.

"You will do no such thing. And do I really smell that bad?"

"You smell like me," he purred.

"I would assume so. I have spent the entire night with you," I said, pushing him away.

He stood, the blanket falling from his body. I decided if he just stayed as he was, maybe we didn't have to worry so much about the hour.

"That is not exactly what I mean," Avenlae said as he began to pull on a pair of black reflective pants, sliding a few knives into the hidden sheaths down the legs.

"It's not?" I asked, fumbling for my clothes.

Avenlae turned to me, plated training vest in place, as he strapped his scabbards across his back. "You know we can smell bloodlines, correct?"

"Yes."

"We can also smell mate-lines."

I stopped mid-tug on the bottom of my shirt, my mind abruptly sharp and very sure that I did *not* like that phrase. "Uh, that's an interesting way to refer to it."

Avenlae's ears flattened over his hair as he dropped his gaze to the floor. "What happened last night—it will not be a secret."

I stared at him, sorting through my emotions to discover how I felt about everyone knowing about us. I didn't like the idea of there being an "us." Even so, now that I had had a taste of him, of the safety in his arms, I couldn't fathom being able to resist him.

Avenlae stayed away from me, arms folded over his chest. Rising out of the bed, I moved over to him, knowing he needed reassurance. Of course, the first thing I said was the wrong thing. "Are you ashamed of me?"

"I have no reason to be. But you do."

I sighed. "I don't know how I'm supposed to feel. I don't even know how to explain to you what I do feel. But I can tell you that shame is not something I have felt with you last night or this morning."

A small smile tugged at the corners of Avenlae's mouth, poking the tips of his canines into his lower lip. "Neither one of us is fully accepted by the tribe. Why should I care what they think now?"

My encouragement was too successful, for Avenlae unfolded his arms and wrapped them around my waist. "Have patience with me then," he said, his voice hesitant.

"And you, me. But keep the sniffing to a minimum."

He chuckled, then purred, "Your scent is intoxicating."

I got him out of the nest within minutes of that statement.

Avenlae stopped by the market in the middle of the tribe while I rushed into my nest to find a clean training uniform. Although I reassured him I didn't care for the opinions of the tribespeople, I was still unsure about having Avenlae's scent on me, marking me as his. There was this soft little voice hissing *get it off* in the back of my mind.

"Xai." Avenlae's voice echoed from the entrance to my nest, filling me with an unexpected calm. Newly dressed in the gray and white marbled training vest and pants, I turned to face him, smiling at the offered *graetae* in his hand. "This is the last time *graetae* will be available until after the cold season. I thought you would like the chance to enjoy it at least once more."

"You thought correctly."

"If you are ready to face the Guard, we should head there now. We are close to being late, and Kaigar punishes tardiness."

"I thought you weren't worried since I was 'otherwise occupied' this morning?"

His dimples poked into his sharp cheeks as he smiled. "I do not have the patience to be belittled by the old man."

When we landed in the training grounds, there was a tangible change in the air as the warriors turned from their social groups to face us. Their eyes respectfully stayed on the ground, but I could see in the shifting of their wings and the subtle tilts of their heads that they knew a dynamic had changed. Avenlae may have been nearly ostracized from the Delfungaye society, but here, among warriors, he was revered.

And he had just mated their most dangerous weapon.

A pair of round navy eyes found mine from within the crowd of lowered heads. Notien's delicate eyebrows were closely knit together, and she sniffed the air conspicuously.

I approached her, my ears twitching at the clicks and soft whistles of the Delfungaye language as the soldiers began to whisper to each other. What used to remind me of birdsong now sounded jarring. Notien's wings pressed against her shoulder blades as I neared her, and her arms raised, fingers fiddling absentmindedly with the elaborately carved handle of a dagger strapped across her chest.

"Why did you not tell me that you were to be mated?"

I flinched at the word, disgust clenching my stomach. I sighed, unable to find words to quell the deepening hurt in her eyes.

"That is why he does not like me," boomed Darinrain's voice as he walked up behind Notien, seemingly unaware of the taboo. "I cannot say I am surprised—there is only ever one reason a *Y'araye* warrior becomes that protective over someone." He held his hands up as Avenlae's ears flattened. "I

216

mean no harm to her. I am no threat to you."

Kaigar's bark reached us from the front of the group, and Darinrain sped away to find his place in the rows of guards. "You have a lot to explain to me tonight!" Notien hissed as she, too, sped away into the formation. I let out a breath, relieved that she would give me a chance to talk through things with her. She was the only person I trusted to make sense of my emotions when I couldn't understand them.

I moved to the back row of the Guard's formation, crossing my wrists to stand at attention. Kaigar spoke to the formation, pacing back and forth along his well-worn path.

"They are graduating warriors today," Avenlae translated next to me. "Giving them a rank and a permanent spot in the Queen's Guard."

"That was quick."

"These men and women have been training for years longer than you have."

"Are you being given a rank, then?"

I heard him scoff. "I am the best warrior they have. I have not needed a rank since I arrived here fifteen years ago."

My mind reeled at the realization of how long these people had been fighting the war. Although I barely remembered a time before the Earth became infested with Voxmor, I'd never spared a thought for *before* the fall of humanity. Avenlae had come to the *Laizuteek* after his people were slaughtered by the Voxmor, which meant the war had lasted longer than fifteen years. And Earth had been sent back to the Dark Ages in just under one year.

I felt a morsel of appreciation for the position Queen Novissime was in. Although I still harbored resentment for the lie I'd uncovered, I began to understand her methods. I had already watched the fall of mankind. Was I willing to watch the fall of Delfungaye, the final stronghold? I belonged to neither species but that didn't mean I was immune to the pain of their deaths. And Novissime's pain, as their queen, would be immense.

The Queen's Guard split to line the bank of the river, and I was pulled out of my thoughts by the movement around me. The whirring of Kaigar's mechanical parts grew louder as he walked up to me, a metallic sliding following him from where the bottom of his lost wing dug into the dirt. He halted, sniffing the air. Slowly, creakingly, his head turned, and deep-rooted anger was in the eye focused on Avenlae.

"What have you done, boy?" Kaigar growled, taking a step forward with his metal hand raised.

One of my wings extended, impeding Kaigar while also preventing Avenlae from doing anything stupid. *"Do not* touch him," I said calmly, keeping my eyes on the General. Kaigar stepped back, ears pinned against his salt-and-pepper hair.

"Like mother, like daughter," he hissed, the suns' light shining off his gold canines.

"What would you know of that?"

For the briefest second, his eyes met mine, a flash of painful nostalgia. "Enough." And then the General was gone, marching down the riverbank.

I tried to watch the ceremony, tried to applaud Notien and Darinrain receiving their ranks and new weapons. My mind kept returning to that flash of nostalgia, that glint of pain on Kaigar's face at the mention of my mother. He had known her, that was obvious, but how well? His reaction indicated something more than a professional relationship, but how much more? Friends from childhood? My curiosity was interrupted by the arrival of Queen Novissime, followed by a lady-in-waiting and a guard.

The Queen's Guard fell to the ground, their heads down, but I stayed as I was. Novissime moved with the grace of vines swaying in a gentle breeze. With one wave of her hand, the Queen's Guard was dismissed, flocking into the sky around her in a whirlwind. Her ebony hair was twisted up that day, and the silver of her wings twinkled with the beadwork that clicked softly behind her. Her arched eyebrows knitted together as she approached, and I realized Avenlae still stood next to me, his intense gaze piercing into Novissime.

"Stand down, Avenlae. Remember your place."

He did not kneel but leaned towards me, turning his head so that his eyes fell on me instead of the Queen. Her eyebrows rose, and she stopped a few feet before us, sniffing the air.

"Ah," she said as she caught the scent. "I cannot say I'm surprised. I will not hurt her, Avenlae."

I side-stepped around Avenlae and joined Novissime, my jaw locked. I couldn't begin to name all the emotions that arose when I remembered our last conversation, but I knew one: distrust.

"I know today is the Ceremony of Ranks and Weapons for the Queen's Guard, so it is fitting for me to come to you this morning," the Queen began, keeping her shoulders back and head high.

"For what reason?"

Her ears twitched at my tone of voice, and a small sigh escaped her lips. "I am not asking for your forgiveness. I don't think I deserve it. Please understand that your mother made me vow never to tell you before she left the tribe."

I tried to soften the venom in my voice. "My mother is dead. You answer to me now."

The sound of the river filled the silence that expanded between us. Novissime lowered her eyes to the grass at my feet. "Then you will have to forgive this older queen for remaining in the past and forgetting to see what is in the present and what will be in the future. I was trying to protect you by guarding your mother's secret, but I see my mistake now."

"I can understand the difficulty of the decisions you have to make."

The Queen gave me a soft smile. "You have wisdom and patience beyond your years, child. I got too caught up in the hope that I had finally found something that would save my people and end the bloodshed." Her silver eyes sparkled in the light of the suns that fell across her face. "I forgot that *something* had feelings and had experienced an entire life before arriving at this tribe."

"If you want to end the war, Novissime, then you need to stop trying to use me and instead let me help you."

"Would you agree if I asked you to?"

I stared into those almond, chromatic silver eyes for a long time. Novissime spoke the truth—it was written in her stature and expression. And her people, they included Notien, the first friend I ever had, Darinrain, an unexpected but no less welcome addition to my tiny list of friends, and Avenlae. *And Avenlae...*

"Without hesitation," I responded, "Not for you, but for the home Silvacastra has become."

"In that case," the Queen said as she turned, "there is something I need to give you. They should have been yours when you first started training with the Guard, but—well, I don't need to tell you twice that I make mistakes."

My eyes widened as she held two rapiers out to me, sheathed in scabbards of deep ruby. Their blackened hilts had twisted, jagged guards that swirled around the pommel, gold interwoven throughout the twists. I pulled a rapier out of one of the scabbards, and the blade, too, was blackened and matte. *Laizuteek* words and symbols were engraved down the blade, shining red as blood.

"They belonged to your mother. It is only fitting that you have them," Novissime said as I lifted the other rapier out of her hand. I swung the first sword, its blade a whisper as it sliced through the air. The *Laizuteek* words glowed as I felt the energy of the Creonex crackle down the metal.

"You are a warrior now, Xiaye. Wear the blades with pride. I know this would have been the proudest moment of your mother's life," Novissime said, a touch of emotion coloring her voice.

I could see the tears of suppressed grief hidden in the Queen's eyes as she watched me test the rapiers and strap them across my back. Despite how regal she appeared, Novissime remained influenced by her emotions and her love for her people. How could I fault her for the flaw that every conscious being shared?

I didn't interpret the gift of the rapiers as an olive branch, but perhaps the seed of trust.

CHAPTER 21

I followed Notien through the tribe to the market, where she insisted on getting me a meal and "at least" one glass of *a'ta'ya*. That meant that she intended to share *several* drinks with me. I accepted the offer, and resigned myself to taking painfully slow sips of the *a'ta'ya*—I needed to be coherent to understand everything that had happened the day before.

We sat on a branch high enough in the trees that we could look out upon the vastness of the tribe, all the way out to some of the farther borders I hadn't yet explored. The combined Delfungaye tribe was much larger than the central hub made it appear. There were different types of nests expanding out from the inner circle, hidden except to the eye that knew what to look for. Off to our left was a hanging farm tended to by several of the *Fyr'aeset* tribe, their white-blonde hair flashing between the multicolored leaves of the crops.

"Are you going to tell me about what happened last night?" Notien asked, sipping her drink before digging into her meal. "I will forgive you this once for keeping me in the dark. But only this once."

I huffed, then began the story of my discovery of my unknown lineage.

Notien listened intently, her eyebrows angling further down the longer I spoke.

"I told you Queen Novissime was hiding something," Notien said when I'd finished, "but I did not know it was something that big."

"I don't think anyone besides her, myself, you, and Avenlae know. Although I'm not sure how much that matters."

"I am not sure how I would feel if I learned that what I thought was true about myself was a lie. That could cause a severe identity crisis."

"It does. But I'm still, well, *me,* I suppose. A part of me is terrified about *what* I am, but I also don't feel any different than who I've been. When I first arrived here, I learned my mother was queen of a civilization in an entirely different universe, so I guess processing this new development is a bit easier than that. Besides, I can't question her now. I can't question anyone."

"You can try. I question whoever I want about whatever I want."

I smiled. "I know you do. But nobody here has the answers I'm looking for."

"Maybe you do not need those particular answers, then," Notien said, searching my face.

"Oh, I definitely do." I raised an eyebrow. "I can't just accept not knowing what I am."

"But it will not change who you are. That is what you just said, right? Your mother hid so much to blend in with the humans, but she was still a Delfungaye, sworn to do whatever it took to protect the tribe, the Creonex, and you."

"She hid many things well," I sighed. "That is what it all boils down to, I suppose. My mother hid all this from me because she thought she was protecting me. Novissime kept the biggest secret my mother had because she thought she was protecting me."

"Her intentions may have been honorable, but does that mean she was right to keep that information from you?"

"In my eyes, it was wrong, but in her eyes, it was right. The Queen is desperate to do whatever she can to protect her tribe, and I cannot fault her for that. But there's pain in concealment."

Notien lowered her navy eyes. "That I know. I am sorry you have to feel this, Xiaye. But it does not change how *I* see you. You are still my friend, and I am still yours. We might discover what you are one day, or we might not." Notien shrugged. "It will take time for you to get used to the idea, but I think either way you know who you are. I feel that is more important than what you are."

I smiled again as she touched my back, resting her head against my shoulder in a small hug. The more I discussed things with Notien, the more I saw the merit of telling her everything as it happened. Our conversation was helping me process my emotions and thoughts better than I'd ever been able to alone.

A determined look entered Notien's navy eyes as she sat up. "That brings us to another topic: Avenlae."

"I'm not sure what more you want to know. I guess what happened between us is pretty obvious." I winced slightly. "To everyone."

"Well, how did it happen?"

"I would think that would also be pretty obvious to you."

Notien rolled her eyes. "You know what I mean. I was not expecting a mate-bond to form between the two of you after the way you fought yesterday."

"That phrase feels suffocating," I said with a grimace.

"Which one?"

"Mate-bond."

Notien tilted her head to the side, confused. "You do not want to be with Avenlae?"

224

"It's not that. It just feels so final when you refer to us like that."

"What would you call it, then?"

I looked anywhere but at her, uncomfortable with where the conversation had gone. "I don't know. I don't know how it all happened. I guess feelings just grew between us, without either of us even aware of what was happening. And then, with everything that went on yesterday, the flow of intense emotions—"

I stopped, my mind reliving the moment in the cave with Avenlae. I sucked in a breath and turned back towards Notien. "He showed me his feelings, Notien. I mean, I saw his thoughts and felt his emotions. It was so real, so raw—and very weird."

"Do you share any of his feelings?" Notien asked.

"I think so. I suppose I've noticed certain, uh, unexpected reactions I've had to Avenlae's presence."

Her eyebrows rose. "Oh, is that what you call them?"

I sighed and rolled my eyes. "I don't know how to talk about this. I'm just letting things happen as they happen. I'm still discovering myself and my role here, and right now, Avenlae is simply a part of that."

Notien nodded, setting her plate aside and picking up her drink. "Well, if he is to remain so, you should probably get used to his protective nature."

"Do I have to? I've already said I don't need—"

"You do not understand. It is not a personality trait that makes him like that. It is his instincts. Above all else, *Y'araye* warriors are most protective of their mates."

I frowned at her. "Are you saying Avenlae's protective nature isn't something he can control?"

"He probably can, but it would be difficult for him and almost an insult for you to ask him to."

"He'll find a way," I said softly as I watched the man in question soar into the Queen's Nest. I lowered my eyes and turned back to Notien, who wore a knowing smile.

"You may not know what to call it, but I still say it is a mate-bond," she said, tilting her head back to finish her drink. "In all the time I have known Avenlae, I have never seen him look at anyone else the way he looks at you."

"Oh, how romantic," I said dryly.

"Xiaye, you need to give yourself the freedom to truly experience what you have with him," Notien responded, stretching her wings as she leaned back against the branch.

"And what is that supposed to mean?"

"It sounds to me as if you are still trying to deny some of your feelings for him."

"How'd you figure that one out?"

She raised an eyebrow. "You will not like to hear this, but you are easy to read. Just let yourself live a little."

"Why? Because 'we don't know how much time we have left'?" I mocked.

"Precisely," Notien said, but she didn't smile as she looked back over the trees. "We do not. More Voxmor penetrated our borders last night in all four quadrants. I am afraid the longer we sit here, the more likely it is that they will make it past the Night Guard and into the tribe."

"I thought the Guard trained every day for the Voxmor attacks."

"We do, but that does not mean we can handle a large-scale attack. That is what I fear—the Voxmor are intelligent enough to have discovered by now that their scouts never come back from a certain point. I wonder, then, how much longer it will be before they send their fighters in to neutralize the threat."

226

Notien's words silenced me as the tribe moved around us. It was unsettling to be confronted with the knowledge that everything I had gained could be snatched away. It was a terrifying thought to find myself stuck on this planet, which I only vaguely knew, with no way to return to Earth, and left utterly alone once again. Or to die here, never knowing what I was, or what I was meant to do.

"We'll stop them," I said, catching Notien's eye as she turned to me. "The Voxmor. We'll find a way to end this. I'm not sure how, but they must have some weakness we can exploit. Tell me everything you can from the boundaries when you're on rotation in the Night Guard. That'll be the best place to start."

Notien smiled at me. "I planned on doing so. You know, you are beginning to sound as if you want to protect your tribe."

"I never said this was *my* tribe. It simply has a few people in it who I prefer would remain alive."

Notien shook her head, her smile still in place. "Whatever you say. Are you up for another drink?"

I glanced down into the crystal bottom of my cup. "Oh, what the hell. Get me another."

Notien took me to the tree that served as a multilevel bar, and to no one's surprise, the majority of the Queen's Guard were already there. I spent an unusually enjoyable afternoon with them, mostly laughing at Notien's antics as she finished off a few more drinks. Darinrain arrived, and his voice boomed louder and louder as he, too, drank down a few glasses of a more potent alcohol he called *gara'ya*. I drank my glass of *a'ta'ya* as slowly as I could since my legs were already becoming unsteady. Fortunately, the more Notien drank, the less attentive she was to detail, so by the time the suns had begun their descent, I was able to pass off the sweeter, non-alcoholic Delfungaye iced tea as a fourth glass of *a'ta'ya* without her noticing. It was just as well, for around that time, Saetyl arrived with a few other burly individuals of the *Hopyroque* tribe. I watched as she approached the bar to order her drink. The rest of the Queen's Guard roared boisterously as she and her companions entered their midst. Deciding that my presence would soon be unwelcome, I began to make my way to the edge of the branch.

Notien, of course, was not as enthusiastic about my decision. "Just one more!" she slurred, trying to form her face into a pout. "You gotta have jus' one more drink. Do not let Saetyl poop on your party!"

I raised my eyebrows, a giggle escaping from my mouth at her attempted colloquialism. "You know, it's probably also about time you started filling your glass with tea or water. Tell me if anything interesting happens when I see you tomorrow. And Darinrain," I said, turning to him as he sloshed a few drops of his own drink down his arm, "try to keep her—and yourself, for that matter—out of trouble tonight. It's no fun if I'm not there."

"Of course!" he yelled, and I tried to smile at him. He clapped me a few times on the shoulder before I turned and leaped from the branch.

The echoes of celebration seemed abrasive to the tranquil chattering and whistling of the rest of the tribe going about their nightly routines. The forest grew chillier as the suns sank, and I reminded myself to ask Notien about what kinds of warmer clothing the Delfungaye wore. The leaves, too, had changed; they were the color of peridot rather than the emerald I had grown used to seeing. I landed on the branch that led to the entrance of my nest, rubbing my hands up and down my arms, thinking longingly of the fire I was about to start.

Before I got there, Avenlae landed in front of me, his wings blowing cool air against my bare skin. I suppressed a shiver as he turned to me, his eyes shockingly silver in the decreasing light of the forest.

"It seems like you enjoyed your time with Notien."

I held his gaze, trying to figure out if there was impatience in his voice. "I did. Did you enjoy your time with the Queen?"

He folded his wings close to his body. "Not as much."

Avenlae's eyes were questioning as he watched me. I was sure he could probably feel the tension between us, as he followed his statement with an almost timid, "Can I join you?"

I nodded, following him in and lighting the firepit in the middle of the nest with a single blue flame. I sat close to the fire, soaking in its heat as Avenlae sat across from me. There was still an uneasiness in the air, but I couldn't understand it. Was it because of the night we had spent together? Was it because *everyone* knew about it? *It's probably because they can smell him on you,* I thought, biting the inside of my lip.

"What did the Queen want from you?" I asked, trying to ignore my thoughts.

"She was asking about you."

"What, specifically?"

"I do not know. I was not paying attention."

I watched as a few sparks flew from the licks of flame that danced before me. Quiet, except for the crackling of the fire, settled over us. I couldn't decide if I wanted Avenlae with me or if I preferred to be alone.

"Are you alright, Xai?" Avenlae asked softly.

I looked at him, but he averted his gaze. I frowned. "I've already permitted you to make eye contact with me."

"Yes, you have. But I cannot read you right now."

I spread my wings to rest on either side of me in an attempt to appear less intimidating. "I'm sorry. I suppose the idea of you speaking with the Queen made me uneasy. Especially after everything that has happened."

"I cannot blame you. She has not made herself easy for you to trust." Shadows danced across Avenlae's cheeks and jawline. They blackened the lines of the tattoos that sliced across his skin and flickered in the gold of the claws hanging from his ears and septum.

"Look at me," I said, catching his eye as he raised his head. "I don't trust her, but I can trust you. And I'm sorry, I don't really know how to, uh, explain myself clearly to you. I guess I had to make sure that no information passed between the two of you that I needed to know about."

"You know my loyalty lies only with you."

"Yes, Notien told me a bit about that."

"Did she?"

"'Above all else, *Y'araye* warriors are most protective of their mates,'" I quoted, attempting to copy Notien's accent.

Avenlae's ears twitched back as he lowered his head again. "Ah, she told you about that."

"Is it true, then?"

"In a way," he said slowly. "I cannot easily explain it to you. I know you are capable and a strong fighter, but I *cannot* let something happen to you."

I loosened the straps on my scabbards, lifting them over my head to give myself time to digest what he'd said. I was about to ask him to explain what he could when a tiny spark from my finger along the serpentine metal triggered flashes of images from the Creonex.

"One day, you'll understand, my Xiaye." A woman's quiet voice echoed as a porcelain hand took a small blue filigree pendant from the pudgy hand of a baby with heterochromatic eyes.

The raven-haired woman was then in a spotless white room, lying on a green sanitized bed under the blazing light of a surgical lamp. They didn't know how their anesthetic drugs would affect someone of her physiology. It was all they could do to hide her screams as her back bled, magnificent wings separated from stubs of bone, muscle, and sinew.

A flash of four figures—one white, one red, one black, and one sickly grey—stood before a golden horizon.

"One day, you'll understand."

I gasped, shoving myself away from the rapier as it clattered dangerously close to the firepit. Avenlae had moved into a crouch across from me, his ears perked up toward me and his eyes wide. My body trembled, and the lump that rose in my throat was so painful that tears stung my eyes.

"What has happened, Xiaye?" Avenlae asked, moving around the firepit with his arms extended.

I pushed myself farther back, shaking my head, unable to speak and still trying to comprehend the images now burned into my eyes. Avenlae's ears lowered against his hair as he paused halfway to me, his body shifting away as if I repulsed him. I was frozen, stuck between terror from the scenes in my mind and the need to hide my vulnerability. But I had no clue how to communicate any of this to him.

"I will leave. I-I am sorry," Avenlae said, lowering his eyes. By the time he reached the entrance to my nest, I finally found my voice.

"No," was all I could say, but my voice cracked in that single syllable. Avenlae moved swiftly towards me, concern softening the hard lines of his face.

"Talk to me, Xai."

"I, I don't—I don't know," I stammered. "Th-the Creonex keeps showing m-me things."

231

"Images? Your eyes were unfocused like you were watching something."

I nodded. "My mother."

Empathy shone in his moonlight eyes as he inched closer. He watched the death of his entire family every night; no one knew better than him what it felt like to relive the trauma the Creonex forced me to see. *He knows, he knows your pain.*

"They t-took her wings." My voice was a whisper. "Th-they took her w-wings, Avenlae. To h-hide her."

I tilted my head up, clenching my jaw so tightly my teeth ached as I tried to stop my cries. The tenderness of Avenlae's touch across my cheeks was so unexpected that I almost gasped.

"This is not weakness, Xai," he murmured, "Let yourself cry. You are allowed to feel these emotions." The silver of his feathers sparkled in my periphery as his wings extended forward to encircle me. "I will hold you so you are safe."

"*You* are t-talking to *me* about feeling emotions?"

"I know. I should take my own advice." He pulled my head against his chest, the beat of his heart grounding me in the present. "I cannot always help myself, but I can help you."

I cried. I sobbed. Curled up in Avenlae's arms, held by the Mercenary, I felt my grief, and he protected me as I broke. *He is safe. He will always be safe.*

CHAPTER 22

A week passed, uneventfully. While I was grateful for the lull in ground-shattering discoveries and memories of self and power, the calm made me uneasy. Notien echoed this when she told me how peaceful her shifts in the Night Guard had been.

"We have gone from fending off several Voxmor a night to not hearing a single scream. I do not like it, Xiaye," she had told me over breakfast. "The Voxmor are only silent when they are planning something."

The calm had lulled the Delfungaye into a false sense of security. Basking in the full light of the suns, I wondered if they were indeed ignorant of the Voxmor threat or so desperate for peace they chose not to care. Out of sight, out of mind. I voiced this to Avenlae, who, too, had become increasingly restless.

"If the people are ignorant, they will not remain so for long," he said, his words tinged with bitterness, "Notien is right—there is a reason for the Voxmor's absence."

"Can Novissime send out scouts to gather intelligence?"

"Yes, but you have just named the problem."

I frowned at him.

Avenlae sighed. "Queen Novissime. During this time of quiet, we should be sending out scouts for reconnaissance to prepare for an attack or go on the offensive to neutralize Voxmor forces closest to us. But the Queen's fear will not allow her to see it that way. She wishes for an end to the violence more fiercely than any of us, so she will do nothing to disturb whatever peace she thinks has entered the tribe."

"The Queen's fear blinds her."

"Yes, but she knows something."

My eyes narrowed. "What do you mean?"

"You can see it on her face, in the worry in her eyes. She knows something, but she is not telling the warriors."

"You think she knows why the Voxmor are quiet, don't you?"

Avenlae nodded once.

I crouched and spread my wings to catch the breeze. "I guess it's time to get some answers."

"Xiaye, wait!" Avenlae called, taking off after me and beating his wings to swoop in front of me. "You cannot expect the Queen to tell you everything."

"That's exactly what I'm expecting."

"Do not be naive, Xai."

"Naive?" I felt my eyes widen. "Naive is sitting in the Queen's Nest and expecting the war to end itself if you ignore it long enough."

"You do not know her like I do. She will fight you furiously if she thinks she is risking the safety of her people by taking action against the Voxmor."

"Will she fight you?" I asked, remembering Novissime mentioning that she took Avenlae in when he arrived at the tribe as an orphaned boy.

Avenlae looked at me sharply. "You really want to ask that of me?"

"No," I sighed, "I really don't. But if I sit here and do nothing like everybody else, then I will be another sitting duck waiting for the Voxmor to kill me. Hell, that's all I've been since arriving on this planet. Except now I actually have the power to *fight back*. So I *will* speak with the Queen to find out what's going on." I moved around him, calling over my shoulder, "You can come with me or wait to hear how it went."

With a grunt of frustration, Avenlae turned to follow me to the Queen's Nest. *Good, I'll need you,* I thought, ignoring a sudden twinge of guilt.

Fortunately for us, Novissime was between meetings and resting in her chambers. Upon our arrival, she called for *anteel*, smiling as if she had invited us in for a chat. Her demeanor, however, could not obscure the shadows under her eyes or her vacant look as she attempted to exchange pleasantries with Avenlae and me.

"You look troubled," I said abruptly. I didn't want to give her time to firgure out how to avoid my questions.

"Why would I be?" Novissime said, concealing her far-off look with a smile. "Surely you have noticed how peaceful the past week's nights have been."

Avenlae's silver eyes flashed, but he said nothing.

I took a breath, knowing how carefully I needed to choose my next words. "You can't think that's because the Voxmor have decided to leave the Delfungaye alone, can you?"

"What makes you say that, child?"

I narrowed my eyes. "When I received my mother's rapiers, you told me there were no more secrets, Novissime. I expect you to keep your promise to me."

The smile fell from Novissime's face as she glanced at Avenlae, as if he might stop me from interrogating her.

Avenlae raised his head, clenching his jaw before looking into the Queen's eyes. "What do you know, Mother?"

235

The use of the specific moniker changed Novissime. The chromatic silver of her eyes softened as she looked at him, no reprimand for the informality of his speech. When she replied, it was to the son she had taken in when he had no one left. "There is a Voxmor hive on the outskirts of our Fourth Quadrant."

"When did you discover it?" I asked.

"Within the week." Novissime held her cup of *anteel* close to her chest like a lifeline, her eyes remaining on Avenlae. "Kaigar reported it to me when the Night Guard spotted one of its funnels."

"Are you planning on attacking it?"

A sad smile suffused her face as she turned to me. "I do not have the warriors to spare for that. I cannot afford to lose lives in a futile attempt."

"Why would it be futile?"

"Hives are large underground webs of tunnels. Each opening to the surface is guarded by multiple Voxmor. The queen stays in the middle, and if she knows there is a threat at one end of the hive, she can telepathically communicate with the rest of the hive to defend that entrance."

Setting my untouched cup of *anteel* on the small table next to me, I leaned forward, my mind spinning with plans. "Couldn't we keep the Voxmor guards distracted on one end of the hive, then, while a team infiltrates—"

"The queen herself is far from defenseless," Novissime interrupted. "She is usually the most vicious of the hive. So you see, it is not something we can simply *do*." Novissime looked into her cup as she swirled the contents. "As relieved as I am to see your apparent enthusiasm, I'm afraid it is pointless. All we can do is continue to defend our borders and hope the Voxmor queen does not decide to mount a full-scale attack until the weather warms up again. It will give us time to prepare for evacuation."

"You'd rather take the chance that the other queen won't wait to attack and kill everyone in this tribe than fight back?"

"I *have* been fighting back!" Novissime nearly rose out of her chair. Avenlae stiffened next to me. "Do you know how many of my people I have seen die from failed attempts to attack Voxmor hives? Why do you think he has no family?" she cried, gesturing at Avenlae, whose silver eyes had widened. "The slaughter of the *Y'araye* was retaliation, Xiaye. The Voxmor murdered the strongest warriors we had because we dared, once, to attack *them*."

Novissime's chest heaved. Avenlae stared, not out of disrespect, but shock. She pushed herself back against the chair, trying to resume her regal composure. "Surviving one day longer than the Voxmor wanted us to *is* fighting back."

Go for her neck. "You have chosen, Novissime, to sit back and accept the blood on your hands?" I said.

The sounds of the forest seemed to quiet under the Queen's steely glare. "You *cannot* speak to me about blood on my hands!"

"I can, and I will! There is not one member of your Guard who remains untouched by the pain and trauma of this war. But still, they train every day to kill the things that have taken everything from them. Your warriors fight with the vengeance born of the bloodshed they have witnessed. Yet you would deny them the chance to avenge their people because of *your* cowardice?"

"You go too far!" Novissime hissed, arching her wings over her head so that her claws were inches from my temples.

"You don't go far enough," I responded, softening my voice and searching her face. "Did you know they took her wings?"

There was a twitch in Novissime's eyebrow, a flash of confusion in her eyes.

"My mother. Did you know the humans *cut off* her wings so she wouldn't be found on their planet? The doctors cut them off right where they were attached to her spine, and she felt every second of it. My mother left her home, her world, and subjected herself to mutilation because she thought she was protecting her people. But you want to sit here and allow that hive to exist inside your borders? You want to make her pain mean *nothing?*"

The Queen's eyes widened, tears sparkling brighter than the silver of her irises. Her lips parted, but she said nothing.

"I know your fear," I continued. "I've looked it in the face my entire life. But now? Now that I'm here? It's no longer just about surviving, is it? You said it yourself when I first arrived in your tribe that I was your hope. I *am* the weapon your people have needed for decades to have even a chance against the Voxmor. Is that not what I have trained for? Not to protect myself, but to fight for you? *Let* me help you. Allow me to find my place in this war and fulfill the purpose of my mother's sacrifice."

The Queen's pupils danced between my heterochromatic eyes. "You realize that if we do this, the Voxmor will retaliate as they have done before?"

"How could they if their queen is dead?"

"You're quite ambitious, child."

"I have no choice but to be."

No one spoke, and a tension so thick I could barely breathe filled the room. My arguments, although harsh, were what Novissime needed to hear. They were things I would've needed to hear were I still in her place, held captive by the fear of losing *more.*

Gradually, Novissime's wings relaxed against her shoulders, and she tilted her chin up to look down her nose at me. "I give you *one* day to put together a plan. Should you fail to prepare, we will move forward with the matter however *I* see fit."

"Tell Kaigar to send Notien and Darinrain to the clearing where Avenlae and I train," I said as I turned away, gesturing for Avenlae to follow me from the Queen's chambers. "And by suns' rise on the second day, I will bring you the head of the Voxmor hive queen."

I could feel Avenlae's anger radiating off him before we even landed in the clearing. As soon as his feet touched the ground, he began to pace across the grass, his wings dragging behind him as if he'd forgotten to fold them. That sting of guilt settled heavily in my stomach—I had known what I was using him for. *And you did it anyway, traitor.*

"Av, I-I'm sorry—"

"How did you know?" he snapped. "How did you know she raised me?"

"I just remembered—"

"Because that is why you wanted me to go with you, right? Did you look too far when you were in my mind, trying to find something out about me you could use?"

"Avenlae!" I shouted, stopping him before his anger could make him say more. "Novissime told me she took you in the first time I spoke with her. You know I would never trespass further into your mind than you allow me to. Don't you *ever* accuse me of that again."

Avenlae's nostrils flared as he held my gaze. I was wrong, I *knew* I was wrong. But I had to do it—why couldn't he understand? It was the only way I could get the truth from the Queen.

Avenlae's muscles relaxed, and he turned his head away, one of his braids flopping over his shoulder to fall against his chest. "She raised me to be a warrior, had Kaigar continue my training, but he was ruthless. Novissime was the only person who showed me compassion, but when she was appointed Queen, she needed a soldier, not a son. I am as abandoned by her as I am by the rest of the tribe." He raised pained silver eyes to me. "But she is the only mother I have ever known, for I cannot remember the woman who gave birth to me."

"I am sorry, Av," I said, stepping forward and cupping his jaw in my hand. "I didn't know what would come up while we spoke with her. I hoped your presence would convince her to speak truthfully with me, but only in the interest of finding out how much danger the tribe is in."

"Do not use me again, Xai. Do not hurt me like that."

My fingers brushed against the stubble along his cheek as I dropped my hand, biting the inside of my cheek. I didn't think I was capable of hurting him. I had seen his pain, his trauma, and because of it, I never thought I could do anything to hurt him. I wasn't that important—was I?

Avenlae looked behind me at the sound of beating wings, and his ears pressed back against his braids. *Only two people cause that reaction,* I thought as I turned. Darinrain landed before us in the clearing, his black wings folding against the staff strapped across his back. While not as broad as Avenlae, Darinrain was just as tall and all lean muscle as he walked up to us, keeping his deep navy eyes lowered out of respect.

"I have been told you have an intriguing challenge for me, Xiaye," Darinrain called, folding his arms as the suns' light flickered across the broken gold of his scalp between his tattoos. "It must be so if Avenlae is allowing lowly me to be here."

"You might as well look me in the eye, Darinrain," I said, stepping away from Avenlae as a low growl rumbled in his chest. "I can't work with you if you can't look at me."

Darinrain rolled his head up, unfolding his arms and clasping his hands

240

behind his back before his eyes met mine. "Allowed to look you in the eye? This keeps getting better!"

A hiss seared Avenlae's throat. "Calm, Mercenary," Darinrain said with a smirk. "Your challenge is enticing enough without the added aggression."

Avenlae's canines flashed as he spat out a phrase in *Y'araye*. Darinrain's eyebrows rose, and he lowered his head, exposing his neck. I was saved from having to step in as shadows blocked out the suns above us—Notien had arrived. My anxiety spiked when I saw the hulking figure of Saetyl behind her. Saetyl's skin burned copper in the daylight, and the forest green of her coiled hair clashed with the cooling of the peridot leaves around the clearing.

"Ah, I am no longer the one you like least, am I, Avenlae?" Darinrain chuckled as Notien approached.

I gestured toward Saetyl. "What's her purpose here?"

"Kaigar sent her," Notien hissed.

"I am here to see if you really can devise a plan worth following," Saetyl said. "Kaigar knows the Queen challenged *you* because there is no way some Earth-raised thing could lead the Delfungaye warriors against an entire Voxmor hive. I agreed to be involved so that I can see how badly you fail."

"I proved you wrong once before, and I intend to do so again."

Darinrain stepped forward. "Ladies, while I am sure more of your banter would be highly entertaining, I did hear a rumor that your plan, Xiaye, must be completed in one day. The suns will not stop moving across the sky to listen to you bicker."

"Do you have anything substantial to contribute, Darinrain?" Avenlae asked.

"Yes, I do, Avenlae. I am glad you see my potential."

"I would hope so. Those are the tattoos of the *Je'quiet,* are they not?" Notien asked.

"Indeed, but it is my brother who followed my parent's bloodline, not me. I still wear their mark, but my interests were a bit too violent for the Masters of Our Stories."

"You were a failure?" Avenlae scoffed.

Darinrain's smile tightened, and his ears twitched back, but he didn't flatten them. He knew not to challenge Avenlae. "I chose to do something more productive with the knowledge I gained from the *Je'quiet*. Would you know anything of that, Mercenary?"

"The suns will not stop moving across the sky to listen to you bicker," Saetyl rasped mockingly.

"Quite the team, Xiaye," Notien whispered, one dark eyebrow raised.

I bit back my retort and addressed Darinrain. "If you have anything of interest to say, say it now. I need all the help I can get and any intel you have."

Ignoring the grunting laugh Saetyl made, Darinrain turned to me, adopting the stance of a guard reporting. "There is not much known about the Voxmor hives. What little we do comes from the *Je'quiet,* who have heard accounts from the few who have survived attacks on nearby hives. And, Xiaye, for those less informed, the *Je'quiet* pass down the stories of our ancestors through their bloodlines—they are our historians."

"I gathered as much," I said with a sigh, gathering my patience.

Darinrain flashed a smile at me before continuing to speak to everyone else—except Avenlae. "The Voxmor possess telepathic communication, and their queen is the only one who can simultaneously communicate with the entire hive. Other members can only communicate with the Voxmor nearby. Multiple guards are stationed at each funnel entrance, and each member knows how to navigate the winding tunnels to reach the queen. The queen possesses an exceptional level of awareness, enabling her to monitor everything that happens within the hive at all times. That makes it difficult to mount a successful attack against the entire hive. While the Voxmor can operate within the hive mind as the queen directs, they also have the ability to make their own decisions on how to attack their enemies. And only weapons reinforced with *exitialium* can pierce the Voxmor's hide enough to cause lethal injuries, so, as you know, we can only use bladed weapons."

"Do all of the tunnels in the hive connect?" Notien asked. "Do they all lead from the funnel entrances to where the hive queen resides?"

"I have not been told they do, but there is no proof that they do not."

"Useless answer," Avenlae grumbled.

"No, we can still work with that," Notien said, turning to me. "Remember your influence on those two Voxmor all those nights ago? The first time they entered our borders?"

"I do. What's your idea?"

"What if you could expand that power?" Notien waved her hands energetically. "Make it a plume of smoke instead of just a bit of mist. You could fill the tunnels with that smoke—then the entire hive would be under your control. You could walk through their tunnels untouched, could you not?"

"You really believe she is capable of such power?" Saetyl asked Notien.

"You, of all people, Saetyl, should know what she is capable of. You saw it firsthand, did you not?" Notien's eyes narrowed as Saetyl glared, the faint scarring of the burns upon Saetyl's face pulling taut across her copper skin.

"If we are to work with that as part of the plan," Avenlae piped up, "we cannot assume the influence of your power will completely affect every member of the hive, especially the queen."

Darinrain nodded. "There will need to be a backup for infiltrating the hive should there be Voxmor outside your control, Xiaye."

"That is what you two will be in charge of, then," I said, avoiding

Avenlae's intense glare and instead focusing on the flicker of worry in Darinrain's navy eyes. "Both of you know more about Kaigar's tactics than I do, so I trust you can formulate an infiltration plan that will be up to his standards. In the meantime, I need to focus on expanding the influence of the Creonex as far as I can. Stay where I can see you." I narrowed my eyes at Avenlae. "I expect respect from both of you."

Darinrain smiled. "I will play nice for as long as he does."

Avenlae searched my face for several moments. "I trust you know what you are doing, Xai," he said, loud enough only for me to hear.

"I trust your suffering will be worth it," I whispered.

A devilish look entered his silver eyes. "Promise you'll make it worth it."

"Tantalizing," Darinrain said dryly. "Come then, my friend. We have a plan of attack to create in less than a day."

"Call me your friend again, and I swear—"

"Be nice, Avenlae," I said through gritted teeth as the warriors moved past us into a more secluded section of the clearing, Darinrain chattering all the while.

"How do you expect anything productive to come from that pairing?" Saetyl asked, her arms so tightly crossed I didn't think they'd ever unravel.

"Avenlae needs to learn to trust Darinrain and vice versa. They are both warriors—their mode of communication is attack tactics, is it not?"

"We will either be provided a brilliant strategy, or Darinrain will die," Notien said.

Saetyl shook her head. "*We* are going to die."

Later in the afternoon, I stood in the middle of the clearing, a bead of sweat sliding down the length of my spine. It had taken an immense amount of energy and focus to produce the smallest puff of mist. I was still far from creating anything substantial enough to be useful, but my body was still feeling the strain.

"Xiaye, perhaps you should rest," Notien said next to me, holding out a crystal bottle of water she had brought back after everyone had gotten lunch. Saetyl sat on the grass on the other side of me, sharpening the blade of her axe and watching my futile attempts with glee. Avenlae hadn't attempted to kill Darinrain yet, but the ground had become more uneven as they used their wings to draw diagrams during their discussion of the infiltration of the hive. Notien had been bouncing back and forth like a nervous grasshopper to check on the warriors' progress and my own.

"No, I just need to focus harder." I sighed, rolling my head back and forth to loosen the tension in my shoulders.

"Is that not the same excuse you have used the past several attempts?" Saetyl cackled. "You have not disappointed me yet, little human."

Don't kill her, you need her, don't kill her, you need her, I reminded myself over and over as I breathed deeply. I closed my eyes, listening to air moving into and out of my lungs. The breeze caressed my feathers and swirled through my hair. Grass crackled under where I sat, dried from the lack of humidity in the air. Trees swayed gently at the call of the wind, and far off in the distance was the language of the Delfungaye.

The Creonex is yours, said a voice in my head. *Use it.* Crackling energy thrashed in my chest, embodying my determination. I pushed it out into the Creonex and knew from the subtle pause in Saetyl's sharpening of her blade that I had created the mist.

I need more. I exerted all my strength, straining my muscles until my hands trembled. I furrowed my brows in concentration, trying to channel the power from my chest to my arms. There was a sense of unease from the Creonex, but I fought to ignore it.

Give me more! My jaw hurt from the force of my clenched teeth. I delved deep into my heart, searching for any sliver of strength or inspiration.

No.

What?

I faltered, just slightly, at the voice whispering behind my ear. Shaking my head, I forced my trembling muscles to dig deeper into my reserves of energy from the Creonex.

No!

A grunt of exasperation forced its way out of my mouth as my skin cooled from the sheen of sweat across my body. I was paralyzed, unable to break from the hold the Creonex had on my limbs as it connected with my blood.

Then a man's voice shouted, "USE YOUR POWER, CREOVIS!"

A plume of indigo smoke burst from my arms, shooting across the clearing. I had only a second to realize where it was headed and pull my hands back, cutting off the connection to the Creonex. Avenlae jumped into the air, trying but failing to pull Darinrain out of the way of the torpedo of influence from the Creonex. The second it touched his skin, Darinrain crumpled to the grass like a sack of potatoes.

I said the first thing that came to my mind: "Oh, shit."

CHAPTER 23

I reached Darinrain just as Avenlae touched back down on the grass. A puff of dust floated by me as Notien skidded into a crouch, watching as I pressed my fingers against Darinrain's neck.

"Is he alive?" she asked.

"He has a pulse," I responded. "I think he's just … asleep."

"Asleep?" Saetyl's raspy voice made my ears twitch. "Why would he be asleep?"

"Because, uh, because I wanted him to be." My gaze passed over the filigree glove covering my left hand. "That plume of smoke? Were we at the hive, it would've rendered the Voxmor unconscious so we could enter without resistance." I turned to look up at where Saetyl stood next to Notien. "I guess that part of the plan will work, won't it?"

"Can you wake him?" Notien asked.

"Must she?" Avenlae grunted.

I glared at him. "I need him conscious again. You two are supposed to

247

figure out a strategy for infiltrating the hive." I placed my left hand on the side of Darinrain's face, letting a jolt of energy pass through my fingers.

The touch of the metal lattice was enough to make his navy eyes pop open. He pushed himself up and wobbled slightly as his eyes focused on me. "I will never refuse the chance to sleep, but Xiaye, at least *ask* first if you plan to force me to."

I shook my head, too relieved to answer.

"Avenlae and I were really getting somewhere," Darinrain continued as he shifted his weight to stand. "Did you see he even reached out to save me from the sleeping smoke?"

I could almost hear Avenlae rolling his eyes. "I did not save you."

"You know, a second longer, and he would have called me his friend," Darinrain insisted.

Avenlae let out a sigh in a long, drawn-out hiss.

"Now that we know Darinrain is alive, you can put him out again," Saetyl grumbled.

"Should we not ensure we have a plan to report to the Queen first?" Darinrain said. "The suns are getting lower, and we need to rest tonight if we are to infiltrate the Voxmor hive tomorrow."

"All you have is a way to get in," Saetyl growled. "You will be leading the warriors on a suicide mission if you take them into a hive with no plan what to do inside."

"Get to the hive queen," Avenlae hissed.

"Wander the tunnels until you stumble across her? Is that all you and the Historian have come up with?"

"You just witnessed the kind of influence Xiaye can have," Notien snapped. "You think it will be difficult for her to find the queen's location within the mind of one of the Voxmor?"

248

"If they are unconscious, she can walk right up to one," Darinrain shrugged.

Avenlae looked at Saetyl. "All the while, teams will enter the hive and slaughter every Voxmor they find littering the tunnels. Only one team will go after the hive queen. Ours. Everyone else will be focused on killing Voxmor."

"I know I can enter the mind of a willing participant," I said. "I don't know what it will be like to infiltrate an unwilling mind."

"Well, is it not fortunate we have an opportunity to do just that?" Darinrain responded, looking directly at Saetyl.

Saetyl reached back and drew her axe, baring her thick canines at me. "If you dare touch my head, I will kill you where you stand."

"Try," Avenlae growled, arcing his wings over his shoulders and advancing on Saetyl. "See how far you get."

Darinrain grinned. "This is a fight I want to see."

"*No one* will be fighting each other," I called out, exasperated.

"That is right. Listen to your mate, Avenlae," Saetyl said.

"I'm not going to practice entering anyone's mind tonight," I sighed. "Everybody go eat, get some rest. Avenlae and I will meet with the Queen tomorrow to review our plan because it's the only one we've got." I returned Saetyl's glare. "Report whatever you want to Kaigar. But understand this: I will still fight to get out to that hive whether or not the Queen gives me sanction. If you want to work against us, you only work in favor of the Voxmor. Who will be the most hated then?"

Saetyl didn't join us as we took to the air to head back to the tribe. I flew straight to my nest, wanting nothing more than to flop (quite dramatically) into my bed and bask in complete silence. I did just that after changing into the loosely wrapped clothing of the *Laizuteek*, but a rustle at the entrance to my nest made me whirl around.

Avenlae entered, two plates of food balanced on his arms. "You cannot sleep until you have eaten, Xai."

I sighed and slid off the bed, unable to deny the savory aroma wafting from the steaming plate Avenlae held out. "No, but I was about to make a decent attempt to do so."

I took the plate, flicking a little blue flame onto the firepit in the middle of the nest before moving to sit near it. For a moment, I didn't notice Avenlae still standing at the entrance to my nest, looking around as if he were checking for threats in the shadows.

"What are you doing?" I asked.

"May I join you?"

"Of course. We're well past you having to ask permission to enter my nest."

Avenlae nodded as he moved to sit near me but not close. I chewed my food, not really tasting it. "What's wrong?"

"I do not like it, Xai."

"You don't like what?"

"I do not like the players in this game. Saetyl has too easy access to you, and Kaigar will do nothing to stop her if she intends to hurt you. I wish I had more time to train you so I would know that no matter what happens, you will be safe. I do not like that you will be out there with me. You are the only thing I have to lose."

That was a thought I had been fighting to ignore. I couldn't describe to Avenlae what he meant to me. But the idea of seeing something happen to him during the attack on the Voxmor hive? That was horrifying. That brought a tightness into my throat and almost shocked me into silence when I felt the warmth of tears swimming behind my eyes. *You are all I have to lose, too.*

"I'm sorry, I'm not used to having another person to think about," I said, knowing it was not nearly enough explanation.

250

"Neither am I." Avenlae pressed his wings even tighter against his back.

I took a breath, then set my plate down and moved closer to him, meeting his silver gaze. "I don't necessarily know what 'we' are, and so I don't really know what it is that needs to be said before this attack in case something happens to either one of us. I am, however, determined to convince Novissime that there will be an attack, so I'll tell you that you are my safety. At the end of the day, I still choose you."

"What do you choose me as?" Avenlae asked, his moonlight eyes shining. "Your mate?"

I felt my eyes widen slightly, although I tried to hide it. I wasn't sure what frightened me so much about the word: its finality, its commitment, its tie to him. But could I really be that scared of being with him? Beneath the rugged walls of the Mercenary was the only person I had ever allowed myself to be fully vulnerable with. He had shaped me into the warrior I evolved into, faced my fears and trauma alongside me, and did not bat an eye. Still, he chose me.

So, how could I be afraid of my mate? Because the suggested love was terrifying on its own.

"I-I don't know," I responded, my pulse heavy in my throat.

Avenlae leaned forward and kissed my forehead softly. "I think it is *you* who should not be afraid of me. Do not worry—I will not ask you that again."

"I don't want you to leave." The words tumbled out as he backed away from me.

"You do not know me if you think I am not as afraid of whatever is between us as you are." Avenlae's lips brushed against mine, his breath hot against my skin. "But I am willing to chase it as far as you will allow me to."

"Even if I hurt you?"

"Will you do it again?"

"Not intentionally."

"Then, yes." Avenlae kissed me again, his lips still too soft, too gentle. "I will chase you even if you hurt me. There will probably come a time when I will hurt you, and you will have to remind me of my place."

Avenlae's words echoed in my mind as he held my gaze, his expression both tender and resolute. A myriad of conflicting emotions swirled within me.

"And you can't let me forget my own." I pressed a hand against his chest. "Here, where it's safe."

Avenlae pulled me onto his hips, wrapping his arms and wings around me as if he alone could protect me from everything that existed outside of my nest. "You have become my safety as much as I have become yours, Xai. I would never take that from you."

I awoke to the feeling of Avenlae shifting next to me. Somewhere during our activities of the night, we had finally ended up in my bed. Something was wrong, though—there was no light from the suns filtering into my nest. A soft amber glow flickered across the grey wall from my dying fire, but that was all.

Even more abnormal was how Avenlae had sat up, his back straight, ears pushed forward as his silver eyes scanned the entrance to the nest. The feathers of his wings lifted gradually the more he listened, and he sniffed the air, the whisper of a hiss in his throat as he flashed his canines.

"Av, what is it?" I asked.

One of his arms shot out and held me down as he whispered, "Someone is here."

"*In* here?" I asked, fighting to sit up, suddenly wide awake.

"Just outside."

I pushed his arm away and looked to the entrance to my nest. I saw no shadow of a figure, but my sense of smell was nowhere near as sensitive as his. I moved to the end of the bed as Avenlae grabbed one of his scabbards. He crept to the side of the entrance, unsheathing his sword and sniffing at the air again. His ears flattened against the tousled braids in his hair, and he growled, "Saetyl."

"You may enter," I called, and Saetyl walked in as I reignited the fire, still dressed in the ragged fur clothes of the *Hopyroque.*

Saetyl wrinkled her broad nose. "It reeks of your bond in here."

"I am sorry you were not invited," Avenlae hissed.

"What do you want?" I asked, ignoring Avenlae's growls.

"I want to speak with you. Alone."

Avenlae and I shared a long look. Neither of us trusted her. Even so, in the end, it was Saetyl's word I needed if I wanted Queen Novissime to mount an attack against the Voxmor hive. If Saetyl said anything to Kaigar to make him think I could not lead his warriors, then it was me alone against the hive.

"Fine," I said, looking away from Avenlae. He stayed where he was for a moment, then walked around Saetyl. He stopped next to her, turning his head and snarling, "I will be outside. If you touch her, I will slit your throat."

Saetyl swallowed. With that, he left me with the one person in the tribe who had nearly beaten me to a pulp.

"Now," I said, sitting in front of the fire. "What do you really want?"

"Vengeance," Saetyl rasped. I leaned toward my rapiers. "Not against you. Against the Voxmor."

She moved across the nest to sit with me by the fire, removing her axe to rest against the nest's entrance. "I had to watch the Celebration of Passing for nearly every member of my tribe," she continued. At my look of mild confusion, she explained, "That is what our funerals are called."

I nodded. "I'm sorry you had to go through that."

Saetyl snorted. "'You are sorry'. I am sure you are. You do not know half of the horrors I have seen. You know nothing of the torture the Voxmor inflicted upon my people. I can still hear the wretched sound of their suffering as though it happened yesterday. I do not stand with the Voxmor. I hate that it is *you* I must follow into battle, but nothing will stop me from having the head of every last Voxmor that brought this pain upon me. You need an unwilling mind to access to ensure your little plan will work?"

"In theory, yes," I said.

Saetyl rolled her shoulders back, massive canines extending over her full lower lip. "You have one."

CHAPTER 24

"Are you sure you want to do this?" I asked, positioning myself across from Saetyl. "I'm not sure if I can control what I see."

"Practice that later, then. For now, you just have to get into my mind," Saetyl said.

"You realize there is also a chance I may enter your mind easily, and you may not be able to stop me from seeing certain things?"

Saetyl was quiet momentarily; her eyes focused on the ground before her. "It is a risk I will take. There is no one else for you to practice on."

"Okay." I raised my hand, keeping my fingers just an inch away from her temple. "Are you ready?"

Saetyl clenched her jaw, then nodded. I pressed my left hand to her scalp and immediately felt fire behind my eyes. My ears filled with screeching, and Saetyl's will to keep me out repulsed me like thousands of tiny, disgusting hands. I couldn't breathe, couldn't see, couldn't hear, and my existence was agony. But I was frozen, held captive by pain. I couldn't move my hand from Saetyl's temple no matter how hard I tried. The only way to stop the torment was forward. I reached deep into the Creonex, drawing forth its power. There was a cry, but I couldn't tell if it was from me or her.

Then, there was blinding white nothingness. The screeching stopped, the pain stopped, and a feeling of peace settled over me. I stared into the ashen abyss, wondering if I had made it into Saetyl's mind or sent both of us into this nonbeing.

Eerie whispers of a memory crept from the fog, and I turned to face a spot in the colorless world that was beginning to shimmer. I tried to move toward it, but I stepped haltingly as if I still didn't have complete control over myself. The sounds of the memory grew louder but remained distorted as images flickered in and out of view.

A cry of misery torched my ears, and I froze. The images came into focus, reaching out to suck me into the time when they'd happened. Lifting the Creonex, I touched the metal lattice to the surface of the images, and the white fog was dispelled around me.

The air was filled with the howls and shrieks of pain, of anguish, of torture. The sound stopped my breath in my throat, and the sight of the world around me being torn apart kept me paralyzed. Bodies lay strewn around me, blood soaking the forest floor. But they were crying. They were still alive. There were gaping wounds along their backs and stomachs, limbs that had been torn off, wings that had been broken in half. These mangled people were left to die slowly, watching as the Voxmor destroyed their homes. My body shook, and bile rose in my throat.

"Saetyl!" A man's voice shouted over the cries. I gasped and turned, saw Saetyl beside me. Her armor was splattered with blood, and her ax hung at her side. Her golden eyes were wide and horrified as she faced the man speaking to her. Blood blotted brown in her hair, the curls lengthened from the weight of the congealed clumps. "You know what you have to do."

"T-to all of them?" she choked out.

"It will allow them to die with honor, Saetyl. We have to. We're the only ones left who can give that to them."

"But… Fentae, there are children." Tears swam in Saetyl's eyes as she began to hyperventilate.

"We can't… we can't let them s-suffer," the man called Fentae stammered, his voice cracking with emotion. "Just do it quickly."

Saetyl and I stared after the man as he turned, dragging himself to the closest body. It was the body of another man, his wings torn from his back. He held an arm over the blood that was pooling from his abdomen, and blood gurgled in his throat as he raised his eyes to Fentae. A zing of Fentae's sword, and the man's head rolled away. I covered my mouth to stifle a scream, realizing what Fentae was telling Saetyl to do. I didn't want to watch; I didn't want to bear witness to the worst of Saetyl's memories.

Slowly, Saetyl approached a woman whose mutilated body shuddered with gasping sobs. "Please," the woman whispered. "Kill me."

Tears traced tracks down Saetyl's cheeks as the ax trembled in her hand. "I'm sorry."

"Do it!" the woman choked on her blood. "End my pain."

The swing of Saetyl's ax felt like a stab in the heart. Every kill broke her more, like knives driven deep into her own flesh. These were people she had grown up with, and memories of each person rose as raw sobs from her throat as she killed them. This was the way of her tribe. This was how each member was meant to die: with honor at their own hand, not the enemy's. But that didn't stop the gut-wrenching wails tearing through Saetyl's body as she collapsed, a body held close in her arms.

It was Saetyl's sister. The last of the tribe to die in her arms, by her trembling hand. A few surviving warriors stood numbly around her, the blood of their people still fresh on their blades.

I ripped my hand away from Saetyl's temple, abruptly pulling the two of us back to the present. We pushed ourselves away from each other, her eyes wide and my cheeks wet. My body shivered as I stared at the woman in front of me.

"Saetyl," I whispered, horrified.

"Now you know," she said, pushing herself up. "Now you see what your mother's abandonment created—a *monster*. An abomination."

I shook my head as I picked myself up off the floor of the nest. "But how?"

"The Voxmor knew what they were doing. I do not know how, but they *knew* that the height of honor in my tribe was to die in battle. Not to be wounded, but to die in a fight or by the hands of your fellow warriors if you cannot continue." Saetyl's breathing became more ragged as her eyes moistened. "They hurt my people, not enough to kill them, but enough to make them suffer and prevent them from fighting back. So, whoever survived had to finish the job. I murdered the people I was supposed to fight for."

I felt as if there was something I should've said, something to validate her pain. Instead, I just stared, still hearing the echoes of her tribe's cries. Saetyl clenched her jaw and headed for the entrance of my nest as if my presence, my knowledge, were suffocating to her.

"Saetyl," I called. She stopped at the threshold, taking a moment to herself before meeting my eyes. "It was mercy."

"Is that what you call it?"

"Yes. That is how I see it."

She held my gaze for a long time, the hatred in her eyes softening. "This stays between us. No one else can know."

I nodded. She lowered her eyes and breathed as if to say something more. After a few moments, however, she shook her head and leaped into the night air. I took a few steps back and collapsed into my bed, my mind reeling. I didn't feel my pain alone, but I hated it. I hated the horror the Voxmor had caused these people. And for what? Because the Delfungaye had protected the Creonex? That couldn't be the only reason the Voxmor had chosen to attack so viciously.

The cloth at the entrance to my nest rustled, and the smell of leather tinged with metal filled my nostrils. "Did she hurt you?"

"No," I said to Avenlae, my voice sounding feeble in the stillness that filled the nest.

"What happened, Xai?" he asked, crouching in front of me and lifting my head with the delicate touch of his hand.

"I-I entered Saetyl's mind. I understand her now. The Voxmor know what they're doing, Avenlae. They attack in a way that will inflict the most trauma upon their victims. It's not about winning to them—it's about domination."

Avenlae shook his head, eyebrows knitting together. "But they fight like animals. There is no intention behind their movements. They just kill everything in sight."

"They're just pawns." I ground my teeth, vengeance filling my mind like flames take to dry grass. "I will force the identity of their leader out of that hive queen tomorrow, and we'll have a new target."

Suns' rise was just a few hours after Saetyl visited my nest. I dressed with gritty eyes but a sharp determination. Avenlae had returned from his nest, where he'd retrieved his black uniform. A warrior's braid twisted his onyx hair down the middle of his skull and between his wings, small rings of gold tucked throughout.

"I don't expect you to say anything more to Novissime beyond an explanation of the strategy you and Darinrain devised to infiltrate the hive," I said, tightening the straps of my scabbards across the front of my grey and white marbled vest. "If you are moved to speak, you may do so, but you are not obligated to."

"How diplomatic," Avenlae responded with a smirk. "You speak to me as if you are already on the throne, Xai."

"I speak to you as my warrior. I don't care if they can smell a bond between us. In this meeting, we have to be whatever the Queen needs us to be to mount this assault. I know how uncomfortable you were with our last discussion with her, so leave most of the talking to me. I won't be leaving that nest without Novissime's sanction."

"You cannot give her any chance to begin to doubt you, then. I, alone, will be a reason for her to doubt you."

"What do you mean?"

"The bond. The *Laizuteek* and *Hopyroque* believe a mate-bond can weaken a warrior. Do not forget, Queen Novissime was a Guard for the *Laizuteek* before becoming Queen of the Delfungaye. Therefore, you cannot look at me for the entire meeting. Do not expect me to make eye contact if you speak to me. They can smell a bond, but if we do not acknowledge the creation of one, the Queen will not think it has been fulfilled."

"'Fulfilled?'"

Avenlae appeared to swallow nervously before saying, "An explanation for another time. If you do not plan on leaving the Queen's Nest without permission to attack, we should go there now. Something tells me this will be a long meeting."

Burying my curiosity, I followed Avenlae across the tribe to the bulk of the Queen's Nest. Its many-layered structure wrapped around several trees like a mother's hand shielding a child. *How accurate,* I thought as we ascended the side of the Nest, nearing a balcony that jutted out of the middle of the structure. Novissime bowed her elegant head as she watched our approach, then turned into the Nest. Upon joining her, Avenlae and I entered a room that was clearly meant for briefings. The top of a rectangular table that dominated the room was a map of the Delfungaye territory within the forest. At one end of the table sat Kaigar, a half-empty cup of *anteel* before him. His silver right eye and damaged left moved past me and narrowed on Avenlae as he moved around to sit across from the General without invitation.

"I trust you have good news for me," the Queen said, inclining her head as I looked into her almond silver eyes. There was no hatred in their depths, but there was no acceptance either.

"Is that what you've been told?" I asked, glancing over at Kaigar.

"That is what we expect," the General snapped.

Novissime's shoulders rose as she took a deep breath before smiling at me and gesturing that I should take a seat next to Avenlae. She moved to sit on Kaigar's right across the table from us. The Queen was dressed in her crisp white uniform, silver diaphanous cape flowing from over her shoulder as she lowered herself into the chair. Her wings were devoid of beadwork and the usual playful clicking they created. Long swaths of ebony braids fell over her shoulders and tinkled from the delicate golden rings within them as they waved with the movement of her head.

"Report," Kaigar barked.

"Avenlae," I said smoothly, keeping my eyes on the General.

Avenlae explained the strategy he and Darinrain had formulated. To execute the infiltration, we needed the strength of the entire Night Guard. Divided into five units, they would enter the Voxmor hive from each of its entrances as soon as I neutralized the Voxmor in the tunnels. As my unit—Avenlae, Notien, Darinrain, and Saetyl—made their way toward the hive queen, it was the goal of the other five units to kill every Voxmor they found in the hive before they awoke from the influence of the Creonex. The rest of the Queen's

Guard would be on standby, encircling the central hub of the tribe to take on any Voxmor that escaped the attack. The combined Delfungaye tribe would need to be prepared for migration should the attack fail, which was why the rest of the Queen's Guard was to stay back.

"You think a migration is likely even with this plan?" Novissime asked sharply, interrupting Avenlae as he took a breath to continue.

"There is a Voxmor hive within the tribe's boundaries, Novissime. A migration is imminent whether we attack or not," I said.

"And you are basing this plan off your ability to control the influence of the Creonex?" Kaigar growled. "This power none of us have witnessed?"

"Saetyl witnessed it yesterday. Didn't she report back to you?"

Novissime turned her attention to the graying warrior. "Why don't you tell me what she had to say, Kaigar?"

"You do not have to hear it from me." Kaigar flicked his head toward the door leading into the Queen's Nest, which opened as if his movement had been some signal. Saetyl entered, her coils of forest-green hair pulled into a braided fauxhawk. She crossed her wrists over her chest, knelt towards the Queen, bowed towards Kaigar, and avoided Avenlae's intense chrome gaze.

"Hello, Saetyl," I said, controlling the frustrated waver in my voice.

Her fiery eyes landed on me. She lowered her arms and, remarkably, tipped her head forward in my direction like a discreet bow. "Xiaye."

"Well, what do you have to say, then?" Novissime's voice was sharp and direct. From how she curled her lip at him, it seemed that throwing Saetyl into the mix had already been a point of contention between the Queen and the General.

Saetyl spoke to the Queen, but her eyes remained on mine. "The plan Xiaye's team created is shaky at best. There is no guarantee of success no matter what angle you approach it from."

My heart sank at the smug look that suffused Kaigar's face as Saetyl spoke. He knew she would never support any attack I attempted to lead. It was just politics.

There was a moment of silence, during which I knew Novissime would dismiss us and send Avenlae and me away. She would threaten retribution should we attempt to disobey her and go after the hive. *Back to being alone, again.*

Then Saetyl spoke. "But I would follow Xiaye. I would follow her into battle to end the slaughter of our tribes. She is the only one strong enough to fight back against the Voxmor we have allowed to take over our planet."

"You go too far, soldier," Kaigar hissed.

"I speak the truth!" Saetyl's voice cracked like a whip. "Is that not what you asked me to do?"

"Enough." The second the order left Novissime's lips, Kaigar, Saetyl, and Avenlae seemed to cringe away from her presence. The men slipped into the backs of their chairs, and Saetyl slipped into the doorway, her eyes on the ground.

Novissime turned to me, her eyes searching. "What is your plan if your powers do not have the effect you're describing, Xiaye?"

"I can't afford to think like that. My powers will not fail me."

"What if they do?"

"They won't." I didn't blink as she stared at me, her flinty gaze threatening to burn straight through me.

Finally, she looked away as she rose from the table. "Fine. Kaigar, find Darinrain. You are to work with him and Avenlae to prepare the Queen's and the Night Guards. Saetyl, I expect you already know where you have to be. The attack must occur at twilight, right before the Voxmor begin to stir in their hive."

Without another word, Kaigar stood from his seat and brushed roughly past Saetyl into the hubbub of the Queen's Nest. Saetyl caught my eye briefly, and nodded once.

263

"Thank you." I mouthed the words to her before she left the room. Avenlae touched his hand to my arm before leaving the room, ensuring that I knew he would remain close by. He didn't miss that Novissime hadn't named me as she dismissed those within the meeting room. Indeed, she moved to stand in front of the doorway before I had the chance to follow Avenlae out of it.

"You understand the amount of trust I am putting in you."

It wasn't a question but a statement.

"You understand the amount of responsibility I'm taking on," I responded. "And those who I have to take with me and protect."

Novissime's silver eyes shimmered as they darted between my blue and silver irises. "Bring them home," she said, the pleading note of a mother's entreaty in her voice. "Dead or alive, bring them home from this."

"I promise you I will."

"And you, too. You must return."

"I won't be a martyr, Novissime."

"I'm not talking about your power or your right to the throne," the Queen said, raising a thin, elegant hand that brushed so lightly across my cheek that tears welled in my eyes. "I need you to return, Xiaye. *You* are more important to me than just the power that you wield."

"But if the suns rise tomorrow and we're not back, you have to leave."

Novissime couldn't hide the fear in her eyes as she nodded. "I will leave. But I will wait until the last second."

"Be strong, Novissime," I said as I walked past her, unable to control my rising anxiety the longer I stayed in that room with her. "Be strong like my mother."

"No, Xiaye," Novissime called over her shoulder. "I will be strong like you."

Within an hour of my meeting with Novissime, the tribe became a flurry of movement. Tribespeople darted in and out of the trees, gathering supplies and accounting for members of their families as they prepared for a possible migration. The discovery of the hive was no longer a secret, and whispers of the Night Guard infiltrating the hive swirled around the gossip circles. The Guard itself was filled with anticipation, as this fight was one they had spent years training for.

Notien met me outside the Queen's Nest as soon as the meeting concluded. Avenlae stayed silently next to me as I detailed the exchange to Notien, who reacted just as excitedly as I expected her to. "I knew when Darinrain was called away to speak with Kaigar that you must have convinced the Queen to go along with our plan of attack. And just in time, too—we'll be able to get your armor before dusk."

"My armor?"

"It is sacred," Avenlae ventured. "Each warrior is taken to *Glae'atii* to receive their armor."

"Come, I will take you there, now," Notien said, already hovering in the air. At Avenlae's nod, I shrugged and followed Notien, welcoming the distraction.

On the edge of the tribe in the Third Quadrant was an ancient tree whose trunk and branches curled with gnarls in the gray wood. It was much thicker than the trees around it but not as tall, like a troll in a crowd of elves. Notien landed on a crooked branch and began walking towards an entrance made out of twisted vines, but Avenlae called me back.

"What is it?" I asked as he neared, his eyes wary.

"I cannot follow you there. I am *Y'araye*, and I already have my armor. I will not be welcome."

I frowned. "You are still Delfungaye, are you not?"

"I am, but *Y'araye* have always been considered outsiders." He touched a callused palm gently against my cheek. "I will be preparing for battle at my nest. You can meet me there if the suns have not started to set when you are finished."

I nodded as he brushed his lips against my forehead before gliding away from the tree. Then I joined Notien on the branch leading to the entrance, where she had been observing Avenlae and me.

"Is it true, Notien?" I asked as we approached the threshold. "Would Avenlae not be welcome here?"

"Each tribe used to have their own armorer who stayed within a *Glae'atii* to dress and arm the warriors. This is the only one left, and it has taken the armorers here a long time to come to terms with servicing the entire Queen's Guard. Avenlae, being the last of the *Y'araye* and already fitted with his armor, would not be treated like a guest if he were to enter." As she finished speaking, I had my first look into the old, sacred tree.

"And you are allowed in?" I asked, taking in the reinforced interior of the tree's trunk. Delfungaye writing glowed gold down the walls, as if they were incantations set in place to keep the tree alive. Clangs of metalwork echoed throughout the space before us, sparks flying out from the shadows. The back of the *Glae'atii* was ablaze with the fire of heated metals, and the acrid smell of smoke laced with rusted iron stung my nose. Workstations were built into alcoves all along the interior of the tree, their shapes organically created by the way the tree grew around the structure.

"I am your escort to bring you to your armorer." Notien smiled. "That is all I can do. I will have to leave once you are united with her."

"Her?"

"Yes. Armorers are traditionally female."

My eyebrows rose as we moved further into the depths of the tree. Indeed, the faces that glanced up from their work as we passed were those of soot-and-oil-covered women with scarred and burned hands. Within a few moments, we came to the workstation of a muscular woman whose onyx hair had been slicked back into two long braids. She towered over Notien and me, and her silver eyes were small and beady. Notien called to the woman in their native tongue. She took her time finishing the decorative details of a chest plate before looking up from her work. They exchanged a few more words, and I watched their interaction with interest.

The woman stopped speaking and turned her beady silver eyes onto mine. I remembered Notien saying that the *Glae'atii* was considered sacred ground and wondered if that meant that the armorers were given a high status in Delfungaye society.

"Your armor has been the most complicated I have had to forge here, Xiaye," the woman said, her voice hoarse from lack of use and her accent strong.

I pushed down the discomfort that rose from her use of my name. "I would apologize for the inconvenience, but I didn't know until recently that I had any armor here."

Notien flashed a look in my direction but continued to back away from us, understanding the armorer's unspoken dismissal. The woman tilted her chin up, appearing to study me. "Apologies are not necessary. It has been the most important point of my life."

"What do you mean?" I asked as she stepped around the side of her workstation, coming near enough to me that I could smell the metal chips coating her hair and skin. She didn't answer, but moved to a large wooden cabinet that leaned against several branches forming the side wall of her workstation. She threw the cabinet doors wide, and I gasped at the sight of the gleaming weapons and armor the shelves inside held.

The woman turned back to me, the slightest smile curling the corners of her lips. "It is the height of honor for one of our armorers to dress and arm the Daughter of War."

CHAPTER 25

A gentle breeze whispered in my ears as I glided towards Avenlae's nest. The black matte blades fitted along the tops of my wings cut silently through the air, and there was no resistance along the smoothed surfaces of my armor. It was all so lightweight I felt as if I weren't wearing anything at all, save for the rapiers crossed over my back.

The armorer had stayed true to the designs of my mother's rapiers. The metal of the armored plates was the same matte black as my blades, intertwined with designs in swirled crimson along the aerodynamic edges. My helmet, which I kept tucked under my arm, was simple and the only part of the set that was shined.

I sank into the dark crop of trees and landed quietly next to Avenlae's nest. He was standing on a branch just outside, his black and gold armor in place and glinting in the soft light of the suns as he sharpened the blade of a sword. His hair had been pulled back into three braids that helped hold his helmet in place—my own had been styled similarly. Avenlae's silver eyes met mine as I reached the branch, and a smile bloomed on his face.

"Look at you, *Le'eseia,*" he called as he walked towards me, reaching over his head to place his sword in its scabbard across his back. He took in every smooth edge of the plated armor covering me, even reaching out to brush a hand over my shoulder and down my arm. He tucked his head down, inhaling deeply at my neck, a gentle purr reverberating from his chest.

"Le'eseia?" I asked.

"It is *Y'araye* for a female warrior—they were few in my tribe. You are my *Le'eseia*. It was time you received your armor," Avenlae said, brushing his lips against my cheek as he straightened.

I nodded, uneasiness flooding my stomach. Standing with Avenlae on the branch, I felt the creeping chill of the setting suns and the apprehension of the looming attack.

"Do you feel it?" I asked Avenlae. "The fear?"

"I feel it more now than I have before. Whether or not I survived never mattered to me in the past."

"It matters to me."

"Xai," he whispered, touching his finger to my chin. "This plan will work. You do not have to worry; I will have your back the whole battle."

"And I, yours," I said with a faint smile. Avenlae touched his forehead to mine, running a hand over the braids down the back of my head. I listened to the tranquil rhythm of his breathing and focused on the warmth of his body close to mine. *He is safe.*

All too soon, however, Avenlae was telling me it was time to meet with the rest of the Night Guard, and we were flying over the trees in the golden glow of the suns as they sank below the canopy of the forest. The anticipation was perceptible around the Guard as we landed. Everyone was quiet but agitated, unable to be still for longer than a few seconds at a time. Notien, Darinrain, and Saetyl were waiting together near the middle of the group, each with their helmets under their arms and their weapons strapped across their backs or hanging at their hips. Notien's navy eyes were round, and she didn't smile when Avenlae and I approached. Before I could say anything to her, Kaigar whistled, and the Guard arranged themselves into their predetermined units, standing at attention. My eyesight had begun to transition into the grayscale of night vision, so I could not distinguish the colors of Kaigar's armor. I could see, though, it was well decorated with emblems of his service to the Queen.

I watched his silver eye pass over the faces of the warriors before him, wondering if he would deliver some kind of morale-boosting speech. Then again, I wasn't surprised when he began barking orders for the Guard to get into position to take off toward the hive. The General was never an effusive man, and as I lowered my helmet over my head, I chuckled at myself for thinking a possible suicide mission would draw inspirational words from him.

I led my unit to the front of the flying formation, with Avenlae and Notien flanking me and Darinrain and Saetyl bringing up the rear. The comms in my helmet clicked on, and huffs of breath, a few quiet whistles and clicks, filled the interior as the other warriors positioned themselves. There was another whistle from Kaigar, and the background noise was extinguished.

"Xiaye, at your signal," he said.

"Notien?" I asked. She was my navigator.

"Ready," Notien answered.

"Let's go."

We stayed low over the trees, our wings barely a whisper in the air as we sped towards the hive. Notien communicated adjustments to our course through the comms, and the warriors on the formation's outer edges noted any movement below us. We didn't come across any scouts before Notien advised that it was time to descend into the canopy. Kaigar's orders crackled in my ears as he directed the

271

different units to separate and surround the area of the hive. Avenlae, Notien, Darinrain, Saetyl, and I continued forward, diving below the canopy and pressing our palms to our chests, activating the camouflage technology of the armor. There were simple reflective cells built into the skin of the armor, allowing the suit to create an image over our bodies that moved in time with us.

After a few moments of weaving through the trees, Notien signaled again, and we landed on the tree branches in front of us, proceeding forward by climbing. It was slow progress, but we couldn't afford to be spotted in flight. A sheen of sweat cooled my skin as I climbed. With a thrill of trepidation, I spotted the funnel of the first entrance to the hive, shooting up from the ground like a termite's nest. I clicked three times in my helmet, and the white noise of my team's movement stilled. Then came soft clicks alerting me that they had moved into position behind me, Avenlae in the lead and Darinrain in the back. Creeping forward, I swung myself onto a branch three feet from the base of the funnel. I clicked my tongue again twice before I leaped down from the branch, using my wings to soften my fall and remaining crouched as the rest of my team leaped behind me.

We stayed silent and still for a few moments, and when there was no movement from the entrance to the hive, I clicked once, and we advanced. My heart raced as the funnel loomed ahead, and energy from the Creonex swirled in my chest. It buzzed through my veins as I began to climb the funnel, the claws of my wings gripping the hardened dirt on either side of me. Avenlae and Notien fanned out to my left, Saetyl and Darinrain to my right, keeping their bodies close to the side of the funnel.

Suddenly, a hiss emerged from the opening at the top of the funnel, and the dirt beneath me trembled. I flattened myself against the funnel wall as the pale reptilian head of a Voxmor protruded from the entrance and swiveled around, a drop of saliva gleaming from its fangs as its tongue flicked out to taste

272

the air. Each of its six coal eyes blinked as it weaved its head back and forth. Soft clicks and whistles were coming through my comms, but I remained focused on the Voxmor guard as it pulled itself out of the funnel. The spikes down its spine glistened in the moonlight as it crawled, and it tilted its head in my direction as it stretched its tentacles out to pull itself closer.

I held my breath, my mind racing. If I did anything to influence this Voxmor, the hive queen would sense an oncoming attack. There would be no point in attempting to continue the infiltration of the hive. But if I did nothing, the Voxmor would find us and the blood of my friends would be on my hands.

Notien made up her mind before I could. Quick as a flash, she pulled a knife from her ankle and threw it at a tree behind the funnel. The thunk of the blade sounded like the crack of a whip, and the Voxmor hissed again as its head whipped toward the sound. It clicked a few times as it began to slither to the other side of the funnel, its serrated tail passing just inches above my head. I slowly released my breath, nodding once to Notien before remembering that she couldn't see me. My hands shook as I continued the rest of the way up the funnel. I had to act quickly, as that guard wouldn't be distracted by a simple sound for long.

The claws of my wings hooked over the edge of the top of the funnel, and I hoisted myself up, only to come face-to-face with the Voxmor guard. There was a moment when we were both frozen, and I *knew* the Voxmor could see me.

Saetyl's ax came flying over my shoulder, and its blade sliced almost all the way through the side of the Voxmor's neck, spraying black blood all over the funnel. It was now or never—as soon as its body hit the bottom of the funnel, the hive queen would be alerted. I plunged my hands into the entrance, reaching deep into the power of the Creonex and willing it to obey. *Please work, please work, please work!* Azure smoke plumed from my palms and raced down the funnel.

No screams burst from the entrance, and the night was once again silent. I gritted my teeth, the word *sleep* echoing in my mind as I pushed the Creonex's influence out of my body and into that funnel. The whistles of the other units of the Night Guard sounded, notifying my team that they had a visual of the blue smoke pouring from the entrances where they were stationed. I panted as I turned my focus inward, drawing the influence of the Creonex back out of the hive so the warriors could enter unaffected.

"I cannot believe that worked," Saetyl whispered beside me. She pressed her palm to her chest, and the camouflage of her armor faded.

"We're one step closer to the goal," I responded as I, too, removed my camouflage. The other members of my team flickered into existence around the edge of the funnel. "Now comes the hard part."

I pressed a small button on the side of my helmet, and lights clicked on around my temple. Avenlae whistled through the comms, and the other units called to each other as they entered the hive. I reached over my head and pulled my rapiers from their sheaths, then jumped into the funnel, the claws of my wings gouging long cracks into the walls as they slowed my descent. I came upon the body of the guard Saetyl had killed, its white scales glowing in the light from my helmet. Seeing no clear place to land, I plopped onto its ribs before jumping to the ground. The tunnel before me was vast and pitch black, but I heard no movement ahead. Behind me came the footfalls of my team as they entered the hive, a beam of starlight reflecting off their blades as they joined me.

"Not that I did not have confidence in you before, Xiaye," came Darinrain's voice, "but I have significantly more faith in this plan now."

I sighed, biting down my response as I scanned the area. Saetyl pulled her ax from the neck of the dead Voxmor, flicking its black blood against the back wall of the tunnel. Notien stepped up beside me, her swords raised into a defensive position.

"The only way is forward," she whispered.

"Are we to kill on sight?" Avenlae asked.

"Yes," I responded.

Avenlae relayed the order into the comms, and quiet responses crackled in my ears as I led my team forward. Slumped Voxmor loomed eerily out of the shadows as we advanced, like bloated bodies floating in a black river. Avenlae, Darinrain, and Saetyl made short work of each Voxmor I passed, and Notien walked with me, serving as a guard in case there was a Voxmor whom the influence of the Creonex had missed. Fear pricked my spine the deeper we infiltrated the hive, and I kept waiting for something to happen, for a Voxmor to leap up, awake, free of my control. None did. For the long stretch deep underground, not a single Voxmor stirred. My uneasiness grew, however—it felt too easy. *Something is wrong, something* should *go wrong.*

"It would appear your control over them is absolute," Saetyl said.

"For now," I responded as we approached a fork in the tunnel. I looked between two tunnels before us, nausea clenching my stomach. There was only one way I would find the hive queen now. A Voxmor lay across the entrance of a tunnel to the left.

The lucky winner, I thought, stepping towards its body. "Avenlae, alert the Guard. I don't know if the Voxmor will stay unconscious after this."

I stepped gingerly around the serrated tail of the Voxmor as I made my way up its body. Its ribcage rose and fell as it slept, the sound of its breathing only audible when I got close to its head. Its six eyes were shut, and its tentacles curled loosely against its front legs. The Voxmor almost looked peaceful in sleep. It no longer appeared deadly, but I know, if awoken, the Voxmor wouldn't hesitate to rip us all apart.

I lowered myself over the Voxmor, positioning myself over the back of its head. Spreading my wings, I pressed the claws softly against the scales above the Voxmor's jaw, holding myself in place. Placing my palms over the Voxmor's temples, I breathed deeply, closing my eyes. I pushed the power of the Creonex into the head of the Voxmor, ready for that screeching agony I felt when I entered Saetyl's mind.

But there was no resistance. I entered the Voxmor's mind as quickly as I had entered Avenlae's mind so many times before.

The Voxmor's psyche was black and empty. Orders and images flitted occasionally, but it appeared the Voxmor had no conscious reaction. There was a kind of buzzing, white noise blanketing a part of the Voxmor's memory, rendering it fuzzy and unclear.

Memory? The Voxmor had *memories*?

There was something else, too. Something hidden in the Voxmor's subconscious, lying dormant and silenced by the influence of the Creonex. Whatever it was, it did not resist me—it *responded* to the Creonex. I wanted so badly to investigate, to understand how the creature had memories. But I had a goal, and I didn't know how much time I had to find the information I needed.

"Xiaye, the Voxmor are stirring." Avenlae's voice entered my ears like an echo. I focused harder on the Voxmor's shielded thoughts. There was so much information there, but it was all muffled. I couldn't spend long trying to decipher each memory, as I could feel faint vibrations against the points of contact I had with the Voxmor's body.

"Whatever you want to do, I suggest you do it quickly." Darinrain's voice sounded clearer as I started to feel resistance from the Voxmor's mind. I knew the plan had felt too easy up to that point. Something had to go wrong, but it couldn't be this part. I *needed* to find the queen for our efforts to succeed.

"Xiaye." Notien's voice was laced with warning. I clenched my jaw, making up my mind within an instant. *Take me to her,* I thought, *Take me to your queen.*

The resistance calmed, and I felt the Voxmor rise under me. I pulled myself out of its mind, calling out, "Grab on!" as I sank the claws of my wings into the Voxmor's jaw. It hissed, but did not try to throw me off.

"Xiaye, what—!" Saetyl gasped as the Voxmor got to its feet.

"Grab *on!*" I ordered as the Voxmor took its first few steps. Avenlae swung himself up to crouch on the Voxmor's neck, and Notien pushed herself off the wall of the tunnel to land lightly on the Voxmor's shoulder. Darinrain pulled himself up the hip of the Voxmor as it moved forward, keeping his right arm free to fend off other Voxmor with his staff. Saetyl hesitated, then positioned herself on the opposite side of Darinrain, her ax at the ready. The Voxmor picked up speed, slithering through the tunnel, unaware of its riders. My pulse thrummed in my vision with the effort it took to keep the Voxmor focused on finding the hive queen.

"The hive is waking up," Avenlae said, echoing the growing calls of the rest of the Night Guard.

"They are still slow," Notien said. "Unit Four reports they are not putting up much of a fight."

"I hope they are right," Saetyl rasped as we entered another tunnel, and several groggy Voxmor shook their heads in the light of our helmets. I gritted my teeth and pushed the influence of the Creonex out *through* the mind of the Voxmor we rode. It worked, and the Voxmor we passed made no attempt to attack us. They didn't have the chance to fight back as Darinrain's staff cracked their skulls, and Saetyl's ax severed their necks.

"If the hive queen did not know where we were before, she knows where we are now," Avenlae growled.

He didn't need to tell me: the resistance from the Voxmor's mind was growing more powerful. The queen knew we were getting closer, and she knew which Voxmor was bringing her enemies into her hive. The other Voxmor wouldn't attack their hive member, but the screams echoing from other tunnels warned that the hive was alert. Calls of the Night Guard became more frantic through the comms in our helmets.

"No casualties yet," Saetyl said as Notien ducked her head to listen to a distressed communication. Saetyl then swung her ax to slice through the neck of a passing Voxmor, splattering us with its black blood. A screech followed the collapse of the Voxmor as another leaped over its dead body, tentacles extended and fangs bared. Darinrain flipped himself over the spines of the Voxmor we rode and sank the blade of his staff into the skull of the one attempting to attack Saetyl.

"I do not know how much longer you will be able to keep the Voxmor away, Xiaye," Darinrain called as he wrenched the blade of his staff out of the Voxmor's head. "I think they are starting to notice we are back here before we pass them."

"We're almost there," I whispered, knowing it to be true from the bubbling fear taking hold of our Voxmor's subconscious. It was alien to feel the emotions of the beast I rode, to know it was capable of feeling anything at all. *How can you feel? How can you kill indiscriminately, yet be capable of feeling emotions?*

We rounded the corner into another tunnel, and I had a mere second's warning before two serrated tails whipped out from the darkness, slicing the head of our Voxmor clean off its shoulders. I was sent into the ceiling of the tunnel, pain blooming across my back as I smacked into the compacted dirt. I caught myself roughly as I plummeted back to the ground, staggering as my head reeled.

Then Avenlae was beside me, his arms steadying my body. Saetyl was yelling about something, Notien hissed through the comms, and Darinrain spun his staff as he moved into a defensive position in front of us. I blinked rapidly, willing my mind to clear so I could take stock of the situation. Slowly, the tunnel came into focus as silence fell. The helmets of my team members darted back and forth as they searched the shadows before us. I reached back and unsheathed my rapiers, rolling my shoulders as the blue crackling energy of the Creonex forked down the blades.

That drew her out of the blackness. A long, drawn-out hiss crept towards us, and the pale scaled nose of a Voxmor became visible in the light of our helmets. Six tentacles, each lined with small jagged spikes, pulled the bulk of the hive queen forward. Her two serrated tails clicked against the sides of the tunnel as she drew herself up to her full height. She began to weave her head back and forth, picking up speed until it almost vibrated.

"Brace yourselves!" Avenlae yelled. The hive queen's jaw dropped, releasing an ear-shattering shriek as a frill extended out from behind the base of her skull. Even with the protection of our helmets, we shrank back, almost paralyzed by the sound. Darinrain swung his staff around, the blade connecting with the hive queen's lower jaw, cutting her shriek short. She smashed her tentacles into him, crushing Darinrain against the tunnel wall. I stared, feeling as if the air had been sucked out of my lungs. There was no time for me to ensure Darinrain was alive, for more tentacles whipped around the tunnel. Saetyl caught one of the tentacles in the blade of her ax and sunk it into the ground, slicing off the end of it.

With a scream of fury, the queen snaked one of her serrated tails around to skewer Saetyl but was blocked by Notien's well-placed parry. The force of the attack sent Notien into the dirt, pinning her down. I sheathed my left rapier and sent a ball of energy from the Creonex into the side of the hive queen's head, knocking her off balance. Avenlae darted forward, slicing one of his blades across the ankle joint of one of her back legs. The hive queen screeched again, turning her attention to him as he brought his other blade across her sternum. A tentacle wrapped around Avenlae's ankle, slamming his head into the ground as she dragged him out from under her.

His cry of pain shot through me like a knife, and I jumped into the air, forks of blue electricity buzzing against the ceiling and walls from my arms and wings. Saetyl's ax flew through the air, sinking into the arm of the tentacles that held Avenlae. The queen's head reared around as she screeched, and I plunged my rapier into one of her six obsidian eyes. Her scream reached a new pitch as she thrashed, and I barely held on to my rapier. The blades of one of her serrated tails cut deep into my right wing, a pain I felt down my spine. I caught a glimpse of Avenlae dragging himself out of the way of the staggering hive queen, the remnants of a tentacle still stuck around his leg. Darinrain remained hunched against the side of the tunnel, and Notien and Saetyl darted back and forth, trying to find a weak part of the hive queen to attack.

As the queen threw back her head, I used the momentum to swing myself on top of her skull, sinking the claws of my wings deep into her scales to hold myself in place. Her shriek reverberated through my body as she reared up on her back legs, trying to smack me into the top of the tunnel. I flattened myself against her scales as Saetyl and Notien sent their blades into the hive queen's leg joints, sending her back to the ground. Her tails arced over her head as she tried to target Saetyl and Notien, who had to launch themselves off the sides of the tunnel like grasshoppers to avoid the queen's tails and tentacles.

"No!" Saetyl, shrieked as one of the queen's tails caught Notien in her lower back, leaving a deep gouge across her armor. Blood leaked out over the shined metal as Notien tried to drag herself to her feet.

Don't freeze, you can't save her if you freeze, I thought as I fought back the nausea of sheer terror. I sent more forks of electricity across the hive queen's scales to draw her attention away from my fallen team. It nearly worked too

280

well, as she shrieked and flailed her tentacles towards me. *You are going die!* The panicked thought ripped through the chaos, giving me one moment where the time stood still. I reached into the power of the Creonex and sent it surging down my arms and into the hive queen's head, my scream joining hers as agony gripped my body. White hot fire blazed across my skin, blinding me, pushing me back like thousands of tiny scalding hands. I could not give up; I could not allow her to win, not with my team injured before me.

A pulse of energy from the Creonex wrapped around my left hand, and suddenly, it all stopped. There was no sound, no movement, no color. There was only blackness, a state of unbeing. But there was also me, standing in the middle of the nothingness. I took a tentative step forward. A small ball of red light appeared before me, flickering like the flame of a candle. It made no noise, gave off no heat—it just hung there. I felt compelled to approach it, to touch it. Its light grew brighter as I neared, but it emitted no sound. I reached out my left hand, the Creonex appearing purple in the red light of the ball. With the touch of my index finger, it exploded into a web that stretched around me, with pulsing beacons flashing at different intersections of the red threads. Then came the sounds, the whispers. Echos of voices slithered out from the pulsing beacons.

I was listening to the queen's entire hive. This was the web of communication between her and all the Voxmor within the tunnel systems.

I took a deep breath, preparing myself for more pain, and thrust my hand into the red ball of light, focusing on the words *Leave. Leave this place and never return.* No pain met my hand, no ache throbbed between my temples. But crackles of white energy spanned out across the threads of communication from the red ball of light to all of the surrounding beacons.

Suddenly, a black cloud poured from the center of the red ball of light. I gasped as something grabbed my hand, and the smoke began to encircle me, swallowing the web. I began to frantically pull at the grip holding me there, trying to wrench myself free of it. A laugh echoed from all directions, and I stopped fighting, paralyzed by the grip of the shadows. Two eyes appeared, red as blood, sunken into a face with skin as gray as death. The cracked lips curled into a smile filled with pointed, yellowed teeth.

"I found you, *Creovis!*" came the singsong voice of the bloody-eyed man.

CHAPTER 26

NOVISSIME

Novissime paced back and forth across her balcony as the first rays of the suns' light shone through the canopy of the trees. The wood on which she tread had the outline of her path pressed into it. After ensuring her tribe was well-protected from Voxmor attacks and her people were ready to evacuate immediately, she had come up to her balcony to wait. Every time a leaf moved or an animal stirred in the trees, she stopped, staring intently, until convinced nothing was there. She had not heard the screams of the Voxmor nor the screams of her Guard the entire night. She wasn't sure if that was a good or bad omen.

Novissime knew she didn't have enough warriors left to defend the tribe if the Night Guard didn't return. She scolded herself repeatedly for allowing the infiltration to happen as the sky lightened above her. How could she have been so naive to believe that Xiaye could neutralize the threat of the hive? The might of Novissime's entire Guard had never been able to do so before. The Queen had kept the tribe alive and safe for so long by doing nothing but defending their location. That had been her problem before—being too quick to action. That was what Kaigar and Lieneata had always told her, anyway. And now, she had probably lost Lieneata's daughter and her General—and the warrior boy she had taken in as a son.

A whisper of cool morning air caressed Novissime's neck. She shuddered. The burden of her last promise to Lieneata weighed heavily on the Queen that morning. Novissime's throat constricted. *Figures you would find a way to love Lieneata's child,* she thought. The Queen felt as if she hadn't ever had the chance to regain Xiaye's trust, and as the light of the suns grew stronger, it appeared that time would never come. Guilt gripped her heart, and she quickened her pace, as if by driving her feet harder into the balcony floor, she could somehow *make* the Night Guard return.

Maybe she should've been more forthcoming with Xiaye. Perhaps if Xiaye had known everything, she wouldn't have rashly gone into the Voxmor hive. *Then again,* Novissime reasoned with herself, *would she have believed everything I told her? What about everything I have yet to tell her?*

Secrets—that was how Lieneata had ruled and raised her child.

"She cannot know," Lieneata had said the night she left the tribe.

"She? You're giving it a gender now, My Queen?" Novissime hissed.

"Yes, and a name." Lieneata's voice had been so stern and determined. She had called the being wrapped in a blanket in her arms a baby, claimed it as her own, and fled to Earth as a result of her actions.

"Xiaye will be the key to everything," Lieneata told Novissime the day before her death. "When I bring her back, I will tell her all she needs to know. I have to ensure she ends this war."

"How is one person supposed to end an interuniversal war?" Novissime asked.

"Because she will believe she can." That was all Lieneata had ever told her. Twenty-four hours later, Lieneata was dead, and Novissime was ushered onto the throne without ever learning what Xiaye was. But she had her guess—it had everything to do with the Prophecy.

The last conversation between her and Lieneata echoed through Novissime's memory as a golden ray of suns' light fell upon her face. She froze, not feeling the warmth of the suns, but an icy touch of fear. She had spent the last of her strength on this infiltration attempt, and now the tribe had no choice but to flee. Panic trickled out to her limbs as she took a shaky breath, preparing to make the migration order.

A flicker of a shadow broke the ray of sunlight. Novissime whipped around to face the suns' rise. Could it be? Could they have survived?

The Queen narrowed her eyes. There were figures in the sky. At first, there were only three. Something hung down from the flier in front of the small group. Then there were five, then ten, twenty, fifty, and suddenly, the entire Night Guard soared over the trees and into the tribe to joyous whoops and calls from her people.

Xiaye landed on the Queen's balcony, slamming the head of a Voxmor onto the floor, its frill lying limp behind the back of the skull. Avenlae landed next, staggering a bit with a prominent limp in his right leg. Xiaye pulled her helmet off, her one silver and one blue eye sparkling with triumph.

"I told you by morning I would bring you the head of the hive queen."

Novissime watched the rise and fall of Xiaye's chest plate, and how her rapiers crossed behind her back: the same way Lieneata had kept them. She stared, speechless, knowing she was looking into the eyes of the Daughter of War, the true Warrior Queen of the Delfungaye.

XIAYE

I checked on Notien and Darinrain briefly, for they had been taken straight to the Healers as soon as we returned to the tribe. I was assured Notien would heal quickly, but Darinrain would have a much longer stay with the Healers. He had finally regained consciousness just before we returned to the tribe, and every time the Healers moved him, his face would pale to the color of sand. I promised both Notien and Darinrain that I would visit often, then left Saetyl with Notien while I went in search of Kaigar for a report on the rest of the Guard. Avenlae attempted to follow me, but his limp gave him away to the Healers. One of them tried to stop him as I reached the exit of the Healer's Nest, and I turned at the sound of him speaking in rapid accented Delfungaye.

"What's going on?" I asked, walking back to him.

"They are trying to keep me here," he growled, swaying his weight onto his left leg.

"You're hurt."

"I can still fly."

"They're trying to help."

"I do not need their help."

"Avenlae," I said sharply as he winced, trying to put weight on his right leg, which only shook and buckled. His ears lay flat against his braids, and he lowered his eyes. "I am fine. You need to stay here and make sure your leg is alright. Nothing is going to hurt me in the tribe."

"I am aware."

I sighed. "I'll return after speaking with Kaigar and the Queen. I hope you won't give the Healers any more trouble."

As I left the Healer's Nest, there was an air of celebration in the tribe, but I didn't join in. I felt relieved that I had survived the night but guilty about the injuries my team—my friends—had sustained. I lead them there, into that hive. And I couldn't get the look of the bloody-eyed man out of my head, the feel of his hand around my wrist, the sound of his cackle echoing all around me…

286

Kaigar was with the Queen when I entered a small conference room situated across the nest from Novissime's chambers. They sat at the end of a long table made from a plank of dark gray wood and polished to within an inch of its life. The room was dimly lit, with only a small round window at the head of the table. A few dewdrop light fixtures hung from the ceiling, casting long shadows from the high-backed chairs against the bare walls. I walked around to sit next to Novissime across from Kaigar, but she rose and wrapped her arms around me. It was almost more than my guilty conscience could stand. *Don't pity me...*

"Avenlae did not follow you?" Kaigar asked.

"No. He has an injury that needs tending."

"Is it serious?" Novissime asked, a tinge of worry evident in her voice.

"No, he'll be fine." I turned to Kaigar, burying my emotions deep. "What's the report on the rest of the Night Guard?"

"Twenty injured, none fatally. Three dead. The Celebrations of Passing will be held tomorrow after everyone has had time with the Healers."

"You should attend," Novissime said, leading me to my seat as she lowered herself into the chair beside me. "You fought with them, and you would bestow honor upon them by attending their Celebrations of Passing."

"I think it would offend their loved ones more if I were there," I responded, fighting to keep eye contact with her.

She furrowed her brows. "Why do you say that?"

"They will want someone to blame, won't they? Wasn't it me who sent the warriors on the mission that killed them? You think their families won't know that?"

Novissime looked at me with a pitying understanding. "You cannot blame yourself, Xiaye. Their deaths were honorable."

"Their loved ones won't see it that way."

"Xiaye, the guilt you feel—"

"You don't know how I feel." Anger, the only emotion I'd never been able to control, sharpened my voice. "I'm not talking about myself; I'm talking about the families of the warriors who died. They won't care whether or not their soldiers' deaths were honorable. But they will want to find an outlet for their anger and grief, and I refuse to be that outlet."

"Xiaye has a point," Kaigar murmured, almost faltering under the look Novissime shot at him. "She was only recently accepted by the Queen's Guard. The people may not accept her into their most intimate traditions."

"That's settled, then," I continued before Novissime could respond. "There are a few more things I wish to discuss. For your peace of mind, Novissime, nearly the entire hive was eliminated last night, and the tunnels are empty."

"What do you mean nearly? You understand those Voxmor are not the only ones in this forest? What makes you think the survivors of that hive will not unite with another and mount a retaliatory attack?"

"Because I told them not to."

"You *told* them?"

"Yes. Through their hive queen. They won't return to a place their hive queen has deemed unsafe, will they?"

A heavy silence stretched between Novissime and me. "There is much we still do not know about the Voxmor. There is no certainty that they will not return."

"Then I have bought you enough time to rebuild your forces and prepare a plan for migration," I said, shifting in my seat. "Now, the bloody-eyed man controls the Voxmor, doesn't he?"

Novissime's eyes widened at my boldness. "To the best of my knowledge, yes. But how did you—?"

"I saw him in the mind of the hive queen. I could think of only one logical explanation for his presence there—he must exert some kind of control over the Voxmor."

"Did he speak to you?" Novissime asked sharply.

I studied her momentarily, my stomach dropping. Something in the inflection of her voice communicated fear. "He did. He told me he found me."

If her face could've paled, the Queen would have blanched at my words. She turned to Kaigar. "Begin preparations for a full migration into the mountains. Send scouts out to find a territory. We move as soon as the warriors with the Healers are able."

"What?" I asked, perplexed by her sudden distress.

"Yes, Your Majesty," Kaigar said, rising from his chair to carry out her order without hesitation.

"Now, hold on just a—"

"I'll speak with my officers to help make preparations run smoothly," Novissime said as she, too, began to stand. "There shouldn't be much to do as I had the tribe ready to flee if the Night Guard did not return this morning."

"Will you just *stop*!" I cried, slamming my palms onto the table as I jumped to my feet. The sound stopped Novissime in her tracks, and she turned constricted, slitted pupils on me. "What are you doing? Why are we migrating right now? The bloody-eyed man didn't do anything to stop me within the mind of the hive queen. He wasn't even in the hive in a physical form. It could've merely been a vivid memory I somehow gained access to that you are so panicked over."

"That man is more dangerous than anything you have encountered," Novissime said, keeping her voice low. "He knows where you are now. We have to keep you safe. *I* have to keep you safe."

"Do you know who he is, then?" I asked as Kaigar brushed past me, heading out of the conference room.

Novissime sighed. "No, I don't know exactly who he is. But I do know your mother told me he had discovered her location, and the next day she was dead. I know she warned me he must never find you. I know she told me it would mean the end of our universes if he ever got to you."

"Could he be another … another thing like me?" I asked, following her as she swept from the room, attempting to dismiss me without saying so.

"No, you are not a *thing*, Xiaye; you are a person, a warrior."

"You don't know that."

She stopped and whirled around, her finger inches from the tip of my nose. "I *do* know that. I don't have to know who your father was to know you are your mother's daughter. I know you have little reason to trust me, and I have done nothing to amend the relationship I broke. But that does not change the fact that I will continue to do everything in my power to protect you and my people. The bloody-eyed man is a danger to both, and the only way to keep you safe from him right now is to flee."

Novissime took a breath, then rested the tips of her cold fingers on my cheek. "For once, Xiaye, let time judge my actions. Trust I am taking them because, in the present, I believe them to be in the best interest of the tribe and your protection." She turned away from me and continued across the walkway, her authoritative voice carrying orders down through the branches of the Queen's Nest.

I stayed where I was, watching her go, trying to understand the sudden change in circumstances. I shuddered, the memory of the bloody-eyed man's vile grip resurfacing. He must have similar powers to what I had gained from the Creonex, but did that mean he was similar to me? Could he instead be some radicalized extremist from another universe capable of telepathy? Could that be all, could he mean nothing?

Or could he mean *everything* in this war?

The atmosphere of the Nest quickly became frenzied, and I was overwhelmed. Desperately craving quiet, I went straight to my nest, realizing as I entered that I still had yet to remove my armor. I began the process of unhooking and loosening the plates around my back, chest, and torso, then moved on to loosening the armor around my arms and legs. My fingers trembled over the dried mix of black and crimson blood splattered against the plates. *Just get them off, be free of it all.*

I had just removed the blades along the tops of my wings and thrown on more traditional harem pants and a nearly sheer wrap when a shadow extended from the entrance to my nest. I turned, my pulse quickening, then let out a huff of relief as Avenlae limped into the nest. A bandaged wrapped around his right leg over the top of a baggier style of pants worn by natives of the *Laizuteek* tribe. His braids had been taken out, so his hair hung in loose waves over a light vest.

"How is your leg?" I asked, adjusting the wrap I wore to fit more snugly.

"I have been through worse," Avenlae said, wincing slightly as he limped closer to me.

"Did you refuse pain medication?"

"Always." He smiled softly at me. I took a few steps back, gently pulling him over to the bed so that he wouldn't have to stand.

"You don't have to be a fierce warrior all the time, you know. I can tell how much that leg is hurting you."

"It will heal quickly enough." Avenlae sighed in evident relief as he leaned back and let his leg rest straight out in front of him. "How is your wing?"

"I forgot about it, honestly," I said, stretching out the wing in question. A long gash sliced down the back of it. The scarred tissue that had already knitted together had no feathers. *A battle scar.*

"You healed yourself again."

"I must have, although I don't remember choosing to do so." A sick feeling settled back in my stomach. "Have you heard anything else while you were with the Healers?"

"I have heard rumors." He gave me a sharp look. "I imagine you are about to explain them to me."

I lowered my eyes, tensing my muscles to stop them from trembling. "Novissime is ordering a migration."

Avenlae's pupils contracted as he stared at me. "But we defeated the hive. Why do we need to leave?"

"There's another threat. There's this man—this man with eyes red as blood. Novissime told me he hunted down and killed my mother and that he will do the same to me."

"I do not understand. We have never heard of this man. The biggest threat to us has always been the Voxmor."

"He controls the Voxmor, whoever he is. I told you they were only pawns: they do as they're told. When I was in the hive queen's mind, I saw the bloody-eyed man. He spoke to me. Told me he'd found me." I shook my head. "Novissime is terrified that it means he knows where the tribe is and will come here next."

"Do you think she knows more about this man than she is letting on?"

"I think she remembers the last time she heard about him. Someone she loved died soon after." I stared at the ray of suns' light that fell across the floor of my nest. "I don't fully understand it either. I don't know who the man is or what he wants from me, but I'm guessing it has something to do with the Creonex. That's what the Voxmor have been after this whole time."

"Then we must leave soon," Avenlae said quietly. I glanced back at him and noticed for the first time that he looked defeated. The glow was gone from his eyes, and there was a tilt of exhaustion to his shoulders. I began to realize what migration would mean to him and the rest of the tribe. Remorse for the amount of pain I caused tightened my chest.

"I'm sorry," I murmured. "I caused this. If I hadn't been so intent on going to that hive—"

"The Voxmor would have attacked us anyway," Avenlae said as he raised his head. His silver eyes softened as a lone tear dripped down my cheek. He lifted his hand, catching the tear on his finger just before it reached my jaw. "You have bought us time to gather supplies and retreat to the mountains without heavy casualties from a Voxmor attack. Do not blame yourself, *Le'esia.*" His fingers brushed against my cheek as his hand moved to cup the back of my head. Gentle pressure pushed against my braids as he ducked to press our foreheads together.

"You wouldn't be hurt right now if I hadn't led you into the hive," I whispered.

"But I would still follow you into battle time and time again if you asked me to." Avenlae kissed me gently, the warmth of his lips calming against the tide of self-condemnation. "This feeling will fade, Xai. It happens every time you go into battle. With time, it will lessen."

"Do you feel it too?"

"Not so much anymore. I have fought too much and have mostly become immune to the emotions of battle—unless you are involved."

A fleeting moment of silence passed between us, the last moment when Silvacastra seemed to be still.

"Do you know how long we have?" Avenlae asked, breaking the silence.

I wanted to reply with a warning, to tell him there was no telling how long it would take for the bloody-eyed man to find the tribe. I wanted to say to him I didn't even know how we would know if the man found us. Another small part of me wanted to ask him to choose to forget about the migration for a brief spell so I could lose myself in his warmth and safety.

I didn't get to tell him anything, for as I opened my mouth to reply, a screech ripped through the tranquility of my nest, and a serrated tail sliced through the wooden walls around us.

293

CHAPTER 27

Avenlae pushed me down as he shielded me from the falling debris with his body. My ears rang with the sound of the Voxmor's shriek. I shook my head, trying to clear it and process what happened. More screams echoed outside, mingled with the cries and whistles of the Delfungaye.

"Xiaye, get up!" Avenlae's voice finally reached me. Adrenaline burned through my veins, and my vision focused. A coat of dust had settled over Avenlae's hair, turning it the color of dry stone. His pupils were contracted, and his ears swiveled as he caught the distressed cries of his tribe just outside the rubble. He yanked me to my feet, using his wings to throw back the debris that had landed on him. I flicked my left wrist, and the Creonex ignited, sending forks of blue energy across my shoulders and around my right hand. Following Avenlae to the branch just outside my nest, my heart plummeted to my stomach.

The trees appeared to slither and writhe with the hordes of Voxmor that climbed them. Fires raced up the bark of the trees from nests that had been flattened or torn down from the branches. The air was thick with smoke, dust, and feathers as terrified Delfungaye darted around, trying to help the fallen and escape the attack.

Voxmor reached out from the trunks and branches to snatch passing Delfungaye out of the air as they flew. Echoing Voxmor screams threatened to burst my eardrums and I had to fight to stay focused. Avenlae leaped from the branch in front of me, diving to a woman below us digging wildly through the rubble of her nest, trying to find her child. I took to the air, shooting a burst of energy at a Voxmor who had raised its tail to attack a family.

"Go, get out of here! Get to the mountains, now!" I heard Novissime's call to my left as I sent a stream of electricity down the tree trunk, and four limp Voxmor plummeted to the forest floor. The Queen swooped into action, guiding panicked Delfungaye into the air and directing them toward the migration point. She twirled her sword around her to fend off two Voxmor that lunged from the branches of burning trees. I swung my left hand around, four blades flying from my palm to land hilt-deep in the temples of the Voxmor, killing them instantly. Novissime whirled around to face me and nodded once, acknowledging my assistance. She tossed a second sword to Avenlae as he flew up beside her and handed off a wounded child to a woman headed into the canopy of the trees.

My sapphire blade extended from my palm, and I dove down to catch up with Avenlae as he went for three Voxmor slithering around the tree trunks. I sliced the tentacles off the first Voxmor as it reached for a Healer escorting a wounded soldier, then shot forks of the Creonex's power down the Voxmor's throat as it opened its mouth to shriek. Avenlae engaged the second Voxmor, but I was too occupied with the third to pay attention to his fight.

The third Voxmor swung its tail up, and a whoosh of air against my skin warned how close its blades had been. It leaped from the branch below me, and I had to spin to avoid its tentacles. As I came out of the spin, my blade broke apart into the chains of the whip. I swung the whip forward, wrapping it tightly around the Voxmor's neck as it clung to the tree trunk, and then dove down, using the momentum of my dive to yank the Voxmor's head straight back. It let loose a scream and then a loud snap, and I had to disengage the whip from my palm as the Voxmor's body fell past me.

I looked up to see Avenlae driving his blade into the skull of the second Voxmor. The wings of his claws hooked around branches above him to support his weight despite his injured leg.

"Av, you need to get out of here!" I shouted.

"We need to get the rest of the tribe to safety!" he called back, climbing to where I hovered.

"I can worry about that. You're injured and at more risk out here than I am. Get yourself to the mountains."

"I am *not* leaving here without you," Avenlae hissed, and the fury in his eyes was frightening. He pushed himself off the branch with a wince and soared over my head to slash his sword across the face of a Voxmor that had sneaked up the tree behind me.

"This is not the time to be stubborn and protective!" I yelled as I sent the Voxmor crashing down the branches with several well-aimed bursts of energy from both my palms.

"This is the *only* time to be protective!" Avenlae flung his sword in a wide arc, the blade sinking nearly up to its hilt into the eye of another Voxmor across from us. I flicked my left wrist and spun the whip over my head as I dove toward the Voxmor. The whip wrapped around the Voxmor's jaw, holding its mouth shut, and I swerved around to the side, pulling its head out of the way as Avenlae wrenched his sword from its eye and drove the blade through the Voxmor's temple. He fell with the Voxmor for a moment as his injured leg gave out from under him. His wings flailed over his head as they struggled to find a branch to grab onto, and a flash of fear shone in his silver eyes. I immediately changed direction and pumped my wings to reach Avenlae before he fell too far.

I was close enough to reach out and grab him when the serrated tail of a Voxmor whipped around and tore across his chest. The force of the attack snapped his head back, and his body fell limply into the shadowed undergrowth.

Someone was screaming. It seemed like Avenlae fell for an eternity, crimson blood blooming across his torso. I felt something damp on my cheeks and arms and realized it was Avenlae's blood that had spurted onto my skin. I retched and gasped for air, and my body shook as I dove into the forest's undergrowth, my heart pounding in my ears. Landing roughly, I staggered, the weight of my crippling terror like lead in my limbs. I caught sight of Avenlae's body lying crumpled in a heap of leaves and sticks. Falling to the ground, I crawled frantically up to him, passing my shaking hands over the deep gash from his ribs up to his collarbone, his flesh jagged from the tear.

"No, no, no, no," I choked out. "Av, no. Y-you can't… C-come on, get up."

I found a place devoid of blood on his left shoulder and shook him gently. "Get up, please. W-we still have to get to the m-mountains."

When there was no response, my voice rose in a panic. "Get up, Avenlae!" I demanded as if I could stir him into action with enough force. "Answer me! Answer me, please!"

Still, Avenlae lay before me, blood pooling slowly on either side of him, his mouth parted slightly, and his eyes half closed. If he was breathing, it was shallow, for there was no steady rise and fall of his chest. I cupped his cheek with my other hand and began to rock back and forth as tears filled my eyes, blurring my vision.

"N-no, you can't l-leave me. I-I can't do this without you," I whispered. Sobs wracked my body as I rocked, pinching Avenlae's cheeks, moving his hair, shaking his shoulders, anything to get him to stir. My chest felt as if it were being crushed, and my lungs heaved under the pain of my anguish.

Suddenly, a hand wrapped tightly around the roots of my hair and ripped me away from Avenlae's body. I screamed and waved my arms above my head, trying to scratch the fist that held my hair, but there was nothing there. My wings flapped as I was dragged backward across the ground, my scalp burning. Another hand wrapped around my throat, pinning me to the dirt, and stars popped in my vision as the face of the bloody-eyed man appeared over me.

"At last, you are *mine!*" He cackled as black smoke swirled around us, swallowing the world and ending conscious thought.

I awoke violently, nearly choking myself with a shriek. Nothing but solid black shadows surrounded me, and the ground I lay on was gritty, like bone-dry earth. My breath came in short, frightened bursts as I reached out on either side of me to feel for walls, but there was only cold air. I folded my wings around me, trembling.

The memories from the battle came roaring back, and I rocked back and forth again, my panting breaths broken with splutters as tears fell down my cheeks. The pain that threatened to cleave my chest in half returned, and I dug my knuckles into my sternum in an attempt to relieve the pressure. I let the grief wash over me in waves, crying desperately until I felt nauseous. I fell onto the dirt floor and curled into a ball, hoping that the pounding of my head might make me pass out again. Anything to stop the pain of loss. I wanted to find every reason I could to deny that Avenlae had died. He couldn't have, not my strong warrior, my protector. *He's not gone, he's not gone, damnit, tell me he's not gone...*

Avenlae's gentle moonlight eyes swam into my thoughts, and the Creonex around my hand glowed softly. The mellow light took me back to the first time Avenlae kissed me, in the cave back on Silvacastra, and pain clenched at my heart and throat once more. As misery spread through my veins, spirals of blue, glowing vines sprouted from my fingertips and moved across the ground beneath me. I wanted to examine them, discover why they grew, but there was no point. Too much effort.

I let the tears fall until my eyes burned dry. I closed them and pretended the pressure of my wings across my arms and legs was Avenlae holding me, but my pain continued. My eyes fell open as the grittiness from the tears became too uncomfortable. The sight that awaited me, however, temporarily drove the worst of my grief from my mind, and I slowly pushed myself up onto my knees.

The blue vines had spread across the small room I was in. They encircled the walls and spiraled across the ceiling, bathing the cube-shaped cell in the silvery light of the full moon. I sniffed a few times as I stood, my eyes following the vines' progress. I reached out a finger and brushed one of the teardrop leaves. A faint pulse of light flowed from the leaf to the outer reaches of the vines. The feeble response of the plant cut a tiny divot into my aching loneliness.

"Remarkable," a voice cold as steel echoed around the walls, "what pain can create."

I ducked down as if struck, my eyes flicking across the small room. Fear buzzed down my arms and tensed my legs as I lifted my wings into a defensive position. Coils of black smoke unfurled from the upper right corner of the room, blocking out the calming light of the vines. A face as gray as death with bloody eyes set deep under a curved bare brow bone appeared. Cracked lips spread into a cold smile. "Incredible, too, that you are capable of experiencing such pain."

The bloody-eyed man swirled gnarled hands tipped with yellowed claws through the air. The smoke billowing from the corner dissolved into long swathes of onyx fabric that hung from the curve of his back and shoulders. The

299

robes still undulated like the current of water as he stepped forward. I crouched lower, passing my hands over my hips, but I had no weapons.

"You reach for weapons created by mortals instead of using the weapon *I* gave you?" He cocked his head to the side, his voice as jarring as the sound of nails screeching across a chalkboard.

"You gave me?" I asked, balling my left hand into a fist. The Creonex clicked together as a metal filigree glove came into contact with itself. *His Creonex... his Creonex lost to time...*

"Yes, my Creonex." The Fifth Creator took another step forward, and I shifted away from him, raising my wings higher. "I had to alter it to respond more obediently to you, but I did not expect it to bond to you."

I shook my head. "My mother gave it—"

"Your mother?" he spat. "Is that what she made you call her?" The Creator began to circle me. "I suppose it explains why you took this mortal form."

"Mortal form?"

The Creator's bloody eyes narrowed. "Are you not aware of what you are?"

I shook my head ever so slightly.

"Intriguing. You have evolved far past what I expected of you."

Sparks of energy crackled over my fingertips. I was getting frustrated with the ambiguity of his speech. "You had better start giving me real answers, Creator."

He cackled, higher and more malevolent than a hyena's laugh. "You are in no position to threaten me, daughter of Sinivir." He drew out the last words, enunciating each consonant as his voice wavered over the vowels. My eyes widened as I stumbled backward, flinching as my wings brushed against the cell's back wall. I breathed deeply, trying to conceal how my resentment made me want to vomit.

The Creator, Sinivir, continued to cackle as he leaned forward, his body appearing to grow larger until all I could see was the way his gray skin was pulled tight against the bones of his skull. "Is that something you can understand?"

I saw his clawed hand in my periphery and acted instinctively, raising the Creonex and letting out a ball of energy. The energy struck Sinivir's palm, but it stayed there, the blue dissolving into the wicked red of his power.

The Creator clicked his tongue. He had returned to his original size and was shaking his head. "No, no, that won't do. Your powers are not strong enough to hurt me here."

In a flash, he sprang across the room and slammed the ball of energy into my head. I was thrown to the ground, the impact forcing the air out of my lungs. My vision went black and my head throbbed. The metallic taste of blood filled my mouth.

"You have convinced yourself that you can be affected by the physical limitations of this vessel you inhabit," Sinivir hissed. "No matter. I will release you, *Creovis*, and I will use you to gain control over the universes of my brothers."

"I don't care what you call me," I said as I spat blood out of my mouth. Electricity forked from my fingers to the ground, causing the vines around us to glow more brilliantly. "I will *never* be yours to control. I will always fight back."

"Oh, Xiaye." His hand whipped out from under his robes, and his claws dug into the skin of my jaw as he forced my head up. "You are so naive to think you are strong enough to resist me. You are only as strong as *I* made you. I know every weakness you have because *I* made it so. Before that thief stole you, you were the most powerful weapon in Creation."

"My mother stole—no, I can't believe—"

"You are what I made you to be, Creovis. You are my weapon, my power. And that is all you will ever be." With one last maniacal laugh, the smoke of the Sinivir's robes absorbed the gray of his face, and he was gone. I hadn't realized he had been holding me in the air until I crashed to the ground, my legs

301

buckling under me. With shuddering gasps, I dragged myself to the opposite corner of the room from where the Creator had appeared, pulling my wings over myself. My body trembled. My breathing quickened until it was painful to inhale, but I couldn't control it. My mind reeled, and suddenly, the glow of the vines was too bright, too hot, and my skin was burning, but it was also frozen with sweat. My thoughts were too loud, too heavy, too painful as they pounded against my temples and ears. My heart felt like it might break my ribs wide open.

Sinivir couldn't have just created me. I couldn't belong to him. I couldn't be nothing more than his power, I couldn't have been stolen, I couldn't be a weapon. Nothing he had said could be true because it repulsed me. I wanted to rip my skin from my body if it was the skin he had created for me. I held my head with my hands, shut my eyes, and *screamed*.

Flashes of light flickered behind my closed eyelids as the flow of emotion caused a surge of energy throughout the little cell. I screamed until my lungs burned for air and my throat ached with strain. The glow of the vines dissipated, and darkness engulfed the room once more. My mind was finally silent, and the trembling began to subside from my limbs.

A tiny voice whispered in the back of my mind. I frowned: Was it my thoughts, or something else? Was I hallucinating? I focused on the small voice, and it became louder but calmer and lower. And then the image of Avenlae's silver eyes burst into my mind, and his voice rang clear in my ears, "You have only ever been Xiaye in my eyes."

A warm glow shone behind my closed eyelids. I opened them, blinking back the tears that gripped my eyelashes. Filling the room around me were small glowing orbs the color of firelight. They flickered as they floated about, bobbing against the vines that still curled around the walls. I reached a finger out and allowed an orb to land lightly upon my skin, surprised at the warmth that spread from the spot it had touched. The orbs bobbed out from behind my feathers, splashing colorful flowers onto the vines. In middle of each flower was the most petite little ball of fire. Within ten minutes, the room was bathed in a welcoming incandescence.

I took a deep breath, feeling a fragile, fleeting calm. *Remarkable, indeed, what pain can create*, I thought, curling myself into a tighter ball in the corner of the room. Just before sleep washed away the trauma of the day, another thought popped into my head.

Remarkable, indeed, what I *can create.*

CHAPTER 28

An ache radiating down my neck and into my shoulders woke me from a fitful sleep. I had no sense of time; it could've been the following day or just a few hours later, but the blooming flowers around me still glowed. Stretching my stiff limbs, I opened my wings, the tips of my feathers touching the walls on either side of me. A rising panic threatened to take hold of my mind. *Get out, get out, be free!* I clenched my jaw as I focused on controlling my breathing and shoving the panic deep into the back of my mind, where it couldn't touch me.

Instead, I let in the pain of loss. There wasn't enough room in the hidden depths of my thoughts to contain everything I wanted to keep there. My shoulders dropped, and energy was drained from my body. I had no motivation to do anything beyond curling back up in the corner I had spent the last several hours in. I didn't know where I was or how much longer I would survive. Hell, everyone I had come to know was probably dead. *You're alone. No friends, no family, nothing.* I had nothing.

The Creonex was dull and quiet around my hand. The metal still shone, but no power was buzzing in my chest. I felt as far away from the Creonex as I had when it first bonded with my hand. I had made the vines and flowers in a moment of pain and panic, but I felt so numb I didn't think I could even produce a spark. Gradually, I began to lose the will to fight. My power was gone, but the Creator wouldn't weaken. *I will always fight,* I thought mockingly. *Yeah, sure you will. With what power? With what strength, you pathetic little human?*

I sat in the middle of the cell, brushing my fingers along the velvet petals of the flowers. I tried to will myself to think of anything to drive away the numbness. With time, I began to contemplate the effect of Avenlae's absence. I didn't want to admit he was dead, so I thought of him as simply elsewhere. I wondered if I would continue to feel numb without him, as if he had taken some giant chunk of me with him. And where was the elsewhere? Could he think of me while he was there? Could his heart break the same way mine was trying to?

I blinked a few times, trying to relieve my dry eyes, and realized how stiff I felt. I removed my fingers from the flowers and heard the soft metallic clicking of the Creonex. Some spots on the flowers had gone dark in the reflection of the lattice. I brought my hand closer to my face, examining the Creonex for damage.

"Come, Creovis," the Creator hissed, sending a chill down my spine. "We have much to do."

I pushed myself to my feet, stumbling away from where Sinivir had appeared behind me. The Creonex began buzzing with energy as I lifted it defensively. *Oh, now you want to work.* "I don't want to go anywhere with you."

The Creator tilted his head to the side. "You do not have a choice."

With the faintest flick of his hand, the scene around us changed. At first, it wavered as if I were observing the cell's walls from underwater. Then they began to fade away, and I found myself standing in the middle of a massive cavern whose walls glowed green with algae that grew within the crevices along the blackened stone. Entrances to multiple tunnels dotted the sides of the cavern all the way up to the ceiling. With a thrill of horror, I realized it wasn't the rock that was moving but was instead thousands of Voxmor crawling along the walls. Hisses and clicks echoed throughout the cavern, with a few soft shrieks here and there.

I raised my left hand, but the crackling energy of the Creonex quieted. *Shit.* My eyes darted around as I attempted to keep my expression neutral, but the dying glow of the Creonex gave away my trepidation.

"This is where I will release you from the mortal ties that bind you, Creovis," Sinivir said as a jolt of red electricity forked down his right arm. Black smoke billowed from under his robes as he rose into the air, and crimson electricity forked across his arms.

"I think you'll find that difficult," I responded, finding a drop of power from the Creonex and forcing blue energy across my skin. Somehow, despite my pain, I was still fearful of death when faced with it. With my attention on Sinivir, I missed the Voxmor slithering up behind me. Its tentacles darted out and wrapped around my arms, wings, and legs. I struggled, trying to pulse the power of the Creonex out from my skin, but to no avail. The connection between me and the Creonex was still weak, and it went dark as the Voxmor screeched and lifted me into the air.

Sinivir's eyes were glowing bright red, and lines like streaks of blood had appeared on both cheeks under his eyes. His power encircled his arms and darted across his chest, originating from two crimson balls of energy that crackled in his palms. His mouth cracked into his emotionless smile, and his voice called me from deep within his chest.

"Come to me, Creovis. Let me access your power so you can fulfill your destiny!"

The Creator's power reached an apex, and the cavern fell quiet and still. The air buzzed with the energy radiating around him as I ceased my struggle against the Voxmor. I knew there was not a damn thing I could do to fight him. *Will it hurt more if I resist, or if I let it happen?* Within a split second of suspended fear, a beam of blood-red energy exploded from Sinivir and slammed into my body, separating my consciousness from my physical form. I was aware but left in a dreamlike state. Something was happening, but was it happening to me, or was I watching it happen to someone else? I was aware of who I was supposed to be, but was it just a memory, an image I had created based on someone else I had seen? Did I have a name, a meaning, a purpose?

Flickers of an image passed before me. There was a bloody-eyed man making commands in a language I did not know. He spoke to an obsidian-haired woman, her wings alight with a fire that burned darker than the blood that flowed through her veins. Forks of rose-colored electricity surged out from her skin and feathers, striking the walls that confined her.

Confined her? Or confined me? I couldn't tell anymore.

The bloody-eyed man made a gesture, and a Voxmor queen emerged from the shadows of a nearby tunnel. The image of the cavern grew clearer as if I were observing memories. The Voxmor queen pulled herself closer to the winged woman, fangs bared and dripping with stringy saliva. I realized I could move, and I stepped closer to the woman. She raised her left hand, a blackened filigree glove enveloping her fingers. I gasped, and the scene froze, forks of electricity appearing as beams from her skin.

She didn't move or acknowledge my presence—maybe she was unaware of my existence. But how could she be when she was ... me?

I reached out a hand and grasped her shoulder. She whirled around, her crimson cat eyes wide with crazed rage. "No!" I screamed, and something yanked at my chest, snapping my head back as my vision went white. My body was screaming in torment. Someone was shrieking, my lungs were burning, my muscles were convulsing. I was back in that state of nonexistence, but this time it was hell. One word echoed, repeating louder and louder until it threatened to crack my skull.

CREOVIS!

"That's not my name!" I heard myself screech into the world, and suddenly the blinding white light behind my eyes disappeared as if it were shut off. The echoing *Creovis* was silenced, and the pain released my body as I crumpled to the floor of the cavern. The cold of the stone shocked me into consciousness. My eyes flew open and focused on the Voxmor queen who cowered before me, her eyes squinted as if expecting pain.

"What have you done?" the Creator hissed from where he floated on a black cloud. The Voxmor queen raised herself back to her full height, a low growl beginning to emanate from her throat. I gradually lifted myself from the floor, keeping my movements slow so as not to startle the queen.

My efforts didn't matter, for Sinivir flicked his hand around and sent the Voxmor queen flying back into the wall behind him, her accompanying screech one of pain rather than fury. "You cannot fight my control!" the Creator roared, his claws curled into fists of crackling energy.

"Is that not what I just did?" I asked, tilting my head in the same condescending way he had done to me back in the cell.

"I created you!" he shrieked, spittle flying from his mouth. "The Creovis is *my* weapon to control! This is what you are destined to be because *I* made it so!"

"I am Xiaye, and *I* will control what I become." The Creonex's power ignited in my chest, finally responding to my call. I didn't know where I was, I didn't know where my friends were, or if they were alive. But I did know who *I* was, and it was the last thing I had left to protect. *Until death.*

With a cry of fury, Sinivir released another barrage of his raw power onto me. I raised my arms and blocked most of it, but it still sent me skidding

308

across the stone floor. He fired more spheres of burning energy at me, some of which I dodged and others I had to shield myself from. My shield, as well as my body, was growing weaker. The final ball of energy hit me square in the chest, sending me head-over-heels into the rock wall. Stars burst in my vision, and a dull ache throbbed through my bones as I lay crumpled at the base of the wall, trying to find the will to move again.

"Ah." Sinivir's voice held a hint of epiphany. "That is the answer."

Something wrapped painfully around my body, lifting me off the ground and over to a darkened corner of the cavern. Bars of metal sprang up from the stone floor and wove around each other to form a small, rounded cage. The Creator released me, and I flopped onto the cage floor, panting through the aching in my limbs.

Sinivir cackled. "Your mortal body will weaken, Creovis, and then you will no longer be able to resist me."

I summoned the strength to sit up and glare at him. "I will always find a way to resist you."

The Creator hissed and turned to where the Voxmor queen had risen from where she lay and crawled over to him. "Guard the Creovis successfully this time, Queen of the Voxmor, and perhaps I will not make you her first victim," he growled at her. She hissed and slithered to my cage, her tongue flicking out in between her fangs as she neared. I pushed myself against the back of the cage, then cried out as the bars burned my wings.

"We will see how long it takes to break you, dear Creovis." Sinivir hissed. The smoke from his robes coiled around him, and he vanished, the echo of his cackles bouncing off the cavern's walls.

A mocking silence filled my ears as I hugged myself, bringing my wings close against my back. The Voxmor queen settled herself in front of the cage, her six onyx eyes focused on me as she tapped her two serrated tails against the stone floor.

"You should be grateful I stopped myself from killing you," I muttered.

She growled back at me, curling her lips.

"Yeah? Well, I don't want to sit here and stare at you, either." I shifted away from her, rolling my eyes as she hissed. I watched as the walls above me rippled with the movement of the other Voxmor. Once again, I had no sense of time as I sat in that small cage, shifting into different cramped positions so that no part of me came into contact with the bars. There was no room for me to lie down, so my back quickly began to ache, and my joints stiffened. I tried to focus my mind on different topics to keep myself awake, afraid that if I fell asleep, I would awaken to the burning of my flesh against the metal.

The Voxmor queen stayed where she was, growling and hissing when I moved.

"If you were forced to remain curled up all the time, you would want to move around, too," I said to her after a drawn-out hiss met my ears. "Savor your freedom while you have it."

She let out a faint screech as she stood to change positions, knocking the cage around so that part of my left leg and arm bumped against the bars before I could move out of the way.

"Just for that, you will be the very first thing I kill when I get out of this damn cage," I spat at her. I could've sworn there was a patronizing look in her black eyes.

Most of my time spent in that cage was filled with quiet introspection, as there was nothing else for me to do. Sinivir didn't make an appearance to check on my progress, and the Voxmor queen wanted as little to do with me as possible. Over time, however, her diligence lessened, and she no longer acknowledged every movement I made.

I refused to feel the pain of my grief, wanting to stay alert enough to defend myself and not fall against the burning metal bars. So, I contemplated Sinivir's goal. There was some kind of power within me that he wanted, but why? As far as I knew, he had destroyed all the other Creonexes, rendering his four brothers helpless to protect their universes. To me, that sounded as if he had already won the war against his brothers. Was it control, then, that he craved? Did the Fifth Creator want to use me to make all four universes subservient to him?

"Seems a little cliche to me," I muttered. The Voxmor queen snarled and lifted her head, flicking her tongue at me. "I wasn't talking to you."

She lifted herself from where she had lain for an hour or two and ambled to where a smaller Voxmor had appeared, holding a bloody hunk of meat in its jaws. The queen hissed and ripped the meat out of the other Voxmor's mouth before returning to her station in front of the cage. She glared at me as she dug into her fresh meal.

"Real mature," I said as I turned away from her, my stomach growling. My hunger was so complete that even raw meat would be delectable.

I figured I'd been in that cage for almost two days. Of course, what felt like two days could've been only several hours. My energy was depleting so quickly that any movement was difficult. I had nonsensical conversations with myself and a few auditory hallucinations where I thought I was speaking with Avenlae.

During one, I became aware so suddenly that I had been hallucinating the sound of his voice that the full brunt of solitude hit me. It felt like my breath had been taken away, and I couldn't catch up. The wall I had built between myself and my grief crumbled in mere seconds. My ribs convulsed with sobs, and tears would have fallen if I hadn't been too dehydrated to produce any. I hugged my knees to my chest, but I was so weak that I lost my grip around my legs and fell against the bars, the metal burning my cheek, shoulder, wings, and hand. I yelped and pushed myself away. I cried harder as my body shook from the pain of the burns across my skin, helplessness growing in my mind.

The Voxmor queen shifted and lifted her head, her eyes meeting mine. I lowered my head and felt my body droop, losing the strength to hold myself up. I felt utterly defeated, as if I couldn't muster the strength to even lift a finger against the Fifth Creator if he were to appear. The idea of surrendering to him was repulsive, but there was no fight left in me through the physical and mental pain. *Maybe I would welcome death, now.*

Something cold wrapped around my hand. I flinched, surprised, but I was unwilling to pull away at first because of how soothing the cool feeling was on my burning palm. I lifted my eyes and saw a tentacle draped across my palm and moving up my wrist. I gasped and attempted to escape the tentacle, but others forced themselves through the cage bars and cushioned my wings against the metal behind me. The Voxmor queen was there. Her tentacles cradled me, preventing the bars from scorching my skin.

I slid down to the floor of the cage, my eyes wide as the Voxmor queen slid her tentacles over the other burns on my arms and legs. Whatever was on her tentacles soothed the aching of my raw skin, and she flicked the tip of a tentacle across my cheek before retracting them out of the cage.

"Why?" I asked as she blinked at me.

She looked behind her and then back at me. I frowned, then realized she had been looking back at the place where Sinivir had nearly forced me to kill her.

"Are you *aware* of what I did?" I asked.

She did nothing but stare at me, her six eyes dark as pitch but not menacing. Had she attempted to soothe my pain because she felt she *owed* me something for sparing her life? Did that mean the Voxmor were more intelligent and conscious than they appeared?

Could they, too, be victims of the Fifth Creator's thirst for control?

CHAPTER 29

A reckless idea sprang into my thoughts.

All the answers were in the Voxmor queen's mind.

Moving cautiously towards the edge of the cage, I summoned what little strength was left in my body. The bars radiated heat as I neared, as if they sensed how close my skin was. Blue mist curled around my fingers as I lifted my left hand, too weak to control its trembling.

The Voxmor queen hissed as the Creonex glowed, and the frill around her neck lifted. I froze, keeping my eyes on her. "I don't want to hurt you," I whispered. "But I *need* to understand. I think you're the only one who can tell me."

I stayed there, my hand held out as if in supplication to the beast I had been raised to fear and taught to kill. The Voxmor queen's frill lowered little by little, as did the curl of her lip. Her tongue flicked out towards me a few times, nearly touching a finger. A glint shone in the black of her eyes—it was awareness. It was recognition. It was confirmation that this Voxmor *knew* me.

The Voxmor queen finally lowered her nose, and her smooth, pale scales came into contact with my fingertips. I was sucked into her mind, thrown into her thoughts and memories as if she'd waited years to show me. She had the black veil of Sinivir's control throughout her psyche, but draped across it was a golden web. Her mind had found a way around Sinivir's influence. Not enough for her to have complete control, but enough.

It was easier for me to filter through her mind than that of the previous Voxmor hive queen. Echos of thoughts and orders flitted around me, each vying for me to listen, to hear, and to understand. One memory was tucked deep within swirls of dark smoke, coated in shadow and threads of the golden web severed around it, as if it was meant to be protected. But not from me. It was what *I* was meant to find. I touched my left hand to the one string of light that dove into the depths of that memory, and I was there, seeing the world through the eyes of the Voxmor.

The control the Fifth Creator had over the Voxmor brought out their feral side, the animalistic aggression that made them kill indiscriminately. But this Voxmor queen was one of the first he had captured, and his control over her was faltering. He was unaware of this, although he kept her close, and she hid her consciousness well. Her telepathic powers were stronger than those of her fellow hive queens, so Sinivir had named her a righthand officer to help control his army. And he trusted her to protect his most precious creation—the Creovis.

To the Voxmor queen, the Creovis appeared as pure energy and power contained in a cage. Forks of red, angry electricity cracked against the bars, making the metal glow. The raw power had no form and tore at itself almost as much as it did the cage that held it. The Creovis had destroyed three of the four Creonexes Sinivir hunted and was the key to controlling all Creation. The Voxmor queen had observed everything from her place next to the Fifth Creator, and even now, she observed the Creovis as it blazed dangerously. She stayed within the safety of a small cave so stray forks of energy wouldn't rip at her scales. She had been tasked with guarding the Creovis, but how could she protect something she feared more than the Creator himself?

The air was suddenly filled with flying debris from a blast at the room's far corner. The shockwave slammed the Voxmor's head into the wall, and her awareness returned as Sinivir's control broke for a fleeting moment. As the dust settled, she tasted the metallic burning of the cage, heard the cracks of raw energy and felt the stifling heat generated from the enclosure. Immediately, the Creovis calmed, its red-hot color fading to molten gold. Its surface smoothed until it appeared no longer as antagonized power but as a resplendent orb of peace and creation. The Voxmor queen beheld the orb, unable to move from the shock of information from her senses.

A woman entered through the jagged hole blown into the corner of the little room. With a flick of her tongue, the Voxmor queen could taste the fear of the obsidian-haired winged woman. There was beauty and a wisp of innocence beneath the grime that coated her fair skin and dulled her black armor. Her silver eyes widened as she moved closer to the Creovis. The feathers along the curve of her wings rustled as she advanced, as if drawn towards the orb.

The Voxmor queen did not attack.

The woman raised a slender arm, reaching for the Creovis. It began to unravel, slowly at first, then quickly, as if the woman was a magnet. A beam of light touched the woman's hand and wrapped around her skin. She froze.

Still, the Voxmor queen did not attack.

More and more of the Creovis left the confines of its cage to wrap itself around the woman's arm. She moved as the light gained weight, and she cradled it within her arms as it took shape. The room dimmed as a creature, a child, no, a baby, appeared in the woman's arms, asleep and peaceful. The infant's skin was as bright as the woman's, and its hair as dark as night. A necklace with a sapphire filigree pendant rested on the baby's chest as it breathed rhythmically in sleep.

The Voxmor queen moved.

The woman's head shot over to the cave from which the Voxmor emerged.

315

The look in the woman's eyes quelled the Voxmor queen's need for action.

"Someday, the Creovis will save you, too. She will release you from your eternal imprisonment if you let me take her." The woman's voice was soft. The Voxmor queen watched as the woman darted out of the room, cradling the baby in a mother's embrace.

The cavern and my cage came back into focus as the image faded. I was still staring at the Voxmor Queen, but she was different. Her first two eyes had become multicolored, like light refracted by stained glass windows, and her pupils shrank to the slit of a snake's eye. Her textured irises tightened as her eyes focused on me. That was *my mother* in her memories. And the baby she held, that child, that creature... that was me.

"Who are you?" I asked, my hand still resting on her nose.

A whisper made the hair on the back of my neck rise. It echoed from all directions as if bouncing off the cavern's walls. The black disappeared from the Voxmor queen's six eyes, and each became just as prismatic as the first two.

Vindicta. The word was spoken by a domineering female voice, and the shock of it made me break contact with the Voxmor queen as I stumbled back to the middle of my cage. As soon as our contact broke, the Voxmor's pupils dilated until her eyes were once again ebony. She shook her head a few times, slunk away from the cage, curled her lip, and growled.

"*Creovis,*" came the hiss of the Fifth Creator's voice. I whirled around, flinching as my wings brushed the surface of the metal bars. My shock was quickly replaced with apprehension as I glanced around the cavern, muscles twitching. Sinivir glided across the cavern's stone floor, his fingers curling together so that the sharpened nails clicked against each other. His bloody eyes watched me as his crimson hair fanned out behind him. A flare of rage burned behind my eyes.

"I know," I said to Sinivir as he stopped inches from the cage. "I know what I am."

316

"*My* power." His voice slithered from his mouth in a harsh whisper. "You understand your destiny, then."

"I'm not going to be your weapon, Sinivir. I won't feed your power to control Creation."

"Ah, you only know the lies the Delfungaye feed you about Creation, don't you?" The Fifth Creator began to circle the cage. "That my brothers tried to take my power because I released evil into their universes, isn't that right? It has been so long since I heard those stories."

I frowned, glancing once more around the cavern before asking, "Isn't that what happened?"

"In the imperious eyes of my brothers, perhaps, it is true." He swirled a wisp of smoke around a gnarled finger. "You see, they wanted to form Creation as a reflection of goodness, peace, and prosperity. A utopia. But there can be no utopia without control. Someone must govern the peace and prevent thoughts of greed, lust, and heinous acts from entering the minds of the intelligent species. Tell me, *Creovis*, what kind of life is that? One in which none of your choices are yours to make? In which you are a puppet, with someone you have never known pulling the strings?"

Sinivir resumed his pacing around the cage. "My brothers, they liked to boast that the mortals of Creation would know nothing but happiness once they discovered the key to utopia. That, of course, was why they each made their own universe, to filter through each organism of their Creation to select which would be compatible with their final product. Surely you see the problem now, *Creovis*."

Sinivir bent so that his face was level with mine, and I smelled the rot in his teeth as he spoke. "How can that be fair? Shouldn't each mortal being of Creation be allowed a chance? A chance at life? Who were they, arrogant wielders of *genepotentia,* to decide who and what lived or died?" He shook his head as he rose.

"No, I did not release evil into their universes. I gave everything that breathed a form of *consciousness*. I gave them the ability to feel, to be aware of the worlds around them. What those organisms decided to do with the awareness, well, it was now *their* choice. I took away my brothers' control over Creation."

"Wasn't that enough, then?" I asked.

"For as long as the Creonexes existed, so did the opportunity for my brothers to seize control over Creation once more. I could not let that happen. While they attempted to hide their Creonexes, I remade my own and built my army. My new goal was to destroy the tools they used to concentrate their raw *genepotentia* so that Creation would be allowed to continue without interference. How could the mortals know of happiness if they did not also know grief and pain? How can there be peace if there is no first war? How can there be Creation without destruction? You see, that is what I am. I am the undoing of everything my brothers made—their antithesis. And you, *Creovis*, are my power, my *genepotentia.*"

"So you're going to war against the 'mortals of Creation'... because you're *jealous?*"

"Have you not listened to—"

"This war has nothing to do with us, then!" I shouted. "You have been sending your Voxmor to kill the people of all of these different civilizations, but your fight isn't even with them! What the hell is the point?"

"Those mortals are part of *their* Creation!" Sinivir screeched. "I will build a new one with *your* raw power. I will create a universe of subservient mortals who will worship the One who made them. I will force my brothers to watch as I, the Fifth, become the most powerful wielder of *genepotentia* without the arrogant control of peace."

"How childish," I spat, the tremble in my limbs that of fury.

"I'm growing tired of this mortal obstinacy you insist on displaying," the Fifth Creator snapped, waving away the cage bars but wrapping a length of his robes tightly around my body before I had the chance to move. "I can sense, however, how weak your body has become. The time to release the *Creovis* is near, and I have a most entertaining way to test your abilities under my control."

With a wave of his hand, the cavern disappeared, its stone walls replaced by lush emerald undergrowth. The smell of fresh earth and dried leaves filled my nostrils as a chilly breeze flowed over my exposed skin, calming the ache of old injuries. The ground lifted above us along the steep incline of a mountain, facing the trees towards the light of two suns.

"No," I breathed, recognizing my surroundings.

"Yes," Sinivir hissed, his lips parting in a malevolent smile. "What better way to test the strength of my control? The Delfungaye are the last intelligent civilization to succumb to the might of my Voxmor. They are the final stronghold preventing me from total control of Creation."

His nails dug into my scalp as he wrapped a hand around my hair, forcing my head back as his power seeped into my body. "You, *Creovis*, will be their destruction."

CHAPTER 30

Figures moved in shadows above him. Voices whispered, but were they hallucinations from his feverish mind? Pain rippled across his chest anytime his body moved, keeping him in a half-conscious state. There were brief moments of lucidity in which he became aware of the smell of damp rock and mildew.

Gradually, he became aware of something else. Every time he awoke, profound loss gripped his heart so tightly he began to wonder if the pain in his chest was grief rather than physical injury. But what caused this despair? What had he lost?

Then came a new voice, a memory. It echoed louder and louder until he heard it even when he saw the figures moving around him. It was the voice of a woman. He knew that voice. He *yearned* for it.

"No, no, no," it kept crying. "You have to get up. Answer me!"

"I can't," he would whisper, but the voice kept wailing.

"I c-can't do this without you. C-come on, get up."

"I'm trying."

"GET UP, AVENLAE!"

His eyes sprang open as a scream echoed through his mind, and he gasped in a lungful of stale air. Pain clenched the muscles of Avenlae's chest as the medical tent came into sharp focus. Sounds of the Delfungaye echoed as if bouncing off soaring ceilings and cavernous walls outside the thin canvas.

Memories flooded back—the infiltration of the Voxmor hive, the death of the hive queen, the migration, the attack on the Delfungaye tribe, and—

"Xiaye." He shot out of the cot, stumbling as the pain in his chest throbbed with each breath. He pressed a hand over his heart and felt the uneven pattern of sewn-together flesh under the bandages.

"Careful, Avenlae," a man's voice spoke from the opposite corner of the small tent. Avenlae turned, falling back onto the cot as the world seemed to spin. Darinrain stood, holding out a hand to offer stability but keeping his navy eyes down. Avenlae shook his head, panting and trying to understand why it wasn't Xiaye who greeted him when he awoke.

"Where is she?" he asked, his voice cracking.

Darinrain frowned, pausing halfway across the room.

"Xiaye. Where is she?"

Darinrain's ears flattened against his temples. "I do not know if I am the person to tell you that."

"I asked you, *where is she?*"

The faint light within the tent glistened across the gold and black of Darinrain's head as he bowed his neck in submission. "We ... we do not know."

Avenlae's nostrils flared as a deep growl rumbled in his broken chest. He shoved himself out of the cot, his wings raised with claws pointed at Darinrain's head. Although Avenlae staggered, his eyes flashed as he towered over the other man. "What do you mean?"

"That is enough, Avenlae," Saetyl snapped from the doorway. Avenlae hissed as he turned towards her, rage building.

321

"Avenlae, please." Notien's voice entered the tent just before she did. She stood in front of Saetyl, her navy eyes round and dark in the dim room. "I have been looking for her. Every day."

Avenlae stared. "Every day? How long?"

"You have been unresponsive for nearly a week."

Avenlae stepped back, glancing at Saetyl and Darinrain, shaking his head. "A week? No."

Saetyl sighed. "We have been taking it in turns. Someone stayed here with you in case you woke up while the others continued to search the forest for any sign of Xiaye."

"I needed to be guarded? As if I am dangerous?" Avenlae growled. Emotions and questions raced around his mind, all manifesting as anger.

Notien and Saetyl glanced at Darinrain, who said, "What would you call this reaction? Your version of a warm welcome?"

Avenlae flashed his canines.

"It is better you hear it from us, is it not?" Darinrain said. He gestured towards the entrance of the tent. "Otherwise, you would have begged everyone out there for answers."

"What have you found?" Avenlae asked Notien, trying desperately to control the violent swell of fear-driven fury that pounded against his skull.

"I found her armor," Notien said, her eyes darting from Avenlae to the floor and back again. "It is with the Queen now. But that is all—and I have gone out on every search, Avenlae." Her eyes swam with tears. "I have barely slept."

"I retrieved her rapiers," Saetyl said, "but that is all we have found. There is nothing in what is left of the tribe to suggest what happened to her."

"It is like she vanished into thin air," Darinrain murmured.

"You are not looking hard enough." A hint of Avenlae's desperation came out as a hiss in his voice.

"What about the bond?" Notien asked, daring to raise her head and hold Avenlae's gaze.

"What?"

"The mate bond, Avenlae. Can you feel anything?"

He stared at her, hating the reason he couldn't feel the bond between him and Xiaye. That was what happened when it was fulfilled. Mates could feel each other's presence, their pain, their happiness—their deaths. Avenlae shook his head once. Notien lowered her eyes, swallowing hard as she stepped closer to Saetyl.

"I have heard rumors that Queen Novissime has a theory of what may have happened to Xiaye," Saetyl said, narrowing her golden eyes at Avenlae. "If you only want to berate us, you might as well continue the abuse to the Queen. That might get you somewhere."

Avenlae curled his hands into fists, finally gaining control over his breathing. Without another word, he pushed past Notien and Saetyl, suppressing a grunt of pain as he forced his stiff muscles into motion. Outside the tent was an immense cave carved into the side of a mountain, the stone the same copper as the skin of the *Hopyroque*. Tents were scattered throughout the rocky terrain, clinging to uneven ledges along the walls and ceiling. Rays of suns' light streamed through the mouth of the cave, casting a golden glow on the scene. White medical tents lined a far wall of the cave where Avenlae stood, surveying the encampment for a sign of Novissime.

He figured she would stay near the middle of the cave—easier to get orders out and collect information. It was strategic, and Novissime would always remain the warrior she was before becoming queen. Gritting his teeth against the pain in his leg and dull ache down his chest, Avenlae made his way into the crowd of Delfungaye flitting between tents. Eyes followed him as he passed, but he didn't pause to intimidate. His sole focus was finding his mate.

The more Avenlae searched for Novissime, the stronger the twisting pain of loss grew. It took nearly all of his strength to control his fear that Xiaye would never be found. He was terrified to process his emotions, much less if the bond between them was severed. Xiaye may have never spoken the words to fulfill the bond, but Avenlae, who had held her in the dead of night while she slept, who had whispered words he never thought she would hear, knew he would feel the pain of the bond breaking. *That means she's alive, at least. But not here, not with me.*

Avenlae caught a glimpse of Novissime in a tent near the cavern's roof. He jumped into the air, faltering slightly from the weakness in his right leg. His landing was just as unsteady, and he nearly fell into the tent where Novissime stood with Kaigar and a group of officers. Avenlae felt eyes on him, but he kept his gaze on the Queen. Hisses of displeasure echoed around the circle, and Kaigar boomed, "Remember your place, boy!"

"I do not care," Avenlae said, brushing past two officers. The hisses turned into growls, but no one stopped him. No male in the tribe, officer or not, was willing to challenge him even when he was injured. Especially when they knew who was missing. Nothing survived a fight against a *Y'araye* when instincts were at play.

"Leave us," Novissime ordered, keeping her silver eyes on Avenlae. The officers shuffled out, but Kaigar stayed where he was.

"Avenlae, lower your eyes," Kaigar growled.

Avenlae looked away from the Queen and focused on the General. "You still smell the bond; therefore, you know I have *every* right to look whoever I want in the eye." He turned back to Novissime. "Where is Xiaye?"

Novissime sighed. "I knew that would be the first thing you asked when you recovered enough."

"That wasn't an answer."

"Respect, boy!" Kaigar roared as he moved forward. In one fluid

324

movement, Avenlae grabbed one of Novissime's swords from her hip and pointed the blade at Kaigar's throat, stopping the General in his tracks.

"Respect that I came here for answers and will not tolerate more lies." Avenlae lowered the claws of his wings towards the Queen. "From either of you."

Novissime raised her hands placatingly. "Avenlae, I understand you distress."

"You know nothing of how this feels!" Avenlae cursed himself for the crack in his voice.

"You are not the only one who cares for Xiaye!" The Queen's voice became sharp.

Avenlae lowered his ears against his hair but did not lower the sword or relax his stance.

"I have tried everything I can think of to find her this past week," Novissime said, her voice quavering with emotion. "I have sent search party after search party back to what's left of the tribe in the forest to find any hint of what happened to her. We've searched through our old territory, and Notien has led groups into the plains in case Xiaye was driven out there. Saetyl, of all people, has led searches around the mountain, but there is nothing."

Tears welled in Novissime's eyes. Swallowing hard, Avenlae lowered the blade he held at Kaigar's throat, his strength leaving him.

"I haven't stopped, Avenlae. I cannot believe she's... no, she isn't dead. I know it. But I don't know what else to do."

The dull ache returned to Avenlae's chest, accompanied by pressure so strong he felt his sternum would break. "She was taken. I can still hear—I can still hear her scream."

"Taken by who?" Novissime asked, her eyes focused.

Avenlae shook his head, frustrated that he could hear Xiaye so clearly but not recall the face of her captor. *She was right there. And her screams...* He struggled to prevent himself from becoming lost in the memory.

"It would have been the Fifth Creator." Kaigar's answer was so unexpected that Novissime and Avenlae stared at him in bemused silence. The General lowered his head and crossed his arms.

"How would *you* know *that?*" the Queen asked.

Kaigar glanced at Novissime with his good eye. "Lieneata did not tell you everything she knew."

"But she told *you?*" Her eyebrows made a bid for the sky.

"You know who I was to her," Kaigar said.

"That is not an explanation, Kaigar."

Avenlae watched the exchange, knowing that, with the General, silence would offer more information than aggression.

Kaigar sighed, lifting his head but keeping his arms crossed. "Lieneata did not tell you everything because she was trying to protect her people. Even though she had given away her throne, she still felt a responsibility to her tribe."

"I can understand that, but knowledge of the Fifth Creator seems too important to keep behind sealed lips." Avenlae could hear the underlying threat in the Queen's voice. He wondered idly if Kaigar could hear it, too.

"She told you who he was, in a way."

Realization widened Novissime's eyes. "The bloody-eyed man?"

Kaigar nodded. "Lieneata had known since she left Silvacastra that the Creator would come after her, but she did not tell you who he was. She wanted you to remain focused on protecting what was left of the Delfungaye."

"Knowing the identity of my enemy would've been an advantage in coordinating the defense of the tribe. You're not making sense, Kaigar."

"My Queen, you cannot convince me that, if you had known who the Fifth Creator was, you would not have gone after him."

Novissime bristled at Kaigar's words, but he did not give her the chance to respond. "As long as you did not pose an immediate threat to him, the Creator was going to leave you and the tribe alone while he attempted to locate Lieneata and—and the weapon she stole from him."

Avenlae's silver eyes darted back and forth between the Queen and the General. It appeared as if Novissime and Kaigar had forgotten he was there, and they paid no attention to the break in his silence as he began to pant.

"So that is what she was?" Novissime breathed, her eyes temporarily unfocused as if she were watching a memory in her mind's eye. "It would explain why I could smell no bloodline on Xiaye when Lieneata first brought her to the tribe."

"It is also why she left so suddenly," Kaigar said. "I do not know how Lieneata found out about it, but she had her mind set on retrieving the weapon the Fifth Creator had made. So she did. And she brought it back with her in the form of a baby."

"No," Avenlae growled.

The General turned to Avenlae. "That is what it is, Avenlae. That is what the Creator made. All that power it had when you were training it, how quickly it learned our fighting style, and its ability to incorporate the power of the Creonex—"

"She has a name!" Avenlae roared, his fury boiling over as he flashed his canines and tightened his grip on the sword in his right hand.

"She isn't a mortal being!" Kaigar shouted back, stepping forward so he and Avenlae were nose-to-nose. "She is an extension of the Creators' power, the *genepotentia* they wield to create. I will never know how it took the form of Xiaye, but it is dangerous nonetheless."

"Refer to her as 'it' one more time, and I swear this blade will find your throat," Avenlae hissed.

"Stand down," Novissime said. "Both of you."

After a moment's hesitation, Kaigar stepped back and Avenlae relaxed his shoulders, neither man able to fight the instinct to respond to a queen's order.

Novissime took a breath before continuing. "Regardless of what Xiaye is or isn't, I am still determined to find her."

"To use her?" Avenlae hissed.

"To *save* her," Novissime snapped back. She gave Avenlae a long, hard look, then nodded at Kaigar. "You are dismissed. Pass my orders to the Night Guard and the next search party."

The General looked as if he wanted to protest, but he turned stiffly at Novissime's glare and left the tent. Avenlae's ears twitched at the loud whirring of Kaigar's wing as he took flight. Avenlae flipped Novissime's sword to offer her the hilt and she took it, and returned the blade to its scabbard without her usual flourish.

"Have you felt the severing of the *lyceliah*, the bond?" she asked, using the name in *Y'araye*.

"No."

"Then Xiaye is still alive." The Queen stepped towards him, searching his face. Avenlae lowered his eyes, clenching his jaw to bite back the emotion that rose in his throat.

"I can see the pain you feel," she whispered.

"My injuries are not an impediment. I'm still capable—"

"That is not the pain I am talking about."

Avenlae felt a gentle hand on his cheek. The touch reminded him so forcibly of Xiaye that traitorous tears welled in his eyes.

"I see your pain because I know you, my son."

Avenlae's nostrils flared as he fought to control his breathing—it was the first time the Queen had called him her son since he was sixteen years old.

"I—I cannot lose her." He shuddered at how weak his voice sounded.

"You haven't yet. You have my sanction to do whatever is necessary to bring

Xiaye home." Novissime sighed. "I will not rest easy until I know where she is."

"You understand, *Mother*," he said as he raised his head to look the Queen in the eye. "Should Xiaye return, I do not care what she is to you. She is my mate, and I will not hesitate to protect her as such, no matter *who* threatens her."

"You have forgotten who I am if you truly believe I care about Kaigar's little story. I am desperate for the return and protection of the child of my spirit, not the Daughter of War."

Avenlae opened his mouth to respond but was silenced by a scream. His head whipped around to the tent's entrance, both of his ears standing straight up as his pulse quickened. Behind the scream was a voice he knew too well.

"*Le'eseia*," he breathed as he leaped out of the tent, ignoring the shock of pain in his right leg. Avenlae didn't even think about where his swords were or his armor—he just soared out of the giant cavern, squinting his eyes against the sudden intensity of the suns' light as he entered the mountain forest. Members of the Queen's Guard were racing towards continued sounds of fighting just off to the left of the cavern. Avenlae's heart leaped at the sight of a raven-haired woman twirling two crimson blades around her body in combat with two Delfungaye warriors. And although she was beautiful in combat, Avenlae knew it was wrong. The crimson of her power, the ferocity of her strikes against each warrior—that wasn't the Xiaye he knew.

Without a second thought, Avenlae dove straight down into the branches of the tree, shoving aside the warriors who attempted to block his way. "Xiaye!" he called to her.

She kicked down a warrior, then spun so that she was facing Avenlae. Her eyes, red as blood, narrowed, and she shot a jet of burning red electricity toward him. He ducked and rolled out of the way, staggering to his feet on his injured leg.

"Avenlae!" a guard yelled, tossing him two swords.

Avenlae caught them, hissing through his teeth at the jolt of pain that rippled across his chest. "Stay back!" he growled to the other warriors. "She's mine."

Ruby energy crackled across Xiaye's arms and down her rapiers as her bloody eyes followed Avenlae's every move. She stepped towards him, then stopped, shaking her head, the intensity of her power faltering.

"I do not want to fight you, Xiaye," Avenlae called to her.

Xiaye said nothing but darted forward, blades slicing through the air. Avenlae parried her attack, but only just. There was strength behind her swords, and Avenlae felt a spike of fear down his spine as pain rippled through his body. With his injuries and reticence to fight her, this might be the one fight he couldn't win.

They flitted across the tree branches, Xiaye's power leaving scorch marks across the bark. Their blades clashed, sending waves of red energy pulsing out from Xiaye's skin. Again and again, Avenlae stumbled away from her, unable to keep his footing against the strength of her blows. The pain in his chest intensified, and he was sure blood was seeping through the sutures that held his flesh together. Still, he fought to keep Xiaye focused on him. He would chase her, protect the bond between them, even if Xiaye killed him.

Xiaye's frustration exploded as forks of blood-red energy. The other Delfungaye warriors scattered to take refuge in the thicker foliage, but Avenlae ducked and twirled just out of reach of Xiaye's power. She screeched, slashing her blade viciously. The tip of her rapier sliced across Avenlae's face, leaving a gash that stretched from the left of his jaw to his right temple. He cried out from the sting of ripped flesh as blood dripped down his skin.

Xiaye paused. Her stance wavered and her eyes widened. She took a shuddering gasp.

"Xai," Avenlae said, spitting blood from his mouth. She blinked at him, and then a look of indignation suffused her face again. He had been so close! The only way to reach her was to disarm her. Take the fight away from her. So he took to the sky, knowing that combat in the air had always been Xiaye's weakness.

Maroon flames raced over Xiaye's feathers as she spread her wings to join him in the air. Avenlae caught sight of the arrival of the Queen, followed by Notien, Saetyl, and Darinrain. He was about to warn them off but had to dive away from a barrage of powerful electrical attacks from Xiaye. He cursed and blinked as blood flowed into his right eye and the pain in his chest made his arms tremble. Avenlae clenched his jaw and flew towards Xiaye, brandishing his swords and throwing all his energy at her. *One more chance, one last time.* Fortunately, the crimson Xiaye had the same weakness as Avenlae's Xiaye, and she couldn't keep up with him in the air. Sword-fighting in close quarters prevented her from using her power to blast him away, so Avenlae was able to rid her of her rapiers in a few swift movements.

Xiaye raised her palms as writhing spheres of power swelled against her skin. Unwilling to give up his advantage, Avenlae dove towards her, dropping his swords and catching her shoulders. He forced her down and against the trunk of a tree, the impact causing her to shriek in pain.

"Hold her!" Avenlae shouted to the surrounding warriors as she began to thrash under his grasp. Notien and Saetyl jumped through the branches to grab her wrists, and Avenlae dug the claws of his wings into the bark of the tree above her head.

"Xiaye!" he yelled over her protesting screams. "Xiaye, look at me!"

Her skin burned under his palms, blistering his skin, but Avenlae did not release her. His leg and chest throbbed, and he was nearly choking on the blood that dripped into his mouth, but his mind remained clear. He knew this was his last chance to get Xiaye back. If not, she would kill him. The Mercenary had finally lost the strength to continue a fight.

"I am not going to hurt you, Xiaye!" he yelled over her renewed screech.

A voice, distorted and warbly, emanated from Xiaye's lips. *"Kill her."*

Avenlae nearly lost his grip on her.

"Kill her, boy!"

"No," Avenlae choked out. "I cannot."

"Protect your people, Avenlae. Protect them better than you did your own family."

"I—no. I can save—"

"She will destroy them!" the voice shrieked as Xiaye writhed. Flames exploded from her wings, and the crimson of her irises grew to encompass the whites of her eyes.

"No, no, I can bring her back."

"KILL HER!" the voice roared, echoing over the trees, wrenching itself from her protesting throat. *"OR SHE WILL BE YOUR DESTRUCTION!"*

"No! Xiaye, look at me!" Avenlae cried, wrenching Xiaye's head around so she was forced to look up at him. She froze as soon as she met his eyes, and the crimson shrank back into her irises. Avenlae's chest heaved with exertion, but his fear calmed as he stared at her.

"You are safe now, Xai," he told her, keeping his voice low and smooth. "I will not let him hurt you anymore."

Her eyes widened the longer she watched him. Slowly, the flames across her feathers shrank, returning to their deep black-to-white ombre. She gasped, struggling weakly against him once more.

"Shh, Xai, I have you," Avenlae said, releasing his hold on her chin to caress her cheek. Xiaye stopped moving, her breathing uneven. He pressed his lips against her forehead gently, and tears welled in her eyes when he looked at her. Gradually, the crimson faded in her irises, leaving her right eye silver and her left flecked with red. Avenlae leaned forward again and whispered, "Come back to me, *Le'eseia*. I will keep you safe."

CHAPTER 31

Consciousness spread over me like water spreads over a porous surface. First, I heard a voice. Then I smelled the forest and felt a breeze against my damp skin. I trembled as I saw the blurry outline of someone standing over me.

"No," I rasped, terror taking hold that it was Sinivir who kept me pinned.

"*Le'eseia.*"

It was the voice again. I stared into two moonlight eyes—the ones I had been focusing on for the entirety of my imprisonment.

"Av?" He released my wrists, and I touched his face. "Y-you're alive?"

He nodded and smiled. My relief was cut short by the blood from a gash that split his face. "How?" I asked as I touched a finger to the ripped skin. "Did—did I—?"

"It is okay, Xai." Avenlae wrapped his hand around mine, lowering it from his face. "I am fine; you do not need to worry about me."

"But you, but you—you were so still and, and y-you wouldn't answer me," I stammered as I pressed my other palm against his chest, flashbacks of his lifeless body during the Voxmor attack in my mind's eye. I could feel the sutures along his sternum under the fabric of his vest. But his heart was beating under my fingers, strong and sure.

A few chunks of bark fell into my hair as Avenlae ripped the claws of his wings from the tree. He wrapped his arms and wings around me. "It is alright, Xai. You are safe now; I can protect you."

"But the Fifth Creator ... Avenlae, he, he wants to kill—"

"I know." His voice rumbled in his chest as he rested his head on mine. "I know."

"Is she—is she okay?" I heard Notien ask, and I cried harder. The knowledge of how close she was when I was in Sinivir's control was too overwhelming. What if I had done something to her? What if I had hurt her, like I had hurt Avenlae?

"I'm sorry," I gasped into Avenlae's chest. "I'm s-so sorry."

"You are okay, Xai," Avenlae whispered. "Everyone is fine."

"Let me see her." Novissime's voice rang out over the chatter of the Guard around us. I felt Avenlae stiffen as he turned his head to watch the Queen as she approached. Avenlae released me when I pressed against his chest, albeit reluctantly. Novissime stopped in her tracks as I faced her, tears still flowing down my cheeks. I gulped down a few more breaths, unsure if the Queen had arrived to defend her people or out of true concern. She approached me, the suns' light glistening in the silver of her eyes. I just watched her, afraid that if I moved, the Guard would see it as a threat to their Queen.

"Oh, Xiaye," Novissime breathed as she ran her hand over my hair, brushing strands away from my face. "What did he do to you?"

"I know," I said. "I know what I am. The Creator told me—he told me what I am."

"I don't care. I do not care what you are." And then she wrapped her gentle arms around me. All of the lies, the lack of trust, the anger melted away as if they'd never really existed. There was just her embrace, a mother's embrace, and the enveloping aura of protection. "I care that you are here and you are safe, Xiaye."

For once, I allowed myself to trust her. I needed her. I finally understood Novissime's reluctance to tell me all, for would I have believed her? I understood her desperate attempts to carve out a place for me in her people's society. I *knew* what my power meant. With these revelations came yearning for her guidance. She had all the answers, as she always did. I stepped away from her embrace and looked into her tearful eyes.

"Will you help me?" I asked. "Will you help me understand all of this?"

"As much as I am able, daughter of my spirit."

I took a deep breath and had just returned her smile when her eyes flicked up, focusing on something just past my shoulder. Her smile dropped, and her pupils contracted as her grip tightened over my wrists. I didn't have the chance to look behind me. Otherwise, I might've been able to stop her.

The world spun as Novissime whirled me around towards the trunk of the tree. There wasn't even time for me to gasp, to ask what she was doing. Then her body convulsed over a black blade that protruded from her chest, dripping with crimson blood. My breath caught in my throat, and my limbs were suspended where Novissime had held them. The sound of the forest, the screams, the color of the trees died away. Nothing existed beyond Novissime as her head rolled around to face the weapon that pierced her heart. Bewildered agony filled her eyes, and a trickle of blood dripped from the corner of her mouth. Then those eyes met mine, and I was suddenly thirteen again, watching my mother climb out of the bunker, hearing the silence spread through the forest. I was alone.

"I—I'm sorry, Daughter." Novissime's whisper pierced the silence before she collapsed, the blade pulled from her chest. Slow motion captured her fall, each moment etched in disbelief. She had to get back up. She had to stand with me, pull her swords out, fight the rest of the war with me. She wasn't fragile enough to be struck down in one blow. Not Novissime, not the Queen.

I staggered forward, one hand out as if to shake her and the other closing around my chest, shuddering gasps echoing in my ears. I couldn't speak, I couldn't cry, I couldn't scream. All I could do was stare, astonished, and will myself to comprehend Novissime's death, her broken body. *Her blood... so much blood...*

"*Creovis!*" The discordant hiss of Sinivir cut into my shock, and I turned to face him. His body materialized from a cloud of sooty smoke, crimson hair flung out around his head like a halo. The black blade stained red from Novissime's blood sank into the depths of his robes as the Fifth Creator grew in size, his gray face twisted into a grimace of hatred. "*Creovis*, you have thrown off my control for the last time!"

"That," I hissed as energy, red as the Creator's eyes, shot down my skin and ignited my wings, "is *not* my name!"

I leaped into the air, my wings alight with the flames of my fury, and my power exploded out of my body. Beams of magenta energy shot towards Sinivir, burning the Creonex violet. For all the damage it did, I might as well have thrown one of my feathers at him. He deflected the attack with a wave of his hand.

"How *dare* you attempt to attack me!" he screamed. "Your maker, your *creator*! You would be nothing without me!" His power, rippling waves of crimson, flowed straight from his palms into my body. My head was thrown back as the power took hold, torching my skin and setting fire to my veins. I saw nothing but red, and I screamed until I felt as if I had torn my lungs apart.

"That's it, *Creovis*," Sinivir hissed. "You have always been and always will be my greatest weapon."

No. The word reverberated through my mind, fighting ferociously against

Sinivir's influence. There was a *reason* he kept failing to control me, and I held on to it with every fiber of my being. The agony of his power diminished, and with immense effort, I brought my head forward and my arms back to my sides, prepared for the attack. Then my body was absorbing his power, my hatred burning behind my eyes. Sinivir's bloody eyes widened, and his look of insane victory slackened.

"My name," I growled, "is Xiaye!" I reached deep into the connection between myself and the Creonex, not to use it but to control it. A beam of pure *genepotentia* erupted from my palms, slamming into the Fifth Creator's chest, the wave of his hand nowhere near enough to protect him. The power was fed by hatred, rage, and *pain*. He smacked into a tree, a hole burnt straight through his abdomen.

I panted as the rush of energy left me and watched Sinivir gasp and stagger, the black of his robes knitting itself together. Forks of violet electricity buzzed over my skin as I dove down to the branch before the crumpled Creator. "You created me. And then you destroyed *everything* I ever knew. You have tried to kill everyone I have ever loved." I advanced, my feathers blazing with lilac flames. "You have created *vengeance*!"

"Is that how you observe yourself?" the Creator hissed as his robes dissolved into black smoke. "Then a weapon you shall remain, *Xiaye.*"

His last words were drawn out into an eerie hiss as his body dissolved. The trembling returned to my limbs, and the weight of grief dropped heavily into my chest, anger evaporated as quickly as it had bloomed. I turned slowly to look back to where Novissime had collapsed, an almost numbing fear drawing me to her. A crowd of warriors stood around her, shielding her body from my view.

I glided back to the branch, landing unsteadily as the world around me seemed to move in slow motion again. I moved forward automatically, pulled as if by a magnet. My body moved, but my mind screamed for escape, dreading the scene of Novissime lying there, lifeless. *It's not real, it's not real.* At the rustle of my wings, the warriors parted, bowing their heads to avert their eyes from mine. I froze, my eyes widening as I saw the ends of the Queen's wings from where I stood. The pure white feathers were more delicate than the snowflakes I had watched fall on Earth. *It's not real, it can't be real.*

I glanced around at the warriors, almost wishing for one of them to take my hand and lead me forward. Finally, I stepped once more, my mind blank, thoughts still. I felt as if I were flitting between the time I was thirteen, curled alone in my bunker, and the present in which I forced myself to step closer to the body of Novissime, the woman who had tried to be the mother I had lost.

The strength left my legs as I reached her, and I fell to my knees. The Queen's unseeing gaze was fixed upon the canopy above, a solitary tear suspended on her pale cheek. Amidst the crimson stain across her chest was a serene elegance within her outstretched wings—a vision angelic and pure. Her obsidian hair lay softly over her shoulders and across the bark of the branch she lay on. She looked as peaceful as if she'd been watching the clouds pass in the sky. A part of me wanted to smile at the thought, but how could I?

Movement sounded in front of me, and Avenlae crouched next to Novissime's other shoulder. I looked into his anguished face, his ears flat against his hair and his pupils contracted so tightly that I couldn't see them. His breathing was ragged as he implored, "Help her."

Remorse rose in my throat and pushed the tears from my eyes. To help her, to make her breathe again, was a power I had never found. How could I explain that to him when he saw me heal superficial wounds on myself?

"H-help her, Xiaye," Avenlae beseeched once more.

I knew his anguish. It made my heart break even more for him to know there was nothing I could say or do that would lessen his grief. I shook my head as I cried, unable to form the words to tell him I could not bring back

339

the Queen he had loved. His eyes searched my face, as if desperate to find an explanation there. At my silence, his eyes widened, and he leaned away from me. Gradually, he lowered his head, his shoulders trembling from sobs he tried to suppress. I lifted my left hand, blue mist encircling the violet filigree of the Creonex, wanting to do *anything* to relieve the pain in his eyes. Avenlae caught sight of my hand before my fingers touched his temple, and he jerked away as if I had burned him. I watched, afraid and confused, as he leaped to his feet, looking everywhere but at me.

"Avenlae," I said, but he just turned and took off from the branch's edge, leaving me alone next to Novissime. I let my hand drop, my fingers brushing against Novissime's cold shoulder. The burning tension in my chest spread into my throat as tears flowed down my cheeks, my jaw, my neck. I mourned the loss of the only person who could help unravel the chaotic mess of what I was and what I was meant to do. I felt alone, left to face the war, the worlds, and the universes. There was no guidebook, no instructions, no help. There was only me, a thing I didn't understand and a power I was still learning to wield.

I cried, crouched like a terrified child, my tears splashing onto the stained white uniform Novissime had died in. I cried for her, for myself, for her people's trauma. After a time, I felt small, gentle hands wrap around my shoulders.

"Xiaye, we must go," Notien whispered into my ear.

"I c-can't leave h-her," I sobbed, brushing a hand over Novissime's cold cheek and down her collarbone.

"I will take care of her," Saetyl said hoarsely.

I shook my head. "We have to move her. I ... she—we can't leave her by herself."

"I know," Saetyl said, grasping my arms as I raised them, pleading for her to understand my distress. "I will have her moved, but you need to go with Notien."

340

"I didn't mean for it to happen!" I tried to tell her, but guilt tightened my throat so much that my voice failed part way through my words.

"I know, Xiaye, I know." Saetyl's voice cracked, and a lone tear slid down her rust-colored cheek.

"Come, Xiaye." Notien wrapped her arms around my shoulders, gently helping me to my feet and guiding me away from the warriors crowded around the fallen Queen. "There is nothing more we can do for her."

Too numb to fight back, I allowed Notien to lead me back through the forest and into a massive cavern carved into the side of the mountain. Tucked into the jagged corner of the ceiling was a white cloth teardrop nest—Notien's home. It was straightforward, only a fire pit and a makeshift bed crafted out of the largest of the mountain trees' leaves.

Notien sat me down by her firepit, lighting the wood and saying something about grabbing a basin of water. It took me a few minutes to realize she had left the nest. Perhaps she couldn't bear to be in the same room as me. Had she watched what had happened to her Queen and held me responsible? Did she think of me as some monster after witnessing what I could do when under the influence of Sinivir's power? I couldn't blame her. I was a monster. *A freak with power no one truly understands...*

Notien returned with a large crystal bowl that she set down next to me. I glanced over, seeing a sponge floating across the surface of steaming water. I blinked, and then there was my reflection in the softly rippling surface of the liquid: matted onyx hair, sunken cheekbones, one silver eye, and one—

I gasped at the sight of my left eye, whose iris had become as red as blood. I blinked again and turned away from the water, watching as Notien lowered herself to the ground behind me.

"What are you doing?" I asked.

"The trauma you have experienced is still caked onto your skin," she said, touching the parts of my arms that still had flecks of Avenlae's dried blood. "Let me help you remove this part of your pain."

"Aren't you needed somewhere?"

"Yes. Here."

I didn't protest as Notien scrubbed my arms and shoulders. She poured water over my head, working out the knots in my wavy hair, and helped me undress and pull on clean, soft Delfungaye garments of gray and black. But I felt no relief as she ran the sponge over my feathers. Or as she combed and braided my hair. I felt nothing but repulsion as she poured the water out of the bowl, and I caught my reflection once more in its crystal depths.

Notien left but returned soon after with *baute* fruits and offered one to me. I stared at the fruit in her hand, remembering the first time I tasted it, on a branch as the suns began to set. Tears welled in my eyes as I yearned to return to a time when the world seemed much simpler. I was surprised I had any tears left.

"Xiaye, you have to eat," Notien said as she cut open the fruit. "This will be light on your stomach but provide you with energy and nutrients."

"I don't know how you're able to eat right now," I whispered as I accepted her offer of the fruit.

The drips of yellow juice from the *baute* clashed with the gold of Notien's skin as she took a small bite of the pulp, chewing slowly with her navy eyes unfocused. "I ... I do not want to eat, but I must." She shook her head slightly, the frame of her platinum bob flowing away from the soft edges of her face. "As much as I want it to, life will not slow down for us to process what has happened. I am still a warrior of the Queen's Guard, so I still have a tribe to protect." Notien reached up and tucked a small whisp of my hair behind my ear. "That means I have to feed my strength and help you to regain yours."

I finally sank my teeth into the *baute*. I wanted to embody the resiliency that Notien spoke of, but how did one move past the numbness? How could I see past the pain?

Saetyl and Darinrain stepped into Notien's nest, avoiding my eyes. A prick of self-resentment stung my thoughts, and I remained facing the fire.

"She has been moved," Saetyl said, sounding exhausted. "The *Matri Me'leiv* is with the Queen now, preparing her ... her body for the Celebration of Passing."

"We met briefly with Kaigar on the way here," Darinrain said. "He is working to control the spread of the news of the Queen's death to prevent panic."

"There will be panic despite his efforts," Notien said. "We have just lost our leader, and she did not have an heir."

There's the fear, I thought as I took another bite of *baute*. There was a brief moment of silence in which I could feel their eyes on my back, but I remained silent.

"Nonetheless," Saetyl breathed, "the Celebration of Passing is to be held tomorrow evening, and—"

"No," I said, straightening my spine, preparing to stand and face them. I didn't have the strength to fight them, but I *knew* the cave would no longer be safe by the next evening. I stretched my wings as I turned to warm them close to the fire. "We need to prepare to leave by tomorrow evening."

All three of them glanced quickly at each other, but Saetyl responded first. "But, Xiaye, we just got here—"

"Sinivir knows the location of the tribe."

They stared, confused, but unwilling to speak up.

"The Fifth Creator. The one who killed the Queen."

Terrified realization spread across their faces. "You deserve to know the truth," I said quietly. "The truth is that the tribe is not safe as long as Sinivir knows where we are."

"But you defeated him, did you not?" Notien asked.

"No, I would feel it. I may have wounded him, and he may need time to recover, but it will take more than one exposure to raw *genepotentia* to defeat a Creator."

"If he needs time to recover, should that not also give us time to prepare a plan for another migration?" Saetyl asked. "You need to give the people time to grieve, Xiaye. It may not affect you, but the death of our Queen is significant."

I rose to my feet and glared at her. "May not affect me? You have no *idea* what I have gone through away from this tribe. And the second I return, the only person capable of guiding me through the truth of this war is killed right in front of me! Your pain may be different from mine, but it is not worse. Novissime's last action was to protect me, and she spent all her time on the throne doing everything she could to protect her people. I will *not* allow her sacrifice to be in vain, which means keeping the tribe out of reach of Sinivir and the Voxmor. He won't return here soon, but he still has Voxmor on this planet. They have probably been ordered to begin their trek up the mountain."

I paused a moment to gather my strength again, then continued. "Novissime's Celebration of Passing will be held tomorrow morning, and preparations to move will begin in the afternoon. Come daylight the next day, we will be gone from this cave. Saetyl, you will speak with the *Matri Me'leiv*. Darinrain, you will need to keep Kaigar out of the way until the morning so we can meet and formally discuss plans for the migration."

"I do not think it is a good idea to send me to head off Kaigar," Darinrain grumbled. "I am not a high-enough ranking warrior to—"

"I wasn't asking," I interrupted. Darinrain raised an eyebrow, and Saetyl rolled her shoulders back. I heard Notien shift uncomfortably beside me.

After a few quiet moments, Darinrain responded, "Yes, Your Majesty."

344

CHAPTER 32

A low-hanging branch with dark, marbled bark jutted out from the top of the entrance to the cavern. That was where I sat the next day, watching the suns rise, breathing in the cool, earthy scent of early morning in the mountains. The rest of the tribe hadn't begun to stir, so I was comforted by the serene silence of life between rest and wakefulness. I watched as a breeze flowing up the mountain sent leaves the color of alexandrite swaying. The trees of the mountain forest were much older than the forest of the valley, as indicated by their size and twisted, gnarled copper bark. Their leaves were broad and jagged, but with the stiff texture of pine. What a beautiful place to live; what a peaceful place to die.

Tears pricked the corners of my eyes, and I took a breath to stop myself from crying again. My sleep had been broken up with random bouts of crying when I awoke from nightmares of Novissime's lifeless body. I had stayed in Notien's nest, and Avenlae had not come looking for me. That had caused another rush of tears just before nightfall, and Notien was patient enough to sit with me through that one as well as all the ones that followed.

When I awoke for the final time, the light of the suns was on the horizon. I stifled the sound of my sob and crept out of Notien's nest, not wishing to disturb her again. She, too, needed time to rest and process her grief.

I dug my nails into my palms and clenched my jaw, forcing myself not to cry. I should've stopped Sinivir. I should've saved her. I should've died. *I should've, I should've …*

I shook my head and raised my eyes to the cloudless sky. How often I had watched those suns rise and set over the past several months, Avenlae next to me. I had sat with Novissime, watching the suns bring forth a new day and hearing her confession of imperfection. Should she have appeared next to me then, I would've forgiven her. That was all—I would've forgiven her.

Novissime was always trying to figure out what she was supposed to do, I thought to myself. *Perhaps I will figure out what I* need *to do.* And damn Avenlae for not being there. Damn him for denying me his reassurance, his guidance, even the simplicity of his body next to mine. My heart thrummed angrily as his betrayal beat a course of red through my thoughts. Avenlae forced me to be alone, not because of my failure but because of the limits of my power. Just as quickly as anger had flared within me, it faded into guilt. Who was I to hate him? Who was I to question or judge his pain, his grief?

Who was I to invalidate his blame for the one person who should've been able to protect the Queen? *You failed. And he knows it.*

"Xiaye."

I gasped and whipped around, the violet blade of a knife materializing in the palm of my left hand. Notien's golden ears pressed against her hair as she lowered her eyes. "I am sorry. I did not mean to startle you."

I sighed and flicked my wrist, the blade disappearing. "No, Notien, I'm sorry. I'm still a little on edge, but I should've recognized your voice."

"You are too hard on yourself," Notien said as she plopped down on the branch next to me. "You have just gone through so much, so you cannot fault yourself for lingering fear."

She pressed a leaf plate into my hands. Upon it was a light, steaming breakfast. I smiled at the gesture—no matter what happened, I could count on Notien to ensure I was taken care of.

"Thank you," I whispered.

"I have a ceremonial outfit picked out for you," she said after a spell. "I know you have never attended a Celebration of Passing, and I did not think you would have the energy to figure out what to wear."

"You are a godsend, Notien."

"The braids in your hair are already traditional, so you will only have to change before the Celebration." Notien looked out over the face of the mountain and forest beyond. "I do not think either of us has the strength to do more."

I set a hand on top of hers, squeezing her fingers together. She glanced down at our hands, and her lip quivered. "I will help guide you through the Ceremony as best as I can. But afterward, you may be on your own with Kaigar."

I rolled my eyes. "Then perhaps I'll spend the entirety of the Celebration of Passing mentally preparing myself to deal with him."

"You and Darinrain both. I spoke with him and Saetyl again this morning before coming to you. They will join us to support you when it is time to discuss the tribe's fate."

"Saetyl will support me?" I nearly choked on my water.

"She has gained more trust in you, especially since we infiltrated the Voxmor hive."

"I'm surprised. I thought she would've found a way to blame the Voxmor attack on me."

"Saetyl told me you two have reached some kind of understanding." Notien took a sip of water, briefly glancing at me out of the corners of her eyes.

347

A flash of Saetyl's past flitted in my mind. "I suppose you could call it that."

"Either way, you will need all the support you can get from the more influential members of the Queen's Guard."

"I never said I was going to take the throne," I said softly, avoiding her gaze, for I knew where the conversation was going.

A muscle tightened in Notien's jaw. "Xiaye, I do not know how much of a choice you have in the matter."

"I have *every* choice."

"*We* do not. Surely, that is something you can understand?"

I stared out over the forest. I couldn't even speak their language. I didn't look like them, I couldn't act like them, I barely knew their culture. Did I even want the responsibility of protecting these people, this dying civilization?

"I just feel alone," I said.

Notien ran her palm down the braids along the back of my head, keeping her navy eyes on me for a moment. "You are my friend. No matter your choice, you will not be alone." Then she stood and wordlessly beckoned me to follow her. I breathed a small sigh of relief that she didn't try to continue the conversation before I pushed myself off the branch, catching the wind currents up the mountain and looping around to accompany her back to her nest. As I stepped over the threshold, a flash of the *Weigt'ri* played through my memory. Once again, two gowns hung from the top of the wall of Notien's nest. For a moment, I was lost in the smells of the bonfire, the beat of the drums, the tickle of *a'ta'ya* on my tongue. *The warmth of Avenlae, his lips, his body...* No, that was too painful.

I shook my head, stepping further into the room as Notien moved around me to take down the gowns. These garments were the color of the emerald leaves, the cloth of the bodice folded in such a way as to imitate the shadows cast by the canopy. The long skirts were coated with traditional beadwork sewn into a layer of white silk fabric. I felt the weight of the beadwork as Notien helped me into my dress, its beadwork sleeves pressing into my shoulders and collarbones. The bodice didn't plunge as deeply as the dress I had worn to the *Wiegt'ri* but resembled an uneven sweetheart neckline.

"Why green?" I asked as I assisted Notien into her own gown.

"It is the color of mourning in the Delfungaye culture," she explained as she adjusted her sleeves. "It represents that when we pass on, we become one with the forest and plants we make our homes."

She turned to face me, holding a masquerade mask of twisted emerald vines. I frowned, taking it from her slowly. "I, uh, is this appropriate to wear?"

"It is traditional to wear these masks," Notien said as she pulled out her own, which had a dusting of gold on the tiny leaves. "They represent that Death does not discriminate—She comes for all of us, one way or another. So we celebrate the passing of our people into the waiting arms of Death in hopes that She will honor the life they had and will allow them to rest in the peace of the forest."

"She?"

"Yes, She. *Fae'yeeriem*, Mother Death, accepts all life and transitions us into the rebirth of continued life once we have finished ours. She is the reason a new forest can grow after a fire."

Notien repositioned my mask over my eyes, placing the band carefully around the braids she had pinned to the back of my head. She let her arms drop to her sides after she placed her own and cast her navy eyes toward the ground.

"I never thought I would experience a Celebration of Passing for a Queen so soon." Notien blinked her eyes rapidly as she took a shaky breath.

I looked to the wall behind her, my own conflicting feelings of grief rising in my throat. We stayed that way for a moment, as I was at a loss how to respond. It didn't matter how much or how little we spoke about it—nothing would change the death of the Queen. Whether we celebrated, fought, cried, screamed, or stayed frozen in time, Novissime would remain unchanged, silent, and still, and we would remain alone.

The Celebration of Passing was remarkably peaceful. It was difficult for me to follow most of it, as I still didn't know the Delfungaye language, but Notien translated what she could for me. She had pushed me to be near the front of the tribe's gathering, and as we moved through the crowd, not a single Delfungaye made eye contact with me. They had always been quick to lower their eyes if I looked in their direction, but now I didn't feel the gaze of anyone on my back. Was it respect or fear that kept their eyes averted? The closer we got to the front of the gathering, the less energy I had to wonder.

A shock went through me at the sight of Novissime's body laid neatly on a marble-white pedestal. She had been dressed in emerald, her hair braided around her head and interwoven with pearl beadwork. The early morning light cast a peaceful glow over her body, an angelic aura.

Movement in my periphery caught my attention. I looked to my right, watching as a tall figure approached, the crowd parting to make way. As soon as I saw the braids interwoven with gold, I knew it was Avenlae. He froze as he came to the front, his silver eyes gazing at the Queen. His ears pressed flat against his braids, and he bowed his head slightly. The gash splitting his face had been neatly sewn together, but its reddened edges were stark beneath his mask. The shadow of the barely healed injury down his chest was visible underneath the black and gold ceremonial beadwork that covered his torso and the tops of his arms. The longer I stared, the more I willed him to look at me, to come to me so that I could release him from the pain he felt, but he refused to acknowledge me. *I should've helped him, I should've gone to him, I should've died...*

My eyes continued to dart to Avenlae for the rest of the Celebration of Passing. Not once did his silver eyes meet mine. He showed little emotion beyond the twitch of a muscle along his jaw or a hard swallow. My distraction prevented me from facing the wave of emotions stirred by the ceremony, but I was not wholly unaware of them. The beauty of the call-and-response song the *Matri Me'leiv* sang brought fresh tears to my eyes. My pain ebbed and flowed with the harmonic response of the tribespeople to each one of the *Matri Me'leiv's* lyrics. All the Delfungaye, whether *Hopyroque, Fyr'aeset,* or *Laizuteek,* swayed with the music, some with their arms outstretched in reverence, others with their heads bowed and their eyes closed. Avenlae remained unmoved, his beadwork a stark reminder of his isolation, the last of the *Y'araye.*

The ceremony ended with a flame passed from a branch to the pedestal Novissime rested on, flame burning as green as the forest trees in the valley. I was struck with the wild urge to run to Novissime and place myself between her and the flames that began to consume her body. As if that would allow me to hear her voice one last time and ask her one final question. Instead, I wrapped my arms around myself, pressing my wings tight against my spine. Ashes from the fire began to drift with the current of the wind. There was no retrieving Novissime from where she was. As the flames calmed, blackening the pedestal with ash, the final barrier between myself and the tribe I was meant to inherit fell. Notien, as always, had been right— the Delfungaye needed me. They had no one else. *I* had no one else.

Notien put gentle pressure on my arm to lead me away from the smoldering pedestal. I looked around once more for Avenlae, and Notien whispered, "Everyone experiences grief differently, Xiaye. You must have patience for how he copes with his."

351

I nodded and allowed her to lead me from the bright entrance of the cavern to the dimmer middle, where a larger, more ornate tent had been set up. A few members of the Queen's Guard left the tent and hurried off into the labyrinth of temporary habitations that dotted the ceiling and stone floor of the cave.

"I guess Kaigar hasn't fought Darinrain too much," I said as I watched them leave, preparing to address the few remaining inside the tent.

Notien shrugged. "Kaigar may be stubborn, but he knows he does not hold rank above you. Although I suspect today he will debate that position."

"He can try," I murmured, removing my mask and entering. Darinrain and Saetyl were already there, both still in ceremonial dress. Avenlae sat in a corner apart from the rest of us, sharpening one of his knives and ignoring everyone.

Kaigar paced back and forth at the front of the tent, his machinery whirring away. I glanced in Avenlae's direction, unnerved by his silence. Steeling myself, I took a breath and spoke.

"I've called you all here today to discuss the future of this tribe. I would appreciate your counsel during this time and in the future. This... position we find ourselves in is unexpected to say the least. I'm not sure what the Delfungaye tradition is for changes in leadership, but—"

"You are doing nothing but proving how unfit you are for the throne," Kaigar growled.

"You can argue that until you die, Kaigar, but it will not change the fact that Novissime had no blood heir and named no other successor," Saetyl responded.

"The *Je'quiet* have always remained clear on this," Darinrain sighed, as if he had repeated this several times to Kaigar. "Leadership must first pass on to the blood heir or named successor before it can be passed down the chain of command."

"*That* is what you want to follow?" Kaigar asked, gesturing towards me. "You've seen what it can do! The power it holds!"

352

Perhaps I was the only one who noticed the stilling of Avenlae's blades, for the others around me continued to argue.

"You followed her in the attack on the Voxmor hive," Notien hissed.

"That was before I witnessed its raw power, its ability to control the Voxmor and harm a Creator! That thing has no place on our throne when it can be used as such a powerful weapon against us!"

A small part of me felt the anger Kaigar's words engendered, but I stayed silent. How could I fight back? I agreed with him.

"She is under no one's control." Darinrain pushed himself away from the wall, rolling his shoulders back. "Least of all yours. Xiaye's power may be beyond our understanding, but all of us here know it may be the only thing we have left to protect the surviving Delfungaye."

"Hiding away in fear from the Voxmor is what got us to this point, and you know it, Kaigar!" Saetyl rasped. "You did nothing to fight for us until Xiaye ordered you to. We cannot continue to cower away from the threat of war, not now that we know who leads the Voxmor and that we have a weapon strong enough to defeat them."

"It is also strong enough to obliterate us!" Kaigar was gesturing wildly, spittle flying from his mouth. "If we cannot control it, what is left for us to do? What if we follow it into a trap? It will be the end of the Delfungaye, and I will not—"

We never learned what it was Kaigar would not do, for Avenlae sprang out of his chair and cracked the hilt of his knife across Kaigar's temple.

CHAPTER 33

Notien gasped, and Darinrain moved to unsheathe his knife, but his arm was stilled by a warning look from Saetyl. Violet energy began to crackle over my skin, Creonex glowing as my adrenaline spiked.

"*She* has a name, Kaigar," Avenlae growled, his canines glinting. A trickle of blood made its way down the side of Kaigar's face. "I warned you to remember it."

"But I will not warn you again to remember your place!" Kaigar hissed as he pushed himself off the ground, using the strength of his metal wing to knock the knife out of Avenlae's hand. He shoved Avenlae back against a support beam that held up the far wall of the tent, the palm of his metal hand pressing hard into Avenlae's sternum. There came a sharp *crack* of bone breaking, and Avenlae's cry of pain sent ice down my spine.

"*Enough!*" I yelled, a ball of energy flying from my palm and slamming against Kaigar's torso. The impact sent him flying to the ground, his metal wing and hand twitching as they struggled to regain connection to his mind. He shook his head several times, his eyes twitching as the wires diving into his neck sparked. I advanced, standing over Kaigar as crackles of energy raced over my skin. "This tribe has just lost their Queen," I seethed. "Do *not* force me to make them lose their general as well."

Kaigar's opaque eye squinted with the uneven whirring from the wires in the base of his skull. After several long moments, he lowered his gaze, his ear pressing back against the blood from his temple.

"I don't give a damn what you think of me," I continued, my voice low. "You have no one else to save you. If you choose to stand with me, go to the Healers to repair your faulty wiring and supervise preparations for migration. If not, tell me now so that I may kill you for treason. Do not allow your stubborn pride to get in the way of your tribe's salvation."

Seconds of silence passed between us, but with the tension in the tent, it felt like a lifetime staring into the eyes of a man I was terrified to kill. Finally, with a growl, the General rose to stumble out of the tent. His right hand remained balled into a fist as he passed Notien, Saetyl, and Darinrain, all of whom averted their eyes, but his metal left hand twitched limply at his side. Letting out a breath, I turned to Avenlae, whose jaw was tightly clenched as he held himself up against the support beam. His breathing was labored, but I knew he wouldn't allow me to help him while the others were present.

"Saetyl, follow Kaigar and make sure he doesn't cause any more trouble." She nodded to me once, then swept from the tent. "Darinrain, you will oversee the organization of the Queen's Guard as they gather supplies and change out shifts guarding the entrance to the cavern. You'll meet me back here late afternoon to discuss the formation of our flight away from here."

"Yes, Your Majesty." Darinrain bowed deeply as he, too, left, but not before issuing me a swift smirk.

I turned to Notien and beckoned her over to me. "Bring a Healer," I whispered to her.

"He will not allow anyone to help him," Notien whispered back, glancing over my shoulder at Avenlae.

"I won't allow him to refuse medical attention," I responded. Notien raised an eyebrow but nodded and followed the others out of the tent.

"I am fine," Avenlae grunted, lifting his head and looking me in the eye. The veins popping in his neck from the strain of holding himself upright told an different story.

"Like hell you are," I snapped. "What were you thinking?"

"He called you *it*."

"And why the hell do you care?" My anger broke through my numb denial in the blink of an eye. "You thought you could just pick a fight with the damn General of the Queen's Guard? What made you think *that* was a good idea? Everyone expects me to take over leadership of this tribe, which means that you, too, have a responsibility to these people since they are apparently able to smell some kind of mate-bond between us. And, of course, your first action in this new role is to threaten the General! The one who still has the respect of the entire Guard! You realize I can't do anything for this tribe without the strength of the Queen's Guard behind me, right?"

Avenlae swallowed but did not answer me.

"But again, what do you care? Until this moment, you couldn't *look* at me. So that mate-bond can't mean much to you anymore, can it?" His eyebrows furrowed, but I kept going, unable to allow him to respond. "You can blame me for Novissime's death all you want, Avenlae, but it won't stop the pain you feel. I—I didn't want her to die. She—she put herself in front of me. And I couldn't react in time. But you can't blame me for that! You can't hate me for something I cannot change."

Avenlae shook his head. "No, Xai—"

"*Don't* call me that!" I raged as angry tears stung my cheeks. "You aren't the only one who grieves for her, you know? You're not the only one allowed to feel the pain of her death. And how cruel of you to ask me to help her when—when we both knew she was already dead. How horrible of you to put that thought, that guilt into my head! And then to just leave me there, alone! Like you have done this entire time! I *needed* you, Avenlae! I have always tried to help take away the pain of your trauma, but when it was my trauma that I couldn't control, you were gone! Probably because you wished it was me who had died instead!"

"Xiaye, *stop!*" Avenlae shouted, the effort making him wheeze. He slid down the support beam, gasping and raising a trembling hand to his chest, finally collapsing to the floor. Fear cooled the heat of my anger as I knelt down to him, instinct taking over. A shadow spread underneath the black and gold beadwork that still lay over his skin. A small lavender blade materialized in my left palm, and I lifted it as I took hold of some of the beads. Avenlae gasped and raised a hand to stop me.

"Av, I have to see how bad it is," I said quietly.

He panted, unable to answer, but his hand slipped from my wrist as sweat glimmered over his forehead. I slashed the blade through several strings of beadwork, the clatter of the beads echoing in my ears as my eyes widened at the sight of his injury. The gash had only partially healed, and his torn flesh bled anew through sutures that had been ripped open. Purple bruising spread vine-like across his chest every time he took a breath.

I cut a length of material from the skirt of my dress and balled it up in my hand. I sucked in a breath, preparing myself. Pressing the cloth to Avenlae's wound, I gritted my teeth as he threw his head back and cried out in pain, his eyes screwed shut in agony.

"I'm sorry," I murmured, my left hand wavering close to his cheek. "I have to, Av. Just until the Healer gets here."

His voice whimpered behind each of his labored breaths. I cooled the metal filigree of the Creonex and spread my fingers carefully over the darkest part of his bruising, hoping the cold might slow the spread of the bruise. Avenlae's moonlight eyes cracked open after a few moments, and the trembling in his limbs diminished slightly.

"I don't think I meant to lash out," I whispered, guilt filling where anger and fear had once been. "I just—I don't know how to do this by myself."

He rested his eyes on me. "I ... I should have ... been there," he said between gasps. "But I do not ... know how ... to be."

"You don't have to know how. Just be with me," I murmured, moving the Creonex to the other side of his chest. Neither of us had any guidance on how to communicate or process the emotions of trauma and grief. They manifested themselves in our actions and words in ways that neither of us could explain but in ways we could empathize with. Neither of us said anything more. But we knew everything, every dynamic, had changed. The glint in the silver of Avenlae's eyes as he looked up at me told me that, from that moment on, he would remain my only constant.

A rustling at the tent entrance announced Notien's arrival with a Healer dressed in white behind her. I stepped back as the older woman knelt beside Avenlae, stabbing a large syringe into the thickest part of his arm before he had the chance to react. He hissed out a breath through his teeth and muttered a word in *Y'araye*, earning him a glare from the Healer. She produced a rounded metal device to scan across Avenlae's chest as I stepped back and stood beside Notien.

"Thank you," I breathed, crossing my arms over my chest in subconscious sympathy.

Notien nodded. "That looks worse than he made it seem."

"You could cut off one of Avenlae's limbs, and he would still look me in the eye and tell me he's fine."

Avenlae's eyes flashed in my direction, but he made no response. He was too busy grinding his jaw against the discomfort of the Healer's device knitting his skin together. After mere seconds, the Healer attached the device to an apparatus on her belt and spoke in rapid Delfungaye to Notien.

"She is telling me about the injury to Avenlae's sternum," Notien translated, respectfully diverting her eyes from the Healer's gaze. "She said it is fractured, but the damage is minimal. Very painful, but not difficult to fix."

"How soon will he be able to participate in the duties of the Queen's Guard?" I asked.

Avenlae growled weakly at the Healer's answer. Notien's eyes widened slightly, and she translated, "If they were to leave it alone, it could take him upwards of three months to heal fully, and he would have to be rested the whole time."

I frowned. "What do you mean, if they leave it alone?"

"The Healer said there is a second option, if you want him to be stronger quicker. It just could be more painful."

"More painful than his sternum being broken?"

"She says bone growth is always more painful if rushed."

"I'm sorry, what?"

"I will be fine," Avenlae said, adjusting his position so that he could stand. The Healer shook her head, placing a hand on his shoulder to keep him down.

"The Healers developed a method of stimulating rapid bone growth," Notien explained. "That is what she is suggesting. I guess it involves"—she shuddered—"an injection of the serum directly into the affected area."

"Is that why Avenlae's protesting?"

"To be fair, Xiaye, I would also protest heavily against that treatment option. She is telling him now that the pain will be manageable with frequent doses of medication."

359

"Tell her to do it," I ordered. Avenlae's silver eyes met mine, and his pupils contracted with fear.

"I think I have more of a say in this than you, Xiaye," he hissed.

"No, I don't think you do. I need you to return to your normal strength as quickly as possible. There is still a war to be fought, Avenlae." I spoke to him in the most autocratic tone I could muster, wondering if he would respond better to that than to the sound of worry. He continued to stare at me, betrayed, but he said no more and did not resist the Healer as she helped him to his feet and led him out of the tent.

"Are you staying here?" Notien asked.

"No. We should change, and then I'll need you to accompany me as I make rounds throughout the encampment. I must ensure preparations for the migration are running smoothly and take stock of provisions and weapons for the Queen's Guard."

One well-trimmed eyebrow rose as Notien settled her round navy eyes on me. "Of course, Your Majesty."

"Don't, Notien." I shook my head as I led the way back into the soft light of the cavern. "I've let Darinrain get away with it, but when you say it, it feels too real."

"You can only escape reality for so long, Xiaye. At some point, you must accept what your life has become."

As I spent several long hours with the tribe that day, her words echoed in the back of my mind. Each time a tribe member lowered their eyes away from me in respect, it drove home that my rank in their society had changed. Their attentive focus on my questions and orders as well as their concise responses spoke of a level of respect they hadn't given me before. I felt a pang of guilt that I had their respect when I still knew so little about them. I had the scent of royal blood, but nothing else.

The suns had only just begun to sit a bit lower in the sky by the time food and supplies had been gathered. The only remaining tents were the large one in the middle of the cavern and a few of the Healer's tents, where patients would remain until the moment we left. Kaigar had stayed out of my way most of the day, finding things to do with the Queen's Guard and organizing units for the migration. Not that it bothered me—the farther I stayed from him, the better for both of us.

Before long, Notien and I had changed out of our ceremonial dress and into our armor. A welcoming relief spread through me when Notien handed me my rapiers to strap across my back. Here were the weapons I knew, the familiar blades I had trained to fight with. The crimson writing down the matte black blades spoke to me like the whisper of an old friend.

I left Notien with some members of the Guard and made my way to the large tent in the middle of the cavern. Alone and fighting off the creeping memories of the past few days, I thought over how to organize the tribe as we moved deeper into the mountains. I knew I would need several members of the *Hopyroque* to lead the flock since they knew the terrain so much better than the rest of us, but I had to ensure that we moved only as fast as our slowest members. I wouldn't lose any more tribe members if I could help it.

Sitting on the cool stone floor of the tent, I mulled over different formations, seeing each in my mind's eye. I could keep the weakest members of the tribe in the middle of the flock to remain protected. Many of the Queen's Guard would be stationed around the perimeter of the group to scout for any attacks from Sinivir or the Voxmor. I was relying on the falling light to help camouflage our movements and the rough terrain of the mountains to slow the progression of the Voxmor, but I couldn't be too careful.

A shoe scraped against the stone behind me. I whirled around, pulling one of my black rapiers from the scabbard across my back. Avenlae raised a hand, keeping his eyes on mine. The gash across his face was a glaring mark over his sharp features, and the top of a white wrap was just visible under his black warrior's vest, but his breathing appeared smooth. I took a deep breath and reached over my head to replace my rapier.

"I'm sorry," I said, struggling to keep eye contact. I didn't feel as if I had the right to look at him, especially with how harshly I had treated him.

Avenlae nodded once, then brought his other hand out from behind his back. My eyes widened as I recognized the clay color of a *j'guaya* seed.

"How did you ...?"

He gave me a soft smile, then cracked it open with his knife. His face tightened, almost a wince, but he hid it well as he handed me half the seed. He moved around me to lean against one of the tent's support beams as he ate his half, the gray juice trickling down his chin. No words passed between us as we ate, but there was a palpable stillness, an uncertainty. I glanced at him as I finished the last few bites of black pulp. Did he want me to worry about him? Did he expect me to still be angry with him? Was I *supposed* to still be angry with him?

"Are you still in pain?" I asked.

"Less," Avenlae responded.

I nodded, then looked around the tent as if a conversation starter might be written somewhere on the walls.

"Did you mean it?" Avenlae asked. "When you said you needed me, did you mean it?"

I tightened my grip on the rough skin of the *j'guaya* seed as if it were some kind of stress ball. "I did."

Avenlae lowered his head, a few long onyx braids falling over his shoulders. "I did not ... I did not know how to tell you I needed you, too." He studied his knuckles before tossing aside the skin of the *j'guaya* seed. "I heard

362

you, you know. The whole time you were gone. For a week, I was in and out of consciousness, but I could hear your voice telling me to get up. You told me you ... you could not do something without me."

I clenched my jaw, feeling as if there was something I was supposed to say to him. But all the emotions pressing in on my chest and throat—it was too overwhelming.

Avenlae spoke through my silence.

"Well, I cannot do *this* without you. This pain, this fear. I could not sleep last night because I knew I would see her again." His voice cracked with emotion. "But I was terrified for you to see me like that, to see my vulnerability. Not when you had the tribe to take over."

"Av, I have already seen the worst of you."

"But is that who you want with you when you lead the tribe?"

"I don't care," I said, shaking my head as I moved closer to him. "Am I really the one who you think the Delfungaye want to lead their people?"

Avenlae tilted his head to the side as he looked at me. "Why would they not want your power to protect them?"

"Are you not as afraid of it as they are?"

He raised a hand to cup the back of my head as his silver eyes searched my face. "Why would I be afraid of you, Xai?"

"You should be, after what you've seen of my power. You shouldn't have let me live."

"No. I will never be afraid of my *Le'eseia.*"

"This is the first time you've been able to look me in the eye for longer than a few seconds since the Queen died."

"It was never you I was afraid of."

"Why? After everything you have witnessed, everything I have done, why

363

did you let me live when I was controlled by Sinivir? Why are you not afraid of me?"

Avenlae's moonlight eyes darted between mine, his pupils contracting slightly with the whisper of fear. *You lied*, I thought, pushing against his arms so I could separate from him, from the pain building in my chest. But he wrapped his wings around me as he pulled me against his body. I began to protest, but he silenced me with his mouth pressed over mine, inhaling my scent as if he needed it.

"You want to know why I had to know if it is me you want with you as you take over the throne? Why I was terrified for you to see my vulnerability? Why I did not kill you to protect the tribe when you would have sunk your blades into my heart without hesitation? Why here, now, I am not afraid of you?" Avenlae's eyes glowed as he rested his forehead against mine. "Because I love you, Xai."

CHAPTER 34

"Well, I am just the lucky member of our little group!" Darinrain's voice rang through the tent, and I jumped away from Avenlae. "Nobody else has gotten to observe the romance between our mated leaders."

"How coincidental," Avenlae hissed, his ears pinned against his temples as Darinrain flashed him a smile.

"Charming, I think." Darinrain looked down at me. "I have a report for you. When you are ready, of course."

I blinked, passing my hands over my armor to ground myself and clear my mind. Darinrain gave me a knowing smirk as he watched me fumble for some kind of royal dignity.

"I, uh, yes, a report. On the Queen's Guard?"

Darinrain's eyebrows rose. "Yes, just as you asked."

"Out with it," Avenlae snapped.

"The Night Guard has fully changed shifts with the rest of the Queen's Guard," Darinrain said, lowering his eyes. "They remain along the outer edges of the cave. The bulk of the Queen's Guard will be rested enough to rotate shifts during the migration. Neither they nor the Night Guard has reported any Voxmor sightings within the mountain forest."

"That's because Sinivir's regrouping them," I muttered.

Notien and Saetyl entered the tent, Notien sipping from a crystal bottle of water and Saetyl checking behind her to ensure that a disgruntled Kaigar was still following her. Avenlae's feathers rustled as he raised them in an intimidation tactic when the General arrived. Kaigar looked between us, then, astonishingly, averted his eyes.

"Preparations for the migration are nearly complete," Notien said after glancing back and forth between Kaigar and me. "All that remains are the Healers' tents, but those collapse quickly."

"Good." I looked around at all of them. "I imagine the formation of the migration will not differ much from what you all are used to. Our weakest members will remain in the middle of the flock, and small units of the Night Guard will spread out on either side of the migration while the rest of the Queen's Guard surrounds the flock. There needs to be a scouting unit to ensure the safety of our destination before the tribe arrives."

"Those units have already been arranged," Kaigar grumbled.

"What is our destination?" Darinrain asked, arms crossed.

"I was hoping to discuss that with all of you. The mountain terrain will only keep the Voxmor at bay temporarily. It may only take a day for them to catch up to us, so we must keep moving."

"That is not something we can easily pull off with the entire tribe," Notien said.

"I'm aware." I looked at Darinrain. "Any chance the *Je'quiet* would know of some well-hidden location where we could lie low for a while?"

Some of the light faded from Darinrain's eyes as he shifted uncomfortably. "If they did, I would not know. What was left of the *Je'quiet* was slaughtered during the Voxmor attack."

I let out a soft gasp. I wanted to show him sympathy, but something told me the warrior in Darinrain would be too proud to accept it. To my surprise, Saetyl spoke up next.

"There are always the Icelands."

Silence met her words. Mine out of curiosity since I had thought most of Silvacastra was warm and tropical.

"We would not survive that far north!" Notien said, shaking her platinum bob.

Avenlae shrugged. "Neither would the Voxmor."

"Great, we go to the Icelands, and everyone dies. Us, the enemy, everything!" Kaigar growled, glowering in Saetyl's direction.

"Is there no way we could temporarily adapt to the colder temperatures?" I asked.

"It is not only the freezing temperatures we would have to contend with," Notien replied. "The weather is severe that far north. We are meant to fly, but not one of us will be able to fly in winds as strong as those in the Icelands. You may be used to walking as one raised by humans, but the rest of our people do not have the endurance to move on foot for so long. The Icelands are a desolate place—nothing survives up there."

"That may not be entirely true," Darinrain said. All eyes turned towards him. His jagged *Je'quiet* tattoos glimmered across his skull as if preparing to tell their own story. "Of everything my parents tried to teach me as an heir to the *Je'quiet,* I remember nothing more clearly than the Fabled People of the Icelands, the *Sloviyankae.* "

"That is all it is, boy," Kaigar said. "Just a legend."

"My brother always said legends are mere exaggerations of simple truths." Darinrain looked me in the eye. "It is not much to go on, but it suggests that a lost ancestor of the Delfungaye found a way to survive up there. If that is true, then there may still be someone out there who can help us and offer the tribe sanctuary."

"Do you have any reason to believe that these Fabled People of the Icelands are real?"

"Just over twenty-four hours ago, Xiaye, part of the Queen's Guard saw the Fifth Creator in the flesh. I do not think there is any reason not to believe the legends told by the *Je'quiet.*"

"Fine. That will be our final destination."

"And if you lead us into the Icelands and there is no one there to watch us die?" Kaigar hissed. "What are we to do then?"

"I will leave you to watch over the tribe on the outskirts of the Icelands while I lead a unit into the worst of it in search of the *Sloviyankae.* Someone has to be left who can keep these people safe. If it is not me, then it should be you."

Not a word of resistance was uttered. Despite the tension between the General and my team of warriors, everyone knew what I said to be true. No one else within the tribe was capable of ensuring the ultimate survival of the Delfungaye.

After a moment of stunned silence, I turned to Notien and Saetyl. "Gather the tribe. I should address them before we leave."

The last rays of the suns' light sparkled against the silver feathers of the *Laizuteek,* glistened along the smooth black sparrow wings of the *Fyr'aeset,* and were absorbed by the matte black of the larger feathers of the *Hopyroque.* Every

Delfungaye tribe member stared expectantly up at me, their silence as loud as the scream of the Voxmor. I tried to calm my trembling fingers and gather my thoughts through the fog of anxiety. Avenlae stood next to me, and Notien, Saetyl, Darinrain, and Kaigar stood a step below me, facing the tribe. *They need to accept you,* a voice whispered in my mind as I looked into the silver, gold, and navy eyes of the Delfungaye people. *Make them accept you.*

I swallowed my fear, then spoke. "I owe you the truth. After all the pain and suffering you have been forced to endure, you all deserve as much. My ascension to the throne is not a choice but a duty, one that many believe will lead our people to victory in the war against the Voxmor. But I cannot offer false promises or reassurances. For this is not a war against the Voxmor, but against Sinivir, the Fifth Brother. This has become a war between Creation itself and one of its own Creators."

I paused a moment as whispers spread through the crowd, fueled by fear and uncertainty.

"The future of the tribe is now mine to decide. Time will judge my actions, and now it's up to you to follow me or part ways. But know this—should you choose to stay with me, I will give everything to protect our people and seek vengeance against the Creator who turned against us. I will not turn away from the fight any longer. Sinivir's Voxmor have taken everything from Creation, but I will not allow them to take more from you! The blood of the Delfungaye will not be on my hands. To ensure this, I have decided to lead the tribe further north to protect the more vulnerable among us. If you choose to stay behind, I will understand and will part with you in hopeful spirits. Either way, a decision must be made quickly, for the Voxmor already know the cave's location."

No one spoke. There was just the rustling of wings as they looked around at each other, fear evident in their eyes. Might they all reject me? I couldn't blame them—my words had been less than comforting and hardly confident.

The crowd parted in front of me as someone approached the raised stone platform. Then Notien, Saetyl, Darinrain, and Kaigar respectfully averted their gazes as the *Matri Me'leiv* stepped forward, making her way gracefully up to me as the beadwork across her wings and chest clinked together. I could see the lines across her golden face, but her watery navy eyes held bright youth within their depths.

"You have many names," she said, her soft voice echoing. "Daughter of War, Child of Creation, *Creovis*—Xiaye. To which name do you respond?"

My eyes traced the lines of her face as I thought over her words. *That answer has never changed.* "My own."

Slowly, the old woman smiled. The *Matri Me'leiv* whirled away and called to the Delfungaye people, her arms outstretched, her voice strong and joyous. They responded back to her in kind, their voices reverberating against the stone.

"They are praising the Queen," Avenlae whispered in my ear.

"Novissime?" I asked.

He shook his head. "You."

As soon as he said it, a roar echoed throughout the cavern as the entire Queen's Guard crossed their arms over their chests in unison and knelt towards me. Saetyl, Notien, Darinrain, and Kaigar each turned and copied the bow. Avenlae stepped forward and crossed his arms as well, but I stopped him with a hand on his cheek.

"They will not bow to me," he hissed.

"They won't have a choice," I responded, coaxing him back to his feet. The Delfungaye still repeated the phrase the *Matri Me'leiv* had spoken to them, *Ayat'ri s'lo Vyslae!* The aged spiritual leader waved her arms to silence the people and spun to face me, her arms still raised above her head. Her navy eyes flicked between Avenlae and me before she said, "Praise be to the Queen."

The *Matri Me'leiv* lifted her wings so the wing joints pressed against each

370

other and bowed forward, her palms open as if in offering. Behind her, in a wave that rippled from the stone platform to the cave entrance, the entire Delfungaye tribe lowered themselves into her stance. I glanced over at Avenlae, whose eyes widened. He had been thrust from isolated Mercenary to mated leader of the very tribe that had shunned him.

A scream sounded in the distance. Fear settled over the tribe as each member rose and turned to face the cave entrance, their ears raised high. The warmth of the tribe's acceptance evaporated, replaced by the cold grips of terror as the violent splintering of tree trunks steadily grew louder.

"Get them out of here!" I shouted to my team, and Kaigar jumped into action, calling out orders to the warriors who stood along the outskirts of the crowd.

"Just go! Get into the air!" I yelled as I jumped down from the platform, spreading my wings to take off.

"Xiaye!" Avenlae called behind me but I didn't break stride. My power was the only weapon the tribe had to stall a Voxmor attack. Taking to the air, the rustle of flapping wings behind me roared like wind in a storm. What little light there was from the setting suns was extinguished in the flock of Delfungaye that burst from the cave. I dove into the alexandrite trees, twisting through the large, knotted branches, one thought driving me forward: *get to them first.*

"Xiaye, wait!" Avenlae called after me again, forcing me to stop and whirl around midair.

"No, Avenlae, you have to leave with the tribe."

"I am *not* going to let you face the Voxmor alone." Avenlae shook his head, his braids flying. Behind him, Darinrain glided to a stop, his staff drawn and held out defensively.

"You're not strong enough to fight them," I said. "The tribe needs you—they need someone to lead them away from here, and now they'll follow you."

"I cannot—I cannot lose you!" His voice was desperate as he shook

371

his head once again, his silver eyes wide under the rising moonlight. Another screech sounded behind me, much louder than the first one. I dove forward, grasping Avenlae's jaw in both of my hands and kissing him fiercely.

"*I* can't lose *you*," I whispered, pressing my forehead against his. "And because of that, I need you to go. Now!" I shoved him away from me and into Darinrain's arms. With his injuries, there was nothing Avenlae could do to fight against Darinrain as the latter began to pull him back towards the flock of Delfungaye that were organizing high above the cavern. I dove back into the trees, determined to protect my people.

"Come back to me, *Le'eseia!*" Avenlae's voice reached me through the sound of the wind roaring in my ears.

"I will," I breathed as I came to a stop once again, watching as the trees trembled before me. I reached over my head and unsheathed my rapiers, bright red forks of energy crackling down their black blades as my wings ignited.

The first Voxmor hurtled through the undergrowth, and one strike of my power sliced its head clean off. Two more vaulted themselves up the trunks of trees on either side of me. Their tentacles extended as they opened their mouths wide, fangs gleaming. I spun out of the way of their leaps, swinging one of my swords in a wide arc so that my blade sliced into the throat of a Voxmor. Its body collided with the second Voxmor in midair, and I sent a jolt of energy into it. They tumbled down into the undergrowth as the tree trunks surrounding me slithered with the white-scaled creatures. Their hisses filled the air as their serrated tails clicked together, a cacophonous clanging in what should've been a peaceful night. I whirled around, trying to guess which Voxmor would attack first.

Finally, one leaped at me from behind, and I was just able to shoot a ball of energy at it in time, its serrated tail missing me by mere inches. The action of the lone Voxmor set off the rest of the hive, and screeches sounded from every

372

direction as they dove from tree to tree, nothing but animalistic hunger in their jet-black eyes. I swerved around, slashing where I could with my rapiers and sending out bursts of power to slow the attack. I pushed myself off the bodies of the Voxmor I killed to change directions fast enough to stay out of reach of the next wave. I felt their black blood as it dripped over my arms and splattered against my face with each new kill. But the screaming did not stop. The attack did not slow, and panic rose in my throat as I felt the burn of fatigue beginning in my muscles. One misstep, and I would be dead.

With a thrill of desperation, a plume of violet smoke burst from me as I yelled, "FREEZE!" into the night. The smoke expanded out from my body like a shockwave, and the Voxmor froze, some of their bodies still extended in preparation for jumping. An eerie silence descended upon the forest, and the night became as dark as it was meant to be, with dissonant stars twinkling in the sky above. A soft breeze danced through the leaves of the trees, twirling around the frozen bodies of the Voxmor.

Then came the sound of something moving slowly through the undergrowth, and a hiss slithered its way up to me. I knew the Voxmor that slunk along the ground before I dropped out of the air—only one could evade the Creonex's influence. The Voxmor queen began to weave her head back and forth as soon as my feet crunched against the dried leaves of the forest floor. A scream was building deep in her throat, the kind of scream that pierced a person's mind and made their ears bleed. Her head vibrated as her frill expanded, and her growl rose in pitch.

"*Vindicta!*" I called to her. Her growl was cut short and her head stilled. The Voxmor queen stayed there, poised as if ready to attack. Returning my rapiers to their scabbards, I crept towards her, careful to keep my movements slow and controlled. I raised my left hand to Vindicta, the filigree of the Creonex glinting softly. Gradually, the Voxmor lowered her head, her onyx eyes never wavering from where I stood until her nose was a few inches from my open palm. I took the final step towards her, my palm flush with the smooth scales just above her upper lip. The pupils of her front two eyes shrank, revealing the prism of color in her irises.

"Find me," I instructed her. "Bring me an army, and I will release you. I promise."

Incoherent whispers flitted around me, getting louder and louder until a word materialized in my mind: "YES."

CHAPTER 35

Trees rippled below me as I wove around the peaks and falls of Silvacastra's mountain range. The world was plunged into gray as the small blue moon rose above the horizon. Vindicta had let me go, unbeknownst to the new hive she led into the mountains. I could only hope some part of her would remember what I had asked of her. It was a deadly risk, gambling on the mind of a sole Voxmor. But if I was right about the hive queen, it could mean the difference between survival and annihilation.

There was no sign of the tribe as I flew deeper into the range. *Idiot,* I scolded myself, *jumping to sacrifice yourself without ever discussing the location of the migration's first stop.* Strategically, I would've chosen to keep the migration high above the mountains to cover more ground—it would offer more time for the Delfungaye to recuperate between flights, as the Voxmor would be severely hindered trying to navigate the landscape. But in the dark, with mist and clouds circling the mountain peaks, I could see nothing of the sky above me.

Come back to me, Le'eseia! Avenlae's words echoed in my head, and the violet filigree of the Creonex warmed suddenly. I stopped midair, my hair flopping over my shoulders, staring at my left hand as the Creonex glowed a soft lavender. Something stirred within my chest, a power that was *new*.

The more I focused on Avenlae, on returning to him, the more volatile this new energy became, compelling me to release it. *The Brothers utilized their Creonexes to traverse between each other's Creations ...*

I raised my hand, trusting the instinct that was driving the power. A sparkling beam of violet light burst from my palm and cracked open the air. It shattered like glass, and trails of light encircled the jagged edges of a portal. There, on the other side, was Avenlae, leading the tribe high above the mountains. I breathed the scent of the wind that twirled through the portal, my heart leaping. *There's still more to discover with this Creonex.*

I dove straight through the portal, tucking my wings in as if the jagged edges were sharp as broken glass. A solemn silence fell below me as I soared above the slipstream of the tribe, and the reflection of the portal's light faded on the wings of the tribespeople. I sent a pulse of energy out along my feathers, and they ignited into violet flames as vibrant as a bellflower. A chorus of whistles and tribal calls floated up to me as Avenlae twisted midair, gliding with a soft smile of relief.

Stern commands in the native Delfungaye tongue echoed around the tribe, and the celebratory calls were quickly stifled. Catching sight of Kaigar's glare from the back of the ranks of the Guard, I extinguished the fire from my feathers, beating my wings a few times to move over the middle of the migration.

I held my position above the tribe for the rest of the night, glancing around the outskirts of the formation to ensure no one fell behind. Children transitioned from huddling down on their parents' backs to gliding along the air currents next to them, and the speed at which the tribe flew was adjusted as necessary to prevent fatigue. Here and there, members of the Queen's Guard would fly in a wide arc around the flock as they changed shifts with the units that would fly ahead, behind, and on either side of the tribe. Many would pass within feet of Avenlae towards the front of the migration and Kaigar towards the back to receive orders.

Healers still dressed in their crisp white uniforms were spread evenly throughout the flock, some helping to support weakened tribespeople already in their care and others handing out water to be passed along the circles of people around them. Members of the *Fyr'aeset*, with a few Delfungaye from the *Laizuteek*, carried extensive networks of netting that held what food the tribe had. Altogether, the tribe was able to migrate as one cohesive unit, and Avenlae had risen to fly alongside me, suggesting a place to rest just before the suns began to lighten the night sky.

"There is an old outpost of the *Hopyroque* still intact just north of us. It will be close quarters, but it will be a safer place for the tribe to rest than remaining out in the open in broad daylight."

"We'll stop there for the daytime, then. Order the start of our descent."

He repeated my instructions to the warriors who had been flying near him for most of the journey. Gradually, the tribe dropped through the clouds, and the full extent of the mountain range was revealed.

Frosted mountain peaks brushed the lowest clouds in the sky. Their jagged inclines were broken up by cliffs bursting with the twisted mountain trees of alexandrite and copper. The setting blue moon appeared to be cradled in the deep ravines carved out by whitewater rivers, angry currents ravaging the shorelines. The air was crisp with the smell of wet rock and spraying water as we neared the side of the mountain on which the outpost rested. Soon, the rumble of a waterfall overtook the wind in our ears, and I caught a glimpse of mist swirling high into the air far behind the skeletons of the buildings clinging to the cliffs.

The tribal outpost had fallen victim to the harsh climate of the mountain range. Tree branches engulfed parts of the structures that jutted out from the uneven rock, but they provided enough space for the tribe to set up shelters. The *Fyr'aeset* and Healers set to work divying up food and water. I didn't immediately join Avenlae, as a Healer approached him when we landed—his medication was due.

Instead, I helped pass along food and water to the exhausted tribespeople as they made short work of building shelters and took quick stock of our supplies with Notien and Saetyl. Kaigar and Darinrain approached us as units of the Night Guard began to surround the camp.

"The Night Guard will stand the first watch over the tribe until the suns have risen completely, and then the Queen's Guard will change shifts over the rest of the day until we take flight again," Kaigar said.

"Later in the afternoon, I will meet with some members of the *Hopyroque* to discuss the next place to rest," Darinrain said as he lifted his staff over his head to place it in its holder across his back. "For now, I need to eat and rest."

"You all do." I handed both men the last two bottles of water in my hand, then turned back to Notien and Saetyl. "Ensure our hunters will be prepared to find a more protein-filled food source by mid-afternoon. I want the tribe airborne again by twilight, but they will need much more energy to make it through the long stretches of flight it will take to get through the mountains."

"Are you sure they can keep up with this?" Notien asked. "Flying all night with only part of a day's rest in between?"

"The sooner we get to the Icelands, the sooner I can guarantee the safety of the tribe," I responded.

"Could you create a portal? Like the one you used to return?" Saetyl asked.

I shook my head—as soon as I had closed the portal, that part of my power went dormant. "I don't have access to that power now. I don't really understand it, and I don't think it's safe to experiment with it on the entire tribe at this time."

378

"Wise choice, Xiaye," Kaigar growled as he took off. I sighed, dismissing Saetyl, Notien, and Darinrain before anyone could say more. Breathing deeply, I made my way through the tribe to seek out Avenlae.

He sat on a branch just outside a small cream tent, watching as the sky turned a vibrant orange and pink. The mountains burned with suns' rise, their jagged peaks the same rust as the bark of the trees.

"Are you alright?" I asked as I lowered myself to sit next to him.

His canines glinted under his lips as he smiled. "You survived."

"I always have." I winced at the gash across his face. "Are you in pain?"

"Not now. I have been assigned my own royal Healer, and she is adamant about ensuring I receive medication at the correct hour."

"You'll need all the help you can get for the remainder of this journey."

His eyes closed as my hand rested against his jaw. "You have something else planned. I can feel it."

"I have a hunch. Time will tell if it is correct."

I sighed, letting my hand drop. "The safety of the tribe is paramount. I don't have the luxury of planning complicated strategies. I only have hopes, risks, and determination. Oh, and the freezing temperature of the Icelands."

"Here's to hoping for once Darinrain knows what he is talking about."

I stood, ready to head towards the shelter and some long-awaited sleep. "You know you'll have to learn to trust him, right? He's the last of the *Je'quiet,* so I'll have to turn to him for advice from now on."

"That does not mean I have to *like* him." The claws on Avenlae's wing joints scraped against wood as he used them to pull himself up. The tent was tiny, just big enough for a simple bed of leaves to be placed in the middle. I collapsed onto the makeshift bed, relaxation spreading through my body. Avenlae lay down beside me, trying not to wince as he adjusted his position to lie more comfortably.

His calloused hands tickled my skin as he ran them over my shoulders and collarbones, starvation having made them prominent. After a moment's hesitation, Avenlae pressed a gentle kiss to my forehead and nuzzled against my neck.

"You still smell like me," he purred.

"Oh, good. I was worried I would begin to smell too much like myself."

Avenlae pulled me closer, holding me despite his hiss when my wrists bumped against his sternum.

"Hold on." I sat up, reminded suddenly of a burning question.

"Yes?"

"This mate-bond. You've said before it can be fulfilled. What does that mean?"

Avenlae's eyes opened wide as if my words had startled him. But he said nothing, staring at me like he was afraid to speak.

"How is it fulfilled, Avenlae?"

His throat fluttered as he swallowed, and he raised a hand to rest his fingers across my jaw. "Love, Xiaye. It is fulfilled by the declaration of love."

I love you, Xai. "Does—does that mean it's already fulfilled?"

"No. The declaration must be spoken by both mates in the bond."

"But you—"

"I can say the words all I want in English." Avenlae shrugged, then winced at the movement. "They mean nothing if they are not in *Y'araye.*"

I studied the shine of his eyes. "What are the words, Av?"

Another flash of anxiety constricted his pupils. *"Lae fleuscythe akeimun."*

The sound of his tongue forming those words, the rumble of his voice speaking his language—it was more beautiful than the birdsong of the Delfungaye language.

"Say it again."

"You have to understand something first, Xai. The human part of you can speak the words of love to whatever and whoever you want, for you will experience only temporary pain should you part from that which you loved. For my tribe, the *Y'araye,* it is more powerful than just words. Once spoken, the mate-bond becomes a *lyceliah*—a life bond. You can choose to walk away from me if you wish, but I …" Avenlae's voice faltered, only for a moment. "I who have spoken the words will never be able to choose another."

I caressed his cheek and jaw with my hand, spreading my fingers through his wavy onyx hair, and watched as his face relaxed. My mercenary, my warrior, my protector—my mate. Never again did I want to feel as if a chunk of my heart had been cleaved out of my chest with him gone. He was all I had left, my constant. Fear faded from my mind as I whispered, "Say it again."

Avenlae stayed silent for nearly a minute, his eyes darting between mine. With a deep breath, he said, "*Lae fleuscythe akeimun.*"

Carefully, with a broken accent, I responded, "*Lae fleuscythe akeimun.*"

The effect was shocking and immediate. Avenlae's pupils dilated completely as his muscles tensed, and suddenly, I could feel his pulse—not through his skin but through his being. I could sense him, his love, his relief, and the dull ache of his pain. I could feel the *lyceliah,* this cord that bound us together.

I touched my forehead to his, listening to his breathing calm and feeling his breaths on my cheeks. "I love you too, Av."

Over the span of three days and three nights, the tribe traveled through the increasingly unpredictable climate of the *Fae'oteek* mountain range. The screams of the Voxmor didn't follow us into the mountains, but that offered little peace.

The Voxmor were intelligent enough to remain silent for an ambush, and the fear of another attack kept the tribe moving. In the back of my mind, I wondered if Vindicta was tracking the tribe because *I'd* ordered her to, or because Sinivir *forced* her to. I spent countless hours in the sky strengthening the influence of the Creonex and reaching for the power that created portals. If she did come to me, I would be ready. Whether or not I could control her, I would be ready.

Halfway through the fourth night of travel, the strength of the wind became too much for the tribe to fly as one unit. Saetyl and Darinrain directed us down to a final waystation tucked deep into a crevice on the side of a small mountain. The tribespeople huddled close together, passing out blankets to protect themselves against the wind roaring on either side of the mountain. Ahead was a sloping landscape of pure white that glowed in the moonlight, the stars above hidden by the swirls of snow. None of the Delfungaye had seen snow before, and their silver, golden, and navy eyes were wide with a mix of fear and curiosity at the opaque landscape before them. We had made it—before us lay the bleak and unforgiving prospect of the Icelands.

CHAPTER 36

I stood towards the front of the waystation, the wind whipping my hair across my face. I was wrapped in the thick black skins of creatures Saetyl called *kreeleurs* that hunted throughout the mountains. Their hide protected me from the worst of the cold and wind, but I still felt the icy bite on my cheeks.

"This waystation marks the beginning of the Icelands," Saetyl said as she walked up behind me. "It was meant as a warning for where our tribe's borders were."

"Did your people never make contact with the people of the Icelands?" I asked. "Surely there were rotations of warriors out this way."

"There were rumors that something moved within the white of the Icelands. But that was it. Nothing more than rumors."

"I hope not," I whispered, following her gaze to where the world seemed to disappear into solid porcelain.

"This is where the real adventure begins, is it not?" Darinrain boomed as he joined us, his staff in his hand and a black scarf wrapped around his head and neck. "This is where legend becomes reality."

"Your enthusiasm is nauseating," Avenlae said. The gold hilts of his swords glimmered in the fires started by the tribe behind us. He also had donned a black scarf over his head and across his face.

"If you die, Darinrain, at least you will die a happy man," Kaigar growled behind us. I turned to face him as he and Notien joined our little group. Notien moved up to me, carefully wrapping a white scarf over my head and neck, exposing only my eyes.

"We should probably leave before one of us stabs the General," she whispered to me from underneath her gray scarf. She then moved to stand next to Saetyl, who gingerly adjusted the scarf around Notien's face, murmuring something about the wind burning her cheeks. I watched them, then turned back to Kaigar.

"If we do not return within the week, move the tribe as you see fit."

The General huffed. "Such specific instructions. And what if the Voxmor get too close, and I have to move the tribe before that time? How will you find us then?"

"I have my ways."

"It is unlikely the Voxmor will get much closer given the cold," Avenlae said.

"But not impossible," Kaigar snapped. "I will move this tribe if I believe our safety is at risk. I hope those ways of yours work to get you back."

Without waiting for a reply, Kaigar turned around and returned to the huddled tribe, the dancing light of fires reflecting off his metal wing.

Darinrain scoffed. "I have to say, a journey into the white abyss of the Icelands seems delightful compared to more time spent under *his* command."

Notien and Saetyl murmured words of agreement as I waved for them to gather closer together. "Does everyone have food and water?" I asked, and they all nodded, gesturing to various packs and bags slung across their shoulders, waists, and backs. "Good. I don't mean for this part of our journey to take long.

384

If we can't find any sign of the People of the Icelands within the first few days, we turn around and head back to the tribe. We're not meant to survive out there, and I don't want to hurt our chances by wandering aimlessly."

"There is not a lot of information to help find the *Sloviyankae* other than some kind of archway that marks the start of their southern border," Darinrain said, "From what I have gathered from your tribespeople, Saetyl, and what I know of the legend, that archway should not be too far north from here. There is no reason to look for footprints in the snow, as the wind will cover them as soon as they are made. But I would look for unnatural structures in the snow and any signs of movement, as I believe the *Sloviyankae* will likely have warriors guarding their borders just like we do." His navy eyes settled on me. "They may have split from the Delfungaye generations ago, but I do not think they will be much different from us."

"Alright." I turned back towards the snow, mentally preparing myself. "Take a moment to take stock of your supplies before we set out." I brushed a hand against the strap of my old backpack from Earth. Somehow, Notien had found it in the wreckage of the Delfungaye stronghold. Inside was enough nutrient-rich food to last a week if I rationed it well and five crystal bottles of water. It was an odd source of comfort to venture out into the dangerous unknown with this backpack. Its weight on my back was familiar, as was the musty scent of the bunker that still lingered within its threads.

"Will you be warm enough?" Avenlae asked, his silver wings appearing on either side of me as he extended them to wrap around my body.

"I will have to be since I can't put on any more layers," I said as I looked up at him, resting my head on the soft furs that covered his chest. "Are you sure you'll be able to keep up? I'm not sure if it's safe with your injury."

"I am not going to fight you in this."

I turned all the way around, one of my eyebrows rising at his tone.

385

"You are still injured. Even if you've gained some strength, you aren't back to normal. And, unless I'm mistaken, you'll be in a world of pain if you don't take the medication your Healer gives you."

"It will be worse if I am forced to sit here and wonder what has happened to you," Avenlae said quietly, lowering his eyes. "I will not go through that again."

I could feel his anxiety spike through the *lyceliah*. I couldn't fault him, for I knew I would be just as stubborn if I were being left behind instead of him. And this time, it would be much worse if he could feel my fear, anger, sadness, or pain.

A wisp of dark hair flopped out from under his scarf and waved in the wind. I reached up and tucked it back in. "I understand. Just promise me you will allow *me* to protect *you.*"

His silver eyes narrowed. "Now, Xai, how can you ask that of a warrior?"

"The love you two share is beautiful," Darinrain called, "but we are losing time, are we not?"

The black scarf over Avenlae's face shifted as he clenched his jaw. "I think you should worry more for Darinrain's safety than my own," he hissed as he followed me to join the others making their way down the last slope of the mountain.

I shook my head but did not answer as I hurried towards the rest of the team.

Darinrain had been right about the wind obscuring footprints as soon as they were made. Within an hour of our trek, I looked back to see nothing but swirling snow and the smooth white ground. Uneasiness settled in my stomach as the bitter wind dried the exposed skin on my face and froze tiny droplets on my eyebrows and eyelashes. We would have no easy way of navigating the Icelands and no way of knowing which direction we had come from. *What the hell have I led them into?*

A few times, we stopped because someone claimed to have seen something in the snow. Every time, there was nothing but the roar of the wind and the shifting snowflakes playing tricks on our tired minds. I could tell from the discouraged sighs of Notien, Saetyl, and Avenlae that they were quickly beginning to doubt the plan. Saetyl kept reaching out to assist Notien through the snow, as she was most unused to traveling on foot. Darinrain stayed ahead of us, his head darting around like a bird's as he watched for any change in the bleak landscape. Avenlae's breathing grew heavier beside me, but he did not slow down nor ask for a break. Whatever physical pain he felt wasn't intense enough yet for me to sense it, but his growing exhaustion was.

The suns began to rise, lightening the monotonous world. No warmth joined the light of day, no sign of the sky flickered above us, and no movement in the snow was easier to see now that the Icelands had gone from dark gray to pure white. I no longer had feeling in my feet or along my thighs, and I had kept my arms so tightly folded my fingers tingled. Tears from the fierce wind had frozen in my eyelashes and down my burning cheeks. My shoulders ached from keeping my wings held up so the snow didn't clump over my feathers as they dragged behind me. Next to me, Avenlae's breathing had turned into a wheeze, and Notien leaned against Saetyl for support as she struggled to move forward. Darinrain seemed to be the only member of the team left unfazed by the unforgiving nature of the Icelands as he continued on, his head darting this way and that.

I stopped, exhausted and sensing a dull ache in my chest that I knew was not mine but Avenlae's.

"Let's rest for a moment," I called out to the rest of the team. Avenlae's chest heaved as his eyes darted around, checking for threats. Notien did not push herself away from Saetyl but instead leaned even more heavily against her as she rested.

I pulled my left hand out from under my arm, regretting it immediately as the wind froze my fingertips. Closing my eyes, I tried to reach for my power, but the cold buffeted away my focus. *Make us warm,* I thought desperately, *just make us warm!* The smallest blue flame flickered to life along my finger. I held on to that little flame like a lifeline and let its warmth spread through my veins. With a deep breath, I forced out a jet of warm blue light from the Creonex, melting the snow in a perfect circle around me. Frozen earth lay deep below the snow, and my team stepped with relief onto the solid ground.

"If I knew you could do that, Xiaye, I would have let you lead the whole time," Darinrain said with a hint of annoyance.

"If I had known, don't you think I would've made this trek easier?" I said through gritted teeth.

"Whoa, Avenlae!" Saetyl called, darting forward. I turned to see Avenlae stumbling backward, a hand on his chest. Darinrain got to him before I did, catching his arm and keeping him on his feet.

"I am fine," Avenlae grumbled, but his ragged breathing gave him away.

"You never should've come with us," I said as I reached my left hand up, placing my fingers along his temple. Intense burning spread through my chest, tightening my muscles and making it almost impossible to breathe. Gasping, I wrenched my hand away from his temple, unable to cope with the pain. His head slumped forward, and Darinrain caught him before he collapsed to the ground.

"Get a fire started," Saetyl said to me as Notien rushed forward, digging through her bag. "If he's in shock, we need to warm him as quickly as possible."

I nodded, unable to take my eyes from Avenlae, his head cradled in Darinrain's hands as Notien removed a small crystal bottle and a roll of bandages from her bag. Panic fogged my mind as I searched for the now silent *lyceliah*. A few meager sparks flew from the Creonex as I tried to turn my focus to warmth and not the stillness of Avenlae's body next to me. Fear became frustration, and I suddenly sent a ball of red flames into the ground that raged along the dead plants.

"Too much, Xiaye, too much!" Darinrain called, trying to move Avenlae out of the spreading flames.

"I know, I know!" I gasped, thrusting my hand into the flames, shoving my panic down as deep as it would go. The fire turned blue and sedate as it reformed into a hovering ball in the middle of the circle. Heat radiated out from the sphere of flames, thawing my skin.

"I'm sorry," I said as I knelt beside Notien. She had opened the front of the *kreeleur* skin that covered Avenlae's chest and unwrapped his bandages. The wound was intact, but the deep purple bruising had darkened.

"Xiaye, can you keep him asleep?" Notien asked as Avenlae began to stir, groaning and panting. "I do not think he will let me do this while he is awake."

"Do what?"

"I have to rewrap his wound, but it has to be done tightly to provide stability to his sternum as it heals." Notien glanced up at me. "His Healer insisted on ensuring someone on the team could care for him."

I nodded and placed my hands on either side of Avenlae's temples. His silver eyes opened, and he looked up at me fearfully. "Xai, please—"

"Shh, Av, just rest," I said, thoughts of calm and peace spreading from my fingertips to his temples. Avenlae's face relaxed as his breathing slowed, and Notien unraveled the bandages she had pulled from her pack. Behind us, Saetyl began pulling some food out of her pack, settling herself close to the ball of flames and watching as Notien carefully wrapped the bandage cloth around Avenlae's chest. All the while, I focused on keeping Avenlae calm even though stabs of pain pulsed through his thoughts and into mine. To remain connected to him was to feel echoes of the pain he felt as Notien worked. When she pulled the wrap tight, I let my hands drop, gasping from the intense pressure.

"Did the Healer send you with anything for his pain?"

"Yes, but it is not as strong as the medication he was receiving with the tribe," Notien said, tipping a small crystal bottle and dropping a red pill into her palm. "It will take the edge off his pain but will not stop it completely."

"Anything is better than what he's feeling right now."

"Xai," Avenlae said weakly as I grabbed a water bottle from his pack.

"I told you not to come," I snapped, shoving the bottle and pill into his hands.

"Wait, Xai," he said as he looked past me and tried to push himself up.

"I knew you weren't strong enough to keep up! This is a result of your arrogant pride."

Avenlae's eyes hardened as he straightened his spine to look down at me. He did not break eye contact as he took a sip of his water and downed the pill. "If you were not so quick to anger, perhaps you would have realized where we are."

I frowned, slowly turning away from him to look around the circle of melted snow we all crouched in. Notien stopped mid-chew of a bite of *baute* Saetyl had handed her and began to look around as well.

"Darinrain!" Saetyl gasped, peering into the ice behind her. "What is this?"

Darinrain rose from his seat next to the sphere of blue flames and joined Saetyl and Notien in examining the ice wall. After a moment of silence, Darinrain raised his head and gestured for me to come closer.

"Can you melt this down more?" Darinrain asked as I bent to investigate what they had found. I could just make out the warped shape of a stone marker sunk into several inches of ice. I raised my left hand, pressing it against the ice, and the Creonex warmed against my skin. Steam swirled as my hand moved deeper into the ice, and the stone marker grew clearer. There was writing along its smoothed surface, the same swirly writing I had seen on the tattoos of the *Hopyroque* warriors.

The closer my hand got to the stone, the brighter the gold of the letters glowed. The instant my fingers came into contact with the marker, a jolt of energy raced up my arm and through my body, and the stone slab flashed as bright as the suns. Startled, we all jumped back, with Darinrain reaching out to save Saetyl from falling into the sphere of flames. Darinrain looked around, his ears up and forward.

"How did you see that, Avenlae?" he asked distractedly.

"I am a *Y'araye* mercenary," Avenlae grunted as he stood, rolling his shoulders. "I am always aware of my surroundings. I saw the shadow of that thing just before I blacked out."

"Xiaye," Notien whispered, looking over my shoulder. She raised her hand and pointed. I turned, barely raising my head over the edge of the snow. Before us, rising far above the desolate Icelands, stood a blazing golden archway created by two semicircular structures. For a moment, they did nothing but hang there, the final harbinger of warning in an unforgiving, deadly landscape.

"I think we may have found a sign of the Fabled People of the Icelands, Darinrain," Saetyl said.

"Their southernmost border," Darinrain whispered as he moved nearer to the edge of the melted snow and ice circle, mesmerized by the glow. Then his deep navy eyes focused on something, and his trance was broken as he reached over his head to remove his staff from where it was secured across his back. "Something is coming."

Notien pulled her thin scimitar from her belt as Saetyl spun her ax around in her hand. Pulling myself out of our melted circle of snow, I narrowed my eyes to discern what was loping across the frozen plateau from the middle of the archway. I reached up and wrapped my hands around my rapiers, pulling the black blades from their scabbards, the metallic sliding awakening the roar of power that crackled in my chest. Within seconds, the rest of my team had joined me. Avenlae stepped up beside me, his breathing still labored, but his eyes determined as he raised his wings, his claws facing the advancing threat.

The bounding shadow grew larger and larger as it made its way across the wasteland. Its details remained a mystery right up until it skidded to a halt in front of us, showering the team in a mist of snow and ice as it stopped its slithering gallop.

The creature towered over us, its six bowed legs covered in thick fur as white as the snow. Its skull was spread as wide as a hammerhead shark's, with four small beady eyes spaced out along the edges of its head. Large, oval nostrils flared up the middle of its skull, right above a mouth whose lips were parted by black tusks long enough to extend over its forehead, almost like pseudo-horns. A mane of wiry gray hair flowed down the creature's neck and back, shortening to a simple tuft that extended like a mohawk down the length of its tail. The tail itself was longer than the creature's lean body, and it cracked the end of its tail menacingly as a sharp clicking sound resonated from its chest. With a hiss, Avenlae darted in front of me, pulling off his scarf as he bared his canines, his ears lying flat as his long black hair flew behind him in the wind.

"Ashi y'gauyat!" a man's voice called from atop the creature. The animal was subdued immediately, and, shockingly, so was Avenlae as his ears perked up.

The creature lowered its head, revealing a slender man draped in an oversized trench coat the color of coal. The length of the cloak billowed out behind him as he leaped down from the creature's back, wing-like appendages from his back expanding out on either side of him to help keep him balanced as he walked over the snow. He lowered his hood as he approached Avenlae, speaking to him in the *Y'araye* language. A single braid of silver hair extended down the man's back, but his face remained covered by a black mask.

"I did not know anyone else could speak the *Y'araye* language," Darinrain told me, keeping his voice low and his eyes on the newcomer.

"Orders, Xiaye?" Saetyl asked, tightening her grip on the handle of her ax. The stranger's head whipped around to me, and he began to lurch forward, the claws at the edges of his bat-like wings pulling him through the snow. My power cracked in anticipation as violet forks of electricity zipped down my blades. This stopped the stranger in his tracks, his head cocked to the side.

He reached a hand up and removed his mask, revealing a face with skin that glowed iridescent. His angled coal eyes studied me as puffs of steam twirled out of three nostrils that rose over top of each other up the bridge of his nose, and long, slender ears swiveled around towards me.

"The Red Eye," he breathed. "The Mercenary." His black eyes slid over to Darinrain. "The Advisor."

"Avenlae," I said. "What did you tell him?"

"Nothing I did not already know," the man answered, his voice moderately high and his accent heavy around the vowels of his words. "You seek refuge?"

"We do," Darinrain responded. I shot a look at him, and he lowered his gaze, realizing he had spoken out of turn.

"You act as if he is wrong, Red-Eye." The stranger tilted his head again, opaque membranes sliding quickly over his black eyes. "Did you not come to the Icelands seeking out my people?"

"Your people?"

The man backed away from me, murmuring a language under his breath that was unlike any of the dialects I had heard from the Delfungaye. One of his wings rose over his head, and the claws wrapped themselves around the long hair of the creature's mane behind him. Each claw moved as if the man could control it individually. "Come!" he called back to us. "I will take you to them."

Saetyl, Notien, Darinrain, and Avenlae all turned to face me, waiting for my decision. I watched as the man used his wings to help him climb back up to his spot on the back of the creature's head. The beast snorted, a plume of mist bursting from its nostrils, and I flinched.

"The *gueirag* will not attack unless I tell her to," the stranger called down to us. "Come, we do not have much time."

I looked at Avenlae, sensing his apprehension calming. Whatever the man said to Avenlae was enough to make the Mercenary relax his protective instincts. I decided to take a chance and trust the stranger, as there was little else in the Icelands that could offer us more than a slow, torturous death.

Avenlae wrapped his dark scarf around his head and face again, moving towards the so-called *gueirag* as she sniffed and shook her broad head. Swinging my arms over my head, I sheathed my rapiers and followed Avenlae to the side of the creature. Notien, Saetyl, and Darinrain moved around to the other side of the *gueirag*, climbing up her legs as she lowered herself closer to the ground. Using her mane, I pulled myself onto her neck behind the stranger, placing myself in a defensive position to protect my team if the man became a threat. Avenlae stifled groans behind me as he climbed up to the front of her shoulder.

"Will you be able to hold on?" I called back to him as he stretched out his wings, using his claws to keep stable.

"Your Mercenary is wounded," the stranger stated.

"I am fine," Avenlae yelled up to the man. The *gueirag* began to move, heading back towards the glowing archway.

"Our doctors will help your Mercenary," the man shouted, but the loud clicking the *gueirag* made as she weaved her head back and forth made conversation impossible. Her six legs allowed her to slither through the snow, and she moved at an alarming rate, fast enough that the rest of us had to tuck our wings in tightly to keep from falling.

One second, we were nearing the archway, which soared so high above

394

our heads that the apex was obscured, and the next, the bleak white of the Icelands had disappeared, darkening to become a warm, humid tunnel carved into rock the color of limestone. The clicking of the *gueirag* boomed against our ears as she weaved into the tunnel, slowing suddenly and quieting her clicks as she realized where she was. The stranger lowered his hood and removed his mask, looking back at us as he directed the *gueirag* through the tunnel with one hand.

"You may loosen your hold now. She will move slowly through these tunnels as we near the city."

"The city?" Notien said as she pulled her scarf from her head, her blonde bob plastered against her dry, cracked cheeks.

"Ah, a Glider!" the stranger smiled, showing off four sets of curved canines. "My people have not had the honor of welcoming a Glider among us in generations."

"Are you going to tell us who you and your people are?" I asked.

"Patience, Red-Eye," the stranger whispered, lowering his face close to mine, membranes flicking over his eyes again. "I will show you my people."

"You can start by telling me your name."

With a tilt of his head, the stranger straightened up, watching us for a moment as the rest of my team removed their scarves and some of the heavier *kreeleur* skins from their shoulders. A soft golden glow flickered along the uneven walls of the tunnel, and I moved to look past the stranger. At the end was a warm light, and I was overcome with a feeling of welcome and comfort. *Safety.*

"What is that, Xiaye?" Notien asked me, her eyes darting between me and the end of the tunnel.

"They look to you so strongly for leadership, Red-Eye," the stranger said, crouching low over the *gueirag's* head as the top of the tunnel lowered.

"She has a name," Avenlae growled, flashing his canines. "And she has asked for yours too many times for you to ignore."

"Ah, the game is up, is it not, Mercenary?" The stranger grinned back at Avenlae as the golden glow of the end of the tunnel blazed against the man's opalescent skin. My jaw dropped as the tunnel's tight walls fell away, opening into the most complex underground city I could have ever imagined.

The stranger slid down from the *gueirag* and threw his arms wide, expanding his wings out to either side of him. "I am Havyeque, and I welcome you to the home of the *Sloviyankae.*"

CHAPTER 37

Before us lay an expansive network of buildings carved into a massive underground cave system. A sedate river clear as glass wove through architecture reminiscent of something plucked from a steampunk novel. The glow was caused by pipes twisting throughout the city, providing light and warmth, including the ground on which we stood. Golden light of small fires flickered through the rounded windows of residential buildings along the top of the cave's ceiling, and artificial light poured out of archways that served as both entrance and exit to the merchant buildings along the river.

Walkways stretched from wall to wall on several different levels, and the *Sloviyankae* people moved acrobatically across them, using their wings not to fly but to climb. Their black wings had evolved to be used as another set of limbs. Because of this, their clothing was tight-fitting with glowing outlines so tribespeople could clearly see who was around them during the climb. The base of the fabric was black, with the only difference between individuals being the design and color of their glowing outlines. Some were more elaborate than others, some more vibrant, some subdued. Each man had a tight silver Dutch braid down his back, each woman two, and they smiled and made eye contact with each other in a familiar way. As Havyeque led us along the river, it was obvious the *Sloviyankae* had been separated from the Delfungaye for longer than a few generations.

"We moved underground quickly after making the Icelands our home," Havyeque explained, gesturing as he spoke. "The environment aboveground is too harsh for us to survive. We were, however, some of the first of the ancient Delfungaye to make contact with the other worlds and universes, so a venture into life underground was not as difficult a transition as it may seem."

"Do your people remain in contact with these other worlds?" I asked him, watching the movement of the tribe around us.

"In a way," he said as he removed his trench coat, placing it over his arm as he walked. The outline of Havyeque's bodysuit was as golden as the pipes above us and coiled around the lines of his body. "We help other civilizations survive in hiding after the Voxmor attacks in all four universes."

"You never helped us," Saetyl scoffed.

"The rest of the Delfungaye did not need our help as desperately as the other worlds."

"How can you say that?" Darinrain snapped. "More than half of the Delfungaye species has been slaughtered by the Voxmor!"

Havyeque shrugged. "Yes, but the Voxmor never found us. Our Queen prefers to keep it that way."

"So you have been here, selfishly safeguarding your tribe, while our people have been dying fighting the Voxmor?" Notien spat. "I do not think your queen is one I will bow to."

"She is not your queen, so I would not expect you to." Havyeque glanced back at me. "You allow them to speak so freely, Red-Eye. I am surprised."

398

"I've never claimed to control their tongues, however incessant they may be," I responded, glancing back at my team in warning. I hoped the *Sloviyankae* would extend their welcome to the rest of the tribe, and offending our saviors wasn't a part of the plan.

"I, on the other hand, am surprised you allow him to continue to call you Red-Eye," Avenlae hissed into my ear, his eyes narrowing toward Havyeque.

Havyeque looked at Avenlae, who stood several inches taller. "She has not extended the courtesy of allowing me to call her by name. Am I not respecting her by referring to her only by how my people know her?"

"How do your people know of me?" I asked, gently pressing a hand against Avenlae's arm to quell him.

"The Prophecy of the Red-Eye."

"I'm sorry?"

"Our *visiocustos* know all of the prophecies ever told by the Oracle of Delf, the first of the Delfungaye. Your arrival among our people was foretold, Red-Eye. We have been looking for you in the Icelands for months now."

"You've been—there's an oracle?" I stammered, looking at Darinrain.

"The *Je'quiet* recorded the prophecies but never put much stock in them," Darinrain shrugged. "The reigning Queens never asked for that information."

"Ah, but I am sure your spiritual leader, the *Matri Me'leiv*, is familiar with this prophecy. To us, you are known as Red-Eye, Warrior Queen of the Delfungaye and Child of Creation."

That stirred something in my mind, the memory of the *Matri Me'leiv* asking to which name I answered. I frowned, wondering if the old woman would be willing to tell me more of the prophecy. However, my train of thought was cut short when Havyeque stopped and gestured towards a well-lit building whose entrance curved around an uneven formation of rock in the cave wall.

"Our doctors are in there," he said, then added, "For your Mercenary."

"I do not need a doctor," Avenlae growled.

I turned towards him, keeping my voice low. "You are injured. Don't make me order you to go in there."

"Do not ask me to leave your side right now." There was a jarring warning tone in Avenlae's voice, and his pupils contracted slightly as he lowered his silver eyes to mine. I felt a prick of his fear through the *lyceliah*—he didn't trust the tribe we had walked into. It wasn't that he wouldn't leave me, it was that he couldn't.

"Red-Eye, if your Mercenary does not want help, we should really continue on—"

Avenlae suddenly darted in front of me, one of his wings pressing gently against me to keep me behind him. The rest of my team each had their hands on their weapons but did not draw them. *Oh, what now?* I stepped to the side and saw Avenlae's hand wrapped around Havyeque's wrist and a knife held to his throat. Haveyque was frozen with his hand held out as if to tap my shoulder. Avenlae's ears were flat against his temples, and his voice came out as a hiss.

"Do *not* touch her."

Havyeque's jet-black eyes darted between where I stood behind Avenlae and the blade held close to his throat.

"I am sorry; I do not intend any harm to the Red-Eye."

"Avenlae," I snapped.

Avenlae's ears twitched, and he took his time sheathing his knife and stepping away from Havyeque. The other man rubbed his wrist, studying Avenlae's stance. I could feel the mood of my team shift—if Avenlae did not trust the man, the rest of them would also stay wary.

"Please continue, Havyeque. We must speak with your Queen," I said, figuring I should get the chance to speak with their leader before anyone on

400

my team caused irreparable damage. Especially since *none* of them appeared to understand a thing about diplomacy.

Havyeque nodded before turning to lead on. I stayed a few steps behind him, trying to distance ourselves. Avenlae stayed close to me, close enough that I could hear the soft clink of his scabbards as he walked. I stayed quiet as we moved through the city, remaining hyper-aware of where each member of my team was. *Keep the peace for just a bit longer,* I begged silently. As we neared the bustling center of the city, my team and I began to receive more stares from the passing *Sloviyankae* people. They were stares of curiosity rather than animosity, but it was still unsettling. Avenlae glowered back at the people as we passed, but they simply tilted their heads, angling their slender ears forward as they began to follow our little party through the winding path along the underground river.

"Should we let them follow us?" Notien whispered in my ear, her navy eyes darting around the walkways above us. I tried to look up discreetly, seeing that the *Sloviyankae* were also climbing along the walkways as nimbly as monkeys climb the branches of trees.

"There is nothing dangerous about their curiosity," I whispered back.

"Yet." She moved her hand closer to the hilt of the scimitar hanging at her hip.

I sighed, hoping the Queen of the *Sloviyankae* was gentle and kind. After everything Darinrain, Avenlae, Notien, and Saetyl had been through, it appeared all it would take was one misstep to set them off.

Finally, we reached the epicenter of the city, a gargantuan piece of architecture that seemed too extravagant to be made by the hands of mortals. A castle reminiscent of a Gothic cathedral stood in the middle of a moat the color of crystal. Across each flying buttress were moss and vines the color of blossoming flora in the spring. The arched windows emitted the golden glow of firelight, yet

401

every archway was outlined in the white glow of artificial light. Walkways led to and from the castle like strands of a spiderweb, each glowing with that same synthetic light as the archways. The peaks and falls of the palace mimicked the outline of the *Fae'oteek* mountains, and the dichotomy of the plant life and darkened color of the architecture spoke of the technological advances of the *Sloviyankae* people despite their spiritual belief in the Oracle of Delf.

The immensity of the castle demanded respect as we approached it, and I felt a fleeting feeling of intimidation the closer we got to its vaulted entrance. Doors two stories high opened just before we reached the threshold, and we were bathed in the sandy light of the interior. Our footsteps echoed on the smooth black marble floor, and it seemed as if even the sound of our breathing was bouncing off the high ceilings. Stalagmites hung off the highest reaches of the ceiling, as if the palace had been carved out of the cave itself. The walls were the color of limestone, and the loamy smell of moist rock was almost overwhelming.

Havyeque led us past a massive staircase into a room whose walls were as ebony as its floor. The room was devoid of color, except for a figure who sat at the back wall upon a throne of the purest white. The fabric of her traditional dress was as black as that of her people, but the design of the orange and blue glowing outline was far more elaborate. Delicate lines of turquoise coiled up her willowy body like the pattern of bark on a tree, with whorls of orange spaced along the natural lines of her anatomy. Her arms remained bare, her skin as opalescent as Havyeque's, but her slender neck was covered by the top of her dress. The material melded into an ostentatious headdress of the same colors illuminating her figure. The top of the headdress fanned out like the feathers of a peacock, but the shapes of the "feathers" reminded me of antlers. Turquoise extensions fell from the bottom of the headdress and cascaded over her shoulders like tentacles. The top half of her face was covered by a mask extending down from antler-like projections of her crown, her forehead a glowing aquamarine pattern, and her eyes and cheekbones gleaming tourmaline. The black of her eyes was made matte by the vibrancy of her glowing attire, and she greeted me with a hard, beady stare as we entered.

Havyeque spoke to her from across the room. I waited for some sign of when I should talk, but the woman was unreadable as she continued to study us with indifference. After a few uncomfortable moments of silence, Havyeque turned towards me to make introductions.

"Red-Eye, this is Klaecyia, Queen of the *Sloviyankae*. You may make your requests for your people now."

It was odd—he did not bow to the Queen or show her any sign of respect. Could it be that there was tension between the Queen and her subjects? Or was their sign of respect something less conspicuous than a bow?

I stepped forward, not knowing if I should bow to show her my respect. I didn't even know if she would understand the words I spoke, for she had remained silent since we entered the throne room. I lifted my chin and spoke as clearly and concisely as possible, hoping I didn't look as anxious as I felt.

"Greetings, Your Majesty. I am Xiaye, recently appointed Queen of the Delfungaye, and I come to you to request refuge for the combined tribes of the *Laizuteek*, *Fyr'aeset*, and *Hopyroque*. We've been driven out of our lands, and our survival depends on the peaceful integration of our people—"

"You have brought only warriors with you," Queen Klaecyia interrupted, her shrill voice cutting across me like a knife. "That does not speak of the peace you seek."

I narrowed my eyes, bristling at her harsh tone. "There is a war raging outside your boundaries, Queen. This war has driven the Delfungaye far from their homes, and—"

"I am aware of the war. My people have spent countless years helping the civilizations of our allied worlds survive the attacks of the Voxmor. This city, however, remains untouched. If I invite your people here, you will bring the war in with you."

"Your Majesty, respectfully, I don't think you and your people are as far removed from the war as you believe," I said.

"If you have spent so long helping your allies survive against the Voxmor, then where were you when the Delfungaye were attacked?" Saetyl seethed.

Queen Klaecyia looked down her nose at Saetyl. "We do not forget those who have wronged us, Climber."

I narrowed my eyes. "Are you telling me, Queen, that you knew of the slaughter of the Delfungaye, but you stood by and watched because you still blame them for the actions of their ancient ancestors?"

"Bad blood runs deep, Red-Eye. Or have you not noticed the treatment of your Mercenary?"

"Whatever grievances you hold, Your Majesty, the fact remains that what is left of the Delfungaye species is waiting just outside your borders. They are in dire need of your help. Now is not the time to reminisce on who wronged who, but instead—"

"You do not know our history, Red-Eye, so it is not up to you to decide what can and cannot be forgiven!" Queen Klaecyia snapped. "I have kept the peace among my people despite the war being fought around us for over twenty years! I have kept them safe by offering *only* supplies to our allies. I will not allow one poor decision to enter my people into a war they have remained untouched by."

"But, Your Majesty, the prophecy!" Havyeque protested.

"What becomes of the Red-Eye and her people is none of our concern."

"None of your concern?" I stepped closer to her, no longer worrying about respect. "When the Delfungaye species is extinct because you wouldn't lift

404

a finger, will it still be none of your concern? When all of Creation has fallen under the control of the Fifth Creator, and war comes knocking on your door, will that be none of your concern? You tell me your people are untouched by the war, yet you admit they have been helping other civilizations. Your people have seen the trauma of battle. They have been amongst those who have watched their families slaughtered in front of them, those who have lost everything. You're in extreme denial if you think that doesn't light a desire to fight back in their hearts. You cannot look upon that kind of suffering and remain *untouched*."

"My people can bear witness, but they do not have to experience it!" the Queen hissed.

"Who are you to say they haven't?" The sound of our argument echoed off the polished walls of the throne room. "What about those the *Sloviyankae* have met in their attempts to help your allies? The ones they have befriended? You think they haven't felt the pain of the loss of their friends?"

The Queen shifted in her seat, attempting to make herself appear taller. I walked all the way up to her throne, placing my hands on either side where she rested her arms. "You may sit here and deny that your people have felt the pain of war, but that does not give you the right to deny *my* people the chance to survive. I can ask you nicely or show you why your people know me as the Warrior Queen. You choose."

"You dare threaten me?" Queen Klaecyia began to push herself off the throne but was stopped by Havyeque's quick interruption.

"I would not, my Queen. The Mercenary is her mate."

The Queen froze, her black eyes focusing behind me. The flash of fear on her face told me Avenlae was poised to attack. The fact he had controlled himself this long was a miracle.

"Well, my Queen," I said. "Which will it be?"

The *Sloviyankae* Queen leaned back against her throne, a frustrated twitch of her eye beneath her mask. I didn't like forcing the issue, but I didn't have a choice. The safety of the Delfungaye would guarantee me time to plan a final attack on Sinivir and his army of Voxmor. And if the *Sloviyankae* really had allies amongst the other worlds, I would have access to my own army.

Finally, she nodded, only once. "Your people may find *temporary* refuge here. Havyeque will assist in the integration of the tribes."

"Good choice," I said, pushing myself off the edge of the throne and back towards my team. Avenlae glared at the Queen while Saetyl and Darinrain gave me grins. We had almost made it to the other end of the throne room when the Queen spoke again.

"Be warned, Red-Eye, if you bring the Voxmor to my people—"

"Then you will provide your people with the chance to avenge the friends they have lost," I called back.

CHAPTER 38

S eeing the look upon Kaigar's face when a portal from the *Sloviyankae* opened was worth every second I had spent in the Icelands. His one good eye widened at the bright crackling hole in the air between us, my reflection clear in the white of his damaged eye. The Delfungaye behind him didn't wait for his permission to move—the warmth radiating from the *Sloviyankae* cave was too inviting. Kaigar was buffeted this way and that as the tribe moved past him, glancing warily around the underground tunnel.

Havyeque had gathered a small welcoming party of the *Sloviyankae's* warriors, doctors, officers, and common tribespeople who met with the Delfungaye as they entered. There were many surprised looks and smiles as my people realized the *Sloviyankae* could speak all of their different dialects. This seemed to ignite a long-lost kinship. *Kreeleur* skins were readily shed in the comfortable atmosphere of the entrance tunnel, and the sounds of greeting grew steadily louder.

Watching the early interactions between the cultures made me wonder how far removed Queen Klaecyia was from her people. Her icy demeanor was the opposite of the warm smiles her people gave to mine as they led them into the city. Delfungaye Healers conversed with *Sloviyankae* doctors as they transported the sick and wounded to their medical building. Calm respect passed between the warriors of the two civilizations, and the eager looks that bloomed on my people's faces told me there was probably talk of a warm meal.

Kaigar finally approached me, overseeing the Delfungaye as they dispersed among the many pathways into the *Sloviyankae* city. "I will admit, you found the tribe refuge much quicker than I had expected."

"That is because she forced them to allow us refuge," Saetyl said, smirking.

"Their Queen didn't give me much choice, did she?" I muttered.

Saetyl chuckled and moved away to join Notien, who was deep in conversation with another *Sloviyankae* woman whose weaponry suggested she, too, was a warrior.

Kaigar raised his lone eyebrow at me. I sighed and said, "Queen Klaecyia of the *Sloviyankae* is not quite as keen to welcome us as her people are. She's terrified of war and is ready to blame us for bringing it upon her tribe."

"We have brought nothing but ourselves," Kaigar said.

"Keep a careful watch on our warriors, Kaigar," Avenlae said. "All that Queen needs is one excuse, and we will be back out in the snow."

Kaigar's eyes shifted between me and Avenlae. I didn't break eye contact, knowing the General wouldn't like taking orders from one who used to rank below him. To my surprise, however, Kaigar gave Avenlae a curt nod.

"I see the way the wind is blowing. I will ensure I am easy to find should you need me, Your Majesty." Kaigar gave me a swift bow and retreated to scope out the city. I watched as he left, the whir of his machinery lost in the sounds of the cave city. When did I earn his respect? Or was it fear that made him defer to Avenlae and my rank?

It took a moment for me to realize that it was just Avenlae and me alone who stood at the entrance to the *Sloviyankae* city. The rest of the tribe had scattered throughout the golden buildings and among the glowing *Sloviyankae* people. I looked over the edifices, hearing laughter, cheers, and general liveliness. It felt as if it had been years since I'd heard the sound, so it hit my ears like sweet harmony. Even so, nostalgia weighed as heavily on my chest as my old backpack did on my shoulders.

"We should find somewhere to stay," Avenlae said, his eyes scanning the cave system before us. I knew I should remain as alert as him, but my eyes felt puffy, my brain sluggish.

"I suppose we should," I agreed. I stepped away from Avenlae, not sure where I was going, but determined to find a bed. Fortunately for me, I chose to walk along the river again, and Havyeque came jogging out of a building whose sounds of laughter and aroma of ale suggested it was a tavern.

"Red-Eye! I am happy I have found you again. The Queen requests that you stay in quarters prepared within her palace."

"Does she? A change of heart, perhaps?"

Havyeque smiled. "More like an understanding of position. Shall I take you there now?"

"We can find our own way," Avenlae said behind me, flashing his canines. I bit my tongue, tired of his stubborn dislike of the *Sloviyankae*. Flashing a tight smile, I assured Havyeque that we would be alright before leading Avenlae along the bank of the crystal underground river. We walked in silence back towards the palace, passing by Delfungaye as they lounged in the entrances of buildings, conversing brightly with the *Sloviyankae*.

Clenching my jaw, I ran through different things to say to Avenlae as we walked. I wanted to talk with him about everything that happened, but I could feel his anger radiating from him. Although he had instincts at play that I couldn't

409

understand, I wasn't convinced he was incapable of at least controlling his attitude. I wondered if the tension in his silence meant that he could feel it, too—the soft rebuttal of the tendrils of the *lyceliah* that had so recently wrapped around us.

The quarters the *Sloviyankae* Queen had prepared for us were similar to what I would have expected in a human's bedroom. I studied my reflection in the polished black marble floors. A queen-sized bed was decked out in a fluffy white comforter with golden pillows and an ornate wooden bed frame. With the knots in my hair and the filth on my skin, I looked too dirty and disheveled to be allowed in such a pristine room. Even so, I was beyond caring. A large golden basin of water with a large red sponge floating in it rested in one corner of the room, its tendrils of steam inviting.

Stepping into the room, I allowed my backpack to slide off my shoulders onto the shined floor. Avenlae followed, his silver eyes scanning the room as I removed the scabbards from my back and the *kreeleur* skins from my shoulders. Finding nothing threatening, Avenlae closed the door behind him and reached to remove his own scabbards, lifting their straps from around his chest. A suppressed grunt of pain escaped his lips, and his arms shuddered as he attempted to lift them over his head.

"Let me," I said, crossing the room and holding my hands out. Avenlae dropped his arms and did not look me in the eye as I gently raised the straps of his scabbards over his head and placed them next to the bed. He couldn't hide the way tension left his shoulders when the pressure of the scabbards was removed.

"Are you okay?"

"As much as I can be," Avenlae responded, keeping his eyes averted as he loosened the front of his vest.

"Do you have medication with you to help with the pain?"

"I do."

"Are you going to take it?"

That was met with a stern look. I threw my hands up in exasperation. "Avenlae, I don't know what you want from me right now. I can see and feel how much pain you're in. But you refuse help. And you act like you need to protect me at all costs when you're not strong enough to do so. You're just so, so angry right now, and I don't know how I'm supposed to respond. I don't know what I'm supposed to do to help you."

Avenlae took a breath, and it seemed as if his entire being deflated. For a moment, it was as if I was back in his head, looking at the broken little boy who had just watched his family slaughtered in front of him.

"I am not angry," he murmured. "I—I am afraid."

I approached him, my frustration melting into empathy as I tried to find the right words to say to him. "I-I know a lot has happened. Everything has changed for you and the tribe for a second time, so I imagine there are a lot of… unknowns you're trying to process." When Avenlae didn't respond, I tried to soldier on, although I didn't feel qualified to console him.

"You've lost a lot in such little time. We all have, I guess. I mean, I've had to step up and lead this tribe that I didn't think would ever accept me, so I probably haven't been as… receptive to you this past week as I should have been." I sighed, shaking my head. "I'm sorry, I'm really not good at this."

"It is you I am afraid for, Xai," Avenlae whispered. "I *cannot* lose you. You are all I have left in this world."

He finally lifted his silver eyes, and the tears that threatened to fall shocked me into silence. The *Y'araye* Mercenary, reduced to tears at the mere thought of losing *me*—how could I mean so much to one person? The memory of the despair that sucked the life out of my body during my imprisonment surfaced. I meant that much to him because—because he meant that much to me. That was the power of the *lyceliah*, wasn't it? The embodiment of love, of its indescribable entirety. I had felt it long before I admitted it to myself or to him—I knew too well the pain he feared.

"Av," I whispered, raising my left hand, the violet lattice of the Creonex reaching for him. "Let me help you."

"You have been doing that a lot lately."

"Allow me to at least once more."

The silver in Avenlae's irises glistened in the soft artificial light of the room. He lifted his arms to rest on my waist as he pulled me closer, dark tendrils of his long hair brushing against my cheeks. I set my hand against his temple, and he closed his eyes, leaning into my touch. This time, I didn't transfer memories of calm, sweet happiness to take away his pain. What I did was more vulnerable—I shared in his pain. I showed him my own grief. I showed him that he was not alone in the suffering that he felt; there was one other person in the world who could understand the whirlwind of emotions that would hit him with such strength he couldn't stifle them. He held me as tightly as I held him, our tears of grief, fear, and shared trauma falling together.

There, in that unfamiliar room, in a completely different position from where we started, Avenlae and I found each other. It was so much more intimate to share in each other's pain than to lie together—it was raw and honest. There was no abrasive judgment, just salty tears on cheeks, gentle kisses, and the cold comfort of shared suffering. Avenlae's arms trembled as choking sobs wrenched themselves from his body, and I brushed the tears from his eyes as I guided his forehead to rest against mine. Gradually, the wave of emotions subsided, but still we held each other—the healing had yet to begin.

Wordlessly, I steered Avenlae towards the basin of water, taking care to remove the wrapping around his chest carefully. Warm droplets of water slid

412

down my arms as I lifted the sponge, tilting his head back so I could wipe away the dirt and old sweat that darkened his face. Avenlae smiled as he closed his eyes, allowing me to pour water over his hair, massaging his scalp, and running my hands down the length of the thick, soft strands as the braids slowly unraveled. I cleaned delicately around the gash down the middle of his face, noticing how his skin had already begun to knit together. With trepidation, I moved the sponge to his chest, wincing at how dark the bruise remained. Avenlae sucked in a breath and stilled as I moved the water over his tender skin, but he didn't resist me. The injury to his flesh appeared halfway healed, no longer an ugly gash but evolving into a pink scar from his clavicle to the end of his sternum. The black lines of his tattoos were only slightly disrupted by the growing scar. There was beauty in how the water sparkled over the deep coal black of each curve and swirl across his skin. Bruising from the fracture still darkened the alabaster of his skin, but, as with grief, it would fade with time.

Moments later, Avenlae had taken the sponge from my hand and dipped it back into the water. With his moonlight eyes on mine, he slid his rough hands underneath the *Laizuteek* wrap I had worn underneath the *kreeleur* skins. My hesitation must have shown on my face, for he leaned forward and pressed his lips against my forehead, right between my eyebrows.

"You are allowed to let go of the control as well, *Le'eseia,*" he whispered. "Let me care for you the way you care for me."

The permission for release brought new tears pricking the corners of my eyes. I took a deep breath and allowed Avenlae to clean the week's dirt and grime from my skin in the same tender way I had done to him. He ran his hands down through my hair, working out the knots and separating the tight waves as they soaked up the warm water. Avenlae's kisses were warm and reassuring against my lips as he massaged the tension in my muscles and cleansed my body of the reminders of the week's long journey. He then stood and moved to a small wooden table at the end of the bed, picking up two folded clothing items and turning them over.

"Courtesy of the Queen, I suspect," he grumbled, unfolding one to show me a black bodysuit with a red glowing pattern of wood twirling up the limbs and bodice.

"Is yours just as beautiful?" I asked, trying to suppress a grin.

Avenlae raised an eyebrow and unfolded the second black bodysuit. The glowing design was as silver as his eyes, but its lines were jagged and severe. It appeared Queen Klaecyia would view him only as a warrior and not as a Delfungaye leader despite the *lyceliah*. I shrugged and opted to dig around in my pack for a *Fyr'aeset* tunic to wear just for the night. I reached up and began to twist my hair into a rough bun but was stopped by the gentle pressure of Avenlae's hand on my wrist.

"Your hair must be braided here."

"Must be?"

"You are our queen, Xai. It will be considered an insult for you to wear your hair any other way, especially among the people we wish to ally with." He led me to the bed and sat me down between his legs. I faced the far wall, about to say I should go to find Notien, but I felt his hands begin to separate my hair into sections.

"You can braid?"

"Did you think my hair braids itself?" Avenlae chuckled softly, his hands moving as nimbly as Notien's did whenever she braided my hair. "I am sorry, though, I do not know the royal styles."

"Will it matter?"

"Not to the *Sloviyankae.*"

"Then it won't matter to me."

A relaxed quiet stretched over the half-hour Avenlae spent braiding my hair. When he was done, four fishtail braids extended from my hairline down my back, their delicate ends brushing against my waist. I brought a braid around my shoulder, running my hands down it to feel its smoothness.

"They're beautiful, Av," I said, smiling at him. I flicked the claw that was pierced through his septum. "Now, what about you? Should we give you some kind of updo?"

Avenlae wrinkled his nose and tossed his long hair over his shoulder. "They do not see me as a leader. My hair does not matter."

"Our people bowed to you."

"Our? I also heard you refer to them as *your* people when speaking with Queen Klaecyia. Do you claim us, then?"

"I have to. The Delfungaye don't have anyone else."

"They do not, or you do not?"

I leaned forward and pressed my lips against his in a long, deep kiss. "I have you."

I felt him smile against me as he placed his hands on my hips and lifted me to rest on his body. He lay back against the pillows of the bed, only a faint groan of pain escaping his lips. "You have me wherever and however you want me, *le'eseia.*"

"Is that so?" I lowered myself down, careful not to lay my full weight on his upper body, and tickled small kisses along the curve of a tattoo that ended just below his ear. A growling purr reverberated through his chest as he angled his head to allow me better access, running his calloused hands over my spine.

"Completely." Avenlae slid a hand up to my jaw and pulled my head around as he kissed me fiercely, desperately. *Well, that was easy,* I chuckled to myself as I allowed him to take control of the moment. I could feel Avenlae's pulse quickening against my chest as he used his free hand to press my body against his hips, as if we couldn't get close enough. Feelings of need feathered their way up my abdomen as I rubbed gratefully up against him, for he had not yet bothered to dress himself in anything for the night.

Avenlae lowered his head to my neck, sucking the skin along my collarbone and licking at the soft discolorations of bruises he left there. The *Fyr'aeset* tunic was pulled from my body as if the fabric had done something offensive, and Avenlae pushed me back against the pillows of the bed.

"Is this really the kind of activity we should engage in before you're healed?" I asked, a slight tremor in my voice as Avenlae moved tenderly on top of me.

"Are you really going to stop me?" Avenlae purred, the intensity of his silver gaze rendering my mind blank as he moved the attention of his mouth to my breasts.

And so, with his mouth otherwise preoccupied and mine incapable of coherent speech, neither of our lips passed protestations for the remainder of the night.

CHAPTER 39

I wasn't awoken by the warmth of the suns' rays across my skin or the sweet smell of morning dew. Instead, the brightening of the artificial lights above me brought me out of my sleep unexpectedly instead of peacefully. It wasn't until then that I realized how much I missed the smell of the forest and the natural light of the suns. I'd become accustomed to life within the Delfungaye's forest enough to feel the dull ache of homesickness as I rolled over to face Avenlae.

He took a long, deep breath as he began to stir, then paused, his eyebrows pulling together as he clenched his jaw. Sighing, I threw back the comforter, realizing Avenlae hadn't taken his medication the night before and feeling a dull ache in my own chest. *Damn lyceliah.* I stepped lightly to where our packs lay crumpled next to the door and rifled through water bottles, food, and bandages to find the pill bottle. It took everything in me not to jump right from where I stood back into the bed, for I hated the feeling of the cold stone floor against my bare feet.

Returning to the bed, I placed a pill into Avenlae's palm. His eyes opened slowly, his silver irises glinting sleepily at me as he turned to push himself up against the back of the bed. His hair flopped over his shoulders as he sat up, taking the pill easily without water.

"I was a little too preoccupied to take this last night," Avenlae said, stretching gingerly and rolling his shoulders. He began to lift his wings to stretch them but quickly learned that there was no room to do so. "I do not like it here," he added, his canines showing briefly under his curled lip.

"I know it's not ideal," I said as I moved to the other side of the bed, grabbing the bodysuit provided by the Queen, "but we are out of reach of the Voxmor for now. It's the best we can ask for."

"For as long as Queen Klaecyia allows us to stay," Avenlae grumbled as he rolled out of bed, finally stretching his wings straight out behind him. Their silver feathers brushed against the wall, even though he stood a mere foot from the bedroom door. He ran his fingers through his hair, preparing to braid it as he returned to the bed.

"We're supposed to be discussing that today. So, I should warn you to hold your tongue until you have thoroughly thought through your responses."

"I was not the one threatening the Queen yesterday, was I?" Avenlae raised an eyebrow at me as I zipped up the front of my body suit, the glowing red design aligning perfectly with the curves of my body.

"Touché," I muttered. Avenlae paused in his braiding, narrowing his eyes at me in confusion. "I did what I had to do," I continued, not bothering to explain the new word to him. "We all need to play nice now that she's willing to discuss the details of the tribe staying here. I have to persuade her to allow the Delfungaye to continue to take refuge here, even if I need to leave with the warriors to mount an attack on Sinivir and the Voxmor."

"Is that wise? Trying to attack the Fifth Creator with just the Queen's Guard?"

"Sinivir won't stop unless someone makes him. He will never quit looking for me just because I moved underground. I suspect he will have no mercy for any who stand in the way of his search as he seeks complete control over all Creation."

"And what makes you think you could succeed in this attack?" Avenlae asked as he tied off the end of his braid. "The Delfungaye warriors have taken a huge hit from the Voxmor attack in our territory, and even combined with the *Sloviyankae*, if we can convince the Queen to ally with us, you will only have an army of roughly two thousand warriors."

"I know not to underestimate the power of the Queen's Guard," I said, crossing my arms over my chest. "Besides, if I can gain Queen Klaecyia as an ally, I'll have access to all the civilizations she claims her people have helped over the years."

Avenlae looked at me sternly as he fastened the front of his suit. "You want to set all Creation against the Creator?"

"I don't want to, I *will*." I stood, straightening my spine as I looked up at him. "One way or another, I will end this war. I'd like to build my army diplomatically, but I'm not afraid to use force."

"Does that make you any better than Sinivir?"

"My goal is to free Creation, not enslave it," I said, my ears twitching back as much as they could.

"Then do so by showing them what kind of leader you are." Avenlae set his finger against my chin, leaning his head down to brush his lips against mine. "Give them no choice but to follow you into battle because there will be no greater honor."

After the first warm, full meal either of us had had in a week, Avenlae and I set out to gather the rest of our team. Notien was easy to find—she was gliding through the city's walkways in *Sloviyankae* garments with soft, swirled designs of a deep blue that brought out the navy of her large eyes. Surprisingly, Saetyl was not far behind with two plates of food, one of which she offered to Notien. I raised an eyebrow at my friend.

"When the fate of the tribe is no longer in question, I think you and I have some catching up to do," I whispered.

Notien tried to duck her head to hide her smile. "I should count myself lucky that I have time to prepare for your questions!"

Saetyl gave Avenlae a curt nod and fell into step behind Notien and I as we began to make our way back to the palace. Within moments, we met up with Havyeque, who shared an early morning drink with Darinrain. I sniffed the air, then gasped as I recognized the scent. "Is that—is that coffee?"

"You are familiar with this drink, Red-Eye?" Havyeque grinned at me, his slender ears twitching forward as membranes slid over his black eyes. "The Voxmor did their best to eradicate the humans on Earth, but they did nothing to the plant life. The coffee bean has become a delicacy in our city and is one of the tradeable items we receive as payment for the support we offer to what humans still survive."

I shook my head, still shocked at the familiar smell. "Humans? You're in contact with humans?"

"Yes, we are. Their governments accidentally made contact with the allied worlds not long before the interuniversal Voxmor attack. We assisted in moving many of their people underground and creating technologies that would allow them to live without the constant threat of the Voxmor."

"It is fascinating," Darinrain piped up, his speech faster than it had been before. "They have engineered these radios that emit a displeasing frequency to the Voxmor. You know, since they communicate telepathically and operate as a hive mind. So, the Voxmor think that wherever these radios are placed, they cannot enter. Sort of like an order from their hive queen that a specific area is off-limits. Amazing, is it not? I cannot believe we did not think of something like that."

"I can't believe your Queen never offered that kind of technology to *all* humans and Delfungaye," I said directly to Havyeque. His smile faltered slightly, and he blinked a few times before answering.

"Understand, please, Red-Eye, the *Sloviyankae* people do not all agree with her methods. But she is our Queen and has kept this city safe while so many have fallen."

"Because you never helped." I narrowed my eyes. "Tell me, Havyeque, have you never drawn your sword to fight alongside warriors and end the suffering you have witnessed?"

"I have. I have fought alongside those I considered my brothers when there was an unexpected Voxmor attack where we were only supposed to pass along supplies. Queen Klaecyia lies when she says her people are untouched by the war outside our walls. Many of us wish to join the effort but do not for fear of losing those we love."

"Will you convince your people to fight with me?"

"And betray my Queen? No." Havyeque raised his cup and gestured toward the palace. "But convince *her*? That I can help you do."

"I would hope so." I nodded to Saetyl and Notien. "Go to Kaigar and tell him to remain on standby. I will want to speak with him as soon as I am finished with Queen Klaecyia."

"Do you want us to join you?" Notien asked, glancing at Havyeque. "Just for support, of course."

"You think I can't handle the Queen on my own?"

Her platinum bob shimmered as she shook her head once. "I am well aware you can handle the Queen. I just thought you would be even more persuasive with your fellow warriors at your side."

I smirked at her. "Do I hear manipulation in your suggestion?"

Saetyl crossed her arms, a rare grin on her face. "It is Notien you are speaking to. What else would she suggest?"

"She may have a point, Xai," Avenlae murmured. "The Queen will need to feel the might of our warriors to be persuaded that we will be a strong ally."

"And you would like to have something there to support any more threats you make," Darinrain grinned.

We all, including Havyeque, gave Darinrain an appraising look. He shrugged and took another sip of his coffee, the green glow of his bodysuit reflected in the cup.

"Someone had to come out and say it," Darinrain said. "And do not look at me like that, Xiaye. You need me in the room. For no other reason than to say everything you are too afraid to."

"Still want him as an advisor?" Avenlae whispered as I gritted my teeth.

"Actually, there is an idea." Darinrain stepped forward to pat Avenlae on the shoulder. "I will speak for Avenlae, so the Queen will think only one of our leaders is aggressive."

"If you touch me again, Darinrain, I will break every one of your fingers," Avenlae growled, and Darinrain's hand hovered just centimeters from the top of Avenlae's shoulder.

"I do not think you speaking for Avenlae will make anyone think he is not aggressive," Notien said, avoiding Avenlae's gaze.

"*No one* will be speaking for anyone else," I said, then pointed at Darinrain. "You, in particular, will not speak unless directly spoken to."

"Fine, Your Majesty." Darinrain shook his head as he stepped away from Avenlae.

"Be grateful I still allow you to be in the room, Darinrain."

"I know it is because of my wealth of knowledge and not my entertaining company." Darinrain winked as he fell into step with Havyeque ahead of us.

"Just say the word," Avenlae murmured as Notien and Saetyl took off to find Kaigar. "I could make it so he never spoke again."

"Calm, Av." I grabbed his hand, an action unexpected enough to shock him out of his glowering. "We need to act as a united front to have any chance with the *Sloviyankae* Queen."

"Fine." He looked at me out of the corner of his eye. "But the truce is only temporary."

Queen Klaecyia met us in a room with a long, solid gold table with stained wooden chairs on either side. The black marble flooring continued into the room, and the lighting came from thin glowing strings woven throughout the panels of silver beadwork on the ceiling. The limestone walls were bare except for the black pillars that stood in all four corners of the rectangular room. I was forced to relive sitting in a similar room in the Queen's Nest with Kaigar and Novissime as we decided what to do with the tribe after infiltrating the nearby Voxmor nest. I had to force down the rising emotion in my throat at the thought that, looking into the steely eyes of the *Sloviyankae* Queen, I would've given anything to have just one more conversation with Novissime, to see her calming smile and hear her soft voice.

Instead, I tried to mimic the regal posture of Novissime as I walked into the room and took my seat at the opposite end of the table. Avenlae stayed on my left, and Darinrain, Havyeque, and a young woman I didn't recognize were on my right. The young woman sat next to the Queen and was dressed similarly but with less flair. A princess, perhaps?

"Have your people been made to feel welcome?" Queen Klaecyia asked without greeting.

I nodded, waiting to see where she would steer the conversation.

"Good. I trust that you and your mate found your quarters satisfactory." She spat out the word as if it were something poisonous. I glanced quickly at Avenlae, watching for a reaction, but he remained silent and still. *Good.*

Klaecyia looked down her nose at me. "You are very reserved for someone who was so verbose upon our first meeting."

I tried a small smile. "Your attempt at small talk is not fooling me, Queen. I know we stand on shaky ground, and I'm intent on securing the safety of my people."

"Let us be succinct, then." She gestured around the table. "I see you have brought your warriors again."

"Only to remind you that, despite how hard you hide from it, there is still a war outside your walls."

"I do not hide. I keep my people out of unnecessary violence."

"Unnecessary? You think we should not fight to defend ourselves against the Voxmor?"

"To attack them is to incite retaliation, Red-Eye." She spoke to me as if she were explaining something to a child.

"No one in Creation attacked first. You should know that, seeing as you claim to support so many of the allied worlds."

"You, however, will bring about the Final Battle, Red-Eye. It has been prophesied." Queen Klaecyia leaned back in her chair. "I will not have my people killed off in your suicide mission."

424

There, again, was the mention of this prophecy I had never heard of. Counting my breaths, I worked to quell my exasperation. "That may be, but I have not made any action to support that prophecy."

"Did you not come here seeking refuge for your people?"

"I did."

"Are you the named Queen of the Delfungaye, an heir by name, not by blood?"

"I am."

"Have you not seen your own red eye?"

"I... have."

Queen Klaecyia turned towards Havyeque, but it was Darinrain who answered. "I hate to tell you this, Xiaye, but that aligns with the prophecy in question."

"Did it ever occur to you to tell me *what* that prophecy is, Darinrain?" I asked through gritted teeth.

"You never asked."

Avenlae pulled out a knife and began sharpening it in Darinrain's direct line of sight.

"You claim to be unaware of the Prophecy of the Red-Eye, told directly from the mouth of the Oracle of Delf to our *visiocustos?*" the Queen hissed.

"I am unaware, yes. Regardless, that is not why we are here today." I shook my head, raising a hand to silence Darinrain as he opened his mouth to speak again. "I need to know if you will continue to allow the Delfungaye to stay here until I have ensured that Creation is free from the control of the Fifth Creator."

Silence met that statement. Havyeque kept his head bowed, and the woman next to the Queen looked startled. The Queen herself looked as if she would've paled if her skin had any color.

I crossed my legs and arms and studied her. "You know of Sinivir, don't you?"

Queen Klaecyia said nothing, but her eyes showed a minute shift.

"You must if you listen so closely to prophecies. Do you think he won't find you as soon as he has squashed the resistance from all other civilizations?"

"If he does not have you, then he cannot be powerful enough to take Creation, can he?" the Queen snapped.

"Do you think that will stop him from trying?" I leaned forward and set my left hand on the table, a soft clink sounding in the silence as each of my fingers touched the gold. "The only reason he has not come to destroy you yet is because he enjoys watching the suffering his Voxmor cause. Sinivir wants to watch the civilizations crumble so that they will have no choice but to turn to him to survive when he presents himself to them. He will take control because there will be no other choice. The cold of the Icelands is the only thing that has saved you so far, but you are living on borrowed time if the civilizations you are supporting are still getting attacked."

The Queen's eyes flicked over to Havyeque, who tried to look anywhere but at her.

"Despite what you may have heard, Red-Eye, the *Sloviyankae* have successfully protected those worlds that are allied with us. If this Sinivir you speak of will only come after my people when we are the only ones left, I believe we have much more time than you think."

"My Queen, I do not believe we do," Havyeque said quietly. Queen Klaecyia's head whipped around to face him as if she had been slapped. He spoke, keeping his eyes on the table—it appeared some Delfungaye habits died hard. "Our allies are getting attacked more frequently. It is as if the Voxmor are preparing for something in all the universes. You do not want to listen, but our allies beg us for more help. Your people are growing restless to do more for our

426

allies, as they are dying faster than we can get to them."

He raised his head to look at me. "Your window of opportunity is closing, Red-Eye. There will soon not be enough of Creation left to support you."

The Queen stared at Havyeque. "Support? Havyeque, what is this? Why have you not told me any of this?"

I leaned my arms on the table and tilted my head. "I think he has been trying to tell you. You have not remained untouched by this war. Your fear of the battles raging outside your boundaries feeds your denial, Queen Klaecyia. People are dying, the universes are being ravaged, and you cannot escape it by remaining hidden here underground. We *must* fight because the alternative is a gruesome, painful death."

"And you think I should ally with *you?*" the Queen taunted, a curl in her lip. "You and what army, precisely?"

At that exact moment, a *Sloviyankae* border guard burst into the room, his silver braid flying and his chest heaving from exertion. He began speaking wildly to Queen Klaecyia and Havyeque while the rest of us glanced at each other, unable to understand their language. Havyeque stood suddenly, his hand on the hilt of a sword that hung at his hip. Avenlae sheathed his knife and moved as if to stand as well.

"Havyeque, what is he telling you?" I demanded.

Membranes flicked over his eyes as he faced me. "There was a Voxmor at one of our border markers above ground."

"Alive?"

"Dead. But not frozen. It had been killed recently and left there."

Darinrain stood, pulling his staff from his back. "Voxmor cannot survive in the Icelands, but there is also nothing alive in the Icelands that can kill them, Xiaye."

I pushed myself out of my seat and turned to the guard, gesturing for Havyeque to translate. "What killed the Voxmor?"

"No. It cannot be," Queen Klaecyia whispered behind me at the guard's answer.

"What? What is it?" I said to Havyeque.

"He says it was killed by another Voxmor."

I turned to Darinrain. "Get me Kaigar. Now!"

Havyeque gestured to the Queen and spoke to her in their language. I assumed he was warning her to take shelter, for she stood and grabbed hold of the waiting arm of the woman who sat next to her. They left through a door that had been hidden in the wall as Avenlae reached over his head and withdrew his swords, moving to join me in the doorway.

"They should not be able to get into the tunnels," Havyeque hissed as he and Darinrain followed us toward the palace entrance.

"The ground is too cold for them to burrow through," Darinrain agreed.

"That, and radios are set up along all the markers on our borders. The Voxmor have never been able to approach us. The frequency dissuades them."

We froze as we heard a familiar screech shake the foundation of the palace, dust and small rocks falling from the ceiling.

"Not her," I said, knowing precisely what Voxmor had left the sign of the dead body near the border marker. Only one Voxmor would've been able to withstand the feeling of the frequency in her head and cloak the minds of her hive. I darted to the palace entrance and pushed open the doors. Water sprayed over me as a Voxmor queen rose from the moat, serrated tails thrashing and tentacles fully extended. The tips of the spikes along her spine cracked against the cave roof as she spun to face the city behind her, weaving her head back and forth and raising her frill.

428

"Brace yourselves!" I yelled as she opened her mouth wide, releasing a scream that reverberated throughout the entire cave system, cracking into our skulls and threatening to make our ears bleed. I cupped my hands around my ears in a vain attempt to soften the effect of her scream, but my head throbbed as my vision blurred. Avenlae fell to his knees beside me, holding onto his head as if he were holding his skull together. *Sloviyankae* fell from the walkways around us, unable to hold on. I knew there was something I had to do, something I had to say, but the pain was so unbearable I couldn't focus. I opened my mouth and screamed through the dizzying popping in my ear canals. In my scream, a word formed.

"VINDICTA!"

The tormenting shriek ceased. The Voxmor froze where she was, quiet, as if her vocal cords had been severed. I panted, my hands still over my ears. Avenlae dropped his arms next to me, trembling as he looked up. Slowly, the Voxmor queen's frill dropped, and she turned, as if in a trance, towards where I stood. I lifted my hands from my head and watched the look of curiosity that glimmered far in the depths of her expression.

"Vindicta," I said again, reaching out my shaking left hand. The Creonex began to glow a vibrant violet, reflected in the black of the Voxmor's eyes as she dropped to all fours, curling in her tentacles and moving towards me. Avenlae stood quickly, grabbing his swords.

"You are speaking its language?" he asked, his voice hoarse.

"No. I am calling her by her name," I responded, walking toward the edge of the walkway from the castle's entrance. The Voxmor queen lowered her nose to me, and hesitantly, she pressed the tips of the scales between her nostrils to my palm. Immediately, the black in her front two eyes resolved into multicolored irises surrounding reptilian pupils.

"I release you," I said and closed my eyes as the power of the Creonex surged from my body into the Voxmor. The pain was almost as intense as that caused by her shriek, and I felt the sharp stab of each burning string I snapped in her mind that represented the control of Sinivir. My skin seared as if it were on fire, but that was nothing compared to when she opened her frill once more and sent a tidal wave of my power out through all of the tunnels surrounding the *Sloviyankae* city. It felt as if my body was being ripped to shreds, yanked in all directions, but I couldn't move. I was rooted to the spot, my hand glued to the nose of the Voxmor, forced to endure the most excruciating pain I had ever felt. Every time I cracked through Sinivir's control over a Voxmor mind, the pain intensified until I felt as if my heart would give out. There was no way my body could cope with this amount of torture, and for the first time, I wished I would die. Anything was better than the pain.

Just as suddenly as it started, the pain ceased, and my eyes flew open as I sucked in great inhalations, stumbling away from the Voxmor. Something caught me gently before I fell, and the dampness against my skin told me it was a tentacle. I looked up at the Voxmor queen as she held me, her six eyes now the most brilliant mix of prismatic colors I had ever seen.

You are powerful, Creovis.

I flinched as the sound of her voice echoed in my head.

Do not be afraid. We will not hurt you now.

"We?"

You asked for an army, did you not?

Vindicta removed her tentacle to allow me to stand alone and turned her head back towards the *Sloviyankae* city, a loud, rapid clicking resonating from her throat.

"Xiaye, what is happening?" Avenlae asked, standing beside me with a sword still in his shaking hand. One of Vindicta's tentacles loosened its hold on him as his eyes darted around the city.

430

Before I could answer, terrified cries rang out from the city as *hundreds* of Voxmor began to crawl out of the tunnels, making their way across the ceiling, through the streets, and over the buildings towards us. Their eyes were not the deathly black I was used to seeing—they were sapphire, ruby, golden, emerald, and amethyst reptilian eyes that all pointed straight at me. When the cave system was filled with Voxmor, turning the walls and pathways through the buildings as white as snow above us, they froze, staring ahead to where I stood in front of Vindicta. Horrified that I had brought a large-scale attack down on what was left of the Delfungaye and *Sloviyankae,* I pulled out my rapiers, backing away from Vindicta and igniting the violet flames of my wings, forks of violet electricity buzzing down my blades. As soon as I did so, Vindicta lowered her head, closing her eyes and opening her tentacles before her nose so they extended straight out like a spiky fan. In a ripple across the cave, every one of the Voxmor behind her copied her stance.

They were *bowing* to me.

"Xiaye, what have you done?" Avenlae asked.

"You!" came the fearsome shriek of Queen Klaecyia behind me.

I turned to her as she stumbled down the steps of the castle entrance, a shaking finger pointed at me. Replacing my rapiers, I let the fire die away from my feathers. Delfungaye and *Sloviyankae* alike stared at the Voxmor, hands on their still-sheathed weapons, darting glances at me for orders.

"I'm sorry, Queen. I believe we were interrupted." I spoke loudly, the strength of my voice bouncing off the cave walls to be heard from the farthest reaches of the city. "You were asking me what army I would be attacking the Fifth Creator with?"

I stepped backward and touched the tip of my finger to the Vindicta's middle tentacle. The effect was immediate. A roar echoed through the cave as the Voxmor shifted, their serrated tails arced over their heads as they rose to stand on

431

two legs, their tentacles curled close to their chests. Avenlae's ears flattened against his temples as he watched them, but it wasn't with fear that he looked at me; it was with admiration.

I lowered my head as I looked at the Queen, her head jerking around as she looked at an entire Voxmor hive within her city. "Is this good enough for you?"

CHAPTER 40

"I cannot believe *that* was how you thought you would convince another Queen to ally with you," Kaigar grumbled as he watched over the Voxmor workers who dug into the back of the cave system, carving out a space for the hive to stay outside of the city.

"It worked, didn't it?" I said, crossing my arms and turning to him.

"In a completely unorthodox, fear-driven twist of events, it did. When were you going to tell us you had that little trick up your sleeve?"

"When I knew it would work."

Kaigar sucked in a breath, then spoke so slowly, I could hear the effort it took him to control his temper. "You invited the queen of all Voxmor to follow you into the Icelands in hopes that you could control her without actually knowing for sure that you could?"

I rocked back and forth on my heels. "Uh, yes, yes I did."

"Do you realize how insane that is?"

"Well, when you put it that way … but it seemed like a good idea in theory."

Kaigar sighed, shaking his head. A few wisps of salt and pepper hair fell from the warrior's braids hanging down his back. "It is the kind of crazy thing your mother would have done."

I watched the General as he looked back out over the burrowing Voxmor. "You loved her, didn't you?"

Kaigar did not respond immediately, nor did he look at me, but he did lower his eyes. "As much as one could love someone with as free a spirit as Lieneata."

"Then why, until now, have you fought so hard against me?"

"You were the reason she left the tribe and ultimately the reason she died. I could not understand what made you, a weapon, so important that she would sacrifice her life. What made *you* worth losing the only person I would ever love? These same thoughts returned after Novissime's death. It did not seem fair that something created to destroy all life was meant to lead the Delfungaye in their fight to resist extinction. However, when you opened that portal, showing that you had secured refuge for the entire tribe—in that moment, I saw Lieneata in your eyes." Kaigar raised his head, both his white and silver eyes on me. "You had become what the Delfungaye queens before you molded you into—not a weapon, but a fierce leader. That was when I finally understood—Lieneata had not foolishly sacrificed her life for some wild tale she believed in. She and Novissime sacrificed themselves to give the Delfungaye the best possible chance of survival, and that chance lies with you, Daughter of War."

I pulled my shoulders back, pressing my wings close to my spine. "That chance lies more with our ability to recruit more warriors and soldiers from the rest of Creation."

"Yes, well, do not forget that an army fights only with a strong leader," Kaigar said, resuming his observation of the Voxmor. Nodding, I began wracking my brain for some excuse to busy myself elsewhere. Fortunately for me, that excuse came in the form of Vindicta, who ambled up to us, clicking to get my attention.

Your mate awaits your presence, Creovis.

"He sent you to get me?" I asked, stepping down from the platform Kaigar stood on.

No, but I can sense that he is searching for you.

"How is that?" She reached out a tentacle for me to grab onto and lifted me onto her back, towards the front of the spikes that wove back and forth along her spine as she walked.

The bond that you two share is strong. I can sense him through you, Creovis.

"I've already asked you not to call me that," I said as she began to slither away from her workers, weaving through a tunnel and entering into the warm firelight of the *Sloviyankae* city. A few Voxmor with sapphire eyes ambled around the streets, assisting with repairs and the collection of supplies alongside the *Sloviyankae's gueirags.* The People of the Icelands and Delfungaye alike had developed a shaky trust in the Voxmor after seeing the control I had over the hive. Queen Klaecyia had relented and allowed both my tribe and the hive to remain within the cave system as she sent envoys out to all the allied worlds requesting a meeting with their leaders. That meeting was supposed to take place in three days, and it would take much preparation to host members from twenty-five different worlds. Fortunately, this provided enough of a distraction to force the tribes and hive to intermingle. The tribespeople remained wary of the beasts, but they knew they had no other options. There was no one else to lead them, no one else to fight for them.

I apologize. Vindicta sniffed and shook her head as she passed a tavern. *It is the name I have known you by for twenty-four years.*

"It's not the name I respond to. Have you felt anything from Sinivir?"

No. Vindicta clicked, and a few Voxmor moved to the side of the street. *He has remained silent. It is odd to have my mind to myself after all these years.*

"Do you think there's any chance you could help me free the rest of the Voxmor?"

Another attempt would break you, Xiaye. It was already too much for your body to handle the first time.

I chewed my lip as we continued down the street, frustrated that my power could do so much but still felt limited. But I knew, too, that the time to push the limits of my power had passed. Sinivir would know what I had done, which meant everyone within the cave system was living on borrowed time.

Up ahead of Vindicta, I spotted Avenlae gliding into a landing on the street. He was wearing his recently cleaned warrior's vest, having traded in his *Sloviyankae* bodysuit the second he got his clothes. White bandages were visible through the vest's V-neck—he had finally visited the Healers like I had wanted him to. I slid down the side of Vindicta's front leg as Avenlae touched down.

"What did the Healers do for you?" I asked as he approached, his wings dragging lightly across the stone behind him.

"They insisted on another injection to stimulate rapid healing. If the injection is successful, I should be back to full strength by the end of the week."

"Good. We have an army to raise in the meantime."

Your advisor approaches. Vindicta clicked, fluttering her frill. Avenlae looked up at her, a twitch of fear flattening his ears.

"Let him hear you," I said to Vindicta.

Behind Avenlae, Darinrain rode atop a Voxmor with golden eyes, an excited grin on his face.

"Does it speak?" Avenlae asked wearily as Vindicta unfurled the tentacles of her front legs.

"She does, yes." I placed a hand on his arm to prevent him from moving away as Vindicta's tentacles brushed across his temples. "And you lead this tribe with me. You need to be able to communicate with her as well."

"Are you—"

436

Avenlae's voice stopped as his eyes unfocused and his muscles tensed. It lasted a mere second, but I felt the connection snap into place through the *lyceliah*.

Vindicta released Avenlae just as Darinrain approached on his smaller steed. "Ah, can you hear them now?" he called to Avenlae.

Your advisor appears much too happy about this arrangement, Vindicta huffed.

Darinrain grinned at me. "Of course I am! We have control over the Voxmor. The *Je'quiet* have never spoken of this before. It is the shift in the war we have been searching for, is it not, Xiaye?"

"Yes, but don't get too excited. We still need to convince the rest of Creation that one last battle is needed to secure our freedom. I don't think it'll be as easy as bringing them an army of Voxmor a second time around."

No, but showing you already have the beginnings of an army may still be an advantage, Vindicta clicked.

Avenlae frowned slightly. "I do not like her in my head, Xai."

Vindicta blinked her six eyes as she turned to Avenlae. *Your reticence is not unjustified. I sense that my hives have caused you significant loss and pain. I cannot take that away, but I can help you to exact revenge on the one who forced them to do it.*

Avenlae's silver eyes studied her chromatic ones. The tension in his muscles relaxed as he cocked his head to the side, his ears swiveling around as if they'd heard Vindicta's voice.

"I hate to interrupt this crucial moment between you two, but there was a reason why I sought you out, Xiaye," Darinrain said.

I do not think your mate appreciates your advisor's disrespect, Vindicta growled. The slightest smirk tilted the corners of Avenlae's lips as Darinrain shot her a furtive look.

I ignored both of them. "What is it you need?"

"Notien, Saetyl, and I are awaiting your orders on how you would like to organize and prepare for battle."

"Is Kaigar not included in the proceedings?"

"Your General seems determined to keep a watchful eye on the construction of the Voxmor hive." Darinrain looked up at Vindicta, bowing his head slightly to expose the top of the tattoos that raced up his neck and skull. "You will have to understand, Queen, he will not trust you as quickly as the rest of us."

He leads your warriors. It is his job not to trust. Vindicta clicked a few times. *Should I meet you back at the hive then, Xiaye?*

"Should you?"

I assume we should meet wherever your General is. If he wishes to watch over my workers as they create a space for my hive, I will not stop him.

I nodded and turned back to Darinrain. "I'll find Saetyl and Notien. If you can collect Havyeque, meet us at the entrance to the Voxmor hive."

"As you wish, Your Majesty." Darinrain executed a slightly exaggerated bow, then was launched into the air by his golden-eyed Voxmor. Avenlae watched him go, then leaned forward and whispered, "Make sure Vindicta is always around when he is."

I was sure Vindicta would've smirked at the comment if she had been able.

Preparations for the arrival of the other leaders went about as smoothly as could be expected. The Voxmor hive was completed by the end of the first day, and unless called upon, the Voxmor remained within the tunnels. That is, except for Vindicta. She, with a select few others, stayed with me, Avenlae, Darinrain, Saetyl, and Notien to create a feeling of kinship between the Delfungaye's new leaders and the Voxmor. This, more than anything, chipped away at the tension between the tribe, the *Sloviyankae*, and the Voxmor hive.

It was Saetyl who suggested that armor be made for the Voxmor. "The Voxmor under the control of Sinivir attack like rabid animals," she had said. "Ours can fight smarter, but they will be outnumbered and need whatever help they can get."

"Armor will also help set them apart on the battlefield," Notien added. "We cannot risk killing one of our own because they look too alike."

So it was that what remained of the Delfungaye *Glae'atii* and *Sloviyankae* blacksmiths began designing specialized armor for the Voxmor. I couldn't hear all of their voices, but from the pitch of the clicks, growls, and soft shrieks they made, I could guess this was one thing the Voxmor could feel excitement about. Over the few days I spent around the hive, it became clear that the Voxmor were more intelligent than we knew. They were aware of themselves and the others within their hive, but released from Sinivir's control, they didn't operate as a hive mind. They could do so in a fight-or-flight situation, but it wasn't their natural state. As individuals, the Voxmor were as unique in personality as different members of each tribe.

Darinrain and Notien began training alongside the Voxmor, as the *Fyr'aeset* had been known for their cavalry warriors when they once ruled the plains of Silvacastra. The *Sloviyankae* who were the most proficient at riding the *gueirags* and remaining members of the *Fyr'aeset* tribe created a new calvary. Voxmor began to deem specific tribe members as their "riders", and they formed a unique relationship. Watching the Riders and their steeds train together was breathtaking, for their bond synchronized their fighting styles in complete harmony.

Through training, we learned that the eye color of the Voxmor helped them distinguish each other. They knew who was considered a soldier, worker, scout, hunter, or breeder based on eye color alone. Soldiers' eyes were red, workers' were green, hunters' were gold, scouts' were blue, and breeders' were violet. The specific shade of the color denoted sex, the more vibrant being female. Vindicta, the most powerful queen of the Voxmor, had all the colors of her hive within her irises. She assured me, however, that the entirety of her hive was more than capable of fighting, as the Voxmor species had been forced to evolve into the most proficient killers in all of Creation.

Avenlae and Kaigar trained the combined Guard of *Sloviyankae* and *Delfungaye*. The *Sloviyankae* fighting style didn't differ vastly from the Delfungaye, so they didn't need to train soldiers from scratch. But, the warriors needed to learn how to fight as one. I watched Avenlae train on the third day, his hair flying behind him as his body moved in tune with the direction of his swords.

He is a true warrior, Vindicta told me as I sat across her shoulder blades. *I am not surprised you chose him as a mate.*

"I, uh, thank you," I responded.

She clicked quietly as a flash from the castle lit up the cave. *I think the leaders you are meant to meet with have arrived.*

I sighed, my stomach clenching with anticipation. "I think so, too. Are you ready to make your big entrance?"

If you are prepared to defend me. She shook her head as she let out a quick screech, getting the attention of Avenlae, Kaigar, Darinrain, Notien, and Saetyl, all of whom were training with the rest of the Guard. *They will not be pleased to see a Voxmor among them.*

"Perhaps not at first," I said as she began to slither along a walkway leading to the castle. The rest of my team separated from the Queen's Guard and took to the air to follow us. "But I am beginning to find that I can be very persuasive."

Your power is intimidating, Vindicta snorted, *and fear is the best tool of persuasion.*

I pushed myself off her back to join the rest of my team, relishing the feeling of the air moving between my feathers again. It was nothing like flying in the open air with the sky above me, but it was enough to calm my nerves. Too soon, my feet were back on solid ground and the pressure of anxiety tightened my chest. Vindicta leaped down to the castle's entrance, remaining on all fours in a futile attempt to appear less threatening. I wasn't sure what Queen Klaecyia had told her allies, so I gave Vindicta instructions to stay quiet, low, and behind my team.

Avenlae stepped up next to me, his hair braided back into a fauxhawk and his swords crossed over his shoulder blades. His claw earrings were in place on his ears, and the gold on the claw septum piercing glinted as he turned to look down at me. "Are you ready?"

"As I'll ever be," I said, and I pushed open the doors to the castle. Once again, I channeled Novissime's regal appearance and swathed myself in it, hoping that some of her strength would manifest within me.

As we crossed the threshold, a crowd of beings of all shapes, sizes, and colors turned to face us. There were outcries and gestures of fear as Vindicta made her way into the entrance hall behind us. I stood silently, waiting for the sounds of shock to dissipate. Queen Klaecyia sat on her white throne at the back of the crowd, her head held high as she observed the reactions of the delegations from each of the worlds. I scanned the crowd, seeing humanoid creatures with skin as brightly striped as a tiger's coat, others with multiple limbs, and still others with beaks as black and shiny as the floor they stood upon. There were beings with hooves, some with various legs, and others who towered over everyone there, their thick hide like leather stretched over the muscles of their four arms as they stared through eyes as yellow as Earth's sun.

There, shockingly out of place, was the human delegation. It was small, just four individuals: a man and a woman dressed in the military's camouflage uniforms and another man and woman dressed in black suits that had obviously not been worn in many years.

Slowly, the sounds of each language quieted, and Queen Klaecyia stood, gesturing around her to seats that rose up from the floor.

"Be seated, and let us begin," she said, and the translation of her words into twenty-five languages echoed from each seat. The delegation dispersed into an oval extending out from the *Sloviyankae* Queen's throne and ended with the seats meant for my team. Vindicta clicked a few times, then settled behind us, blinking each of her six eyes as she watched the proceedings. Several of the beings from the delegations refused to take their eyes off Vindicta, leaning around to whisper to each other while keeping her in their periphery.

"As you can see, the Red-Eye has come to our city," Queen Klaecyia began, extending her elegant hand to me.

"Does this mean the prophesized time of the Final Battle is upon us?" a bespeckled green creature said, clasping his long, thin fingers together in front of his face.

How many civilizations know about this prophecy? I wondered. It seemed as if I was the only one who had never heard it in its entirety, yet I was its subject.

"Is it wise to enter into a Final Battle?" said one of the humanoids with the striped skin.

A dull ache began in the back of my head. I rubbed my neck and tried to pay attention to the debate.

"What would you know?" shrieked a hooved creature whose bug eyes spun as it spoke. "Your people are cowards! You have never fought alongside any of us!"

"Let's not forget that many of us do not have the numbers to offer to the cause," the human man said, his voice laced with haughty indifference.

The ache turned into a throb that began to make its way up the back of my skull. I massaged my scalp where I could around my braids, trying to release some built-up pressure.

"You have the numbers, human. You are just too greedy to give up any within your military," a hulking, leather-skinned creature roared.

"I'm sorry, most of our military is concerned with protecting our own people," the human woman in the suit snapped.

"*And* stealing any extra supplies you can get your little hands on!" hissed a creature with coral-colored scales and a long, slender neck.

The throbbing headache grew more severe, to the point where I was squinting my eyes against the pain. I rubbed my temples, trying desperately to remain present as my vision blurred.

"Have the *Sloviyankae* finally decided to join the fight?" came a deep voice, but I couldn't see who spoke.

"That would be perhaps the only thing that would convince me to even consider a Final Battle," a slow, crackly voice added, "given how conservative their war efforts have been thus far."

"If the *Sloviyankae* are fully involved, that means there is little hope left for us!" someone cried, the shrillness of their voice driving a spike into my skull.

"I thought the Delfungaye were the final stronghold?"

"Haven't they lost their queen?"

"Is that not who sits before us?"

"Xiaye?"

The world spun around me as the corners of my vision faded to black, and the castle's entrance hall disappeared. The splitting headache suddenly stopped, and I found myself standing in the middle of complete blackness, the only color being the red glowing from the wooden pattern of my bodysuit. I spun around on the spot, willing my eyes to see something in the darkness or my ears to hear the whisper of something in the shadows. It was so eerily similar to being within the mind of a Voxmor hive queen that I worried for a moment I had somehow slipped into Vindicta's mind.

"You are becoming the biggest thorn in my side, *Creovis*," hissed Sinivir's voice. I spun once more to come face-to-face with his bloody eyes set deep into his death mask face. Crimson hair flowed down his shoulders as he paced around me, gritting his yellowed, pointed teeth. "First, you escaped the clutches of my Voxmor, and now you have taken my most powerful queen from me? You think you can do these things without retribution?"

"Where is it?" I snapped. "Your retribution, where is it? Why have you not appeared, releasing your wrath upon me and my people, then? Is it because you're afraid, Sinivir? Afraid of the weapon you created?"

Red forks of energy buzzed across his fingers as he raised a clawed hand to strike me. I caught his wrist on the down-swing, my power whirling angrily in my chest. What was stopping Sinivir, however, was the glowing golden cords wrapped around my wrist. Their length led back into the shadows behind me, and their glow acted as a protective shield around me. "Or," I said slowly, twisting his wrist, "have you already tried? Is that what this is? Did I stop you, Creator?"

Sinivir hissed as he wrenched his wrist from my grasp. "Your powers are evolving, *Creovis*. Exactly as *I* created them to do. That bond you've created with the little Mercenary added a bit more power than expected. But no matter, *my Creovis*—"

"You have no control over me, Sinivir. You've lost that battle."

"I will not lose the *final* one." He smiled as I swallowed. "Yes, *Creovis*, I am aware of your futile attempt to build an army." He cackled, a dribble of spittle dropping out of the corner of his mouth. "What is an army of mortals against the power of a Creator? Have you told them yet that you are leading them to their deaths?"

I thought quickly, acting on Sinivir's arrogance to buy myself some time. "No mortal could wish to wield even a fraction of your power. But who will be left subservient to you if you unleash your raw power on Creation? Where's the fun in complete decimation?"

Sinivir narrowed his eyes. "Will not my demonstration against your army be enough to eradicate any further thoughts of resistance?"

"Perhaps. But my army will consist of what is left of Creation. Should you kill them off, won't the victory behollow? There will be no fight, no honor. No one left to bow to your power." In a split second, I made my decision. *Trap him*. "Let's make things more interesting, Sinivir. This is your game, after all."

Sinivir remained silent, pacing around me as he considered. "What do you propose, *Creovis*?"

"It's me you seek and me alone. Creation is what you wish to control. Allow Creation the chance to fight for their freedom against your army of Voxmor, and you fight me like a mortal. Your victory will be even sweeter. To win upon the sweat off the back of Creation, to crush their resolve by weakening their fighters—will that not give you better servants?"

The Fifth Creator paused in his pacing, a sly smile parting his cracked lips once more. "It is true, perhaps, that the Final Battle could lay the groundwork for complete subservience among all of Creation, to know that they cannot defeat me no matter how hard they fight." He stopped, his bloody eyes sliding back to me. "My trophy, however, will be you, *Creovis*."

I held my breath. "Yes. Should your Voxmor beat Creation, you will have me. I won't fight you then. But should Creation win against the Voxmor—I will destroy you."

Sinivir began to cackle, quietly at first, then he was bent over from the cracking sound of his laughs. "Prepare yourself, my weapon! You shall soon be within my grasp." He straightened and pointed a yellow claw at me. "The plains of Silvacastra will be the location of our Final Battle. You shall have three days to prepare. If you are not there at dawn of the fourth day, *Creovis*, I will come for you. And I will kill every living thing I come across on the way."

CHAPTER 41

I returned to consciousness as if shoved back into my body. Stumbling backward, I shook my head, blinking my eyes against the light of the room. I gasped when I felt a hand on my back, but I let myself be held in place. Two moonlight eyes swam into my vision, and with them came a fierce determination I felt through the *lyceliah*.

"Three days," Avenlae hissed.

"Did you hear anything more?" I asked. Those golden cords, those had been the *lyceliah*. Avenlae had been partially aware of the presence of the Fifth Creator.

Avenlae shook his head.

Vindicta's voice entered my thoughts. *Sinivir is gone now, but even I could sense him in you. He is strong, Xiaye. Be wary of anything he said to you.*

"You brought us together to follow this … this thing, Queen Klaecyia?" the human man cried. "Was that performance supposed to incite confidence? There is no way I will allow any of my men to follow something into battle that cannot control itself!"

"Call her a thing one more time, coward," Avenlae growled as he stepped away from me. "I dare you to see how long you would last in a fight."

"Listen to yourselves!" I said as I looked around at the delegations, my anger and desperation redirected as I pushed myself away from Avenlae. "You're bickering like children! Are you all so self-righteous as to think what matters most is who helped when, or who has what supplies? Have you not one thought to spare on the survival of the entirety of Creation?"

"An interesting accusation coming from you, Red-Eye," the scaled creature hissed. "Is that not a Voxmor behind you?"

"*Vindicta* is a true Voxmor queen, released from the control of the Fifth Creator."

Whispering and murmuring rose up the crowd. Queen Klaecyia leaned back on her throne, a sly smile visible under the ornate mask of her crown. She seemed to believe I had the situation well-handled without her, for she remained silent.

Vindicta rose and wove around the chairs to stand behind me, blinking her six eyes at the creatures who began to cower before her. "I control her and her hive now," I said. "This is an advantage no one in all of Creation has had before. If, for one second, you can all find it within yourselves to consider the survival of your people, I propose we devise a plan of attack for the Final Battle. The Fifth Creator will allow Creation one last chance to fight for their freedom, and we have no choice but to take it!"

"Was that what you were doing, Red-Eye?" the bespeckled green creature asked. "Were you communicating with the Creator when you became unresponsive?"

"I didn't choose to, but I did what I could with the situation. We've been given three days to prepare."

"How are we supposed to believe that?" the human man snapped, gesturing angrily. "What evidence do we have that it wasn't some kind of sick show?"

"You can choose not to believe anything I say, but it'll be *you* who will be remembered by your people as the one who turned their back on salvation. This battle will not be easy. Victory will come at a heavy price for all of us. But, should you choose not to fight, you and your people will enter into servitude to the Fifth Creator."

"How do we know that is not what is supposed to happen? Should Creation not serve the Creator?" the human woman said. I gritted my teeth. I may have considered myself one before, but at that moment, humans were beginning to become the most frustrating species I had encountered.

"I believe you, of all people in this room, should understand the importance of free will," I responded.

"While your argument is intriguing," the tiger-striped leader began, "I, for one, cannot ignore the fact that the Creator's Voxmor have reduced the populations of all of our civilizations to barely half of what they were before. Why do you think that engaging in direct combat with the Voxmor will be any more successful now than before?"

"Because we have our own Voxmor." I took turns looking into the eyes of every leader in that room. "And I know we want it *more*. The adrenaline from fighting for your life will always be stronger than fighting for a prize. We have everything to lose but also everything to gain. Let us show the Fifth Creator the true power of Creation when it seeks *vengeance*."

"Vengeance will only fuel the fight so far," Queen Klaecyia said, sitting up.

"If not for vengeance, then fight for those you love," I said, calming my voice. "Fight to provide a world in which they are free to live without the fear and pain of war. Fight to let them live on with the memory that every breath they take was rewarded to them by the strength of your blade in battle. Fight to give yourself the legacy of a warrior, not a coward."

449

My statement was met with silence from the worlds' leaders. It was not a silence born of fear but rather of thought.

I continued. "Finally, you have me. You have my power. The Fifth Creator will choose to target me in battle, leaving the rest of our army to fight the Voxmor without the full might of a Creator behind them. I call that leveling the playing field."

"And you are sure a Creator has been behind the interuniversal war? This is not just some myth, some story?" the scaled creature asked.

"You know it to be true, Gryscythe," the bespeckled creature huffed. "We all know it. There may be much we leaders disagree on, but you've all heard the rumors as much as I have. We've all witnessed the same unspeakable acts of the Voxmor." The creature turned towards me, its voice softening. "There is not one individual in this room who has not known immense suffering at the unforgiving hands of the Fifth Creator."

"Then let us take these three days!" I called to them. "Give us your soldiers, your warriors, your strongest fighters. Sinivir is arrogant enough to allow us time to prepare, if only for his own entertainment at what kind of army Creation will build. But his arrogance will be his downfall. Will you hide away and watch as the rest of us sacrifice ourselves for the chance to grasp a future of freedom? Should you do so, I hope you'll remember that choice when the Fifth Creator slaughters you and your people in his thirst for complete control. This," I said, igniting the violet flames along my feathers, "is Creation's last chance at salvation. Who are we to deny it?"

"Who are you to ask that sacrifice of us? You who has allied with our enemy!" Gryscythe raised himself out of his seat, his scales flashing as he hissed.

Before I could answer, Vindicta clicked behind me. *Let me show them.*

I turned back towards her as more whispers and jeers echoed through the room.

Let me show them what the Voxmor have been through under the control of Sinivir. Send out your power, Creovis, and I will do the rest.

Determination strengthened in the colors of her six eyes, but I stayed still for a moment longer.

"Do it, Xiaye," Darinrain said. "Let them see. It is the only way they will understand."

"See what, exactly?" the human man snarled.

Gritting my teeth, I pulled from the fire of my wings and let a plume of blue smoke flow from my hands to fill the throne room. "This."

The gasps from the creatures were cut short as Vindicta pressed a tentacle to my temple. Suddenly, every single leader from each delegation felt the crushing pain of the Voxmor, imprisoned within their own bodies and forced to kill everything in sight. They watched the torture Vindicta was subjected to as Sinivir attempted to break her. They felt the guilt and the horror each Voxmor experienced as they watched themselves destroy the worlds of Creation, unable to do anything to stop it. They realized the intelligence of each member of the hive, their awareness, and their loyalty to the one who freed them—me. Vindicta said nothing to them through our connection, but her message was clear without words.

I pulled the influence of the Creonex back into the glove around my left hand, panting slightly at the effort it took to keep the telepathic pathway open between so many individuals. Avenlae pressed a steadying hand against my back as other leaders stumbled, gasped, clicked, squawked, and growled at the release of the Creonex's connection. A stunned silence settled over the gathering.

Then, Queen Klaecyia moved.

She stood and stepped down from her throne. Eyes turned away from Vindicta and watched the *Sloviyankae* queen as she made her way towards me. But she did not look at me. She stared at the Voxmor Queen behind me, and Vindicta stared back.

Queen Klaecyia raised a trembling hand.

Vindicta lowered her head.

"I will follow you, Tortured Queen," Klaecyia said, pressing her palm to Vindicta's scales.

The encampment on the back of the cave system was as interesting to watch and walk through as the *Sloviyankae* city had been when we first arrived. After only an hour of deliberation, all twenty-five worlds had agreed to send forth their armies. *That is what you weren't betting on, Sinivir,* I thought as I watched the arrival of warriors from multiple portals. *The determination of those who have everything to gain.*

The cave became more colorful as each group of soldiers displayed the colors of their people, and I became fascinated with the different fighting styles I witnessed as I walked by the encampment early in the morning. Avenlae and I didn't see each other as much in the days leading up to the battle, as he was called to join Kaigar in meetings with other generals to formulate attack plans. Kaigar seemed to defer to Avenlae as his own right-hand in battle, a decision I did nothing to discourage.

Notien oversaw the creation of weapons tipped in *exitialium* and the collection of supplies that would be needed by Healers on the battlefield. She updated me regularly on what was still required by the different soldiers from each of the allied worlds and on the progress of the training. She, of course, would also ensure that I was well-fed before she was done with her report, and her optimism carried me through the three days leading to the Final Battle.

Saetyl ensured the *Glae'atii* and blacksmiths worked round the clock to finish the armor for the Voxmor. However, many times she would join Notien to report to me on progress, and there was a growing playfulness between them. I couldn't decide if I should be happy at the prospect of a new relationship or saddened by the prospect that the relationship could be so short.

Darinrain worked with soldiers from many civilizations to match each Voxmor with a Rider, and by the second day, every Voxmor had been bonded, rendering our cavalry incredibly deadly. The Riders' connection with their Voxmor appeared to be as close as the one I held with Vindicta. Darinrain, in true fashion, boasted that the success of the cavalry rested upon his own golden, broad shoulders, but only when neither Vindicta nor Avenlae was around.

A quiet apprehension was building throughout the city as the battle drew near. The fires glowing from within each building no longer seemed warm and inviting. The smiles I had seen so often on the faces of the *Sloviyankae* faded on the second day and all but disappeared by the third. The taverns were filled at night, but they were quiet. It was as if each individual within the caves felt the fragility of their mortality. I couldn't blame them—by the third day, my own anxiety prevented me from eating, as I was sick with the swirling thoughts in my mind.

On the eve of the third day, I found myself walking along the underground river, contemplating the insanity of what I planned to do. Just when I wanted time to slow so I could savor every breath, every heartbeat, it seemed to race forward at an alarming rate. The immensityof the battle plan felt suffocating, and I wanted nothing else but to run, escape to the opposite end of the universe, and hide so entirely that I would never have to fear the bloody eyes of Sinivir again.

The frantic buzzing of my brain came to a halt as I noticed that I was not alone on the shore of the river. The *Matri Me'leiv* stood with her toes just touching the edge of the crystal water, swaying and humming to herself. Beadwork along her wings and down her neck clinked softly as her white hair flowed. Her eyes were closed, and a sweet smile pulled at her lips, deepening the wrinkles around her eyes, nose, and cheeks. Up close, she looked frail, but I knew better—her strength was not in her muscles but in her influence.

I cleared my throat to make her aware of my presence.

"There is no need for that, My Queen," she said, her eyes remaining closed. "I heard you walking several minutes before now."

"I'm sorry, I didn't mean to disturb you."

"Ah, but isn't it fortunate that you did? I feel that uncertainty is weighing heavily on your shoulders, Your Highness." The *Matri Me'leiv* twirled into a deep bow before opening her bright navy eyes to look at me. She only had to tilt her head down slightly as age had shrunk her stature.

I held her gaze for a moment, thinking hard before answering. "Why did you ask me what name I responded to?"

The aged woman tilted her head to the side, her voice much younger than her appearance suggested. "Surely by now you have heard of the Prophecy of the Red-Eye? To the Delfungaye, it is worded differently, and is known as the Prophecy of the Daughter of War."

"That was what the armorers called me."

"Yes, our people are very familiar with it. Of course, no one truly believed it, as the Delfungaye pride themselves in being advanced enough to move past things such as prophecies and oracles."

"And yet you hold a critical position within their society."

The *Matri Me'leiv* laughed. "I did say they pride themselves that way, not that they *are*. That particular prophecy, however, gained traction once again when you arrived at the tribe before the season changed. People began to ask if the prophecy was made about you."

I frowned. "Was it not?"

"The wording was broad enough it could have been about anyone. It all depended on Novissime's final choice."

"Her choice—her choice to die so that I could live?"

The *Matri Me'leiv* nodded, looking back out across the river. "*The final Delfungaye Queen shall have an Heir, not by blood, but by name and sacrifice. That Heir shall either be the salvation or destruction of all Creation, contingent upon what name the Heir chooses to take—the name of love or the name of vengeance.*"

I felt my eyes widening. "That was why you asked which name—I must have answered correctly."

The old woman shook her head, and I felt my stomach drop.

"I didn't? Then why—"

"You answered unexpectedly," she said, glancing at me and then turning to walk away back up the river.

"Wait a second! What does that mean?"

"It means, Your Majesty, that you cannot make decisions based on prophecies because the Oracle of Delf does not really know what she is talking about." The *Matri Me'leiv* stopped suddenly and whirled around, pressing her palm against my chest, right above my heart. "You are the observer now, My Queen. It is up to *you* to show us what the final line of the prophecy will be."

On that enigmatic note, the *Matri Me'leiv* turned on her heel and leaped into the air, leaving me alone by the river. I felt an urge to rip my hair out and scream, but instead, I leaped into the air, heading in the opposite direction. Her words had done nothing to alleviate the weight of the uncertainty, but they did remind me of one last thing I had to do before dawn. It was the kind of thing Novissime would have done—had done. It was a fail-safe, a final wish—a beg for mercy.

CHAPTER 42

Dawn of the fourth day began with Avenlae holding on to me tighter than he ever had before. I breathed in the smell of leather, metal, and open skies, savored the feeling of his skin, and how his chest rose and fell with each breath he took. I stared into those silver moonlight eyes as if I would never see enough of them, ran my fingers through his long, ebony hair. I listened to the steady beat of his heart, relishing the miracle that it continued the rhythm on its own without reminder, without help. Avenlae folded his wings around me so I was enveloped in his warmth and strength.

He pressed his lips against mine for a long, deep kiss, and I tasted the salt of tears on his skin. "I love you, *Le'eseia*. I always have, and I always will."

"I will have loved you forever, and it still will not have been enough," I said, running my fingers along his cheek.

"No, Xai, you *will* love me forever," Avenlae corrected.

We assisted each other into our armor, tightening the straps of our scabbards and checking that the armor's integrity was intact. Avenlae braided my hair straight back so that it would tuck into my helmet easily, and he braided his own as I sharpened my rapiers. Then we stood, facing each other, our hearts thrashing against our chests in a desperate fight to stay together. Silence had never been so loud, so heavy, so terrifying. I raised my left hand to rest against his temple, and he leaned into the comfort of my touch, closing his eyes tightly. There was little I could do to calm his fear, for I couldn't calm my own.

The light of fires blazed in the crimson writing of my armor. Black blades glimmered along the top of my wings as I met with the rest of my team at the castle entrance. It was odd—someone always had something to say, but at that moment fear held our tongues hostage, and Notien, Saetyl, Darinrain, Avenlae, and I could do nothing but nod to each other in greeting. I raised my helmet over my head and waited while the rest of my team did the same. They didn't speak to me and didn't speak to each other. There was, however, a sudden spark of dauntlessness keeping our spines erect as we turned to join the army of Creation, for we had begun this journey together, and we would end it in the same way, remaining by each other's side.

Just outside the palace was my army, standing at attention, ready for their orders. In front were the Voxmor with their riders on their backs, shaking their heads and hissing in anticipation. They wore silver helmets with a blade that stretched from their noses to the back of their skulls, and the serration of their tails was reinforced with *exitialium*. Plates of flexible armor covered their vulnerable flanks and underbellies, and spikes lined the inside of their tentacles.

Vindicta flared her frill as I approached, her armor the same matte black and crimson as my own. *So, Xiaye, are you prepared for battle?*

"I believe I was born for it," I said, reaching up and allowing her to lift me onto her back. Notien and Darinrain pulled themselves onto the backs of their own steeds as Avenlae and Saetyl leaped into the air to hover on either side of me. I signaled Kaigar, who hovered over the middle of the foot soldiers and in front of the Queen's Guard, the sounds of their beating wings like war drums.

457

I held my left hand out, feeling the buzz of my power as it moved down my arm. *Take me to my Maker,* I thought slyly, and a burst of energy left my palm, splitting the air in front of us into a wide, crackling portal that opened onto the golden plains of Silvacastra. I led the advancing army through the portal, smelling the sweetness of the fresh, open air and the warmth of the rising suns' light on my body. The sky was a blazing orange and pink above us, so beautiful and deadly. The long golden grasses waved in the wind, rippling as we entered, but the peace was shattered by the warning screams of the thousands of black-eyed Voxmor that reared back on their hind legs, tails thrashing and fangs dripping with saliva. A cloud of black smoke materialized above the white-scaled creatures, and Sinivir's cackle was heard before his figure was seen. An uneasy rustle of fear moved through the army behind me as the Fifth Creator revealed himself, crimson hair braided back to mock the styles of the Delfungaye warriors.

"I was beginning to worry that you would not arrive, *Creovis*," Sinivir called to me, a malicious grin plastered across his face. "Actually, you've already spoiled some of my fun. I was looking forward to the prospect of killing so much in my search for you."

"Your fight is with me, Sinivir," I called back, tightening my grip on Vindicta. "Remember our deal."

"Of course, *Creovis*, for what am I but a man of my word?" Red forks of electricity cracked down his fingertips. "Besides, my Voxmor are too hungry for me not to allow them the chance at an easy feast."

At his last word, every Voxmor in his army opened their mouths wide and screamed, the wall of sound hitting us like bricks. Fortunately, Havyeque was quick-thinking enough to deploy the frequency they had used on the boundaries of the *Sloviyankae* city, so the scream was cut short after just a few seconds. Our Voxmor, however, remained ready for battle—their helmets blocked the frequency.

Vindicta reared onto her back legs, opening her frill and screeching a war cry that echoed far past the plains. I pushed myself up so that I crouched right over her neck as she began to bound towards the Voxmor, my wings primed and ready to take to the air. The shadows of the Queen's Guard flitted across the golden grass ahead of us, and showers of arrows penetrated the scales of Sinivir's army. Vindicta took one bounding leap, thrusting me into the air as I pulled my rapiers from their scabbards. Sinivir was ready, ruby crackling swords extending from his palms as I dove towards him. A deranged look of glee suffused his deathly pale face as he whirled around, parrying and attacking nimbly with smoke swirling around his limbs.

"Ah, *Creovis*, you learned the Delfungaye blade well!" he cackled, parrying my attack close to his left shoulder. He spun my rapier away from him and struck out with his sword, causing me to flip backward to avoid injury.

"Just well enough to kill you!" I seethed as I darted back up to him, swinging the blades of my wings around and slicing a gash into his cheek.

Sinivir's bloody eyes widened as he touched the black blood that dripped down his skin. "You drew first blood. How ungrateful, *Creovis*."

The Creator bared his yellow teeth and hissed as he struck again, his crimson power forcing me back. I spun my rapiers, igniting the violet forks of electricity that danced down their matte blades. "I guess we're cheating, then," I said, and every attack I made sent daggers of energy into the smoke that swirled around Sinivir. He cackled madly as ruby-red sparks flickered within the smoke, supercharging his power. Branches of electricity dove down into the ground below us, sending sprays of debris several feet into the air.

Screams, shrieks, and screeches echoed across the land as the battle raged. The stench of death grew stronger the higher the suns climbed into the sky, and sweat dripped down my temples as I darted, twisted, flipped, and spun around Sinivir, locked in intense combat with the unwavering strength of his blades. The plains turned brown and red from blood and scorch marks, the golden grass burnt to ash and swirling around dead bodies.

For the second time, the Creator sent me flying away from him with a burst of energy from his swords, and I caught myself on the ground, my rapiers digging deep trenches in front of me. Pushing myself back up, I ran into the fray, ducking under clashing Voxmor and darting out of the way of soldiers as they ran to defend their own. Blood sprayed across my body as a Voxmor's tail sliced through a soldier next to me, and I had but a fleeting breath that it was not a soldier I knew. My steps splattered through the mix of mud and blood as I raced toward where Sinivir had landed, the smoke around the bottom of his robes growing and beginning to glow with the red of his power.

"Come, *Creovis*!" he shrieked, spittle flying. "Let's put the power of a Creator against his creation!"

Sinivir lifted his hands to the sky, lightning as red as the blood of Creation crackling across the sky and into his body. I shoved my rapiers back into their scabbards, reaching deep into my being to take control over the Creonex as a charge built along my wings. I planted my feet and let my violet power explode from my body while the Fifth Creator directed his stream of red energy toward me. The two beams of energy collided in the middle of the battlefield, a shockwave blowing away all who were within a few yards of Sinivir and me. My entire being burned with the effort it took to hold back his power, crackling and forking across the ground in glowing red ripples. I gritted my teeth, then screamed through the exertion as I tried to force more and more of my energy into the beam, but it wasn't enough. Gradually, the red of Sinivir's power began to swallow the violet of my own, the promise of my destruction creeping ever nearer, and I was helpless to stop it.

460

I heard a cry to my left. I tried to ignore it, but Sinivir's eyes flicked over, and his grin deepened. He sent a swirl of sharpened smoke towards the sound, giving me a split second to throw myself onto the ground and shoot off a ball of energy to deflect his attack. Notien rolled out of the way as Sinivir's smoke spear dissipated over her head, then stood and took off towards a Voxmor with Saetyl in its tentacles. I rolled back to my feet but immediately had to dive again to dodge a burst of power from Sinivir.

"Dance, *Creovis*, dance!" he screamed, his eyes popping out of his flushed sockets. "For you know your power is no match for mine!"

I shielded myself from another strike of his electrical power, then leaped into the air, cracking my violet electrical whip across Sinivir's face as I spun. His crimson hair flew as his head snapped around, and I flung the whip back to wrap around his neck. Diving back to the ground, I wrapped the whip around the metal of the Creonex several times and pulled back with all my strength. Surge after surge of electricity shot down the length of the whip, buzzing over Sinivir's face and burning his skin. Clumps of singed crimson hair fell to the ground as he wrapped his long-fingered hands around the whip. His bloody eyes widened as his skin turned from deathly pale to charred black.

Suddenly, a jet of red energy shot through the whip and hit me in the chest like a bullet, sending me flying back into the ground as my helmet was knocked off my head. Stars burst throughout my vision as I coughed and sputtered, trying to catch my breath.

"*Creovis!*" Sinivir spat as I rolled onto my stomach, gasping for air. The cries of battle had subsided, and instead I heard hisses and clicks growing louder above me. Dragging myself onto my knees, I panted as I saw the tight circle of Voxmor that had closed around the Fifth Creator and me. The Voxmor of my army were being forced to the ground, including Vindicta, black blood coating her scales.

461

Notien and Darinrain were both being restrained by a Voxmor to my right next to Kaigar, whose metal wing had been ripped off. What made me freeze as I stood was the sound of Avenlae thrashing against the two Voxmor and the sound of his cry of pain as they smashed him against the dirt.

"No," I whimpered.

"Ah," Sinivir hissed, his bloody eyes focusing on Avenlae as he growled and tried to fight against the Voxmor again. A jet of black smoke shot from Sinivir's palm and coiled around Avenlae's body, lifting him into the air and carrying him to where the Fifth Creator stood.

"Everything has a weakness, Creovis," Sinivir hissed as he carved a sharpened nail into the fresh scar across Avenlae's face. "How interesting that you would develop one of your own."

"Stop!" I shrieked as Avenlae's blood poured down his cheek. His chest heaved as his wide, terrified silver eyes met mine. "Please," I whispered, keeping my eyes on Avenlae, "I'll do anything."

"Anything, *Creovis*?" Sinivir cackled as he lowered his hand, pressing his claws into Avenlae's chest. Avenlae's mouth opened wide as he threw his head back in an anguished cry.

"Anything! Please!" I yelled, my body trembling. The Fifth Creator removed his blood-soaked fingertips from Avenlae's chest, licking a drop of the crimson liquid from his claw. "Just don't hurt him anymore. Please."

"Broken by love," Sinivir mocked, his pointed teeth stained by the blood from his fingers. "How mortal of you, *Creovis*."

"What do you want?"

"Surrender to me, Weapon. Return to your Creator, and I shall let your people live. For now." His eyes slid over to where the smoke of his robes still coiled around Avenlae. "Should you choose to continue the fight, I will have every last soldier in your little army slaughtered right in front of you. This one will be first."

The Creator's hand jerked Avenlae's head up from where he had dropped his chin to his chest. Those silver eyes were filled with pain and terror as they looked at me from across the field, blood dripping on either side of them.

"Okay." I swallowed. "Okay, I sur—"

Something silver flashed through the air, and I heard the *thunk* of a blade embedding itself in armor. An immense pressure spread across my chest as I stumbled backward, confused. Avenlae's pupils contracted entirely, and he *screamed*. The gut-wrenching sound pierced my ears and stopped the struggle of the soldiers of Creation. Slowly, I lowered my head and caught sight of the hilt of a jagged knife sticking out from my chest. Drops of my own red blood began to drip down the front of my armor, and only then did I feel the intense pain of my heart trying to beat when it had been pierced through. My lungs spasmed, unable to fill against the constricting pain of the blade in my chest. I held my hands in front of the hilt of the knife as my knees gave out, and I fell to the ground, trying to understand if the knife was real. Then came the fear. Did that mean I was going to die? I wasn't ready to die! I didn't want to!

"And the resistance dies from within!" the Fifth Creator screeched, his abrasive laughter echoing in my ears as I lifted my head, my vision blurring with tears. To my left stood Saetyl, her throwing arm still extended, tears flowing freely down her cheeks.

"Mercy," was all she said.

"Mercy? Mercy!" Sinivir cackled, releasing Avenlae. He fell to the ground, scrambled to his feet, and darted over to me, his breathing ragged from the sobs that racked his bruised body. I fell back as Avenlae caught me, tasting the metallic copper of blood in the back of my throat as I coughed and gurgled.

"Ironic, dear *Creovis*, that you should die by something so simple," Sinivir hissed. "Let the strength of Creation die with you, my weapon."

Avenlae pressed his bleeding forehead to mine, unable to speak through his cries. His muscles trembled as he held me, gasping as tears mingled with the blood that dripped down his cheeks. His shrieks and sobs of anguish echoed far past the plains of Silvacastra—Creation stayed silent to listen. I couldn't tell him how scared I was, how I wasn't ready to know what it felt like to die, how much I didn't want to leave him. *Wait, I want more time! I need more time!* The voice in my head called frantically, but there was no energy left within my body to fight. To even take one final breath seemed to be an insurmountable task.

Mercy. Why was it that I had asked Saetyl for mercy?

"How dare you ask such a thing of me!" Saetyl had shouted, loud enough I was afraid the entire cave would hear.

"Because you're the only one strong enough to do it," I had whispered, fighting to hold her gaze, "should you think for one second that Creation no longer has a fighting chance, you're the only one who can stop Sinivir from taking his prize. He won't kill me—he needs his weapon."

"But he will kill me! If he does not, the rest of Creation will! Xiaye, think. Why would I want to become that monster?"

Notien's smile flashed before my eyes. The sound of Darinrain's booming laughter echoed in my ears. My skin warmed at the memory of Avenlae's embrace.

"Why?" I whispered.

A memory of my mother removing her necklace with the blue pendant played in my mind's eye. The pendant morphed into the book, the book I had kept for thirteen years before ever knowing its true form. "One day you will understand, Xiaye," she said, kissing the forehead of her sleeping toddler. "One day, you will understand, Creovis."

"Because," I said to Saetyl, tears filling my eyes, "it will be merciful."

"Creovis," I whispered, my vision going black. "I … I am power."

464

Flashes of the golden orb played behind my eyes, the golden orb that became a child. A child who was stolen by a desperate Queen. A child who was raised mortal, but …

"I … I am the *Creovis,*" I said, my voice stronger as my vision and hearing returned. New energy, wild, untamed power pulsed from my chest and through my veins. Avenlae's swollen eyes widened as a golden glow began to emanate from where Saetyl's blade pierced my heart. The pain was gone—the weight of my dying body lifted.

"What?" Sinivir's voice had a twinge of uncertainty. "What is happening?"

As if pulled by strings in the sky, I stood, pulling the knife from my chest, facing the Fifth Creator as realization sent wave after wave of power coursing through my body, causing my skin to emit that golden glow.

"You can't kill power," I said, throwing the knife to the ground. "You can't kill me."

And, suddenly, I *knew* I was the *Creovis*, the salvation of Creation. I began to move towards the Fifth Creator, leaving Avenlae where he crouched, my glow growing brighter with each step. My wings extended as the golden hue suffused my feathers, arching them high over my head so that the tips of the feathers could brush the tops of the trees behind the battlefield. The feathers were shimmering flames that flew in the wind. The power reached my face and shone gold through my eyes, creating an aura of pure energy that radiated around my body. My hair wrapped around my head in a headdress of spiraled vines of gold and white pure as snow that fell and wrapped around my body.

"This is what you wanted, isn't it?" I asked as I neared Sinivir. "You wanted me freed from my mortal form."

"My *Creovis!*" the Creator called, raising his hands as my figure grew taller, the glow from my body growing ever brighter, more intense than the suns. "You have come back to me!"

465

"No," I growled, stopping a few feet in front of the Creator. "Not your *Creovis*. I was never yours to control, Sinivir."

"But I created you!" he shrieked. "You only exist because I allow you to!"

"You created vengeance! I am what you made me! Your thirst for control, your needless destruction, your arrogance gave Creation their weapon."

"We made a deal, *Creovis!* You are mine!"

"You made a deal with Xiaye."

The Fifth Creator roared out his fury and sent a beam of blood-red energy towards my chest. I raised my hand, catching the beam of power in my palm, absorbing it. I was the embodiment of *genepotentia,* the power the Creators wielded. Sinivir's power flowed out of his body and into mine, but the glow of my skin intensified until he couldn't look me in the eye. He threw his arms up over his head, his power fizzling out of his skin and his smoke disappearing. Cowering before me was a feeble, pale old man who stumbled back into the ground, into a puddle of blood.

"You allowed me to evolve, Sinivir," I said. "You created the weapon that would destroy you."

"But, *Creovis* …" he whispered, his pale lips shaking as the color drained from his eyes.

I pressed a finger to his chest. "I can sense you, now. All of you is here. You can be killed. You really are imperious enough to believe you could fight the very power that makes you a Creator."

"Who will stop my brothers from regaining control over the universes, *Creovis*? Was that not what I was doing?" Sinivir pleaded.

For a half second, an image of an eye, one eye, created by the stars of the universe, lit up my mind.

466

"You think your brothers are safe from my power?" I asked, cocking my head to the side, the image gone as quickly as it had appeared. "This is only the beginning. I will be ready when they come. They will face the most powerful of their Brother's weapons and will be defeated in the same way you were."

With one surge of energy, Sinivir was no more. His body melted into the pool of blood in which he lay, as insignificant as dust floating away in the wind. Silence fell over the battlefield. There was a stirring among the mass of white scales as the control of the Fifth Creator died within the Voxmor. Color returned to their eyes as they looked around, confused and afraid. I straightened and turned to look at the Army of Creation as they pulled themselves out of the grasp of the Voxmor, appearing just as stunned. The circle that had formed around Sinivir and me split as Voxmor and soldiers alike stumbled back to stare up at me, their dirty, blood-stained faces masks of awe. Still crouched in the ground, however, was Avenlae. His silver eyes looked up at me, not with awe, but with peaceful happiness.

"Are you not afraid?" I asked him.

He smiled, his canines flashing in the light of the golden glow from my skin. "How could I be afraid of my *Le'eseia?*"

Despite everything, despite the power reverberating through my body, despite all the blood, the pain, the trauma, I smiled back at him. I crouched down to join him, my body shrinking and my glow diminishing. When my knees touched the dirt, my eyes were again mismatched, one silver, one red. My hair fell in messy waves down my back, and my wings boasted their normal black-to-white gradient. I cupped the sides of Avenlae's face and pressed my lips over his. The war had finally been won after decades of fighting. Avenlae wrapped his arms around me and pulled me as close to his body as his armor would allow, kissing me back fiercely and filling his lungs with my scent.

467

A call of celebration went up from the warriors closest to us. Soon, the plains of Silvacastra were filled not with the sounds of battle, but with the sounds of Creation's freedom. I stood, helping Avenlae up with me, and turned to a beaming Notien just as she ran forward and threw her arms around my neck.

"It is done! We have won, Xiaye! We have finally won!"

Tears of joy poured from her navy eyes as Notien released me, replying to the celebratory calls of her people, the *Fyr'aeset*. I looked around, searching the crowd for the golden eyes of the one who finalized my sacrifice. There were many more hands I shook, embraces I gave, and words of affirmation I spoke before I found Saetyl alone, overcome with grief-stricken sobs. When she saw me with Avenlae following behind, she collapsed to the ground, her hands out to me placatingly.

"Mercy, My Queen," she gasped, bowing her head low. "Have mercy!"

I cocked my head to the side, watching as she folded her warrior's body into subservience. All of Creation cried out their joy around us, their shock at their own survival still fresh enough to push tears from their eyes. But I knelt to the ground, blood seeping through my armor and touching my skin from the battlefield. In time, that blood would serve as food to the plains, whose golden grasses would soon wave not only at the call of the wind, but also from the slipstream of the *Fyr'aeset* returning home.

But now, the blood was fresh. Now, it still flowed from the bodies that lay half-buried in the mud.

Now, it was only Saetyl and I who felt the flow, and understood its warning.

468

Acknowledgments

I am still in shock that *I've* made it to the acknowledgments page. This novel began as a dream in the mind of a thirteen-year-old kid, and now it's a story that has been published and shared with you. It's amazing that I've reached this point, but what's even more incredible is that I had the support of so many people who helped me get here.

First and foremost, I want to express my heartfelt gratitude to my family and friends, the ones who joked about wanting my autograph years ago so they could "sell it when I become famous!" They believed in me long before I realized how much I could believe in myself. To my husband, who never doubted me for a single second and wouldn't let me voice my own doubts—thank you for building my writing space and sharing with everyone that I "write books", even when all I had was an unedited manuscript. This success is shared with you.

I also want to thank my editor, Mr. Rich, who taught me that I can describe something without taking up an entire page. I am truly grateful for your patience with this new author.

A huge thank you goes to Vendera Publishing, which has always been just a call away. Your dedication to supporting debut and indie authors is commendable. The compassion with which you operate is hard to find in the publishing world, and I feel fortunate to have had the opportunity to work with your company.

I must also acknowledge my mentor and close friend, Karisa. The countless hours we spent discussing our works-in-progress helped me reshape many of my plots and discover "the third option." Your brilliant mind has been a valuable resource, and I am so grateful that you shared it with me.

Finally, as an indie author, I want to thank you, dear Reader, for joining me on this journey. Your choice to continue reading is what keeps me going. Your support means everything, and I promise to keep my books on the shelves and in your hands.

About The Author

Willow Grace discovered her passion for creative writing at the age of thirteen, igniting a lifelong love for storytelling that blends the realms of science fiction and fantasy. A proud nerd at heart, she grew up captivated by tales from iconic series such as Star Trek, Lord of the Rings, Harry Potter, Avatar, and The Dark Crystal, which continue to inspire her imaginative worlds. Residing in sunny Florida, Willow cherishes her time away from the keyboard snuggling with her beloved furbabies, all of whom she has lovingly rescued. Alongside her husband, she enjoys spending time outdoors, or building intricate Lego sets, crafting mini dioramas, and playing games—often with him patiently awaiting her discovery of the elusive jump button for her character. Willow's creative endeavors reflect her vibrant personality and her deep connection to the fantastical worlds she loves to explore.

www.ingramcontent.com/pod-product-compliance
Lightning Source LLC
Chambersburg PA
CBHW020629020726
47494CB00001B/108